Newsletter

Get several of my books for free when you sign up for my newsletter here:

https://books.bookfunnel.com/idjohnsonnewslettersignup

CORDIA'S WILL: A CIVIL WAR STORY OF LOVE AND LOSS

Forever Love Book One

ID JOHNSON

For my dad, Levi, who took me to the places where men fought and died so that our country would remain united. One of our favorite places was Wilson's Creek in Springfield, Missouri.

CONTENTS

Chapter One

SUNSHINE PEEKED through the tops of the elm trees that lined the thoroughfare that was Broadway Street, the warm rays invigorating the sparrows who bounced around from branch to branch without a care in the world. As she passed beneath them, however, Cordia Pike could not help but think of all the worries that may be coming in the not so distant future. She made her way along the brick sidewalk, her long gown swishing back and forth. Occasionally, she waved at a familiar face within one of the wagons or carriages that made its way down the busy street from the town square. Conveniently, Cordia's family lived only a few blocks from the Lamar Square, the geographical center of the town and the economic and social heart for its residents. So, she could easily walk the short distance between their home and any business she could possibly need to visit. The year was 1860 and Lamar had been settled for less than twenty years. It was the county seat of Barton County, Missouri, and it was thriving. Two railroad tracks kept the people employed and the visitors coming in streams. But Cordia could not help but wonder how much longer this peaceful life they had laid out for themselves would last.

She made her way across the busy intersection on the southwest corner of the square. Her father was the President of Barton County Bank and Trust, which was located on the northwest corner of the square. She nodded her bonnet at strangers and greeted the many faces that she knew as she made her way across the final street and into the two-story building. Her father, Isaac Pike, had moved to the area that was now Lamar as a young boy. His family had done well, and he was able to found the Barton County Bank and Trust, with a little bit of help from a few state senators and congressmen he had befriended over the years. He and his wife, Jane, lived in one of the most beautiful houses in town, and he was well respected, both for his work at the bank and his dedication to the city. Cordia swung open the thick mahogany doors, *Overly ornate for such a country settlement*, she had always thought, shaking the dust off of her light-blue gown.

"Well, hello there, Miss Cordia," a familiar voice called from across the black and white checked marble floor.

"Good day, Mrs. Adams," Cordia replied, smiling at the older woman who was crossing the hall toward the exit. "It's so lovely to see you," she added, shifting the basket she was carrying with her so as to offer her hand.

Margaret Adams beamed as she took Cordia's white-gloved hand delicately into her own. "Cordia—it is always a pleasure to see your beautiful face. I was just getting some business out of the way for Arthur. He is very busy planting these days, you know. Has every single one of those boys of ours out there in the fields as well. You know what he is always saying, 'Nothing quite like a long day's work to make a man proud.' Are you bringing that pa of yours some dinner?"

Cordia nodded and stepped out of the way so that others could make their way in and out of the doors. "Yes, I try to bring him something at least a few times a week. It is hard for him to find time to eat these days himself. The town is booming right now."

Margaret's face lit up. "I know! Isn't it wonderful? Who would have imagined a railroad would have had this kind of impact on a little old town like ours?" She reached up and adjusted the bow of her bonnet. Margaret was a workingwoman whose hands and face showed what sun and weather could do. Her dress reflected this as well, Cordia noted, thinking of the difference between her own stylishly cut bonnet, and Margaret's simple, homemade bonnet, designed to keep the sun out of her eyes, not the eyes of the men on her. Although, the Adams family had done quite well for themselves as local farmers. In fact, they were some of the wealthiest folks in town, though you could certainly not tell by their demeanor, or in the way they presented themselves to the rest of the citizens of the town. "Well, you give our best to your dear father," Margaret smiled, embracing Cordia quickly before stepping toward the door.

"Yes," Cordia replied, a little surprised at Margaret's show of affection. "Please send my best to your family as well."

"All right, dear. We'll see you on Sunday." Margaret stepped through the door and out to her wagon that was tied to the post not too far away. Cordia watched her briefly before turning back around and proceeding to her father's office. Sunday. Just three days from now. She would be attending church at the First Baptist Church as always. But afterward, she would be joining Margaret's oldest son, Jaris, on yet another afternoon stroll. She had been on many such walks with Jaris lately. Was Margaret's embrace some indication that this Sunday would be different than other Sundays?

"Miss Cordia? Is something the matter with you, dear?"

Cordia looked up to see Mr. Sulley, one of the bank tellers, looking at her curiously from behind the banking counter. She blinked, wondering if he had been speaking to her and she had not heard, lost in her thoughts. "Good day, Mr. Sulley," she said, a polite smile turning up the corners of her mouth.

"Well, that's more like it, dear." The old man chuckled, adjusting his wire-rimmed glasses. "You must have been dreaming of your mama's ham. I could smell the sweet aroma the second you walked in the door. Boy howdy, is your daddy in for a treat today."

"Yes, sir," Cordia said over her shoulder as she continued toward her father's office. She stopped and turned slightly to add, "If I ever do get it to him." She smiled back at him and ascended the staircase. Her father's office was on the second floor, giving him a view of the town as it spread out from the square. The door was slightly open so she only rapped her fingers lightly on the glass and peeked her head inside. "Hi, Daddy." Her father was hunched over a stack of papers, one of which he was examining closely with a magnifying glass. He saw Cordia noticing this and quickly shoved the tool into a drawer. Both his wife and his daughter had been on him for several months saying that he needed to have Dr. Walters check out his eyes and get him a pair of spectacles. He refused. He was only fifty-three and that was no age to have to wear glasses, he insisted.

Cordia pretended not to notice, though she mentally noted that she would mention this to her mother when she got home. She sat the basket down on the edge of her father's desk and opened it up. "Mother has sent you some ham and a few other things." She began to take the items out of the basket, but her father seemed famished and began to take them out himself.

"Wonderful," he stated, digging into the basket. "I'm starving." Cordia laughed. Her father had a reputation around town as quite an eater, though you wouldn't be able to tell just by looking. He was still a fairly fit man for his age. Her mother, on the other hand, had become quite plump as she aged. As her father dug into the well-prepared meal, she removed her hat, revealing her dark brown hair. Normally, she would have preferred to keep it down all day, but her mother insisted that if she was going to the bank, she had to have it pinned up properly. It seemed ridiculous to Cordia, especially in a town where all of the farm girls and their mothers seemed to be so much more practical, but it was not an argument she wished to have. So here she was with all three feet of brown wavy hair piled underneath her new blue and white flowered hat, direct from New York, which she had received a month before on her eighteenth birthday.

Cordia wandered around her father's office as he continued to eat his lunch. She peered out the window and could see dozens of houses spreading out from the square. She found it interesting to see how the town was growing. Just a short while ago, it seemed that the houses were only a block or two away from the square, with a sparse dwelling here and there dotting the distant horizon beyond. But now, houses stretched well past her line of sight, new ones popping up even as much as six blocks away from this main artery of life. And that wasn't even counting all of the new farms that had sprouted up out in the countryside. These houses belonged mostly to new residents, which the railroad had brought this way. Some were craftsmen, others traders, businessmen, such as her father, who were now able to make their way in this thriving little community. And Lamar wasn't the only such town. Lots of little places that weren't even on the map not so long ago were spreading all over Missouri and into Kansas, the border of which was only about 25 miles to the west. It was amazing what the mines over near Minden, and the railroads that were needed to bring the coal out of them, had begun, bringing a flourish of growth to the area.

Once again, Cordia realized she had not been paying attention. Her father was talking to her, and she had not heard a word he was saying. She tried to pretend she had heard the first part of the story and figured out what she had missed by catching the rest of it. "Then I told old Mr. Liverpool that he could take his farm and move it to China for all I cared, but I was not going to support him giving money to any cause that had anything to do with ol' John Brown's supporters," he was saying between (and occasionally in the middle of) bites of ham. "I'm all for supporting the Union cause but not by the means that fellow employed." Her father had always stood behind the idea that the Union should be protected, though there were other men in the county who thought otherwise. This debate seemed to be taking place more and more these days. "Boy, this is good! Your fine mother has really outdone herself this time," he mumbled more to himself than to Cordia.

John Brown. There was a name that Cordia could have done without hearing for the rest of her life. It seemed that most people around here were just now slowly beginning to realize what a name of significance that would be for the future of Kansas and Missouri. Though they certainly didn't want to admit it. It seemed to Cordia that the days of pretending away the affairs of the nation were numbered. But, like everyone else, she was not likely to begin any conversations with notions of what that might mean for their way of life in Lamar.

"I am sure that he didn't take that kindly," Cordia noted, walking back over toward her father's desk.

"Oh, no, he stormed out of here faster than you could believe a man of his age could ever move," he replied, the grin on his face marred a little by the wrinkle that grew between his eyebrows. "Oh, well," he said, smiling. "That is not a matter to discuss with a fine young lady such as yourself, my dear."

Cordia sighed and smiled at her father. Sometimes she was very offended by the way men treated women and their ability to partake in such conversation. But, in this case, she knew that her father was simply trying to protect his little girl from the concerns of the outside world. She wondered how much longer that would even be possible. And then it occurred to her that it might be her husband who held those concerns in the not so distant future; which prompted her to hesitantly say, "You know, Daddy, I bumped into Mrs. Margaret Adams downstairs." She watched his face for a reaction as she sat down in the chair across from his oversized oak desk.

His face didn't seem to change too much, although she thought she saw a hint of something in his green eyes. "Such a lovely woman. So kindhearted. Wonderful family," he commented, still eating his lunch.

"Yes," Cordia agreed, straightening the pleats in the front of her dress. "She said to tell you hello and that they would see us on Sunday." Again, she studied his face for some sort of clue—perhaps Jaris had come to him, asked him for her hand, given an indication that maybe he intended their courtship to come to an end and a wedding to take place soon. But Isaac Pike only nodded and took a bite out of the roll he was holding in his hand.

Sighing again, Cordia stood and walked away from the table, back to the window. She thought she heard her father chuckle quietly. Her head turned quickly, and she gave him a questioning look. Finally, he said, "Oh, Cordy, always has to know the future. Always has to find a way to pick everyone else's brains. Why can't you just let things unfold my dear?" He stood then, walked to his daughter, and hugged her. Instantly, at his touch, she became his little girl again and even laughed at herself. She turned and crossed back to the desk, wrapping up the leftovers, and packing them back into the basket.

"I'm sorry, Daddy," she agreed, nodding her head. "I guess the Good Book does warn us not to go looking for soothsayers and the like. Just wondered if there was anything you could tell me." She closed up the basket and put it over her arm.

He joined her at the desk, leaning a strong hand against it. "And what if there were? Would that be my place, dear? No, I think not. Now, you go on home and practice that new sheet music I got for you. All the way from Boston, you know. I will want to hear you play when I come home."

"Yes, Daddy," she said, leaning over and kissing him on the cheek. New sheet music. Maybe she could think about that on the way home, instead of all of the other things that had been preoccupying her mind this morning. "Have a good afternoon," she added as she closed his office door. She made her way down the stairs and back toward the entry, waving goodbye to Mr. Sulley, who was now with a customer.

On her way back home, the thought of running her fingers over those piano keys did occupy some of her thoughts. But other ideas also sprang to mind. What would happen if this notion in the south that they needed to be an independent country escalated? What would happen if more John Browns raided along the border of Missouri and Kansas? And of course, she could not help but wonder what would happen this Sunday on a stroll through the park with Jaris Adams. If he asked her to be his wife, would she say yes?

"YOUR HAZEL EYES are as bright as the sky, and as vast in their reach, Miss Cordia Pike. Now, please don't leave me in suspense any longer. What do you say? Please say yes. I don't know what I will do if you won't have me."

Cordia continued to look ahead of her, down the little lane that led out into the countryside and past the little town of Lamar, out into the expansive state of Missouri, and beyond. Thoughts of those distant places should have no bearing on whether or not one simple girl in a small town should accept the hand of marriage from a local boy. Yet, in these trying times, how could she not consider all that was going on around them before making such an important decision? She continued to walk, her red and white striped parasol protecting her delicate face from the sun. She had known Jaris Adams her whole life. She had attended church with him every Sunday since what seemed the dawn of religion. She had even run through his father's farm fields at dozens of parties and social gatherings, all the way hollering, "You'll never catch me, Jaris Adams!" He and his younger brothers, Zachariah, Peter, and John, as well as his slightly older cousin, Carey, had chased her numerous times, until she was trapped by the creek or a dense forest, or so out of breath she would collapse on the ground. Now, it seemed, he had finally caught her in a way she could not possibly outrun.

And it wasn't necessarily that she wanted to outrun him. The Adams family were mighty good people, and no one in Barton County could argue with that. Jaris was not only a kindhearted, loving, intelligent person; he was also very nice to look at. He had striking features, beautiful blue eyes and dark brown hair, though not quite as dark as her own. Their children would be lovely, strong and bright. Independent, just like both of their parents. And maybe that was part of the problem. Cordia wasn't sure she was ready to be anyone's wife. She loved Jaris in a way that no one could possibly understand—a love of familiarity, a love of friendship and respect. But she knew in her heart that she did not love him with the passionate love of a Jane Austen character. It was that storybook romance that she had always longed for. She did not think herself capable of ever loving Jaris in that way.

"There are other ways to fall in love with a man," her best friend Susannah had commented just the day before. They had been sitting on the back porch of Susannah's house, shelling green beans, and watching her two little sons run around and play in the backyard. "When James proposed to me, I didn't really know if I loved him either, but I knew I would learn to love him." Cordia had to hold back a small chuckle at that comment. That was a complete fabrication. Susannah Dixon had been denying the very existence of James Brooks since she first laid eyes on him at the ripe old age of four. But Cordia had always known that she had her eye on him. She was more surprised to see that he had reciprocated, as he had spent the better part of his teenage years avoiding Susannah. But she did understand what Susannah was saying. She had heard a lot of women admit that they weren't really in love with their husband when they first met them but that they had grown to love them over time. Maybe that was the best she could ever hope for. Lord knew she wasn't going to just fall in love with anyone else in Barton County. Jaris was certainly the best man she could possibly hope to meet around these parts. So, if she were going to marry, it would probably be to him--sooner or later.

But, in Cordia's mind, as she walked along beside a very nervous suitor who was shaking worse than the time when they were seven or eight and they had come across a copperhead in the woods beyond his father's farm, she could not help but beg the question of--was this the right time to get married? "Jaris," she began, "you are one of my very best friends. You are a good man." She thought she saw his face start to fall as she peeked up at him over the edge of her bonnet. "Let me finish," she said, stopping and turning to face him just beneath one of the widest poplar trees in the county. She couldn't help but notice all of the initials in hearts carved all over the trunk as she began her explanation. "I think marrying you is a very wise choice. And yes, I intend to do so. But do you think that now is the time for people to be pondering a peaceful future together, on the eve of a war?"

Jaris leaned back against the stately trunk. "Cordia, always considering things that don't directly concern you," he mumbled. "Cordia, we don't know for sure that there is even going to be a war, nor do we know that we are going to have to fight. We're so far from Washington and all that politicking. South Carolina is about as close to Lamar as the moon. What does it matter what those men decide thousands of miles away? I want you to be my wife. I want to plan a life together. I love you, Cordia." And with that, he placed his hands gently on the sides of her face. For a brief moment, Cordia thought for sure that he was going to lean down and kiss her, right on the lips. Then, she would know for sure if she could ever love Jaris Adams. But he didn't—that would be too bold for him. Instead, he leaned over and kissed her on the top of her head, knocking her bonnet backward in the process, almost sending it to the ground. Then, he looked at her awkwardly with those big blue eyes, as if to say, "All right—I'm awkward, but don't you love me anyhow?"

He turned around to face the tree, something easier to look at than Cordia, as she straightened the hat he had toppled over. He was wearing his very best suit and the bowler hat his father had given him for Christmas last year. It was his favorite and he only wore it for special occasions. So, Cordia knew when she saw him at church that day that her suspicions had been correct and that he would have an enormously important question to ask her after Sunday meeting, on their weekly stroll. She had been wondering what to say for weeks, especially these last few days since seeing his mother in the bank on Thursday. Now, here she was, unsure of every word that was coming out of her mouth. She placed her hand on his shoulder, and he turned his head to look at her.

"Jaris, I'm not saying 'no.' I'm just saying, I know you, and I know if there is any chance that you can go enlist in an army and fight for what you think is right that you will do it. You'll do it in a heartbeat, regardless of what I think. And what if we had children? What if we had little ones left at home while you were off fighting? I just don't think it's a good idea right now."

He spun to face her. "Cordia, what if we did?" he asked, his arms flailing out in exasperation. "That would be wonderful. You and your family could raise them for a little while. Heaven knows my mama would be there, more than you could ever wish to see her, at the idea of grandchildren. I'm not saying that if there is a war that I won't go fight. But even if there is—and that's a big if, in my opinion—it's bound to be a short war. Everyone is saying so."

She could not help but throw her head back in a sarcastic "Ha!" before continuing. "Yes, everyone is saying so. Everyone who wants good men such as yourself to enlist for the duration. This is an issue thousands of years old. I do not rightly think that it will be decided in a battle or two. It hasn't been decided by old men deliberating and discussing it for over two hundred years. It sure won't be decided by young men dying much faster." The passion in her voice and the glint in her eye made him realize that this was something she had spent many hours thinking about. It was amazing for him to consider that a woman would put so much thought into issues like war and slavery. But then, Cordia Pike was no usual woman. And that is why he finally decided to let her have her way.

"All right, Cordia," he began. "Just what do you believe we should do then?"

She had spun around at the end of her speech so violently she was shocked to hear him speaking so calmly. She put her parasol down, point resting on the ground, and turned to face him. She cleared her throat. "Well, I think that it would be in our best interest to wait until after the war. If there is a war," she added, before he could even open his mouth to throw that idea in. "If they do get all of this decided peacefully, and South Carolina does not secede—which it will," she commented quietly, more to herself, looking at the ground. She looked back up at him, "Then, we can plan an earlier wedding. But if there is a war--and I don't see how there is anyway there won't be—and you enlist, then I propose we wait until your safe return before we carry out our wedding plans." She was looking him straight in the eye now and she could see that he was beginning to accept the fact that, though not under his most choice circumstances, she had, in fact, agreed to be his wife.

Jaris nodded. "Yes, ma'am," he agreed, a smile beginning to grow across his face. After all, when you were asking someone like Cordia Pike—and there weren't too many women like Cordia Pike in this world—to be your wife, you had better reckon on something not going directly as planned.

"Do not call me ma'am," she said, eyes open wide, only half kidding. This was a little game they had been playing for about six years, ever since the day that Jaris realized he was infatuated with Cordia and wanted to marry her. He would call her ma'am because he knew that it irritated her. Eventually, he knew that she would hit him, which had been about the only way that Cordia Pike was likely to touch a member of the opposite sex. He would take what he could get.

He smiled at her and she could not help but smile back. "Oh, I almost forgot," he said, digging around in the pocket of his jacket. He pulled out a small gold band with a very tiny diamond adornment. Cordia gasped. She had forgotten all about a ring. Likewise, she was surprised to see it included an actual diamond. "This belonged to my great-grandmother, Helen Teal Adams. My ma said it should belong to you because you are just as strikingly beautiful and just as prone to fits of reason as any woman she has ever known since." Cordia's eyebrows rose at these last comments. His mother thought that she was difficult. "Cordia," he continued. "You shouldn't be surprised that you have a reputation as a strong-willed woman. My ma meant it as a compliment. She will be extremely happy to hear that you have accepted my proposal." He thought, but did not admit out loud, that his family would have a hard time accepting an indefinite date for a wedding. Cordia wasn't so sure that calling her strong-willed was a compliment, but she stuck her hand out for him to take and he slipped the ring delicately onto her finger.

"Now it is official," he said, proudly. "Someday, we will be married."

She laughed and actually reached over and put her arms around him. "Jaris Adams, you are something else."

"So are you, ma'am," he said, turning to walk back toward her house where his horse was waiting.

"Don't call me ma'am!"

"Sorry," he started, but couldn't help but add, "ma'am."

Cordia balled up her fist and punched him in the side. He pretended that it hurt and doubled over in pain. "Help, my wife-to-be is beating me!" She laughed and pulled him back up.

"Stop it! People are going to start looking at us," she said quietly.

Jaris spun in a circle. There was no one in sight. "There ain't no one around, Miss Cordia. But don't you already know that people can't help but look at you, the prettiest girl in town."

Cordia actually felt herself blushing. She'd never had a young man say anything quite like that to her before.

"But, I reckon you had better be careful about hitting me," he continued. "You know, once you are my wife, I will be able to hit you with a stick, so long as it's no wider than my thumb." She knew he was teasing, and when he started to laugh that confirmed it. Still, the very idea that he would have control over her once they were married was a little alarming to her. He saw her eyes widen and stopped, turning her around to face him. "Cordia," he said, no longer laughing and with a very serious look in his eyes, "I can promise you that I will love you until the day I die."

She looked deeper into his eyes. Yes, she could see that. He would love her always, until the day he died. She did not know if she could say the same. "I know you will," she admitted. And then, Jaris Adams did something he had wanted to do since he was 14 years old. He leaned over and kissed Miss Cordia Pike right on the lips.

Chapter Two

April 1861

Will Tucker was startled. He sat up in bed quickly; sure that he had heard something. Not quite sure what it was. And then he heard it again. It sounded like the thump of horses' hooves moving through the woods just in front of the Tucker cabin. His brother, Nolan, must have heard the noise, too. Will could see him standing at the window, his rifle in one hand. Will sat up and pulled on his pants and boots as quickly as possible. In the moonlight, he could see that Nolan was already dressed. His sister, Julia, was still asleep on her cot across the room.

"What is it?" he whispered, crossing to the window to join his brother.

"Not sure," Nolan replied. "Thought I heard branches breaking, hooves. Maybe three or four horses. Don't see anything though." Just then, Julia began to stir. Will glanced back over to see his sister pulling on her robe.

"What's going on?" she whispered as she crossed the room. Just then, out of the trees appeared four shadowy figures on horseback. They entered the front yard of the little log cabin, guns in hand. Nolan shuddered, and walked to the front door. He stepped out slowly.

"What can I help you with?" the oldest brother asked, squinting in the moonlight, trying to make out any of the marauders' faces.

Atop a sorrel stallion, one of the men, who seemed to be the leader, cocked a double barrel shotgun. "This the Jones place?" he yelled down. The other three riders fanned out beside him. It was hard to see in the pale light, but all of the figures seemed menacing. He continued, "Word has it that the Jones family has been harboring Union raiders."

Nolan stepped out of the door, gun in hand but not raised. "No, sir," he answered. "Name's Tucker. Jones place is a few miles up the road."

Will wondered what these people could possibly be planning to do with the Joneses. Peaceable family, older man and his three daughters. The leader leaned over to one of the other riders and whispered something. The other man laughed out loud, and then spat on the ground.

"That's funny," the first man continued. "We were right sure this was the Jones place. Folks down the lane said so."

Now the other three men seemed a little restless. Will stepped out the door as well, trying to get a better understanding of exactly what was happening. Julia was still concealed in the darkness beyond the threshold.

"Neighbors must have given you wrong directions, sir. Like I said, name's Tucker. My daddy built this house with his own two hands about twenty-five years ago, and we've worked the land ever since." Nolan and Will both stepped farther out into the yard. An old well, long ago dried up and since that time used mostly to collect trash, not to mention a hiding place that gave their mother fits before she died, was all that stood between the boys and these strange riders.

"Where is your daddy?" a third man asked. He seemed not quite as old, but something about the tone of his voice seemed very evil to Will, as he stood behind his older brother, wishing he had grabbed a gun himself.

"Dead," Nolan replied. "Our ma is dead, too. Both died about five years ago."

"You all that's left?" the first man asked.

"Yes, me and my brother and my sister," Nolan replied. Will assumed Nolan thought he had better tell the truth right up front.

"Sister?" the final man asked. "I like the sound of that word, sister." He looked at the other men and they all began to laugh in a purely devilish fashion, all but the leader, who kept his cool.

At her mention, Julia stepped out the door, holding her robe tightly around her. Nolan continued. "We ain't the Joneses, and we ain't looking for trouble. We've got some provisions, if you want to take them. Some ham, a few beans. They're yours if you want. Otherwise, please be on your way."

"Provisions?" The younger man repeated. His horse seemed restless, and it began to bounce around a little bit. "Is your sister there a provision?"

The other man who had seemed so interested at the idea of a woman began to laugh. He commented, "I like the idea of that, too."

Nolan shifted his position, stepping between Will and Julia, who was now closest to the old well. Will took a step backward, thinking he could dart into the house to get his gun if need be. "No, she ain't." Nolan said, taking hold of Julia's arm.

Now the leader chuckled. "We'll see about that. Manny, get the girl," he said, looking at the younger of the men. Manny was more than happy to oblige. He quickly dismounted.

Nolan started to raise his gun, but then realized that all three of the other men had their guns drawn on him. Once again, he began to verbally protest, but all he got out were a few words. "Wait a minute now, let's talk about this." Then, in a flash so bright, the sky seemed completely lit up, the leader's gun went off. Will could see the whole thing unfolding, as if in slow motion. Before he could even register what was happening, he saw his brother's head snap backward, and a tiny bead of blood start to roll down his forehead. His brother's expression changed from a look of total shock and surprise to anguish. And, just before he began to fall, he turned his head slightly, and looked right into Will's eyes.

Horror swept over Will. He knew he had to react quickly because he would be next. Acting instinctively, he snatched his brother's rifle out of the air with one hand and pushed his sister into the well with the other. Fortunately, Julia, though equally stunned at the fate of her oldest brother, had the same idea, and she was already jumping into the well herself. In one fluid motion, Will turned the gun on Manny, the closest marauder, and shot him, right in the chest. Then, with no time to reload his own weapon, he grabbed Manny's shooter and trained it on one of the other men, at the same time dodging behind the well, using it for protection. He exchanged fire with the other two mounted raiders as their leader reloaded. His second shot hit one of the men square between the eyes, and he slumped backward, nearly falling off his mount. Both of these two men's shots had missed, hitting the cabin behind him.

Just then, Julia popped out of the well, handing another gun to her brother, and training her own weapon on the leader. By this time, the large man had reloaded and fired in the general direction of the well, but his horse had been startled by all of the noise, and he missed. Julia, as good a shot as either of her brothers, hit him in his stocky chest, knocking him to the ground.

Will had his gun trained on the remaining gunman, but seeing the fate of the rest of his company, the man took off into the woods. Without even considering letting him go, Will ran to Manny's empty horse and leaped atop it. He took off after the final assassin. Branches snapped back, hitting him in the face as he began to close in on his prey. He didn't feel them, though, nor did he feel the blood trickling down his sallow face. Finally, the two riders came to a small clearing and the outlaw ahead of him drew his steed to a stop.

Throwing up his arms and dropping his gun, he turned his horse partially around. "Please," he begged, and Will could see in his face that he knew he could not escape. "Please let me go. I got a wife. I got two kids."

But Will was not listening to the dirt-covered bandit's pleas. "Yeah, I had a brother once," he said, his face void of all emotion. Then, the marauder, seeming to understand his fate was sealed, began to weep, his face turning from an expression of hope, a pleading look of distress, to wide-eyed terror, as Will raised his newly reloaded gun and blew the scoundrel's brain matter all over the trees behind him.

The horse whinnied loudly and tried to buck the lifeless rider from its back. Finally, the corpse's grip slipped from the reins, and he fell to the ground, what was left of his head hitting first. The horse slowly began to trot out of the woods, stunned, but aware of his freedom. Will Tucker turned his borrowed horse around and headed back to the cabin he used to call home.

As he entered the yard, a realization of all that had just taken place began to creep at the corners of his consciousness. He pushed it aside, knowing he would have to act fast. Gunshots echoed for miles around here and it was not likely that this small band of four were the only raiders around. They usually rode in bands of twenty or more, or so Will had been told by neighbors who claimed to have seen them. Until now, he wasn't quite sure he believed them. Talk of looting and burning had traveled up and down this borderland for a few years now, since the idea of war had spread into so many folks' heads. And while he knew that such things were going on over in Kansas, he had yet to hear of any families actually being attacked this far into Missouri. Until now.

He could hear his sister crying softly as he climbed off of the horse. She was leaning over Nolan's body, trying to wipe away an endless trickle of blood that continued, no matter how many times she brushed her handkerchief over it. "Julia," he said softly as he approached, "we need to get going. There will be others looking for us soon. We don't have much time."

At the sound of his voice, Julia looked up, the expression on her face frantic, almost as if she wasn't sure who was talking, someone behind her, or her dead brother in her arms. "Will?" she asked, bewildered. Then she repeated herself. "Will? What are we going to do?"

He gently placed his hand on her shoulder. Poor girl was only fourteen and she had seen too much death. Their parents had both died of consumption within a few months of each other when she was nine. Julia had suffered from the illness ever since. Even now, she began to cough. Will kneeled down beside her, next to the lifeless body of his brother, and handed her his handkerchief, knowing she could no longer use her own. He looked at his brother's face. Julia must have closed his eyes, which was good because he didn't think he could bear to look into them again. Nolan had taken care of them, practically raised them both, since their folks had died. He was only three years older than Will, and just twenty-five, but he had shown the strength of character and the endurance of any man Will had ever known—just like their pa. Now, they would need to leave, leave their home, leave all the memories that they had behind and try to outrun the closing darkness that was taking over these parts of the land.

Again, he repeated to Julia that they needed to get going. And this time, as if she had snapped out of a trance, she nodded, gently resting Nolan's head on the ground as they both came to their feet. "I'll go inside, get dressed, and gather up what I can. You'll get the horses ready?" she asked. Will nodded. Then, she looked back at her dear brother's body on the ground. "We can't leave him," she added.

Agreeing, Will nodded again. "I'll saddle up the horses and hook them to the wagon. We can bring shovels and bury him up in the family plot before we leave the wagon and ride out of here."

"Where will we go?" she asked, a solemn look on her young, pretty face.

Will sighed, where would they go? He could think of only one place where they might be out of danger. "We'll go to Aunt Margaret's. I think we will be safe there. Now go, get dressed. We need to hurry if we are going to make it out of here before sunlight and before any of these outlaws' friends come a'lookin' for us."

Disappearing inside of the cabin with a nod, Julia went to put on a dress, find her boots, and grab the little provisions they had. She took the ham and beans that Nolan had promised to his murderer and then managed to find some bread. She stuffed it all in a knapsack, along with a change of clothes for her and her brother, all of the ammunition they had for the rifles, and a stack of drawings she had made of her parents before they died, as well as some drawings of her oldest brother. That would be all she would have to remember them by.

As she came out the door, she could see that Will had the horses all hitched up and ready to go. She went back inside and grabbed a bed sheet to wrap around her beloved brother's body as Will tossed some shovels into the back of the open wagon. "Can you help me with him?" he asked, sadness welling up in his deep brown eyes. She nodded, pushing a stray blonde curl behind her ear. They carefully wrapped the sheet around their brother, as delicately as if he were a newborn baby, and loaded him into the back of the wagon, Julia taking his head and laying it down as gently as possible. Then, they rode out to the lane that would take them up the hillside to their family plot. As they left the little homestead, neither of them could bear to turn their head and glance back at what remained from the life they had known before that horrible night.

ON APRIL 13, 1861, Jaris Adams turned 21 years old, just a few days after Fort Sumter fell to the Confederacy. Of course, word of what had happened so far east traveled slowly and it was unclear to the residents of Lamar just exactly what had happened. Still, the townsfolk knew there would be implications that would affect all of them.

It was a cool spring Saturday afternoon, and his parents had invited over many neighbors for a birthday celebration out in the yard beside their house. A fine hog was roasting, his mother bustling around readying all of the other fixin's. His brothers were setting up tables and chairs and carrying on like young men do.

As of December of 1860, seven Southern states had seceded from the Union, South Carolina being the first to do so. Texas was the latest, seceding in February. Since then, there had been lots of speculation as to whether or not the so-called Border States would follow in the Deep South's footsteps. Missouri and Kansas were both torn between the two sides of the issue. Many in both states wanted to stay with the Union, while others wanted to join up with the Confederate States of America, as the new Southern government was calling themselves. And Barton County was divided about half for one, half for the other. Most people were still avoiding talking about the issues. It was amazing, Jaris thought, as he strolled about the yard—he had offered to help but his family wouldn't let him lift a finger on this special day—how people around here were still refusing to talk about these issues, as if pretending there was nothing to talk about was going to keep them safe. Even though the residents of Barton County, Vernon County to the north, and Jasper County to the south, bordered along some of the bloodiest counties of "Bleeding Kansas," many people still seemed to think that the bands of marauders and raiders would simply stop when they got to the border. Jaris thought it was just a matter of time before they began to pour over the rim and saturate this state like an overturned cup of poison.

He glanced over his shoulder and saw his father helping his mother with the tablecloth. His father had worked hard his entire life, provided a good home for his family, and made some money doing it. But, even though Missouri's State Guard was active in the area, and some of the young men of the town had even ridden off to join their appointed sides, Arthur did not even want to hear Jaris speak of joining up. Jaris had thought long and hard about which side of the issue he truly supported. It was difficult with so many friends and schoolmates choosing different sides. Finally, both Jaris and, even more strongly, his older cousin, Carey, had decided that they would join the Missouri State Guard, and support Governor Claiborne Jackson in his effort to dismantle Missouri from the Union.

Though Jaris did not necessarily believe in slavery, he did believe that every state had a right to be independent, to make its own choices, independent of the Federal government. Lincoln had been very adamant in stating that he would not let any of the Southern states go without a fight, and that just didn't seem right to him. So, unbeknownst to his parents, he and Carey had enlisted the day before. And though he had discussed enlisting with his fiancée, Cordia, he had yet to tell her he had done so. He would announce it to her along with the rest of his family over his birthday dinner. He knew his parents would be sad to see him go, but he truly believed they would be proud of him for supporting his cause. As for Cordia, well, he wasn't exactly sure how she would react. Just as he was thinking of her, he saw a wagon coming up the road. He could see her dark brown hair blowing in the wind, and knew it was the Pike family, first to arrive. He couldn't help but think of how her mother must have carried on at the idea of her coming to a social event with that hair down. He laughed and walked toward the hitching post where he knew the vehicle would be headed.

"Miss Cordia, Mr. and Mrs. Pike," he said as the horses came to a stop just in front of him.

"Hello, dear Jaris!" Mrs. Pike called. She looked, as always, the picture of respectability, in a fine gown, her hair tied up nice and properly beneath her bonnet. Cordia was also dressed very fashionably, but her hair was blowing around in the April wind such that she almost looked like an Indian Princess. "Happy birthday!" Mrs. Pike called, as she stood to dismount. Mr. Pike called his greeting and congratulations as well, and it took both gentlemen to help the very plump Mrs. Jane Pike down from her seat. As she was climbing down, Margaret crossed the yard to greet them, and the parents went off to chat.

When Jaris turned back to the carriage, Cordia had already jumped out and was standing beside him. "I'm sorry," Jaris said, studying Cordia's stunning, fair face. "I would have been happy to help you down."

She smiled, her hazel eyes gleaming in the bright sunlight. "Quite all right," she said. "I can manage."

"I reckon you can," he agreed, taking her by the hand and leading her across the yard, toward the rest of the family. "I can't help but notice your hair is down today, my dear."

She sighed. He knew that her hair was always a touchy subject with her mother. "Yes, she insisted that I put it up, pleaded with me, even used the wind as an argument. I just hate putting it up, though." Even as she was speaking, the wind was whipping through it, leaving it tangled and a bit messy. "I did bring a bonnet," she added, reluctantly. "Just in case it starts to drive me batty." The bonnet strings were wrapped around her arm, along with her fan and a small purse. Jaris couldn't believe how much baggage these fashionable ladies had to carry around with them, but he knew better than to comment.

Within a few minutes, several more carriages, wagons, and horses had shown up and many of the women were helping Margaret set the food out and make sure everything was in place, including Cordia and her best friend, Susannah. The men were sitting around, several smoking pipes, sharing news about their families. Finally, someone dared to bring up the topic of Fort Sumter and even secession. It seemed that, just like the county in general, those attending the party were split down the middle, fifty-fifty, half for Missouri leaving, half against. Jaris and Carey, who had arrived shortly after Cordia, looked at each other, wondering if this would be a good idea to announce their enlistments. Carey's mother had died when he was born, but his father, an older, more rigid man, was present, and was sure to support his son in his decision to go off to fight. Just as Jaris began to open his mouth, his father stood up, looking over his shoulder toward the road.

Two riders came into view, making their way toward the hitching post. "Who could that be?" Arthur Adams asked. "I believe all of the families that we invited are here."

His mother had also noticed and had walked over to where the men were gathered. She was staring intently while wiping her hands on her apron. "Why, that looks like Julia and one of the boys, come down from Vernon County."

Arthur stood, and he and Jaris started walking toward the unexpected visitors, Margaret just behind. Though his cousins were certainly welcome, they seldom came to visit, since the trip was rather long, and they had little time for such things since their folks had died. This was a clear indication that something must be wrong.

Sure enough, as they drew nearer, they could tell that it was in fact Jaris's cousins, Julia and Will. But why wasn't Nolan with them?

"Julia?" his mother called. "Why, tarnations, whatever are you kids doing here?"

The looks on his cousins' faces should have been enough to tell them that all was not well. As they each dismounted, Julia looked near to collapsing. It was quite evident that she had been crying and both of them were streaked with fresh dirt. "Oh, Aunt Margaret!" Julia cried, running toward her aunt and throwing herself into her wide-open arms. "It was just terrible. I can't believe we are finally here. Those awful men!" Then, she began to cry.

Jaris could hear his mother's soothing voice repeating, "There, there now, it will be all right child," as she held his younger cousin in her arms.

"We were attacked by raiders, early this morning. We rode out quickly, trying to put some distance between the guerrillas and us," Will was explaining. Though he did not appear to have been crying, he looked exhausted, worn, covered with dirt, and relieved to have finally reached his destination.

By now other visitors had come over to see who the strangers were.

There was a crowd of people standing around. Jaris glanced back to see only a few women still standing behind around the table. "Where's Nolan?" his father asked. At these words, Julia's wailing grew even louder, and the question was answered before Will could even reply.

But he gave a brief explanation anyway, apparently all he could muster. He removed his filth-covered hat, smoothed back his hair and said, calmly, almost matter-of-factly, "He's dead. They shot him."

Jaris's head fell. He knew that Nolan had done so much to help raise his younger brother and sister after his parents had been stricken down so young. His cousin had been a very good man. Sadly, he was probably the first of the good men he knew who may not survive the impending war. "I'm so sorry," he and his father said, almost simultaneously.

Will nodded, clearly not able to think of any sort of reply to their remarks. "We took him up to the cemetery, buried him by our ma and pa. Then, we thought we should head out of there right quickly, before any of the raiders' friends made their way back to our home. On the way, we saw two of our neighbors' houses, burned to the ground, and no sign of any survivors. We were lucky to make it out of there alive."

Before either of them could even ask, Margaret generously extended their home to her niece and nephew. "We have plenty of room for both of you. Now, let's get you some clean clothes and you'll probably want to freshen up. You both are just covered in. . . ." she paused, realizing the dirt must have been from the grave they just dug, "Well, we need to get you all cleaned up. Follow me into the house, and we'll get things sorted out."

Both Will and Julia, who was still sobbing on her aunt's shoulder, made their way into the house. Though Will was still in a state of shock and not thinking too clearly about much of anything, the image of a beautiful long-haired girl rounding the corner of the house with a bucket of water in her hand, did register in his mind as he entered the home. But he had no time nor need to think about anything right now except for the welfare of his sister and the sort of governors who would let men maraud around burning down the homes of perfectly law-abiding citizens.

Cordia had gone back behind the house to get a bucket of water, with Susannah tagging along behind, and had missed Jaris's cousins arriving. She noticed two strangers accompanying Margaret into their house. For a brief second, she caught the dark, haunting eyes of the man, and blinked in surprise. *"How could someone just a few years older than her have that much sadness in his eyes?"* she wondered.

"Who is that?" Susannah was asking her husband, James, who was walking toward them, followed by Jaris, Carey, and several other men.

"That was Jaris's cousins," James explained. "They were just attacked up in Vernon County somewhere. Their brother was killed."

Cordia's eyes widened in horror. How awful! Though she didn't know these people, the thought of what they must have just gone through was inconceivable to her. She dropped the bucket of water, a small portion of its contents splashing her leg, and ran to Jaris, who still looked a little stunned himself. "My goodness!" she exclaimed, grabbing her betrothed by both hands. "How terrible. What happened?"

"I'm not exactly sure," he replied. "Will doesn't seem to want to talk about it, and Julia is too out of sorts. They lived ten or fifteen miles from the town of Nevada, no other towns close by, just some neighbors here and there. Pretty close to the Kansas border."

"We are pretty close to the Kansas border," Cordia exclaimed.

Carey actually laughed at her, causing her to turn her head and look at him, stunned that anyone could be laughing at a time like this. His dark eyes were menacing even when he was amused and Cordia had difficulty looking directly into them. "Your woman scares easily, Jaris," he said crossing back to where they had all been sitting peaceably only moments before.

She started to follow him, wanting to know why she shouldn't be alarmed at this news, but Jaris had her hand and pulled her back, well aware that she would be ready to argue with Carey at the drop of a hat. "They were closer, Cordia," he explained, although not so sure she didn't have reason to be concerned.

"Still," Cordia continued, staring at Carey who no longer seemed to be paying her any attention at all. In fact, he had drawn out a pipe and was smoking, nonchalantly, as if nothing had happened. Jaris led Cordia back over to where the majority of the guests were congregated. "I don't think we should just be casual about this. Are there some authorities in Vernon we should notify? Isn't there something we can do?" she asked.

Jaris sighed, not knowing what to say next. Luckily, he didn't have to. "Cordia," her father was saying, "I don't think there is too much anyone can do about these raiders. You know they have been riding through Kansas for years. If people are going to make their homes out there, practically in the wilderness, then they will need to be careful of them. It is a shame that Jaris's cousin has died. Let us help him by tending to his brother and sister. Especially his sister. Poor girl. So young to have lost so much." He sighed, turning to Arthur who began to fill his guests in on the history of the family. Isaac Pike had his hand on his daughter's shoulder, and he pulled her with him as he crossed back to the chair where he had been sitting.

Cordia sat down on her father's knee, as if she were still a little girl, without even realizing it, half listening to the story, half lost in her own thoughts. There must be something that she could do to help that poor girl and her brother. She just needed to figure out what it could be. Meanwhile, she felt the icy eyes of Carey Adams crawling up her skin. She had known Carey her whole life and never cared for him. Unlike his gentle cousin, Jaris, Carey could be mean spirited. He had sandy blond hair and a handlebar mustache, which he was often seen twirling between his fingers. When they were younger, he would find it funny to catch an animal and threaten to torture or kill it in front of Cordia. Usually, Jaris could convince him not to harm the animal, but occasionally, he would break its neck, or cut it open, just to hear her scream. There was something not right, in her mind, about people who liked to cause pain to other living creatures. In fact, she was surprised that Carey hadn't enlisted in one army or the other yet. She had thought he would be the first to sign up when it came to causing bloodshed.

As she sat there on her father's knee, Carey continued to stare at her, and she began to wonder if he wasn't thinking of all of those times when he upset her so as a child. Perhaps he was wondering what she would sound like if he cut her open or rang her neck. A chill went down her spine, and then, thankfully, she realized that Susannah was calling her to come back to the table and finish the task they had been working on before the visitors had arrived. Margaret was coming out of the house as well. The hostess forced a smile, and Cordia knew it was only because she did not want to ruin this special day for Jaris.

Cordia crossed back over and picked up the bucket where she had left it. She glanced over her shoulder and noticed that Jaris watched her walk away. Carey, however, was no longer staring at her. He was sitting in his chair, looking bored with Arthur's tale of his wife's brother and the woes of his children. Then, she realized she must have been listening to the story more than she had originally thought. She did know that it was Margaret's brother and his wife who had moved up to Vernon about twenty-five-or-so years ago and eventually started a family. She also knew that they had died of tuberculosis, which the girl, Julia, still suffered from, and that Nolan and Will were hardworking, respectable men. She had heard that they had only been to visit a few other times, when Julia was very small, though Margaret and Arthur had gone up to visit them several times. As she began to pitch in with the necessary chores, she wondered if she had ever met these folks before. Chances were that she had if they had visited the Adams Farm.

Susannah was asking Margaret how her niece and nephew were doing. "Those are strong kids," she said, proudly. "Julia is resting, and Will is getting cleaned up. I don't know if he will be joining us, or if I'll just bring them some food later. They must be famished. Can't imagine they are much in the mood for celebrating though, and I don't want to spoil this day for Jaris, if it can be avoided."

Finally, the finishing touches were done, and Margaret picked up the triangle, to ceremoniously call everyone to eat, though it wasn't really necessary as they were all gathered relatively close together. The men made their way over and Rev. Jacobson, who had come along with his wife, said a short prayer, not only blessing Jaris on this occasion, but praying for the welfare of his extended family and for his beautiful young wife-to-be, which caught Cordia by surprise. She opened her eyes and looked at Jaris, who just happened to be looking at her. She blushed and closed her eyes again, feeling like a little kid who had been caught with her hand in the cookie jar, though in all fairness, he had his eyes open, too.

As the others dug into the bountiful feast that the Adams family had spread before them, Cordia wandered off toward the horse corral, too much on her mind to eat just now. Jaris's horse, a big appaloosa named Sam, came over to greet her, and she absent-mindedly began to stroke his long nose. She still felt an overwhelming sadness for those poor people who had lost so much. First their parents, now their brother. She was still feeling Carey's eyes on her, though he couldn't possibly see her now, as he was around the other side of the house with everyone else. Finally, she was thinking about Jaris. She wanted so badly to be in love with him and in many ways, she really did love him. But not in a way that was satisfying enough for her.

So many times in the past months, since he had asked her to be his wife last June, nearly a year ago now, he had asked her to set a date, to pick a month. At one point, he asked if she even thought it would be this year. But she had explained to him over and over, she had to see how the war was going to go, if there was going to be one, before she felt right planning a future. Though he had given in at first, he didn't seem to understand that she was serious about this issue. He seemed to think that she would change her mind. And, maybe she would. But right now, she just couldn't dream of marrying someone who was bound to enlist at a moment's notice. She sighed and ran her fingers through Sam's long main. The wind had died down and her own hair was actually beginning to look like human hair again, rather than a horse's mane. Just then, she heard someone calling her name. It was Jaris, of course, approaching her from around the house, the same way she had come. She turned and walked toward him giving Sam one more stroke as she went.

"Are you hiding?" he asked, a cup of coffee in his hand. Had she been gone that long? Were they already drinking coffee?

"No, just thinking," she said, forcing a smile.

He looped his arm through hers and began to walk back the way they had come. "Well, I have some news I need to tell everyone, and I think you ought to be present for it."

"News?" she asked, shielding her eyes from the sun. Perhaps that bonnet did some good after all. "What kind of news?"

"You'll see," he said, smiling broadly.

"But shouldn't you tell me first? I'm practically your wife," she inquired. It ought to be good for something.

He laughed. "Cordia always has to know everything first." By then they had made it most of the way back to the table. "Ladies and gentlemen, friends and family, I have a few words to say," he began, letting go of her arm, and raising his cup in the air, as if that would somehow draw everyone's attention. At first few people looked up, but then, when they realized it was the "guest of honor" speaking, the idle chatter stopped and all eyes were on Jaris as he made his important announcement.

"First of all," he began, "I want to thank my folks for this delicious birthday meal. And I can't wait to try the cake." Everyone laughed and his mother beamed proudly. "Second of all, Carey and I have an announcement." He looked at his cousin, who had also been standing, and was now walking over to stand on the other side of Jaris. "Carey and I enlisted yesterday. You are looking at Lt. Carey Adams, and Lt. Jaris Adams, Missouri State Guard." At first, everyone seemed to draw in a deep breath simultaneously. But then, there was a round of applause.

Cordia looked at the other people in the crowd—some were clapping wholeheartedly, others, who clearly wished he had enlisted for the Union—were only clapping in support of this young man on his birthday. His parents actually seemed to approve and were nodding proudly. Soon, everyone was standing and offering Jaris and Carey their congratulations. Even Carey's stern old father seemed not at all shocked or surprised at the announcement. So why was it that Cordia seemed to be the only one horrified at the thought of her fiancé joining in the war effort?

Just then, she noticed one other person who was not joining in the backslapping; Jaris's cousin, Will. He was sitting on the porch rail of the cabin, looking out past the pasture, past the woods beyond them, seemingly past the horizon itself. She studied him for a moment, seeing that he still seemed haggard and weary, but that he had changed into clean clothes, maybe even bathed. As she stared at him, he turned his head and looked at her, again, catching her eyes in that deep, almost mystifying stare. She caught her breath and looked away. Jaris was taking her arm again and was looking at her for some form of approval to his announcement. She smiled and nodded at him, as if to say she understood. She had known all along that she couldn't stop him anyway. And then, she couldn't help but peek back over her soon-to-be-husband's head to see if his cousin was still looking at her. But when she turned to look, he was gone.

WILL HAD CLEANED HIMSELF UP, as had Julia. He had even considered going outside and being sociable, as he was sure that is what Nolan would expect him to do. But he was not in any mood for introductions, nor was he ready to tell anyone about the ordeal they had just been through. His aunt had brought him in a plate of food—which he had devoured. Julia's sat untouched, waiting for her. He was hoping that she would sleep awhile. She could use the rest.

Eventually, he had wandered outside, hoping the fresh air would clear his head a little. But he did not dare venture into the crowd of strangers. It was hard enough for him to talk to a group of people he didn't know, and the events of the day would make doing so even more difficult. He stood on the porch for a few minutes, looking around the farm. His uncle had some good land here and had done a fine job of clearing it and turning it into food and profit. He sat down on the porch rail, looking out beyond the farm, and thinking about all that had happened in the last few days. For a moment, his mind slipped away, and he was not in Lamar anymore. He was back on their farm.

"Come on, get down!" his brother was yelling at him. "Ma is going to see us!" In his vision, Nolan must have been about eight, he no more than five. They were standing on a board they had nailed across the inside of the old, dried up well. He could hear his ma's voice calling to them. Why did she fall for this same trick every time? She would come out the door, and her sons would jump up and scare her. They must have done it a dozen times since the well dried up the year before. He turned his head and looked into his brother's eyes. But suddenly, they were not the mischievous, carefree eyes of an eight-year-old anymore;

they were the eyes of a dying man as he fell to the ground, blood running trickling down his forehead....

Will turned away from the vision, trying to shake the idea out of his mind. But as he turned his head, he caught another pair of eyes. Clear, curious, hazel eyes that must have been watching him as he sat there, transfixed. Suddenly, she remembered herself and turned around. Will could clearly see that she was with his cousin, Jaris, by the way she was standing next to him. This was confirmed when he took her arm, and she smiled up at him. Will went back inside then, thinking maybe he should lay down himself. Maybe some sleep would help him to get beyond the awful visions dancing around in his weary mind.

Chapter Three

THE NEXT DAY WAS SUNDAY, and like every Sunday, the Adams family and the Pike family sat in the same pew of the First Baptist Church. They were surrounded by friends, family, townsfolk, and this Sunday, even some visitors from out of town, though not the two strangers Cordia had seen yesterday at Jaris's birthday party. Margaret explained that both her niece and nephew had been literally exhausted, and she did not think she should wake them, not even for church service. Of course, no one disagreed, knowing what the two had been through.

Still, Cordia was disappointed. Not only did this Will intrigue her almost to the point of alarm, but she also wanted to offer her assistance to poor Julia. She had even asked her mother if she could dig through the attic and look for some of her old dresses which might fit the young girl. Her mother agreed that her idea was a good one but insisted that Cordia let the housekeeper, Frieda, do the actual digging. So, Cordia sat through the service in her usual place between her mother and father, listening to Rev. Jacobson preach the Bible's warning not to go to war without the proper spiritual armor.

Occasionally, she would glance past her father and past Mr. Adams to see if Jaris was paying attention. She thought this sermon may actually be for his benefit, and for Carey's, after yesterday's announcement.

While Jaris certainly seemed to be listening, he also seemed to be preoccupied in his thoughts. He even caught her looking at him a few times, and barely smiled, which was unusual for him. Her father, however, caught her looking at Jaris as well and gave her a most disagreeable look. She knew she couldn't explain to her father that she wasn't looking at him in a "wanton" way, that she was just curious as to her betrothed's ideas about the sermon, so she decided she had better stop glancing at him altogether and focus her own attention on the sermon, though she wasn't quite sure what it had to do with her directly. She wasn't planning on fighting any battles anytime soon.

After the sermon, Cordia stopped to talk to Susannah while her parents lingered to discuss the sermon with the reverend. Susannah's youngest son was digging in the dirt, and her other boy was running around with a few other children. She hadn't gotten a chance to talk to her friend yesterday after Jaris's announcement. Now, as she waited for her parents, and Susannah waited on her husband, who was talking to several of the men who had just enlisted, including the Adams boys, she finally had an opportunity to discuss her concerns. "Well, what do you think of Jaris signing up?" Susannah asked, as if reading her mind.

Cordia sighed. "I don't like it," she admitted. "But then I guess there really ain't much a girl can do about it either."

Susannah nodded in agreement. "I think James is going to do it any day now. He keeps talking about it. There he is standing over there talking to the State Guard boys. I'm sure he'll go." She reached down to straighten her little boy's hat, which did no good as he promptly knocked it catawampus again. Then, as if she didn't realize she was talking out loud, Susannah added, "I'm sure that if he goes, he'll get killed."

Cordia paused, not sure she had heard her friend correctly. Susannah straightened back up, looking a little ashamed. "What did you say?" Cordia asked.

Susannah sighed, not quite able to look her friend in the eye. "I don't know, Cordy. I just have this feeling that if he goes, he ain't coming back. Don't you ever think about that? "

"Of course I think about that," Cordia admitted. "But I don't go around saying I think it's going to happen. Why in the world would you say such a thing?" Cordia knew her friend, understood that she was very superstitious, and also realized that Susannah wouldn't say such a thing if she didn't really, truly believe it was a certainty.

"I don't know." Her friend looked over at her husband, and then down at the ground. "I just have this feeling. And I don't know what I will do if it comes true. I'm not like you Cordy, not able to pick and choose who I'll have. I would be on my own, with two small boys, for the rest of my life."

Now Cordia was a little offended, though she didn't know what gave her the right to be. "Susannah," she began, "I have had one proposal, same as you. If something happened to Jaris, I would most likely die an old maid. But that's not the point now, is it? We shouldn't be concerned that our men won't return because of how it will leave us. We should be concerned about our men not returning because what it means for them."

Again, Susannah looked ashamed. "You're right, Cordy. I'm sorry— such a terrible thing to say. Still, I do have my boys to think of."

"I know," Cordia said, wrapping her arm around her friend's shoulders. "I know. It will be all right."

Then, as if out of nowhere, Susannah added yet another bit of superstition. "You know, they say that, if'n your loved one dies away from home, you'll know it before word ever reaches you."

Cordia's curiosity, always at its peak, now had the better of her. "What do you mean?" she asked.

Susannah continued. "They say that their spirit will leave them and make its way back to you. People have told stories about looking out a window, or down a lane, and seeing their loved one comin'. Then, they just disappear. And then, hours later, they find out that, at the time they thought they saw them a'comin', they were already dead."

Cordia looked at her friend with a great amount of skepticism. "I don't reckon I believe that, Susannah." Then, she went further by saying, "And I ain't sure that's the type of thing people should discuss in the churchyard."

"Maybe you're right, Cordy," Susannah admitted, "But if you see Jaris comin' down the road someday, and then he disappears, you'll know something has happened."

Just then, Cordia noticed her parents motioning her over. They were ready to go. "See you later, Susy. Let me know if you need any help with those rascals of yours." As she made her way toward the wagon, Susannah's words replayed in her head. *"Ridiculous,"* she thought. In the back of her mind, she raised the question of whether or not this superstition applied if you weren't sure you truly loved the deceased, but she fought that thought back down and shook her head at the silly story.

Just then Jaris came running over to help her into the wagon seat. "I guess you know we won't be seeing you for dinner today," he said as he took her hand and helped her up.

She did not know that. She looked at him with a blank stare, expecting him to continue, which he did. "My ma wants us to have a meal with my cousins, just the family today. Kind of a remembrance."

Cordia nodded. This must be the first time in nearly two years that their two families had not met for dinner on Sunday. "I see," she stated. "Well, Frieda was going to gather up some dresses of mine for your cousin. Julia, is it?" He nodded, and she continued. "I was thinking perhaps I would bring them by later, maybe see if there is anything that I can do for her."

"Cordia, you're one of the sweetest people I ever did meet," he said, still clutching her hand, though she was already in her seat. "I think that would be a wonderful gesture toward my cousin. I know she would dearly appreciate your friendship."

Cordia could feel her face turning a little red. She hadn't really thought it would mean too much, just giving someone some old clothes. "Well, maybe I'll see you later then." She smiled at him. Her father and mother said their goodbyes as well and waved to some remaining friends outside the church. Just before Jaris let go of her hand, he kissed it very quickly, about the boldest thing he had done to show his affection that year. Cordia was surprised but had no time to even see Jaris's face as he stepped away from the carriage, as they were on their way. She glanced back over her shoulder as they made their way the few blocks toward their home. He tipped his hat to her, and she waved. Maybe one of these days, before he off and left for the war, he would actually get up enough nerve to kiss her lips again.

That April afternoon was wet, as many April days are in that part of Missouri, and Cordia was having a little bit of trouble steering the wagon down the muddy dirt path that led to the Adams Farm. It was only a few miles out of town, but the wind was blowing up the rain a bit, and she didn't think she could possibly make it there without being absolutely drenched, even with a hat and with Frieda attempting to keep the umbrella over their heads. Her mother had practically forbidden her to go, saying the dresses would be too wet to wear by the time she got there anyhow, but Cordia was about as stubborn as they came, and she had insisted that she would not leave that poor girl another day without some proper clothes and a proper friendship. Jane had finally realized she was arguing on a losing side, as most people were if they ventured to argue with her daughter, so she had let her go, as long as she took Frieda along with her. Cordia agreed, and much to Frieda's dismay, here they were.

Frieda was one of the few people on the planet who ever attempted to put Cordia Pike in her place. She was a middle-aged woman who had been looking after Cordia, and her parents for that matter, since Cordia was born. Frieda had no family of her own, being the only child to survive when typhus hit their cabin when she was twelve. She had buried both parents, three brothers and two sisters, and she had never married. So, though she did not necessarily like being out in the rain assisting this foolhardy young lady, she did understand how the girl they were trying to help was feeling. And she understood that, while she often had the mind of a mule, Cordia Pike had a loving heart, and she was set on showing some love that day.

As Cordia made the last turn into the drive that led up to the Adams Farm, she could see that there were cows loose all over the place. "Must have had a fence break," Frieda was saying. Surely the Adams's knew, but Cordia sped up a little, dodging a few strays, as she neared the house, hoping to inform them of the breakout as soon as possible. She tied up the horses as Frieda grabbed the bundle of dresses, which they had been keeping in a wooden box to help keep them dry.

Cordia knocked on the door, but no one answered. She looked at Frieda and then knocked again, this time more determinedly. "I wonder if they aren't all out trying to get those cows put back in," she yelled over the wind. Frieda just nodded. But surely someone had to be home. Would Julia be out helping in her condition? Frieda knocked one more time, and finally, the door opened, just a crack.

"Who is it?" a frightened voice answered from within. Cordia could barely see pale blue eyes peeking out at her. It was Julia. She was white as a ghost and looked petrified to open the door to strangers. Cordia could understand why she might be concerned, after her ordeal, but she was a little astonished that she might think these two women could do her some harm.

"Julia?" she called, softly. "Julia, my name is Cordia Pike. I am a friend of your aunt and her family." She paused, wondering if the girl would believe her and let them in. Though the porch offered a little bit of protection from the blowing rain, they were still getting drenched. Julia did not make a move, so she continued. "Julia, I was here yesterday for Jaris's birthday party. Perhaps you saw me? I know you weren't in a state to be paying much attention." She thought maybe she had overstepped her boundaries and again Julia didn't move.

Frieda seemed to grow impatient. "All right," she said. "Now Miss Julia, this here is Jaris's fiancée. She has brought you some nice dresses because she is concerned about you and wants to be your friend. Now, you can either stand there and stare at us until we drown out here, or you can let us in where it's dry and warm, but we ain't going away."

"Frieda!" Cordia began to reprimand her caregiver, but just then the door swung open, and a seemingly very small, terrified girl gestured for them to come in. "Thank you," Cordia said as she began to remove her rain bonnet. Frieda brought in the dresses and set them down by the fireplace, which provided the only light in the room, except for the little sunlight that was pouring in through the three windows. Cordia never remembered seeing the cabin so dark and musty. She could barely see past the room they were standing in. Though it was a wood-frame farmhouse, there was plenty of room. The kitchen was in the back and a small staircase led up to the boys' rooms. Their parents' room was just off the living room to the right, a curtain separating it from the main living area. There were two more small rooms off of the kitchen, one in the back and one to the side, which led out to a porch. Cordia thought maybe they had made one of those rooms into Julia's for the time being. Julia seemed a little lost. She wandered across the room and sat down at a small table in the corner of the room, across from the fireplace, her head in her hands.

Cordia waited a moment before she spoke. "Is everyone else out trying to wrestle up the cattle?" she asked. Julia seemed not to hear her at first. Then, she slowly nodded her head. "Julia?" Cordia asked, walking slowly toward her. "Julia," she repeated. "Is there anything at all that I can do for you?"

The girl looked up at her then. And for a moment it was as if this was the first time she had noticed she had company. Then, she said quietly, "You said you were gonna be Jaris's wife?"

Cordia looked at Frieda, who was still standing by the fireplace, trying to warm up. Cordia didn't even feel the cold herself. She was too preoccupied with helping the girl in front of her. She nodded at Julia, who turned her head and looked at the table again. "May I sit down?" she asked, her hand on a chair.

Julia nodded and Cordia sat down beside her. She could feel the water dripping out of her dress, probably making a puddle on Margaret's clean floor. But she didn't care at the moment. She could help her clean it up later. "I'm sure Mrs. Adams is taking very good care of you," she continued, hoping the girl would relax a little bit. "She's so kindhearted. You've eaten already then?" she asked.

Once again, Julia nodded. Her blonde hair looked all out of sorts. She had it pulled back into a loose ponytail, but Cordia could tell she had slept on it that way and hadn't bothered to fix it. Cord thought it looked as if she had also slept in her dress. It was wrinkled, and the bow was untied in the back. Cordia continued. "Good. I'm glad you've eaten. Well, I just wanted you to have some of the dresses that I have outgrown. I thought you could use them." Julia didn't say anything. She seemed to be staring out the window, out past the woods, much as her brother seemed to have been doing the day before.

Cordia stood up. "I guess we'll head out then," she began, looking for any sign from Julia that she wanted her to stay. She didn't move, so Cordia nodded to Frieda, who started toward the door. "If there is anything at all that I can do to help you through this troubled time, please don't hesitate to let me know," she added as she turned to go.

Just then, Julia's hand shot out and grabbed her arm. Her fingers were ice cold, and they caused Cordia to jump at their touch. "Wait," she said. "Please don't go until my brother gets back. Or my aunt. I don't want to be alone."

At first Cordia was too startled to say anything. She couldn't believe the girl had said so many words to her at once. But then, she put her hand on top of the frail little one that still clung to her arm. "Of course I will stay," she said, sitting back down at the table. Julia looked grateful and for a second, it almost looked as if she was going to smile. But then the smile faded and that look of woe returned to her face. Once again, she held her head in her hands. But this time, having broken through a little, Cordia reached over and smoothed the tangled blonde hair. She was greatly relieved that Julia didn't put up a resistance. She heard Frieda behind her sitting down in a chair by the fire. It seemed like ten or fifteen minutes that Cordia sat there, running her hand over the young girls' hair, not saying a word. Finally, Julia looked up at her. "I haven't brushed it for a few days," she said. "I haven't really found the strength, nor the need, I guess."

Cordia hesitated for a second, but then ventured a suggestion. "I have a brush in my bag here. Would you like me to brush it and tie it up for you? You have such beautiful, light hair. I promise to be very gentle," she added with a warm smile.

She was surprised when Julia overzealously nodded her approval. She was expecting her to ignore the question, or at the very least tell her not to touch her. But it seemed this young lady really needed someone to reach out to her right this moment, and thanks to a few hundred cows, Cordia was the only one in the position to do that. She drew her brush out of her purse that hung from her wrist and set her fan and the purse on the table. Then, she took the ribbon out of Julia's hair and began to brush it as gently as possible. Shortly, she realized that Julia was crying. She stopped for a second, thinking maybe she had hurt her. But Julia motioned for her to continue, so she did. Finally, between her tears, Julia began to talk. "My mama used to brush my hair for hours," she wept. "After she died, sometimes Nolan would try, but he would always come near tearing my head off than getting out the tangles. Of course, I could do it myself, but there's just something about having your mama brush your hair."

"I know," Cordia agreed. She could remember when she was little how nice it was to sit on her mama's lap as she brushed her hair. Of course, often enough it was Frieda who held the brush, but there was something special when it was your mama.

Julia continued, "It was so kind of you to come on a day like this, all this way, in the rain and mud just to bring me some dresses. And you don't even know me."

Cordia carefully wound the ribbon back into place. "You're right, I don't know you. But I know your family. And there's nothing I wouldn't do for them. And that means there's nothing I wouldn't do for you, Julia." She sat back down, fished a handkerchief out of her purse and wiped Julia's tears with it.

Julia seemed to want to say more but couldn't think of the words. She whispered, "Thank you."

Cordia smiled letting her know she was most welcome. She gently patted the younger girl on the arm. Just then, there was a sound at the door. Both girls turned to see Will walking in.

Cordia's look of surprise was only out done by the expression on Will's face. He had volunteered to repair the break in the fence while his cousins and aunt and uncle gathered up the stray cattle. They were just about finished and he had come back to check on his sister. He hadn't even noticed the wagon tied out front and was greatly astonished to see that his sister was not alone. Cordia, likewise, was shocked to see him walk in for some reason, though it made perfect sense, since he was staying there. She simply stared at him, dumbfounded, until Julia jumped up and ran over to hug him. "Will!" she exclaimed, as she attempted to throw her arms around him.

He stepped back, keeping her at arm's length. "Hold on, Jules. I'm soaked and you don't need to be getting all wet." She nodded, knowing that any amount of wetness could easily cause her consumption to flare up.

She stepped back away from him. "Sorry," she began. "I was just really excited to see you."

He smiled at her, glad to see that she was sounding a little more like herself. He had been extremely worried about her the last few days. She hardly ate, hardly talked. When she did sleep, it was restless. Then, he noticed her hair. "Your hair looks beautiful, Jules. I don't think I've seen it that pretty since Ma used to fix it."

Her hand automatically went up to touch her hair at his mention of it. "Cordia brushed it for me," she said, nodding in Cordia's general direction. It was then that Will remembered that they were not alone. He wasn't exactly sure what he was supposed to do. It wasn't often that he was introduced to a young lady, especially one of the social status of Miss Cordia Pike, whom he had learned much about from his cousin in the day or so he had been living there. According to Jaris, she was a goddess, the sweetest, smartest, prettiest girl on earth. And though he had yet to speak to her, he was sure Jaris was right on at least one count. She was strikingly beautiful. Which made it even more awkward. Luckily, Miss Cordia Pike seemed to know what was proper in this situation. She had already stood up while he was wondering what it was he was supposed to do. She gracefully crossed the room and offered him her hand. He looked at Julia who seemed to mime to him to just take her hand. But was he supposed to kiss it or shake it? He didn't know. Once again, he didn't have to decide, as Cordia gave his hand a polite shake and then let it go.

Cordia was nervous to do such a thing in her own right, especially knowing he had seen her staring at him yesterday on at least two occasions, yet she did know what was fit and proper. She curtsied briefly and said, "Pleased to meet you, Mr. . . ." then she realized she didn't know his last name. She knew it wasn't Adams because they were cousins on Jaris's mother's side, but she didn't know her maiden name. And he wasn't helping. He didn't fill in the blank as she had hoped, he just stood there, dripping and looking at her with those brown eyes, deep as a well.

Julia seemed to have finally gathered all of her wits about her. She chimed in, "Tucker. Our last name is Tucker."

Cordia nodded her thanks and tried a greeting again. "Please to meet you, Mr. Tucker."

"Uh," he began, glancing again at his little sister. She had read enough books to know how men and women were supposed to act around each other. He, on the other hand, was practically clueless when it came to these sorts of proper things. Finally, he got out, "Likewise, Miss Pike."

Cordia wondered how he knew her last name. Had Julia said it when she introduced her? No. She knew she hadn't. Maybe Jaris had said something about her. Then, she heard Frieda clearing her voice from over by the fireplace. At first, Cordia thought that she was simply trying to get Cordia to introduce her, but then she saw her nodding her head toward the door and realized she was trying to get her mistress to leave. After all, they had come and done the appointed task, and Julia had asked them simply to stay until her brother returned. So now, they should be free to go.

But Cordia knew that Jaris would be unhappy if he didn't get a chance to see her while she was there. So, rather than acknowledge that she had seen Frieda's head nod, she went with her initial instinct. "I'm sorry—where are my manners? Mr. Tucker, Miss Tucker, this is Frieda Gardner. She takes care of most everything at our home. I apologize for not having introduced her earlier."

Frieda looked extremely annoyed. They all exchanged how-do-you-dos and then a moment of awkward silence resumed. Once again, it was Julia who found something to say first. "Will, you should come over by the fire. You're dripping all over the floor."

Will looked down and could see that he surely was. He had taken off his hat but still held it in his hand. He now placed it on the hearth, next to the dresses Cordia had brought. "What's this?" he asked his sister.

Julia looked as though she had forgotten herself at first. Then, it came to her. "Oh, Cordia brought me some dresses. Wasn't that nice of her?" She went over and looked at the bundle for the first time. "They sure are fine-looking," she added.

Cordia smiled. "I hope they fit. There's about ten of them there, I think." Then, she hesitantly turned to Will, for some reason nervous to ask him anything. "Do you know if Jaris will be coming back anytime soon?"

Briefly, Will had hoped that Miss Pike was actually lingering to talk to him. He didn't know why he would care, but the thought had crossed his mind. Now, he realized she was waiting to see her betrothed. Without turning to look at her, he answered. "He should be home in a minute or two. They were getting the last of the cattle herded back into the pen as I was leaving. Would have stayed to finish the job, but I was a little worried about you, Jules."

Julia nodded in understanding. "I am feeling better," she assured her brother. He nodded, clearly seeing that whatever it was that this Cordia Pike had said or done for his sister had snapped her out of the trance she seemed to be in when he left her a few hours ago.

"My goodness, it's wet!" Arthur was exclaiming as he flung open the door. Behind him trooped in all four of his sons and his wife, all soaked to the bone. Puddles quickly began to form on the floor, and Cordia wondered if they might form a river, what with so many drippy people all entering at once. The three younger boys all ran to the fireplace, stripping off coats and hats as they went. They didn't see Frieda there at first and almost knocked her over, much to her chagrin. Julia scooted over to help her aunt get out of her wet things, and Will simply slid over to make room around the fire. Meanwhile, Jaris had yet to notice Cordia standing across the room. He was also trying to get out of his wet coat, hat, and gloves. It was Margaret's cry of surprise that first made him look up and realize that she was there. Cordia was beginning to wonder if their wagon hadn't floated away. Normally, people noticed when someone else pulled up and hitched in at their house.

"Why Cordia Pike! Look what the rain has washed in!" Margaret exclaimed. "I'd hug you, but I'm soaked."

Cordia smiled. "That's all right, Mrs. Adams. Frieda and I just came to drop some dresses off for Julia. Now, we better get going before the road gets washed out."

The whole family seemed astonished, even Jaris who knew she had planned on coming by. "You came all this way in this storm on a mission to deliver dresses?" Mr. Adams asked.

Cordia nodded, catching Jaris's eyes. Even though he was dripping wet, he was beaming with pride at Cordia's act of kindness.

"I do declare, you are an angel," Mrs. Adams said, crossing the room to take Cordia's hand in hers. "It is a wonder your mother ever let you leave the house," she added.

"She didn't want her to come," Frieda was explaining from her new position practically in the corner of the room. "But it ain't an easy thing to tell Miss Cordia Pike no and have her listen."

Cordia gave Frieda a harsh look but chose not to try to defend herself. She knew she had a reputation for being strong-willed, or mule-headed as her father liked to call her, but she wasn't about to back out on her word that she would be a bringing those dresses this day.

"At any rate," Cordia began, "Frieda and I had better be a getting on our way."

"Now, I don't know," Margaret began to protest. "It is mighty wet out there. Maybe you had best wait out the storm here."

Cordia felt very uncomfortable, all of a sudden, in the presence of Jaris and his cousin. She wasn't sure why. She didn't even know Will Tucker. Why should she be ill at ease in his presence at all, let alone with Jaris also nearby? Yet, she couldn't help but feel as if she had somehow wronged Jaris by simply conversing with Will. Maybe it was the way she couldn't help herself but to look at him that made her feel this way. All she knew for sure was that she wanted to get out of there as quickly as possible. "Mrs. Adams, thank you, but we made it this far, and I think the rain has actually let up a little. We'll be okay—it's only a few miles."

Margaret opened her mouth as if to protest, but before she could say a word, Jaris stopped her. "Ain't no good to quarrel with her Mama, her mind's made up." His mother looked at him, as if she was about to argue with him, but she relented. Jaris promptly put his hat and coat back on. "I'll walk you ladies out to your wagon," he said.

Cordia had already picked up her things and was tying her bonnet back on. "No, that's okay, Jaris, you don't have to do that. We'll be all right."

But he was already halfway out the door. *"Maybe there is someone I can't argue with,"* Cordia thought. Then, out loud she said, "Well, you all have a pleasant evening."

Before she could even say goodbye to Julia, the girl had crossed the room and taken her by the hand. "Thank you most kindly, Cordia," she said quietly.

Cordia pressed her hand in hers. "If there is anything I can do, please let me know," she said smiling. Then, before she knew what was coming out of her mouth, she yelled across the room, without really looking at him, "It was nice to meet you, Mr. Tucker."

Will was a little startled at first. He was not only surprised to hear her speaking to him again; he was more surprised to hear her call him Mr. Tucker. He wanted to say something, acknowledge her in some way, but the words got stuck in his throat, and before he could get anything out, she was through the door and out into the rain, Frieda following close behind.

Jaris took her arm and tried to lead her around the puddles that were slowly washing away the dirt path to the hitching post. "You sure you're going to make it back to town all right?" he asked.

Cordia could barely hear him over the wind and rain. "Yes," she yelled. "We'll be fine." The horses had gotten some shelter from the rain by a large tree that hung over the hitch. In retrospect, she probably should have untied them and put them in the barn nearby, but it wasn't too cold, and they seemed to be all right.

For the second time that day, Jaris helped her up into the wagon. "Be careful," he said. She nodded, the wind, blowing the rain almost directly in her face. Then, he shocked her again. He put one foot onto the carriage mount, pulled himself up, and kissed her lips. She was so astonished; she couldn't have kissed him back if she had had the presence of mind to even think of such a thing.

As Frieda led the horses down the path, Cordia sat in shock, wondering what had possessed him to suddenly become so bold. This world was becoming an awful surprising place.

She didn't know that Will had been watching from the cabin. If she had, she would have been even more astounded to know how much it bothered him to witness that kiss.

Chapter Four

WEEKDAY EVENINGS WERE GENERALLY quiet in the town of Lamar. Cordia usually spent the time after supper reading in her room or playing the piano for her father in the den. Occasionally, a few of the elder men in town would meet with her father in the parlor, the door closed, voices low and secretive, and the only indication of what was going on in there was the continual smell of pipe smoke that seeped out from around the door. Of course, Cordia knew they were discussing the imminent war and the defense of the town, which was a welcome idea, at last. By late April, there seemed no way around it. There was a fight coming, and they could no longer pretend it away. Several men were leaving the county every day to meet up with regiments from one side or the other.

The State Guard continued to drill on the square, and sometimes, when she was bringing lunch to her daddy, Cordia would see Jaris drilling right along with them. He was very good, too, she had noticed, never seemed to miss a beat. Most of the time he was too consumed by what he was doing to realize she was there, but from time to time, she'd see him catch her out of the corner of his eye and a crooked grin would pull at the corners of his mouth. Eventually, the men were drilling every day and Cordia knew it was just a matter of time before

Jaris left, went off with his unit to join up with Claiborne Jackson's men.

It had been several weeks since Jaris's birthday celebration, and Cordia had not seen his cousin, Will, since that day in the rain. At church, she had gotten a chance to talk with Julia, who was still very thankful for all that Cordia had done to help her regain her composure after her brother's murder. She had said only that Will was not in a religious mood these days. Then, she said that she was pretty certain that he would be joining up with Franz Sigel's Union men, who were now encamped somewhere between Lamar and Springfield. Cordia couldn't help but ask why Julia thought he wouldn't be joining the Southern cause like his cousin, but Julia explained that Will felt like it was the Confederate Army that was partially responsible for Nolan's death. Guerrillas of Southern sympathy had been terrorizing the area, and there was no doubt that the men who had shot their brother were in support of "the cause."

Though she had not seen Will for many days, her mind had wondered to him many times. She wasn't sure why. There was just something about him that made her want to stare into those infinitely deep brown eyes. At first, she had tried to put him out of her mind. She had concentrated on Jaris—even tried to make herself think of all the horrible things her poor fiancé may have to go through in battle— so as to avoid thinking about his cousin. But, eventually, she gave up trying not to think about Will. Now, it seemed almost every time someone began to talk to her, she wasn't listening. She was daydreaming about a time when there was no war, and Jaris had decided upon marrying someone else. Then, Will (who hardly knew her and surely had not thought of her at all since he saw her last) could declare his love for her and they could ride off on a white horse....

"Cordia!"

"Fiddle," she said under her breath. She had done it again. Here she was, up in her room, supposed to be reading her Bible, and instead her mind had wandered off to the point that she did not hear her mother yelling for her. She could tell by the tone of her voice that this was not the first time she had hollered up the stairs at her.

"Yes, Mother," she said running to the landing that overlooked the staircase. She could see by the expression on her mother's face that she was not amused at having to stand there and scream.

"Jaris is here! Please come down!"

And then, Cordia saw him, standing behind her mother, his hat in his hand, looking at the ground. "*Strange*," she thought. "*Why would Jaris be here on a Thursday?*" He had never shown up in the middle of the week before—ever. She began to think maybe something had happened. "I'll be right down." She ran back to her room to straighten her dress, and then bounded down the stairs. Her mother was still standing in the foyer, smiling at Jaris, who seemed to be making polite conversation. Her father and several men were in the parlor, doors shut, smoke billowing.

"Jaris," Cordia began, "what on earth are you doing here in the middle of the week?"

"Now, Cordia," her mother reprimanded. "Is that the way to greet the man you love?"

Cordia had meant no disrespect, and Jaris could see that. "That's all right," he replied. "I thought you would be surprised to see me, but I need to talk to you."

Once again, Cordia's mind was spinning with imaginative explanations for his presence. Was there a battle? Had his home been attacked? He looked too calm for that. What could it be?

"Would you mind joining me on a short stroll, Miss Cordia? If it's all right with your mother, of course?"

Cordia looked at her mother, who nodded her approval. She grabbed a hat from the hook by the door and stepped outside.

At first, Jaris took her by the arm and led her out into the moonlit sidewalk without any explanation at all. In fact, it took him several minutes before he even spoke. It was all Cordia could do to keep herself from asking questions, but she was trying to downplay her role as the curious girl who could not be patient. And Jaris was intrigued, so he kept her in suspense for as long as he could, wondering what was wrong with her that she hadn't started asking him questions.

Finally, he turned to her and asked, "Well, don't you want to know what I'm doing here?"

"Of course." Cordia blurted out, no longer able to control herself.

"I was trying not to be nosey, but if you aren't going to explain yourself...."

He was laughing at her now. She expected as much. She wasn't sure why so many people found her curiosity so amusing. "Cordia, I am going to miss you something awful," he said.

Now she understood. That's why he had come. He was finally going to join up with the army. Though she had known he was going, and though she only loved him as a friend, it was still a little difficult for her to bear. She let go of his arm, walking a little ahead of him at first. But he caught up to her and took her arm again. "Cordia, don't be cross," he said pulling her back toward him. "You knew I was going."

"Yes, yes, I did," she admitted, turning to face him. "But that doesn't mean I have to like it." She looked at him, straining to see his face in the dim moonlight. "I'm not mad, Jaris. I'm sad. I'm sad for all of us, sad that this war ever had to happen."

"I know, I know," he said, putting his arms around her. "Me, too. But I have to go. We're leaving this Saturday. All of us, riding out together. Only leaving about forty militia behind to guard the town."

She rested her head against his chest, something that, before, would have seemed too strange to her, but now, on the edge of this cliff, it seemed right and natural. At first, she wanted to ask why he couldn't just be one of those forty left behind, but there seemed no use in arguing. Obviously, his mind was made up. She was a little confused. "I thought you were in the infantry," she said, more as a question.

"I am. But there's no railroad that joins up with Jackson's men. Besides, as an officer, I will be allowed to keep my horse. We'll ride over—then there will be plenty of walking. Then, the enlisted men will likely donate their horses to the artillery. They need us pretty badly, we hear."

All so complicated, she thought. So complex. She was amazed that people could even keep track of where they were and what they were doing, let alone their enemies. She let the news sink in a bit more, and then turned to walk back toward her house. "Well, I guess I have no say, so, thank you for letting me know," she said a bit tartly. But Jaris was pulling her back toward him.

"There's one more thing," he said, still clutching her arm. Her hazel eyes looked up at him, questioningly. He continued. "Skeet Cooper and Samuel Wilkerson, well, their girls have consented to take their hands before they go. Rev. Jacobson has agreed to marry them Friday, before the big bonfire celebration they're a'plannin' to send us off." She stared at him in confusion, wondering what it was he was getting at exactly. Jaris let out a sigh, as if he'd hoped she'd figure it out on her own. "Cordia, is there any chance at all that you would change your mind? Be my wife, before I pull out of here on Saturday?"

The fog had lifted. Now she fully understood what had made him come to her house in the middle of the week. Once again, Cordia was put in a position in which she felt most uncomfortable. She knew how much it meant to Jaris to have her for his wife before he left. And if she were in love with him the way he was so completely in love with her, then she would have wanted nothing less. But, as she looked into those blue eyes, lightened by the moon above her, she knew that she did not love him, not like that. She could not marry him—not now, not ever.

But she couldn't come out and tell him that just before he left for war. So, instead, she shook her head "no" and began with her usual excuses for delaying the wedding.

He cut her off though, not wanting to hear again why they should not be planning their future together at such a time of turmoil. Shaking her head was all he needed. "All right, all right," he said, letting go of her and walking back toward the house.

"Jaris," she said, following behind him. "It's not... I don't mean to..." but she didn't have the words to say.

He spun around then to face her. "Cordia, don't you think I know that you don't love me the way that I love you?" Her eyes grew in astonishment. In fact, she had assumed he did think she loved him the same way. Why would he propose to her if he didn't? "Every day since I was fourteen I have dreamt of the day that you would take my hand as my wife. I know that you don't love me like that, that you don't spend your hours dreaming of me, or wishing we were together." She shook her head in bewilderment, amazed that he had ascertained this sentiment. "But Cordia Pike, I promise that, if you'll have me, I will make you the happiest woman in the world."

Cordia was awestruck; she didn't know what to say or to do. Now, he was on one knee, as if he was proposing all over again. What should she do? She couldn't bear to break his heart—she wouldn't dare to marry him when she did not love him. She did the only thing she could think of. She started to cry. And it wasn't that simple womanly pitter-patter cry, either. It was an all-out bawl, her body shaking with each sob. She sank to her knees beside him.

At first, Jaris seemed shocked as if he wasn't sure what in the world would cause her to do such a thing. Cordia began to blubber through her tears. "You leaving...." She could tell he was straining to make it out. "Don't know what I would do to be a widow, so young. Can't think of marrying now. Not now."

"Cordia, Cordia," he was stammering. "Please stop. I'm sorry. I am so sorry." He drew out his handkerchief, handed it to her, and rested her head on his shoulder. Within a few moments, she calmed down and simply seemed to vibrate occasionally, as a stymied sob tried to escape. Eventually, he began to talk again. "I didn't mean to upset you, love. It's all right. We can wait. We can wait."

That is what she had been waiting to hear. And she began to piece herself back together. He helped her up and walked her slowly toward her home. She did feel a bit ashamed of herself, having practically thrown a fit to get her way. But she had done it for the right reasons, or at least that is what she was telling herself. How she was going to get past marrying him when the war was over, she wasn't quite sure. But she did know that war changes everything. Perhaps she would not be the same person after the war. Perhaps she would want to marry him then. All she could be certain of was that she could not rightly marry him without loving him. And she did not love him that summer night as she made her way back to the solace of her home.

ON FRIDAY AFTERNOON, the whole town seemed to shut down early. When Isaac Pike had heard that there was to be a big send-off for all of the boys going out to fight, he insisted on hosting it at his house. And no one protested, as the Pikes were known for throwing some of the best social events in the county. After the double wedding at the First Baptist Church, they all walked or drove their horses and carriages the few blocks to the stately, two-story brick house on Broadway. Frieda had stayed behind to ensure everyone would have plenty of libations when they arrived. It was almost like a parade, Cordia noticed, as she walked along beside her parents making their way back home. Some of the fighting men were in their uniforms, many carrying their guns, sometimes firing them up into the air. And though not all the uniforms were the same, some for one side, some for the other, no one seemed to be disagreeable or ready to fight the folks from their own town. This was the last celebration before the war, and they did not mean to spoil it by discussing the issues as of yet.

As they made their way into the yard, Cordia's role switched from member of the audience to hostess, and she hurried about trying to make their dozens of guests as comfortable as possible. Her father had arranged for several bales of hay and benches to be set up in the yard. A trio of musicians was playing the fiddle, guitar, and accordion. The fire was a blazing, cooking several hogs, enough for everyone. Cordia scurried about, handing glasses of water and ale off to her guests, careful not to trip over the children running back and forth throughout the rolling green yard. Her mother and Frieda were awful busy as well, making sure the number of beverages was enough to go around. In her hustle and bustle, Cordia barely had time to think. At one point, she turned so quickly, taking drinks to more guests, that she ran smack into someone. She looked up, stunned to see that it was Will.

He grabbed the cup in her hand, as well as most of her fingers, trying to keep the vessel from spilling. "Miss Cordia," he said politely.

She was shocked to see him there. He had not been at the weddings. Of course, he didn't know anyone getting married. Still, she had just assumed he would not be joining them for the celebration. Yet, there he was, out of nowhere, as he always seemed to be, and now he was practically holding her hand. Finally, she gathered her wits a little bit. "Mr. Tucker," she said. "I am surprised to see you. Do you care for a drink?" she asked. He was wearing his Union uniform, which told her that he, too, must have been leaving the next day.

"Actually, I think I'm wearing some of it," he said, wiping a few drops off of his jacket.

She just noticed that she had, in fact, spilled some of the water she was carrying on him. "Oh, dear," she said, handing the cups off to Susannah, who just happened to be standing close by. "Let me get that for you," she pulled a hand towel out of her waistband and began to dry him off.

"That's all right," he said. "It will dry." She noticed he was smiling at her and imagined it was because she seemed so concerned over just a few drops of water.

Will inhaled deeply; Cordia was leaning in close to him in her attempt to amend her accident, and he could smell the scent of lilac wafting from her perfectly exquisite neck. This was the closest he had ever been to her. He began to notice how delicate her skin looked, imagined that it must feel like silk. A few of the curls from her dark brown hair had come loose from the combs that held it up and the ringlets fell just behind her pearl earrings. And for some reason, he noticed, he was not nearly as uncomfortable being this close to her as he had been weeks ago in the presence of his sister. Why, he did not know, but when she began to back away, he was disappointed the moment was over.

Cordia suddenly realized how closely she was standing to him. She could feel his breath on her neck, could smell his cologne. She found herself feeling a little dizzy. How long had she been standing there? It seemed like time had stopped for a few moments, but then she remembered herself and her duties and regained her composure. "Mr. Tucker," she said, not quite meeting his eyes, "Please let me know if there is anything that I can get for you, sir."

He wasn't sure why she was being so formal, she a fine lady, he nothing but a farmer. "Please, call me Will," he said, just as she was turning to walk away. She turned and smiled over her shoulder, a little nod to say that she would try to oblige from now on. Will then saw Jaris standing across the yard, next to Carey and some other uniformed men, some in Union, some Confederate. He made his way over to where they were standing, and Cordia disappeared into the crowd.

The night was full of dancing and singing, gallivanting, and general merriment. Cordia danced with Jaris for the first time since they were kids and forced to do so at school. He was a good dancer, and he whirled her around as if he had not a care in the world.

Eventually, people seemed to tucker out and head for home, leaving only a handful of close family and friends sitting around a campfire, remembering the good old days and boasting of the glory that was to come. Many of the young men seemed particularly sure that they would be killing several of the members of the opposing army, probably as soon as tomorrow.

Cordia did not like to hear men sit around and talk about such things. She was seated next to Julia, who had been nothing like the solemn child she was when Cordia first met her. She had even danced with a few of the men earlier. Will was also still there, standing across the campfire from them. Her eyes wandered to him more often than they should have, but a few times, she thought she saw him looking back at her. Or maybe he was just checking on his sister. She couldn't be sure. How was it that she could be just as upset about him leaving, someone she hardly knew, as she was about the man she was to marry, someone she had known her whole life? She was hoping that, before he left, she would get just one more chance to talk to him. Perhaps, she could write to him, maybe under the guise of keeping him informed of how Julia was doing.

Jaris was sitting a few benches away from her telling a story, and everyone was listening intently. She glanced back up to where Will was standing, but he wasn't there. She looked around, and suddenly realized he was standing in the shadows behind an old shed. At first, she thought her eyes were tricking her, but then she could see he was motioning for her to come over there. She looked back at Julia, thinking maybe it was her he was wishing to speak to, but her eyes were fixed on Jaris, and she didn't even notice her brother had left.

Cordia was bewildered. What could he possibly want? She slowly got up and tiptoed away, hoping no one would notice. She carefully glanced back over her shoulder and could see that everyone else was hanging on Jaris's every word. Eventually, she was out of their sight and lost in the shadows behind the shed.

Will was standing there, leaning against the old, rusty tin. Neither of them spoke at first, and she thought maybe he was going to tell her that he had wanted to speak to someone else. What could he have to say to her? But eventually, he started to speak. "Cordia," he began, quietly, "I have a favor to ask of you."

She took another step toward him. The moonlight caught his eyes, but she could barely make out the expression on his face. "What is it?" she asked, almost a whisper.

"This is not an easy thing for me to ask, but it is necessary," he continued, shifting his weight and standing up straighter. He looked away from her, looked at the ground.

She was mystified. What could it be? "Well, whatever it is, please go ahead and ask," she reassured him. She put her hand out, instinctively, wanting to touch his arm, but she stopped herself, and rested it on the shed instead. The memory of touching him early had not faded, and though she wanted to do it again, she could not muster up the courage to do so just yet.

He cleared his voice. "I am not exactly sure what it was you said to my sister that day when the cows got out that made her regain her usual demeanor, but I am very thankful that you took the time to come and see her." He looked at her now, and she began to understand what it was he wanted to ask of her. She wasn't too sure herself what it was about her conversation with Julia that had brought her back around, but rather than venture an explanation, she let him continue. "My sister now thinks the world of you. She has been through more than any child her age should ever have to go through." Again, Cordia nodded. She certainly agreed with that. "Would you be so kind," he hesitated, as if he wasn't sure he was in any position to ask her for a favor, "to look after her while I am away?"

Cordia did not even pause to think about it. She had planned to all along. "Of course I will. She is a wonderful girl."

Will seemed relieved at her words; it was as if his whole body relaxed. She realized it must have been a terrible burden for him to leave his sister and go off to fight. She knew he was determined to do all that he could to avenge the circumstances of his brother's murder, and she thought him very noble for it. Now, was her opportunity to let him know that she would also be thinking of him. She wasn't sure how he would react, especially since he was well aware of the contract she had with his cousin. Nevertheless, these were days when men had to stand up for what they believed in, and that meant that women should have some opportunity to embrace their convictions as well. "Will," she said, finally reaching out to him, placing her hand gently on his arm. "I think it would be comforting to you for me to write and let you know how she is doing."

He seemed surprised to hear this suggestion. "Oh, you don't need to go to all of that trouble. I'm sure she will correspond herself," he began.

"Yes," she agreed, her hand still resting precariously on his arm. She glanced down at it, not sure why it was there, or even how it had gotten there. She had already been bold. What was stopping her from continuing? "*Apparently nothing*," she thought as she heard her voice proceeding, "But I am not sure she will let you know exactly how she is doing. I am sure her illness will preoccupy your thoughts. If I write and let you know how she is getting by, maybe it will put your mind at ease." He was looking her directly in the face now, his eyes meeting hers. For a moment, she thought she could see a hint in his eyes of the same feelings she held in her heart.

"I don't know what Jaris would think of that," he said, though Jaris's feelings were not exactly the most important thing on his mind at the moment. He was very aware of her hand resting on his arm. Now, he realized that he had moved his own hand to her elbow. He glanced over her shoulder at where the others were gathered around the campfire. No one had moved. They all seemed to be laughing as Jaris continued his story, totally unaware of what was happening between his fiancée and his cousin.

"Well," Cordia said, her forehead furrowed in thought. "I guess he wouldn't rightly have to know, though I don't think he would mind. I am sure, as kindhearted as he is, he would understand me keeping you informed about your sister."

Will continued to stare at her, memorizing her face, hoping he could look at her long enough to call her image back whenever he needed to in the weeks and months ahead of him. How could it be that this angelic creature had left her wealthy, doting fiancé, to sneak over and speak with him in the shadows? And how could he possibly tell her he didn't want to hear from her? "Yes, please do write me. Let me know how things are going," he consented.

Now, she glanced back over her shoulder at the campfire. The story seemed to be coming to an end, and she was sure they would be missed momentarily. She looked back up at Will, wanting to tell him what was in her heart, but unable to explain it—it was so foreign even to her. When she realized how deeply she was looking into his eyes, she had to look down, blushing.

"You're about the finest woman I ever did meet, Miss Cordia Pike," he said, drawing his hand away from her and stepping back further into the shadows.

And then Cordia did something so bold; she could not believe it was she who was doing it. She felt as if she were standing beside herself, watching it play out. Without a thought toward the potential consequences, she stepped up to him, closed her eyes, but then felt them widen beneath their lids in surprise at her own actions as she realized she'd pressed her lips to his.

So many thoughts went thundering through her mind as she time seemed to stand still once more. How could she do such a thing? What if Jaris found out? How would she explain herself to Will, who would obviously be outraged that she should violate him in such a way?

But then, she realized, he was not outraged. He was kissing her back. And then, she felt his arms around her, a smile spreading over her face like none she had ever felt before, and she was kissing him even more passionately.

There was noise behind them, people standing up, getting ready to go, and it brought them back to reality, brought them back to war. He released her then, and she had only a moment to look into those mysterious eyes before she gave his hand a gentle squeeze and turned to walk back toward the others, still feeling the warmth of his lips on hers.

A glance over her shoulder told her Will had gone the other way, which gave Cordia enough time to make it back to the fire undiscovered.

Will stood in the shadow of the shed, trying to collect his thoughts.

He had no explanation for what had just happened, what had caused Cordia to act so boldly, but he also knew he didn't really need to understand. Whatever it was that had made her react this way, he was feeling it in his heart as well. He ran his hand along his jawline, the scent of lavender lingering in the air and knew he'd never forget that moment for as long as he lived.

Amazingly, Jaris had not noticed where Cordia came from. Because she was walking toward him, he knew she had left, but he seemed not to even wonder where she had gone. Actually, as he took her hand and started to walk toward his horse, he appeared to be totally at ease with the world. She could not help but ask, "Jaris Adams, what's wrong with you? I have never seen you so content."

He smiled. "I have just realized, my dear, that tomorrow I leave for war. Which means, the next time I see you, it will be when I return for our wedding."

Cordia's eyebrows rose. She hadn't given much thought to that. But then, if that was enough to send him off to battle without a care, then so be it. She smiled at him as they approached Sam. "Is this it then?" she asked. "Will I not see you tomorrow?"

He shook his head. "We pull out at dawn. Which is in just a few short hours." Then he smiled at her, that winning Adams smile that seemed to make him capable of conquering the world. "I will be awaiting word from you. I hope to hear from you as often as possible."

"Of course," she assured him. "I will write everyday if I get the chance. Hopefully, all of my letters will reach you."

He nodded. "It will be your face that gets me through the horrors of war," he said, in a manner that made her realize he had not yet mentally accepted that he was, in fact, going off to war. Even now, on the eve of their leaving, most of these boys still had it in their heads that this was a game. They thought they'd be back in a few weeks. She could not believe it. Nevertheless, now was not the time or place to discuss such matters. Again, she nodded in agreement.

Jaris Adams then leaned over and kissed her lips. She kissed him back, though it was nothing like the kiss she had just shared with Will. "I love you, Cordia," he whispered in her ear.

She squeezed him tightly, and said, "I love you, too Jaris," which was true. She did love him and hoped for his safe return. She would miss him, couldn't imagine going more than a week without seeing his smile, without hearing that gentle laugh of his.

Jaris climbed atop Sam, and then reached down to take her hand. "I'll see you soon," he said.

"God be with you." She looked into his eyes, meaning every word. He kissed her hand, turned his horse, and rode away, pausing just briefly enough to glance back at her from a distance. She was still standing there, watching him ride away. She raised her hand, and he waved back before disappearing down the road.

Cordia continued to stare across the yard long after Jaris had disappeared from sight. Then, she saw something else. It was Will on horseback behind a grove of trees in the woods across the street. She knew he, too, was giving her one last look, one last goodbye before he left for battle. And, unlike Jaris, Cordia knew that Will was aware that this was no game, that this was real. He had seen it firsthand. How she wanted to run across the street, kiss him again, tell him she would think of him every second until his safe return. But, she could hear her mother calling her name behind her. She needed to help clean up the remains of the celebration. Slowly, she raised her hand, placed it on her lips, and blew a kiss across the span that separated them. He tipped his hat to her and watched her turn and walk away.

Will sat atop the hill overlooking the Pikes' yard for a few moments until Cordia's form had disappeared into the shadow of trees near the dying embers of the fire. Again, he was mesmerized by all that had taken place that night. At this point, his life was so full of uncertainties, so full of unknowns. But as he turned his horse to ride back toward the Adams Farm for one last night, there was one thing he was sure of. He would love Cordia Pike until the day he died.

Chapter Five

MAY 16, 1861

Dear Jaris,

I hope this letter finds you well. I decided to wait a few days before writing to you because I wasn't sure how long it would take for you to meet up with your unit and get settled. And, until today, I really couldn't bear to think that you were gone. The town has changed in the last few days. It seems all the young men are gone, all the old men are politicking, and all of the women are trying to keep their minds preoccupied with something other than the fact that their sons or their sweethearts are off fighting. Rumor has it that your side is planning an attack soon, that Gov. Jackson has decided to take the state back from Union hands. I pray that you will be safe, no matter what lies in the future. I hope that you will find some solace in thoughts of me and of your home, which awaits your safe return.

Your fiancée,

Cordia

Cordia sighed, rereading the letter one more time. She hoped that it didn't sound too formal, but she wasn't exactly sure what to say to Jaris. She wanted to be uplifting, encouraging, hoping for the best, but she didn't want to be too personal. She stuffed the letter into an envelope, sealed it, addressed it to Jaris's unit, and shoved it out of the way.

Then, she began to write the letter she had been thinking about writing for the last few days.

The thought of writing to Will made it too real that he was actually gone, and until now she had not been able to face that thought. But then, he was almost a vision to her, something she had invented with her own imagination. There had not been too many real moments between them, so in a way, it was almost easier to write to him than it had been to Jaris, someone who had been a very real part of her whole life.

She paused for a moment to gather her thoughts before filling the blank piece of paper before her. She was hesitant at first to say what she felt, but then, in times like this, she could see no use in dancing around the truth. Her only concern was that some other eyes might read these words and tell Jaris. That would be more than she could possibly bear. However, she didn't think there was much chance of that, considering they were on opposite sides of the war. So, she began to pour out her heart, hoping that Will would find serenity in her words.

May 16, 1861

Dearest Will,

I cannot explain to you just how much I have missed you these past few days. It has utterly surprised me that I could long for someone this deeply when I have spent such little time in your presence. Nevertheless, the few moments that we spent together were enough to assure me that the feelings I have within my heart are true and strong. I have often dreamt of meeting someone with eyes so deep I could peer into them for ages, arms so strong, they could hold me for a life-time, lips so soft, I could feel their touch days after a kiss has faded. You have taught me, in a short matter of time, what it is to truly love someone. If by chance you should be surrounded by this overpowering darkness that threatens to overtake us, please let the undying love I hold for you in my heart pull you through.

I await word of your safe journey to your station.

All my love,

Cordia

This time, Cordia did not dare to re-read what she had written. She slipped it into an envelope, addressed it, and grabbed her bonnet to take it promptly to the mailbox before she changed her mind. She hadn't even bothered to mention Julia, nor had she given any explanation of her relationship with Will's cousin. He probably assumed she was telling Jaris the same thing. He must think her utterly ridiculous! Yet, she thought he needed to hear these words first. There would be time for further explanations in the days and weeks to come. She dropped the letters in the slot, knowing that the post would collect them promptly, and hopeful that they would make their destinations.

The next Sunday, Cordia was amazed at how few men were attending church. It seemed most all of them had joined up and emptied out. There was word that even the forty men who had stayed behind would be relieved of their duties and replaced by Union troops from other parts of the state soon, but Cordia had heard so many rumors in the last few years, she didn't even pretend to speculate on what would happen.

That day after church, the Pike family joined the Adams family at their farm for Sunday dinner as they did most every Sunday. This week, as last week, of course, Jaris was not present, which seemed odd to Cordia in every way imaginable. His mother went on about how she had written him every day since he left and asked if Cordia had gotten a chance to write him yet, which she assured him she had. Julia also said that she had written to Jaris and to Will, who she said should have joined up with Col. Franz Sigel and his men by now. It seemed that no one in town had heard from any of the men who had left just yet, but Margaret was sure that Jaris would write as soon as possible.

Days passed. Everyday Cordia checked the post for a letter from either Will or Jaris, but by the next Saturday, she had heard nothing from either of them. She had written to Jaris a few more times that week, nonchalant little letters—"I hope you are doing well, how is the drilling," etc., but she had not written to Will again. She intended to spend some time with his sister before she wrote to him so as to provide some of the information she had actually promised to him to begin with. With that in mind, she made her way over to the Adams Farm to check on Julia and to bring Margaret some bread that her mother had baked earlier in the day.

"Cordia! What a lovely surprise!" Margaret exclaimed as Cordia climbed the porch steps. Mrs. Adams had been sweeping off the front porch and put her broom down to hug her.

"Hello, Mrs. Adams. I thought that I might spend some time with Julia today, if she is feeling up to it," she said, handing Margaret the bread. "Mother baked this for you."

"Lovely! Thank you! Yes, come in. I am sure that Julia would be happy to see you." She pulled the front door open and held it for Cordia. Julia was sitting at the table. She seemed to be sketching something.

Noticing Cordia was there, Julia jumped up in surprise, quickly crossing the room. "Cordia!" she said throwing her arms around her.

Margaret set the bread down on the table. "Cordia's come to visit you," Margaret explained. "You should show her your drawings," and then to Cordia she said, "I have never seen someone who could draw as well as Julia."

Cordia could see by the few sketches that were spread out over the table that what Margaret said was true. "They're lovely," she said, studying them, though they were upside down from her vantage point.

Margaret rested her hand on Cordia's shoulder. "Have you heard anything from Jaris?" she asked, a look of concern marring her face.

Cordia shook her head and watched his mother's face fall. "I'm sure he will write as soon as he gets a chance," she said, managing a small, reassuring smile.

Margaret nodded. "Well, I will leave you two girls alone and get back to that porch. It is a never-ending battle against dust around here!"

Cordia sat down at the table next to Julia. "How did you get to be such a fine artist?" she asked the younger girl.

Julia's face was beaming. "I don't know. I just always liked to sketch things. Would you like to see?"

Cordia nodded, and Julia carefully picked up each of the drawings lying on the table. "This is my ma and pa," she explained. "I did this sketch a long time ago. It's not as good, but it helps me remember how they looked." Cordia was captivated by the images on the paper. Not only did this young girl do a good job of capturing the expression on her parents' faces, now Cordia could put the names and faces together of Will's family. "And this is Nolan," Julia continued. Funny, he looked almost exactly how Cordia imagined he would. A lot like Will, though a little older, perhaps a little more worn. "And this is Will," Julia went on. Cordia's eyes went to the paper; she almost couldn't believe what she was seeing. There he was before her, that face she had been dreaming about for all of those nights. Her eyes were, once again, looking into his—though it wasn't quite the same. Still, she had not imagined she would have this opportunity to see his likeness when she had planned her trip earlier today.

Julia took the picture and set it aside, but Cordia's eyes followed it. Then, she caught herself, and realized that Julia had moved on to the next image. "This is a picture I am working on," she said, opening a sketchpad. It looked new, and she wondered if Mr. or Mrs. Adams hadn't gotten it for their niece. "It's a sketch of me. I'm going to send it to Will so that he can remember me by it." The picture was only half done but already Cordia could see that it was going to look just like Julia when it was finished.

"That's a very good idea," Cordia agreed. "I am sure he will treasure it."

"I have an idea," Julia said, her face lighting up. "Maybe I could draw you and send it to Jaris! I am sure he would love it!"

Cordia knew that he would—what she wouldn't give to confiscate that picture of Will and take it home. But she wasn't sure she really wanted to sit for a sketch. "I don't know," she began to protest.

But Julia was already flipping to a fresh sheet of paper. "It will only take me a few minutes," she said matter-of-factly. "Here," she said, standing and walking to the window. She dragged a chair into the sunlight. "Sit here so that I can capture your image just right."

Cordia knew there was no sense arguing about it. She stood up and walked over to the window, sitting up nice and straight. Just before Julia began to draw, however, the girl began to cough. She picked up a handkerchief off of the table and held it to her mouth. "Are you all right?" Cordia asked as the cough continued. Finally, the young girl stopped coughing, took a drink of water, and went on about her business as if this was a normal occurrence. And Cordia thought, *"Perhaps she's used to coughing so violently."* She did notice that there were a few drops of blood spattered on the clean white surface of the handkerchief. But, Julia was asking her to sit still and look straight ahead, which she was inclined to do.

About a half an hour later, Julia was finished. She hadn't had anymore coughing attacks in that time, which put Cordia a little at ease. Still, she felt obliged to mention this one small incident to Julia's brother. The portrait looked just like her, Cordia agreed, though she noticed a bit of sadness in her own eyes she hadn't before and wondered how Julia was able to see it when she hadn't herself.

Realizing her mother would be missing her, Cordia told Julia she'd come and visit again soon. Taking the drawing, she hugged the young woman and headed out the door. She said her goodbyes to Margaret in the yard and made her way back toward town, her mind poring over the words she would use to compose her next letter to Will.

It was not until a few days later that she finally decided exactly what to write.

May 21, 1861

Dearest Will,

Forgive me for not having written in the past few days. I wasn't sure what to say after my last letter revealed so many of my thoughts and emotions. I hope that you have not found me too bold. I would think that having not heard from you must mean that you do not share the feelings I have disclosed, except that Julia says she has written to you several times and she has yet to receive a reply. I do not know why I find comfort in that, only that, hearing nothing from you is far better than hearing that you do not return the feelings I have admitted to you. I am sure that you are safe, as they tell us that any word of casualty will be posted on the courthouse door, should it ever come to that. I pray that no man from home will suffer in this conflict, though I don't see how that is possible.

There are a few things I feel obligated to tell you. Firstly, I have spent some time with your sister, not just after church with the family, but also on our own. While she did have a little bit of a coughing spell while I was there, she seems strong, and I know that she is anxiously waiting to hear from you.

Secondly, I think you have the right to know exactly what the situation is between your cousin Jaris and myself. I love Jaris, but only in the way a person loves someone they have had a friendship with their whole life. I know that he hopes to make me his wife upon his return, and I am sure it will be one of the hardest things I will ever have to do to tell him that I cannot marry him. Though at first I intended to try to love him, as time passed, I now know that that would not be fair to him, to me, or, perhaps, to you. I am putting off telling him until this war is over. I hope that you can understand why. I do not think it would be kind of me to send him into battle with the knowledge that I am not waiting for his return; at least, not in the way he would choose.

Your sister has made a drawing of you, which I wished so much to have as my own but could find no way to ask for it without her asking why I would want such a thing. But just looking at your face for a few moments has renewed my love for you.

I long to hear from you, but if you are only given a few moments to write, please send word to your sister that you are doing well. I know that she worries about you, as we all do.

All my love,

Cordia

Once again, Cordia hurried to the post with her letter before she changed her mind. She had begun to wonder if, perhaps, she had misread Will's intent. Maybe he had no interest in her after all. Perhaps he just saw her as a foolish girl who had betrayed his cousin. She dropped the letter into the slot, along with another letter to Jaris, which also contained the picture that Julia had drawn of her.

As she was walking out of the post office, she heard the postmaster, Mr. Wheeler, calling her name. She turned around and he handed her a letter. "It's from your sweetheart!" the old man exclaimed. At first, Cordia's eyes lit up, thinking it was from Will, but then, she realized that he—of course—meant Jaris. She glanced down at the letter and could see that the envelop stated it was, in fact, from Jaris. Though she was disappointed that it was not from Will, she was still glad to hear from her friend. She rushed home to see what he had to say.

ARMY LIFE WAS NOT AT ALL what Jaris Adams had thought it was going to be. He had been in camp now for just over a week, and he hated every minute of it. Though he was raised on a farm, he could not get used to sleeping on the ground, using a latrine, eating hardtack.

And he hated the noise. The men all seemed to be in high spirits, which he knew was a good thing. But they were up playing music, gambling, carousing, until all hours of the night. As an officer, one of his duties was to try to enforce curfews, but it was damn near impossible at this point in the war effort. They had word that Franz Sigel's men were headed toward them and that there could be a skirmish, maybe even a full-blown battle, any day. That was enough to keep morale—and noise—at an indescribable high.

His days consisted mainly of drilling the troops. As a lieutenant, he was in charge of a certain number of men. Of course, he had officers above him as well. A good portion of the day was spent drilling—practicing following commands, stepping in line, even shooting. Some of these men were bankers and businessmen who had never even handled a gun before. Part of his duty was to make sure that they knew how to take care of their weapons and how to use them when the time came. And then, on some days, they would pick up camp and move. Sometimes they would only go a couple of miles. Other times, it seemed they would march the better part of the day. It was on those days that Jaris wished that he had joined the cavalry. Though he was allowed to ride his horse, trying to keep the stragglers in line tried his patience considerably.

He had hoped to write to Cordia everyday if possible, but in his first few days of camp, he had been too busy or too exhausted to write her even once. Before he knew it, over a week had passed, and he had yet to write to anyone. He received a letter from his mother a few days after he arrived in camp. She had sent her love and the love of the family. She had mentioned that Cordia looked so sad lately. She knew it must be because she was missing him something awful. This was actually good news to Jaris. He was hoping that "absence makes the heart grow fonder" would have its effect over his fiancée. Still, he had not heard from Cordia, which was surprising, because she had promised to write often. Perhaps her letters had not made it through just yet. There certainly was no reliable way to get letters to constantly moving men.

Carey's regiment was camped nearby, and the cousins spent time together whenever they would get a chance. Unfortunately, that wasn't too often, what with all the drilling and marching. Jaris often wondered how Will was making it. He prayed that, if the time came where he would be engaged in battle, his cousin would not be standing across that line from him. Still, he did not have much time to think about that either.

Finally, he had the opportunity one afternoon to try to compose a letter to Cordia. It was raining outside, so there was really no way to get the men to drill. Though some of the officers had been lucky enough to be issued a cot, he was still sleeping on a mat on the ground. He tried to get comfortable and prop himself up enough to be able to write without spilling his ink. The light from a lantern was all that he had to see by, that and an occasional flash of lightning that came in the tent flap. His tent mate—another officer—had taken this small break from drilling to try to take a nap.

Jaris thought for a moment before he began to compose his letter. Finally, he put his pen to paper and began.

MAY 25, 1861

Dearest Cordia,

I have arrived at camp and can't say that these first few days have exactly been what I had envisioned. Most of our time is spent drilling and marching, with an occasional meal break in between, which is not to indicate that anything we have to eat tastes much like food. Though I am still supporting the cause with all my heart, I hope that I can grow more accustomed to these conditions. Else, there is not much to stop me from coming home to you. Of course, I exaggerate. But I do miss you something awful. How I long to see your face. I hope that everyone is well back in Lamar, which, though is not very far away, seems a million miles or so from here. Please tell my mother I intend to write her back as soon as I find time. I hear them calling us to drill now, though it is still raining. Please do not worry over me. I will return to you shortly, when this war is over.

Love,

Jaris

He quickly stuffed the letter in an envelope and dropped it in the post box on the way to drill.

❀

IT HAD NOT TAKEN EVEN a full day for Will and the rest of the Union men coming out of Lamar to locate their regiment of Union soldiers in camp near the Spring River, just a ways south of Barton County. He had taken to camp life very quickly, made several friends, and didn't even mind the drills they practiced over and over. The long days helped to keep his mind off of his brother, his sister, and Miss Cordia Pike. His sergeant, Teddy Bolder, had commented on his very first day in camp that Will was a natural as a soldier. He said he saw a promising future ahead for the young man. And though Will truly enjoyed the army life, he wasn't so sure that he would ever want to be promoted much beyond the private he was now. It was one thing to be responsible for yourself on the battlefield. It was quite another to be responsible for the lives of thousands of other men.

A few days ago, Will had received a letter from his sister and one from Cordia. Since he had left Lamar, his mind had often drifted back to the conversation he had had with Cordia the night before he left. On several occasions, he had thought, perhaps he had dreamt the whole occurrence. Maybe it was just one of those moments that he had created in his own mind to ease the pain of losing his brother or of this coming war. But then, he received her letter, and not only did it become clear to him that he had not invented what had happened between them, but that she actually did have feelings for him. Though he wasn't sure what that would mean, considering she was engaged to his cousin, just the idea of that angelic woman waiting for him at the end of this war was enough to put a smile on his face, even when drilling in the rain.

The officers had given them a break that day because of the weather, and he was hoping to write a couple of letters himself while he had a chance. But just as he was entering the tent he shared with two other soldiers, he heard the buglers blowing. Time to drill—again.

He made his way through the muddy lanes between the tents. The rain hadn't exactly stopped, but it had lessened. He was able to use his own rifle as his weapon, the same one he had used to kill some of the raiders the night his brother had died, so he was extremely comfortable with the piece in his hands. He took his place in line between a couple of other Barton County boys, Frank Glen and the newlywed Skeet Cooper. They were not supposed to talk during drill, but Will could see that Skeet had a letter sticking out of his pocket. Frank was so busy peeking over Will to get a better look at it that he almost dropped his weapon a couple of times. Finally, Will couldn't help but whisper to him, "Pay attention!"

Frank looked up at him, his eyes wide, his unshaven face covered with grime. "He's got a letter!" he said back.

Will could see the sergeant coming. He definitely did not want to have to do any running in this mud, so he chose to leave Frank and Skeet to their own demise. "It's from my wife," Skeet said, leaning over Will.

Will shook his head in dismay. And then, he couldn't believe Frank didn't have enough sense to let it go. "What's it say?" he asked.

Just then, the sergeant jumped into Frank's face. "Boy! We are drilling here! There is no talking during drill! Do you understand?" Frank looked puzzled, as if he did not understand. He just stood there, perplexed. "Do you hear me, boy?" the sergeant yelled again. This time Frank just nodded his head. Of course, that wasn't good enough for the sergeant. He yelled to the entire company, "That's it—we're moving out. Attention Company! About face! March—double time!" Moans and groans went in waves down the line as they all started to run as fast as they could, while still maintaining their ranks. Carrying heavy rifles while running through the mud was no one's idea of the glory of war.

Later that night around a campfire, Frank was retaliated against non-stop. Some of the men only called him names; others couldn't help but knock his hat off of his head, or worse. And it wasn't until then that he found out what Skeet's letter said—none of which seemed to truly interest or concern him.

The next afternoon at mail call, Will received another letter from his sister, and another letter from Cordia. He didn't get a chance to read the whole correspondence before he had to go drill. Still, just knowing that she was thinking of him was enough to get him through —even though Frank's mouth did cost them all another sprint.

ALL OF MAY had passed and then most of June. It had been so long since Cordia had seen Will or Jaris. She had found some comfort in the few letters she had received from Jaris, but she still longed to hear from Will. She had now written six letters to him and more letters than she could count to Jaris.

She had been spending a great deal of time with Julia. Almost every day they would get together in some fashion or another. A lot of the women folk were hosting different sorts of bees at their homes, some to make socks, others to make blankets for the men in the winter. And then some days, Cordia and Julia just sat out on the swing in Cordia's yard and exchanged stories about their childhoods. This was a great comfort for Cordia because she often got to hear about the adventures of Will's youth. Julia told her of all the different times her brothers had hidden down in their old, dried up well and jumped out and scared their poor mother. She also talked about the time that Nolan had held her upside down over the new well, behind their house, threatening to drop her in if she didn't give him back a shiny rock he had found. Cordia felt as if she knew Nolan now, though she was heartbroken that she would never get to meet him. She also realized that she probably knew more about Will than he could possibly like for her to know at this point in their relationship.

One day, near the end of June, Cordia was sitting out under a shade tree in her yard, trying to read *Wuthering Heights* when, she heard Julia screaming as she came flying up the lane, her horse charging at full speed. At first, she thought something was the matter, but when she saw Julia's face, she knew that it was good news. Then, she saw a letter in her hand. Cordia's heart skipped a beat—it had to be from Will.

Sure enough, her screams of glee confirmed it. "Will sent a letter! I got a letter from Will!" She almost doubled over trying to catch her breath.

Cordia took her arm, trying to keep her from falling on the ground. She was afraid that she might start having a coughing fit now, which she had had quite a few of lately, but she didn't. As soon as she caught her breath, she pulled Cordia over to a bench, and they both sat down to read it together.

MAY 26, 1861

> *My Dear Sister Julia,*
>
> *How are you Jules? Scarcely a minute goes by that my thoughts don't return to you. I have been in camp for quite some time now. It's not too exciting, but I have made a lot of friends. We do a lot of drilling and some marching, but mostly drilling. There is a rumor that we may be headed out of here soon and into another county, though we are not supposed to say which one. At any rate, army life seems to suit me pretty good. I hope that you are finding ways to pass the time. I know that you have a good friend in Miss Cordia Pike who will take very good care of you. Have you heard from Jaris? I hope he is safe and that I do not see him anytime soon, if you gather my meaning. Well, you know how I am about writing letters. Not too good at it. But I did want to let you know I am safe and hope to see you soon.*
>
> *Love,*
>
> *Will*

To Cordia, simply seeing those words, that he was safe, was almost enough to make tears fill her eyes. But, she would not be able to explain to Julia why that might be. Somehow, she managed to hold them back. Julia, on the other hand, had tears streaming down her face. "That's my brother," she said. "Cordia, I am so proud of him."

Cordia wrapped her arm around her friend. "You should be," she said quietly. "You should be."

ON THE NIGHT of July 4, 1860, Franz Sigel's men found themselves in camp north of the city of Carthage, Jasper County, Missouri. Unbeknownst to them, Gov. Claiborne Jackson's men, under his own command, lay in wait, just over a ridge further north. Though the Confederate forces had Sigel's men grossly outnumbered, almost six to one, nearly a third of Jackson's forces were not armed. Still, the Confederate soldiers who had weapons and were ready for battle had a great advantage on the Union Army. On the dawn of July 5, Jackson drew his men into formation along the ridge. Sigel had been chasing him across the state. Jackson wondered if Sigel would take this opportunity and attack. It did not take long for the governor to receive an answer.

Will's regiment had been part of the encampment that settled down in Carthage the night of July 4. There were plenty of rumors going around that Confederate soldiers were in the area. Of course, they had heard this several times in the last few days. As they began to eat their breakfast early on the morning of July 5, the troops were alarmed to hear their officers telling them to fall out. They quickly gathered up their supplies and fell into ranks.

Skeet Cooper looked a little nervous as he was standing in line next to Will. "Do you think this is it?" he asked. "Do you think we're going to see the elephant?"

Will wasn't sure what to say, but it turned out he didn't have to. Frank had an answer for him. "Course not," he said, still chewing the remains of his breakfast. "This here is just a drill, to let us know what it would be like if we were suddenly surprised in the morning."

But Will wasn't so sure. He could hear some officers shouting commands in the distance. And then, he thought he heard the *pop, pop* sound of rifle fire. Soon, Sgt. Bolder was giving them a command to march forward. Then, they were told to hold their line. It suddenly became quite clear to all of them that they were about to engage in battle.

JARIS WAS TRYING to hold his line together. It wasn't exactly an easy task considering the Union had a canon trained right in the middle of his men. Still, he had been engaged here for nearly forty minutes and had received no orders to fall back or to press on. He wasn't exactly sure what Gov. Jackson had in mind. In front of him, he could see some Union soldiers gathering together, as if they were about to make a charge up the ridge, directly at his men. He looked back at his soldiers, some of which seemed terrified. "Hold your ground! Hold your ground!" he yelled as he made his way down the line.

Some of the officers had mentioned to him that Jackson was counting on a diversion. He planned to send some two thousand unarmed men into the trees on the left of the Union line. The plan was to use these men to make Sigel think he was vastly outnumbered, which hopefully would cause him to call a retreat. Then, the Confederates would swarm down over the fleeing Union soldiers, routing them, and with any luck destroying the army.

That was not happening right now, however, and Jaris could see that the Union forces directly across from him were making their way over that deadly ground between them. They charged up the ridge, and he gave the command "Fire at will!" At first the Union line seemed to waver, but soon the men began to make it up the ridge. Some of Jaris's green recruits looked as if they might turn and run. He made his way down the line, reminding them that they must hold their ground. Soon, the Union line, though much weaker now than it had been when it first began its charge, was at their position, and they were engaged in hand-to-hand combat. Some of the men had the presence of mind to use their bayonets. Others were using whatever they could get their hands on to force the Union back.

Jaris drew his pistol and his sword and jumped into the fight. He shot one man in the gut, and then turned to face another one, stabbing him through. Another soldier lunged at him with a fixed bayonet. He was able to step out of the way before shooting him with his handgun. His men were rallying; they were fighting back. Soon, he heard the Union yelling for a retreat. At first, his men began to cheer, but he reminded them they must regain their composure. It was quite possible the Union soldiers might be coming again.

THOUGH WILL HAD NOT BEEN one of the men to charge Jaris's company, he did attack the ridge outside of Carthage that day. He had successfully wounded and shot down several Confederate soldiers. On their portion of the battlefield, they had nearly taken the ridge. He was actually leading the charge up the side of the incline when he heard the order to fall back. He wasn't sure why, but he had no choice but to join the rest of his regiment in doing so. They retreated past their encampment, all the way back to Carthage, ten miles from where they had started.

Later that evening, Sgt. Bolder, who had been cut on the head by a piece of enemy shrapnel, came through the encampment to notify the troops of exactly what had happened and to give their orders for the next day. Apparently, Col. Sigel had seen another movement of troops in the woods to their left. Rather than surrender the town, he decided to fall back and try to hold it. They could all plainly see that they had been extremely outnumbered. Still, it was hard for Will to sleep that night, knowing they were giving up ground to the Confederacy.

As he slowly started to fall asleep, he heard Skeet in the tent next door exclaiming, "We saw the elephant Frank! And we done come out alive!" Will sighed. There would be many more elephants to come.

In the morning, Sigel's men retreated even farther into southern Missouri, finally encamping near Sarcoxie. Jackson's men seemed to have turned the tables, and the hunter became the hunted.

Chapter Six

CORDIA, like most other citizens of Barton County, spent much of July 5 standing around outside of the courthouse, waiting to see if a casualty list would be posted. Of course, everyone was fairly sure that it was too soon for anyone to send a telegraph with news of the engagement from Carthage that day. All they knew was that Jackson's men had attacked Sigel's somewhere north of Carthage. They also knew there had been another skirmish, a little farther south, near the town of Neosho.

While Cordia was taking all this news in stride, Susannah had spent the better part of the day crying herself sick. Her young boys had stared at her at first, wondering if something had happened to their pa. Eventually, their grandmother came to take them to her house, and Susannah and Cordia spent the rest of the afternoon sitting on the courthouse lawn. Julia was camped there as well, along with her aunt and many of the other women. Some of them Cordia did not recognize, and she assumed that they must have been from outlying farms.

Eventually, Mr. Ward, who ran the post office and was usually the first to receive telegraphs, came out to announce that they might as well all go home, as he was not expecting to hear anything that evening. Reluctantly, Cordia and the others headed back toward their houses, planning on returning the next morning.

Cordia was up with the rising sun. She made the short trip to the town square and the courthouse, which sat in the center. She could see from a distance that there was, in fact, a list posted on the door. As she approached, she noticed a few women in tears, others trying to console them. She felt her stomach tighten a little as she walked up the steps, though, for some reason, she felt calm, as if she didn't have anything to be too worried about.

Her eyes darted down the list, skimming it first. She did not see either of the names she was looking for the first time through. Then, she looked again, more closely this time. She read every name—all 200 or so--of the wounded, missing, and killed in action. Jaris's name was not there. Neither was Will's. She let go a deep sigh of relief. But then, the woman next to her began to wail. She turned to see if she recognized her face, which she was glad to say she did not. "My baby!" she was screaming. "Dear God! Why? Why?" Another woman put her arms around her, as she collapsed. Cordia wasn't sure what to do. An older man who was standing nearby came to assist the other woman in carrying the poor mother down the steps. She was still screaming. "Joseph! Joseph!"

Cordia felt tears of sympathy welling up in her eyes as she turned to go. Just then, she saw Susannah coming up the lane. She had been sure to check and make sure that James's name was not on the list either. But when Susannah saw the tears in Cordia's eyes, a look of panic overtook her. Cordia shook her head, "no" and waved her arms, as if to say, "Don't worry," but Susannah didn't seem to be calming down. So, Cordia ran over to. "He's not on the list—Susy. James isn't on the list."

Susannah took a deep breath, seeming to relax at least a little bit. "Are you sure?" she asked.

Cordia nodded, but her friend continued toward the steps, wanting to check the list for herself. "None of our men are on there. Not James, not Jaris, nor Skeet, nor Frank or Carey, or Will." And that's when she saw Julia and Margaret climbing down from a wagon across the street. She wanted to make sure they were not confused. So, with a big smile on her face, she ran over to greet them and let them know the good news. Their men had made it through the first battle without having their names written on the list.

❧

ON JULY 6, Sigel's men began a retreat toward Springfield, where they planned to join up with General Nathaniel Lyon's men, making their way down from the northern portions of the state. The going was slow, and Will intended to take this opportunity to write back to Cordia. He had not come anywhere near being shot the day before, but he had been engaged in battle, which was scary enough. He wanted to make sure she knew how he felt about her, just in case something was to happen next time.

His regiment paused that afternoon along the banks of a little creek. While many of the men took advantage of this opportunity to clean the grime of battle off in the water, Will wanted to ensure he got that letter done first. And he also hoped to find time to write his sister. He sat down beneath a spreading oak tree and found a few scrap pieces of paper he had been saving in his knapsack for this occasion. He wrote to Cordia first, pausing to think just what to say several times before finishing. He was never good at writing letters, and she always seemed to know exactly what to say to warm his heart. So, it was not an easy task. When the letter was finished, he put it in an envelope and placed it back inside of his bag. Then, he began to write to his sister.

July 6, 1861,

Dear Julia,

I guess you have probably heard by now that we were engaged yesterday. We fought near the town of Carthage against Gov. Jackson's men. I do hope that Jaris was as lucky as I and made it through unscathed. I hope that you have not been too worried about your brother. You know that I am a scrapper and can make it through most anything. I guess there probably wasn't much of a July Fourth celebration this year. We celebrated with extra rations. Or at least we thought we were celebrating. Maybe they were just giving us extra food before the battle. At any rate, I think on you daily. I hope to see your beautiful smile again soon. I have received four letters from you and am anxious to hear from you as often as possible. In your last letter, you mentioned a drawing you had sent. I have not received that yet. Perhaps it is caught up in the post. Maybe you can send another one, if you have time to finish? I am glad to hear that you are spending so much time with Miss Cordia. She is just the type of woman you should aim to emulate. Please give my love to Aunt Margaret and the family.

Love,

Will

Will had just finished addressing the envelope when the postman came by. "That a letter?" he asked.

Will nodded and handed it to the man. "I have another one in my bag," he said, anxiously digging around for his letter to Cordia, but he couldn't find it in time and the man disappeared into the crowd. *"Oh, well,"* he thought. *"I'll mail it later."*

ON JULY 7, Jackson decided not to follow Sigel's men on their retreat toward Springfield. There were Confederate soldiers, under Gen. Ben McCulloch and Gen. Sterling Price, already stationed there. However, with the growing call to arms from the Confederate Army, a number of men decided to detach from the Missouri State Guard, and enlisted with the Confederate troops, officially becoming part of the Confederate Army. Jaris Adams was part of that regiment. He made the long, slow trip toward Springfield, along with a few hundred other men, many of which were also from Barton County. He had hoped to find time along the trip to send word to Cordia and his mother that he had survived his first engagement, but free time was hard to come by. Eventually, they found the Confederate Army and were enlisted. Jaris retained his rank of lieutenant and was soon drilling with a whole other set of men.

Throughout the rest of July, both armies were relatively quiet as far as fighting was concerned, though they both seemed to be doing quite a bit of moving. To look at Missouri from afar would have been quite like watching a giant chess match. Lyon was desperately working his way toward Sigel, force-marching his men for many days to reach Springfield. Jackson and McCulloch were also shifting their troops around. It seemed only a matter of time before a major battle would have to take place. The soldiers on both sides began to brace themselves for the impending doom of combat.

THERE HAD BEEN rumors of raiders attacking some of the settlements in Vernon County, north of Lamar. So far, Cordia had not heard of anyone in Barton County being attacked. But the small number of militia drilling on the square every day was a reminder that it was possible that those marauders could burst into town at any time, a threat that kept the townsfolk constantly on guard. She went by the courthouse everyday now. Usually, there was nothing new posted. Sometimes, there would be news of troop movements or of wounded soldiers being discharged. She never saw mention of either Jaris's name or Will's—which was exactly what she was praying for.

The post office was also a daily stop for her. Most days nothing came. On this day, July 30, she received a letter from Jaris, telling her that he had transferred into the Confederate Army, that he was no longer in the Missouri State Guard. For Cordia, all this meant was that she now needed to be looking for the names of Gen. Sterling Price and Gen. Ben McCulloch when she was checking on engagements, rather than Gov. Jackson. It alarmed her quite a bit to hear that these principal Confederate armies were converging near Springfield at the same time that the Union armies of Lyon and Sigel also seemed to be joining together there. Hopefully, they would miss each other and continue to dance around the state without actually fighting. However, this was a war, and it seemed fairly certain that, eventually, they were going to collide.

That afternoon at the Adams Farm, Julia read to her a second letter that she had received from Will. He was also marching to Springfield, it seemed. Julia was so happy to have heard from him again. His words seemed to reassure her that he was going to make it through this war just fine. While Cordia was also happy to have heard from Will, she was a little saddened that he had now written his sister twice and had yet to send any correspondence to her whatsoever. Once again, she thought perhaps she had been foolish in ever thinking that Will had feelings for her, although this letter, like the last, did speak highly of her. Still, she did not find the same amount of comfort in his letter as his sister did.

❦

ON AUGUST 9, Franz Sigel's men were camped south of Wilson's Creek, near Springfield. Will took a few moments that evening to write Cordia another letter. Though he had yet to mail the last one he had written to her, he had a strange feeling about what might happen the next day. It was difficult to gather much information from the officers; however, he was fairly certain there would be a battle tomorrow. He had heard enough to know that the Confederate Army, under Gen. McCulloch, was bivouacked nearer to the creek. He also knew that Lyon's men were camped just north of the creek. Now, he was not a military specialist, but it would seem like a good idea to him to try to catch McCulloch in between. He imagined that was probably what the higher-ups were thinking as well. He wasn't sure exactly how many men the enemy had, but he knew his side was probably outnumbered. So, he took a few moments to write Cordia another letter—not insinuating he thought he was going to die—but he did want her to know that, the night before this battle, his mind was on her.

It seemed Will had only been asleep for a few seconds when he heard men whispering. Once again, he had been dreaming about Nolan. They had been hiding in that well again. This time, their mother had had enough and chased them around the yard with a broom. He tried to shake the image of his brother's laughing eyes out of his head and bring himself back to reality. "Time to get up," Frank was saying in his ear. Will groaned. The sun wasn't even up. "Be quiet," Frank continued. "We don't want to wake the snoozing Rebs."

Will wiped the sleep out of his eyes. The stars were still shining above him as he rolled up his blanket and gathered up the rest of his belongings. "What time is it?" he whispered to Skeet, who looked to be still half asleep himself.

Skeet carried a pocket watch, which he pulled out and attempted to focus his eyes upon. "Three o'clock," he finally said, almost a ques-tion. Apparently, he couldn't believe how early it was either.

As they began to fall into line, Frank leaned over and whispered, "Elephant's waking up mighty early this morning."

IT HAD BEEN A SURPRISE ATTACK. Around four o'clock that morning, Jaris was awakened to the sound of panic. "They're coming!" men were yelling. Soldiers were scrambling for their guns, trying to form a line, trying to stop the Yankees as they poured over the high ground in front of them.

Though Lyon's men had used the element of surprise, it had not taken long for the Confederate forces to regroup. The fighting was extremely intense. Jaris's men spent a great deal of time combating in a cornfield. He had done tremendously well, killing a number of Union soldiers, while still managing to keep his men from fleeing the field. Suddenly, about an hour into the attack, a large number of fresh Union soldiers swept over the hilltop, charging toward Jaris's company. They seemed to be outnumbered. He looked around to see if any other troops were available to help, but then he realized the rest of the Confederate soldiers were giving up the ground, retreating toward a small, brick farmhouse. Jaris thought perhaps they could reform there, get some sharpshooters into that house. He fell back with his men, yelling for them to reform. Just as his men were getting into line, he felt a sharp stinging pain in his chest. He looked up and saw the Union soldiers closing in on them. He gave another order to charge, and his men went forward, moving the Yankees back the way they had come.

But Jaris couldn't make the charge with them. He looked down at the place on his chest where the sting was now turning into a throb-bing pain. He was amazed at first to see so much blood on his uniform. A lump formed in his throat. He wasn't quite sure why there was so much blood. It was oozing out of his uniform now, spreading across the gray fabric, dripping off of the buttons. He felt his knees weaken. Sinking down to the ground, he reached up with his hand and wiped at the blood, only managing to smear it all over his white glove, which he stared at for a moment in disbelief. Suddenly, he couldn't sit up anymore. He had to lie down—but how could he lie down in the middle of a battlefield? He tried to stand but couldn't. He heard noise behind him. It sounded like some men were coming. Maybe they would bring a litter, get him to a medic. He was having trouble seeing. His vision was fading in and out. He couldn't seem to understand what was happening.

And then, he saw her. Cordia, standing over him like an angel—her face hovering above him, outlined by the bright blue sky. And she was smiling that perfect smile of hers. He knew that he would be all right now. He knew that he would be fine because Cordia was with him.

WILL and the rest of Sigel's men had probably spent as much time standing around as they had marching, or so it seemed to men anxious to get on the battlefield. At 5:30, they approached a smaller creek, known locally as Tyrel's Creek. The Union forces had mostly used their artillery to route the Confederate cavalry here. Will had gotten a few shots off, but he wasn't sure that he had hit anything. Then, they advanced to another position near an old red farmhouse. Here they stood for some time, and the men were growing impatient. Finally, they saw gray uniforms coming toward them. The men steadied their guns, ready to open at the command. But their officers were very slow in giving their orders, and the gray-clad soldiers drew closer and closer. At last, word was passed down the line that those weren't Confederate soldiers, but it was the First Iowa Infantry, who also wore gray. Though Will knew that not all of the uniforms were, in fact, uniform, something in the pit of his stomach told him that those soldiers coming at them were, indeed, the enemy. And his feeling was confirmed when those "friendly" soldiers opened fire. Some of the officers were stunned; others were hit in the first volley. Eventually, either someone gave the order to fire, or the enlisted men had enough sense to fire back, but now there was a battle on.

There wasn't much to hide behind. They were essentially in open ground, standing across from each other. *"A stupid way to fight,"* Will thought to himself as he fired and reloaded his rifle. Next to him, he heard Frank scream in pain, and he looked down to see his friend bleeding badly from the leg. The Union line began to break. Will grabbed his friend and tried to help him fall back with the rest of the men. Frank was slowing him down, but he managed to make it back over a little hill, further out of the line of fire. There, one of the lieutenants was trying to reform a line. While Frank managed to hobble toward the rear on his own, Will joined in with the rest of his regiment, just as the gray storm cloud came into view. The Union soldiers fired, sending the first wave of Confederates back. But the Rebels regrouped and came again. This time, as Will pulled the trigger, his rifle jammed. He pulled the trigger again, but nothing happened. Around him, the line was breaking. The look of panic on the other Union soldiers' faces, as they began to scream and run in horror, was demoralizing. Even the officers seemed to be breaking.

Will was determined not to run. He grabbed a weapon from a fallen soldier on the ground beside him and fired it into the onslaught of gray uniforms. Just then, he felt a pain in his upper right arm. He couldn't tell exactly where he had been hit at first. He looked down to see if it was in his arm or his chest. Then, he felt another shot. This one hit him just below the neck, near the center of his collarbone. He stumbled backward, and then fell to the ground. He heard Skeet yelling his name, but he knew his friend could not get to him now. He saw a blur of boots flying around him as the Confederate charge carried the ground. He did his best to roll out of the way, trying not to be trampled. As the last of the boots went flying overhead, he suddenly began to feel intolerably cold. The thought occurred to him that he might be dying. Just before he slipped into unconsciousness, his mind wandered back to Lamar, back to Cordia's arms, back home.

Chapter Seven

THE HEAT of the August sun was blazing. It was only a short walk from the large two-story house on Broadway Street up to the town square, but even with a sunbonnet on, Cordia could feel the sweat running down the back of her neck. Maybe it was just because there had been rumor of another fight, a big one near Springfield, but she felt like she was being burned alive.

Her heart was pounding as she neared the courthouse. She could see a crowd forming there. News had just made it to her father at the bank, who had sent word by one of the young boys who worked at the newspaper to go tell Cordia. Yet, already, there must have been close to fifty people standing around, staring at the courthouse door. Nothing was posted yet, and most likely nothing would be that day—nothing that really supplied any pertinent information. Nevertheless, Cordia did not have the best of feelings this time. Her stomach was tight, her palms sweaty, her heart raced, ready to burst out of her chest. Regardless of whether the news came today, tomorrow, or next week, she was determined she would not be leaving until she had some word of how many casualties there were and the names of the dead and injured.

Cordia looked around the crowd for familiar faces. Though she recognized many of the town folks, she did not see any of her friends.

She found a spot in the shade, but even that did not help with the overwhelming heat she was feeling. Her mother had wanted to come with her, but Cordia insisted that this August sun would do her no good. Likewise, Frieda volunteered to escort her mistress. Cordia knew she had work to do and felt that, at twenty years old, she ought to be able to manage this trip by herself. Now, she was wishing she wasn't alone. What if they put that list up there, and she saw Will's name on it—or Jaris's—and she just fainted straight away? There'd be no one there to help her. She would be just like that poor woman calling for her Joseph after the last battle, with no one to come and lead her home. She didn't want to think about that, and rightly shouldn't. It would be far better to faint in this burning inferno than it would be to be lying on a battlefield somewhere bleeding to death. And while she prayed that neither of her men were in that situation, she felt fairly certain that some of the Barton County boys must be.

At any rate, she was extremely relieved when Julia showed up about an hour later. She had ridden in on horseback, tied up her horse, and then spotted her friend where she was now seated on the ground under an oak tree. "Any word?" she asked.

Cordia shook her head. "Not much. Mr. Jenkins said that he received a telegraph earlier this morning from some relation of his who lives down around Springfield. Said that Lyon and Sigel had attacked McCulloch and Price early, early this morning. Didn't have any idea on casualties or who had won or anything like that." Julia sat down in the soft grass beside her. Cordia continued. "Then, Mr. Ward came out a little while ago and said that he couldn't confirm anything, but he had a cousin who lived down around a creek, Wilson's or something, not too far from Springfield. Said his cousin had sent word that Lyon was dead and that the Confederate Army had overrun what was left of the Union forces, which he estimated to be outnumbered about two to one. But, I don't rightly know what we can believe at this point."

Julia nodded her head. "Aunt Margaret wanted to come, but I just thought it was intolerably too hot for her out here. Can't imagine having to fight in this kinda heat."

Cordia had to agree with her friend on that point. For one of the few times in her life, she was actually using the fan that hung around her wrist. Not that it was doing her any good. Julia must have noticed. "You don't look so good yourself, Cordia. Are you overheating?"

"No," Cordia reassured her, though she thought perhaps she was about to boil. "I'm fine. I'll be fine."

The look of skepticism on Julia's face made it clear she didn't believe her friend, but she didn't say any more about it. "Do you think there's any way that they will have a list of casualties today?"

Cordia shook her head. "The Battle of Carthage was about twenty miles from here and, from what we're a'hearin' nothing more than a skirmish compared to this recent encounter. I will be greatly surprised if they have any indication of who is wounded or killed today. Frankly, I don't expect them to know anything by tomorrow." Julia was nodding her head that she agreed. "But, honestly, Julia," Cordia went on, looking her friend in the eye, "I don't have a very good feeling about this."

At first, Julia looked surprised to hear Cordia admit that. But then, she shook her head. "I know what you mean. Something just don't seem right." Then, she mustered a small smile. "I'm sure Jaris is just fine, Cordia. He's a strong man. Good with a gun. He's made it through. I'm sure of it."

Cordia nodded in agreement, but she didn't venture any guess at Will's fate or any words of support. All she knew was the pit of her stomach was telling her that something was terribly wrong.

Around seven o'clock that evening, another telegraph came in, this one also from Mr. Ward's cousin. He basically repeated what he had said before, and then gave a quick account of the dead and wounded, saying only, "I have never seen so many dead and bleeding men in my life. Churches, barns, farmhouses, any structure nearby has become a hospital. Dead and dying littering the ground all around."

These words were extremely unsettling to Cordia. She was happy that her father had come over after work and had joined them. Susannah had also come by to bring some cool water and to see if there was anything else she could do. She was not worried about James in this instance because he had stayed with Jackson's men and was not engaged that day. Mr. Ward had told everyone he did not expect any more word that evening, but he would stay and watch the telegraph for another hour or so. Then, he was going home and would be back in the morning. He also warned them that, if the casualties were truly as high as his brother had said, they most likely wouldn't send a report by telegraph, but by news reporter or carrier, and that may take a few days.

At that point, Cordia's father tried to get her to go home, but she insisted on staying. She watched as Mr. Ward locked up the courthouse at 8:15. She watched as the crowd dispersed. She even watched as Julia rode away around 9:00. Finally, her father talked enough reason into her to get her to walk back home. She knew she wouldn't sleep that night and that she would probably be one of the first people at the courthouse the next morning. If it had been up to her, she would have spent the night sleeping underneath that oak tree.

As soon as there was enough light to see the brick sidewalk, Cordia was out the door, flying to the town square. As she approached the courthouse, she saw just a few other people standing outside. There was nothing new posted on the door. Her shoulders slumped as she went back to the same spot where she had spent the better portion of the day before, underneath the oak tree. She hadn't figured on there being any news. As a matter-of-fact, she could tell that Mr. Ward hadn't even made it to the building yet. Still, a part of her had hoped to have some sort of relief from this awful wondering.

The majority of her night had consisted of tossing and turning, flailing about on her bed. She had spent hours on her knees, praying to God that neither Jaris nor Will had been injured, and if they had been injured, that He wouldn't let them be dead or suffering and dying. Her mind had envisioned so many different scenarios. She imagined them reeling on the battlefield, still lying there after nightfall. She envisioned herself reading that list on the courthouse door, falling over in a faint. Finally, she wore herself out enough to fall asleep. But it was the most restless sleep she had ever had. When she did dream, it was a haunted dream. She could see Jaris, and then Will, lying dead in a pile of mud, blood running from their cold bodies. In her dream, she just had a feeling that they had shot and killed each other. She hadn't seen it, but she had gathered it, just from the way they were lying. Then, in another version of the dream, it was she who had shot them both.

Jarred awake from the images, she was relieved to see that the sun had risen above the horizon. And now, here she sat, waiting. Hoping and praying that none of her awful dreams had played out and that both of the men she loved were somewhere off in camp now, reading letters from home and talking about the battle with their friends.

She didn't have any idea what time it was until the church bells on the First Baptist Church, just a block away, began to ring. Only five o'clock? She realized she was probably going to be sitting there for a few hours before Mr. Ward even showed up to unlock the doors. Most folks who worked at the courthouse didn't arrive until at least 7:00 or 8:00. She was hoping he would be a little hastier today, what with so many people waiting. But he had seemed pretty sure yesterday that they were not going to be finding anything out that day.

Around 6:30, Cal Markson, a boy of about fifteen or so, showed up on a horse. "I'm riding toward Springfield," he announced. "Surely there has got to be word in the Springfield paper or someone who can tell me something."

"Be careful!" one of the old-timers standing around warned. "You don't want to be made a casualty yourself, boy. You know them scouts is liable to shoot anything that moves."

Cal looked determined. "My older brother fights with Price. I'm going to go see what I can. I mean to be back before the sun comes up tomorrow." He rode off with such fury his horse's hooves kicked up dirt along the road that lined the square, and then all they could see was a trail of dust in his wake.

Though Cordia was concerned for Cal, being such a young boy, she was glad to know that someone was going to do something proactive to find out some information. She couldn't believe that Julia wasn't here yet. Wasn't she concerned about her brother? Of course, Cordia knew she was being a little hard on the young girl--in fact, Julia was probably thinking that it wouldn't make much sense to go sit and stare at a locked courthouse. Still, she needed something to be angry about, and right now, anything would do.

It seemed like an eternity before Mr. Ward finally arrived around 7:30. There was now a crowd of about forty people who all gave a big cheer when his horse and wagon came into view. "I declare," he said, as he fumbled with the keys to the building, "I do hope there's some kind of news come soon, or else I don't know what you early-risers might do to me."

Again, Cordia was aggravated. It was easy for the old man to have such a nonchalant attitude. He didn't have any relations in the war as far as she knew. *"Still, you'd think he'd have a little compassion for all the boys he knew who may well be dead."* Once again, Cordia was glad she was keeping her opinions to herself. It seemed every thought she had was unwarranted. She knew it was just this awful uncertainty that was eating away at her. She made a mental note to be careful, if ever she did open her mouth, as she may likely bite some innocent person's head off.

At a little after 8:00, Cordia's dad stopped by to check in with her on his way to the bank. "No, Daddy," she said aggravated. "We've not heard a word. Mr. Ward's in there, but I guess there must not be any news because he hasn't bothered to come out and tell us."

"Calm down, sweetheart," he assured her. "I am sure that every-thing is fine and that you are getting all worked up about nothing."

Cordia felt her face turn a little red. How she hoped he was right. "I'm sorry, Daddy. I just have this awful feeling."

He put his arm around her. "I know, child. You have always been sensitive to the ideas of the suffering of others, or of losing those people that you love. But it will all work out in God's way, my dear." She had thought on that a lot. *God's way.* She supposed he must be right, and again she nodded in agreement with her father's wisdom. "I know that a normal person would be all worked up, wondering what had happened, but you, my child, the most inquisitive person I have ever laid eyes on, well, this must truly be eating you up. Why don't you go back to the house and rest, and I will come over and check every so often to see if they have any news?"

"No, Daddy," she said very adamantly. "I need to stay here and find out for myself."

Having known Cordia for all twenty years of her life, her daddy knew there was no sense in arguing with her. He kissed her lightly on the forehead and then was on his way.

A few minutes later, Mr. Ward came out, though they could all see he had no papers in his hands. "All right," he announced, "this is what I have done. I have telegraphed my cousin and asked him to go down to these hospitals he was speaking of yesterday and see if he can compile a list of the Barton County boys who are dead and wounded." There were now close to one-hundred people standing around, and most of them were very happy to hear this news. "Now, I can't promise he'll get the message or be able to do it today, but I reckon that's about all I can do at this time."

"There's no other news?" someone shouted from the back of the crowd.

"No, I'm afraid there ain't been no news, nothing I didn't already tell you about." Mr. Ward confirmed. Then, he promptly turned around and went back into the courthouse.

Conversation began to build now, something else to talk about. Some people thought this was the best idea they had ever heard. Others were already declaring that it couldn't possibly work. It was then that Cordia saw Julia making her way through the crowd toward her. She waved and the younger girl came over and joined her.

"Please tell me you ain't been sitting here all night," the blonde said, plopping herself down beside her friend.

Cordia was already annoyed, and Julia had just gotten there. "Course not," she said, a little snippy. "I'm not wearing the same dress, am I?"

"Well," Julia said, obviously offended. "Sounds like someone didn't get much sleep last night."

Cordia was ashamed of herself. "I'm sorry," she began. "No, I didn't get any sleep. This waiting is about to do me in."

Julia accepted her apology by pulling Cordia over to rest her head on her shoulder. "Have faith in the Good Lord, Cordia. It'll be all right."

"How can you, of all people, say that?" Cordia asked, literally amazed that her friend could think that way after all that she had been through. And yesterday, she had agreed that something about this situation wasn't sitting right with her either.

Julia smiled. "I've been thinking, most all night long. I know that the Lord has a plan for each of us. I can see that now. I don't think that He would take my ma and pa, Nolan, and Will from me. I really don't think He would. But, if'n He decided that was best, I know I would be strong enough to make it by because the Lord don't give us anything that we can't handle."

Julia was staring off into the sky now, and Cordia could see that the girl really wanted to believe her own words. "Well," she sighed, "I hope you're right. But, I have always had a reputation for being stronger than I think I truly am. I am praying that the Good Lord don't overestimate me."

The hours passed so slowly. Cordia could imagine that if there was an hourglass before her, its contents would be dripping down like molasses. At first, there had been a lot of conversation around them. But, as the blazing August sun filled the sky, discussions had died off. Some people grew weary of sitting there and actually went home. Others had found a place in the shade to take a nap. By two o'clock, Cordia's mind was so weary of thinking on all of the horrible possibilities, her body ached from sitting on the hard ground, and it was almost as if she just gave out. She hadn't fainted, but she had fallen asleep so quickly that Julia had to catch her from falling over and lay her down on the shaded ground. Then, Julia promptly rested her head on her friend and fell asleep herself.

The girls awoke to a commotion. At first, Cordia had forgotten where she was. She couldn't believe she had fallen asleep on the lawn in front of the courthouse. When she opened her eyes, she could see the sun going down. The crowd of people seemed to be pushing their way toward the courthouse door. In a panic, she reached over and nudged Julia. The girl stirred slightly. "Julia—wake up!" she said, clambering to her feet. Julia didn't seem to know where she was at first either, but soon enough she was standing next to her friend. "What is it?" she asked someone standing near the back of the crowd.

The older man didn't take his eyes off of the people in front of him but replied out of the side of his mouth, "List. Mr. Ward's cousin sent a list of dead and wounded boys from Barton County."

Cordia's eyes opened widely now. Then it *had* worked. "Is he sure it's right?" she asked the same man.

"Don't know. Sure he didn't put anyone on there who isn't dead or wounded. Might of missed a few, I reckon." The man moved forward as people began to come down off of the courthouse steps. Some women were already screaming and crying. Others looked as if they were going to faint. At least one woman had begun to cheer, and then remembered where she was and solemnly walked away. "Mr. Ward said his cousin went around to different hospitals gathering names, talked to a few of the Confederate units still near Springfield and some Union soldiers. Said he didn't know who was dead or who was wounded, but these are the ones that got shot." With that the man was lost in the crowd.

"Dammit!" Cordia exclaimed. So, even when she saw that list, even if Jaris or Will had their name on it, she still wouldn't know if they were dead, dying, or wounded, or if someone just gave Mr. Ward's cousin the wrong name. She was beginning to think that Cal Markson had a better idea when he rode to Springfield early that morning. Maybe that's what she should have done.

She looked around for Julia and saw that she was still standing close behind her. "Did you hear what he said?" she asked. Julia nodded. "Still won't tell us much."

Julia was obviously in a much more optimistic mood. "Let's just hope we don't recognize any of the names, and then it won't matter."

Cordia nodded and finally made her way to the courthouse steps. She still couldn't see, and people were pushing up here much worse than they had been when she was at the back of the line. Word had gotten out, and many people were showing up now on horseback and in carriages. She knew she shouldn't have fallen asleep! She was one of the first people here, and now it was taking forever for her to see that blasted list.

But then, she thought, maybe she didn't want to see the list after all. Maybe she should take a moment to think for a second before she looked. The information on that piece of paper could change her life forever. As she made her way the last few feet to the dreaded posting, a thousand thoughts rolled over her all at once. Jaris, chasing her through the fields around his house, skipping rocks on the family pond, that laugh of his peeling off into the sky. She remembered holding his hand one time when they were only young teenagers. She remembered the day he had asked her to marry him. The first time he kissed her. The day he had left, and how he had kissed her goodbye. And then she thought of Will. He had kissed her that day, too.

Now she was standing right in front of the list. The sun was going down, but someone was holding a lantern nearby, and she could faintly make out the names. This time, a quick skim did not leave her with a feeling of relief. There it was, Lt. Jaris Adams, CSA. Her heart began to sink in her chest, like a ship struck by a cannonball. And then, she heard a small cry beside her, and she looked down to see Julia, her hands over her face. Cordia knew that Julia would be concerned to see her cousin's name, but she also knew that there was only one thing that could make her friend's face turn that pale. Her eyes flew back to the paper. Yes, sure enough, a few more lines down, Pvt. William Tucker, USA.

Julia, who had been so strong all day, was now sobbing. Cordia put her arm around the girl and led her down the steps, pushing her way through the people who were still trying to get their eyes on that horrendous list. She could feel tears brimming over her own eyes, but then, something in her had known all along that this day would not be like last time. She saw her daddy now, standing over by the oak tree. The look on his face told her that he could plainly see by his daughter's reaction that things were just as she had thought they would be. Cordia was almost afraid to go near him because she knew the moment he touched her, she would be his little girl again. And she wouldn't be able to hold back her tears—for Julia's sake or anyone else's.

She took a deep breath as she approached her father, who was now holding his hat in his hand and staring at the ground. "Is he... is he dead?" her father asked.

"Don't know. Doesn't say. Just know they were shot," she replied.

"They?" he asked.

"Yes. Both of them."

Mr. Pike nodded his head and then offered to take Julia home. She could not have ridden a horse in this condition if she had wanted to. He dropped Cordia off first. Her mama took one look at her face and didn't bother to ask if she had any word. As Cordia dragged herself up the stairs, she heard Frieda assuring her mother not to bother Miss

Cordia, but that she would run down to the courthouse and find out what had happened herself.

Cordia collapsed on her bed, numb. She hadn't begun to cry yet. She hadn't let the news register. All she could think of were those three simple words she had said to her daddy. She was in disbelief. How could it be? *Both of them.*

THE SKY WAS LIKE A PAINTING, portraying the end of the world. Dark red at the horizon, lightening to pink and orange, before it finally spread into a thick yellow that covered the rest of the sky. Smoke billowed through the air, sometimes pervasive enough that simply breathing would make a person gag and choke. It seemed that not a single blade of grass could still be standing. The ground was thick with mud, small rivers flowing through it, the same color as that horizon. The stench of death and dying hung in curtains, wafting around on the breeze, churning stomachs, causing nostrils to flare. Standing here, one no longer needed to imagine what hell must be like.

Cordia was picking her way through an endless sea of dead men's bodies, piled to her knees and higher. She looked into the eyes of every single one of them. Sometimes, she had to turn them over to get a good look at their faces. Occasionally, parts of their corpses would stain her hands with blood, body tissue, maggots. She would try to wipe the stains away on her dress, but they would not come off. No matter how hard she tried to make them clean, her hands stayed dirty.

A little way in the distance, some men were digging a pit. They were throwing some of the bodies inside, mostly the ones dressed in blue. They would topple down the slopes, falling on top of each other, like marionettes whose strings had been cut. She tried to yell at the gravediggers not to go so fast. She hadn't checked those men yet. She didn't know if they were tossing in a familiar face. But they continued their work as if they could not see or hear her.

Then, it didn't matter. She looked down, and there he was. He wasn't piled on top of anyone else—just lying there on the filthy ground, almost as if he was asleep. Except, his eyes were open. Open and staring into the sky. As she studied his face, she began to think how peaceful he looked. But then, she was horrified to see his face twist in an angry grimace. He was looking right at her now—his blue eyes squinting up at her in a way she never knew they were capable of doing. "Why didn't you come?" he demanded. Cordia began to back away, but his icy eyes trapped her. Again, he yelled at her, "Why didn't you come? I called you—but you didn't come. You just left me here!"

She began to back away now, tears pouring down her cheeks. "No," she whispered, but he did not listen. He was still lying there, most of his body lifeless, unmoving. But he continued to bombard her with angry words, insisting that she answer. "No, I didn't mean to hurt you," she sobbed. Then, she began to scream. "I never meant to hurt you!"

Cordia was still screaming as she shot upright in bed. She heard a commotion in the hall, and before she could even register what was happening, both of her parents and Frieda were in her room.

"What is it?" they all seemed to be asking at once. Cordia's eyes darted around the room. Where was he? Where was Jaris? She had just seen him—he had been here, yelling at her. But then, she looked around and realized she was not on a battlefield. She was in her own bed, drenched with sweat.

By now, her family had realized she had just had a bad dream. Her mother sat down on her bed, smoothing her hair, as Frieda poured her a glass of water. "There, there now," her mother was saying. "Darling, you were just having a nightmare. It'll be all right now."

But what she had just seen would not leave her, and Cordia was well aware why that was. Though what she had dreamt did not really happen, Jaris and Will had both been on that list of casualties earlier that day. And she still had no idea of their status. How could she possibly sleep under these circumstances?

She took the glass of water from Frieda and drank the whole thing. Her throat felt as if she really had been choking on smoke. She looked out the window and could tell the sun was nowhere near coming up. "What time is it?" she asked.

"I don't rightly know," her father said, standing behind her mother. "Don't usually wear my pocket watch to bed." He was smiling at her, trying to make her feel better.

Frieda went out into the hall and looked at the clock. "It's a quarter past three, Miss Cordia. You had better get back to sleep, child. You are likely to have another long day ahead, if I know you."

A quarter past three. Almost three hours until the sun came up. And not likely to be any more word until who knows when. She could not possibly go back to sleep. She could not possibly stay in that bed, or that house, or that town one more day not knowing.

"No," she said. They were all looking at her blankly. Frieda was just about to turn and go back to bed, but now she stopped and stared at her, along with her parents. She said it again. "No. I can't go back to sleep. I won't go back to sleep."

Her parents looked at each other uncomfortably. Her father gave a little chuckle. "Why, Cordia, sweetheart, what do you mean? Are you saying you just intend to get up this early?"

Before she could answer, Frieda chimed in. "Child, you know that there won't be any word from anyone this early. And even if there was, Mr. Ward ain't gonna open up the courthouse where the telegraph is any time soon."

Cordia was already putting on her robe and trying to free her legs, though it was rather difficult with the weight of her mother on her blankets. "No, I am tired of sitting on the courthouse lawn. I am tired of waiting." She managed to free herself and stood up. "I'm going to Springfield."

Again, the rest of the people in the room were dumbfounded. "Cordia," her mother was saying, "you can't possibly be serious." To look at her, however, they could tell that Cordia was definitely steadfast. She had already gotten two traveling gowns out of the closet and a bag for her essentials.

"Cordia, calm down," her father said, lightly grabbing her arm, in her mind causing a loss of precious time. "You can't just go galloping off to Springfield in the middle of the night. It wouldn't be safe."

"I don't care," she insisted, shaking her arm free. "I'll be fine. I know how to shoot a gun. I'll take one with me. I am not going to sit here for one more minute waiting for someone to tell me that the man I love—or his cousin—is dead!" She turned around and flung open a drawer and began to pack her bag. Her parents were talking to each other quietly, but she didn't take the time to listen to what they were saying.

"Fine," her father finally relented. "I'll go with you."

"You can't go, Daddy. This town would fall apart if you left it for even one day. I'll go by myself." Once again, her parents were whispering. Her father knew as well as she did that he could not leave the bank without people thinking there had been some sort of run on it. Not with things the way they were in the state just now.

"Listen," Cordia said, pausing her packing for a moment. "I don't know why y'all are bothering to argue with me. You been telling me my whole life there ain't no use in arguing with someone as strong-willed as I am. I love you both immensely, but I can tell you right now there ain't nothing you can say that's gonna stop me from going to Springfield today."

It was Frieda who spoke up next, "Lord A'mighty!" she declared. "Don't either one of you have enough sense just to tell the girl no?" All three of them stopped and looked at her now. Frieda was known for speaking her mind, but they were all very certain she had forgotten her place this time. Yet, she continued. "I'm sorry—I mean no disrespect. I know better than anyone what good people you all are. But I have to say, I think you're all plumb out of your minds if you let Miss Cordia go riding off to Springfield in the middle of a war, all by herself."

"Frieda's right," her father was saying. "I'll go down to the bank in a bit and let them know I won't be in for a day or so. We will ride to Springfield together. Now, go back to bed and rest, and I will let you know when it's time to go. All right, darling?"

Cordia looked from one face to another. She knew she could not win this argument. Reluctantly, she nodded, putting the garments she had gathered down on top of her dresser and crossing back over to the bed. Her mother stood so that she could climb back between the sheets. "Now, there, there, dear," her mother said soothing her hair.

The three of them turned and walked back out the door, still lamenting Cordia's state of mind. Cordia waited until she heard all three doors close and her father snoring before she arose and began to go back about her packing. She was willing to do whatever it took to get to Springfield immediately, even if it meant sneaking out.

Cordia had the horses hitched up, her bag, and a shotgun she had procured from her father's gun cabinet mounted beneath the wagon seat and was just about to climb aboard when Frieda came flying out the side door, moving faster than Cordia had ever seen her short little legs carry her. "Now, what in the world do you think you're doing, Miss Cordia?" she was yelling.

Without pausing, Cordia shouted over her shoulder, "I think you know precisely what I'm doing."

Frieda grabbed her by the arm. "You know I can't let you do that!" Frieda replied sternly.

Shaking her arm off, Cordia climbed atop the seat. "There's nothing you can do to stop me," she replied. She grabbed the reins and gave them a quick shake. Frieda looked around in despair. She had to know she wouldn't have time to go back in and get Cordia's father. She must have realized her options were dwindling. Without another moment of hesitation, she threw herself into the back of the wagon, refusing to let Cordia go alone. "What are you doing?" Cordia asked once she realized what Frieda had done.

"I'm a'comin' with you," she replied, out of breath.

"I don't think that's a good idea," Cordia replied, not slowing the carriage a bit.

"Well, you've left me little choice, young lady," Frieda replied.

Though Cordia was reluctant to take Frieda with her, she was glad that she would not have to make the journey alone. She gave the reins another jerk, pushing the horses forward, ready to find out exactly what had happened to Jaris and Will once and for all.

The sun was still not up as they made their way out of town. Cordia had slowed down enough to allow Frieda to crawl over the back of the seat and join her in the front portion of the wagon. She knew the way very well until they got outside of the county. Then, she would have to rely on Frieda's familiarity with the roads. Many years ago, Cordia and her mother had gone on a short trip to visit some family friends in Springfield. At the time, her father had given them the names of some business relations of his who would be happy to let them spend the evening at their home. Cordia hoped that they still lived in the same vicinity, and that Frieda, who had accompanied them, could remember the way. But she honestly had little intention of stopping until she found the hospital in Springfield where her answers lie.

She had considered stopping by the Adams Farm to see if Julia wanted to go with them. But she remembered how pale and fragile her friend had looked yesterday, and she didn't think this trip would be good for her tuberculosis. And, though Cordia had never been on a battlefield before, if it was anything like the one she had walked in her dream, she knew the air would quickly get to delicate Julia. So, here she was, driving the horses before her with a purpose, Frieda beside her, rambling on about stubbornness and the likelihood of them both getting killed. Cordia ignored her, deep in her own thoughts.

Frieda mentioned that she was glad they had taken the whole cart. She said she was only doing this one time, so if there was something (and by that, Cordia knew all too well that she meant *someone*) to haul back, she was doing it now. She also mentioned she was glad that this way they would have to stick to the roads, which Cordia would be much more likely to do in a wagon then if she were riding on horseback, where she might be liable to try to take shortcuts. Springfield was about 75 miles from Lamar. They would be close to arriving there that evening. But she had been warned against riding into an army camp yesterday when Cal was leaving town, and she assumed that applied to an army hospital as well, particularly after dark. Cordia decided she would cross that bridge when she came to it. For now, she was just leading the horses on as fast as she could.

August 12 was not any cooler than August 10 or 11, and had Cordia been capable of feeling anything, she might have known just how boiling hot it was. Frieda kept going on about it, but Cordia wasn't even listening to her. She was lost for hours at a time in her own thoughts. She kept replaying that dream in her mind, wondering what did it mean? She just could not sort it out. She was hoping and praying that Jaris was not angry at her and that he would know, somehow, that she was coming for him.

The sun was rising high in the sky when they saw a single rider coming down the road ahead of them. He was at a full gallop, and both women were alarmed at first. Frieda reached under the seat and grabbed the rifle. Cordia squinted and shaded her eyes and realized that she recognized him. "Cal!" she yelled, standing up. At first, the boy looked just about as scared of them as they had been of him, until he realized whom it was. He slowed his horse down and eventually brought it to a stop alongside the wagon.

"Cordia Pike?" he said in disbelief. "Where are you going?" he asked.

"Well, we're headed to Springfield," she explained. "Got tired of waiting. Same as you. Did you find anything out?" she asked.

"Some," he nodded. "Found my brother. He's okay. I don't know about Jaris though, I'll tell you that right up front." He took off his hat and wiped his head. Her face fell with the news. His horse seemed thankful for the moment's rest. "My brother's all right. Said he ain't never imagined war could be as bad as that."

Cordia nodded. His brother was in the Confederate Army. She had hoped he would know something about Jaris. She was certain that if he hadn't heard about Jaris, he wouldn't know anything about Will, but she had to be sure. "Did your brother know anything about any of the Union boys from home?"

The boy nodded. "The McCarthy boy, George, serves in his unit. Said that he got his head banged up a little. He went to get it bandaged up. Saw Frank Glen, shot in the leg. Okay though. That's all I know."

"I see," Cordia said. Well, it was worth a try.

"Why do you ask? I can't figure on whom you'd be asking about from the Union side."

"My friend Julia Tucker's brother's fighting for Col. Sigel," she explained.

"Oh, that ain't good," Cal said, as his horse became restless, telling him he was rested up now. "My brother said most of them boys didn't make it out of there. Said that a whole regiment of Confederate soldiers walked right across the battlefield in front of them, and those Sigel boys never even fired a shot, till it was too late. Then, most of them got it when they was high-tailing it out of there. That's how Frank Glen got shot, I reckon. He's one of Sigel's boys."

Cordia felt her stomach turn over. All the blood seemed to be draining from her face. Frieda seemed to have suddenly remembered that she was there to take care of her, rather than give her a hard time. "You all right, Miss Cordia?" she asked, placing a hand on her shoulder.

She took a deep breath; her eyes had gone blurry for a moment. Finally, she recovered herself. "Yes, I'm fine. Probably the sun," she said, trying to force a smile. She could tell then that Cal was ready to go. "I'm sorry to keep you," she said, turning back to him. "Can you tell me, once I get to Springfield where I will need to go to find the hospital?"

"Oh, it ain't inside Springfield. Here, I got a map," he said, pulling his horse over closer to Cordia's wagon so she could see. "When you get to about here, on this here road, you're gonna cross a creek. Called Wilson's Creek. Around there, that's where most of the dead and wounded still are. Very few of them actually got moved with the army back to Springfield. Some of the Union wounded got left behind in town when they retreated to Rolla yesterday, but most of them are out here in the farmhouses and buildings nearer the battlefield. There's the Ray house, and a little church, some other houses. Some of them are in tents; some of them are just out on the ground. Really not something a woman probably needs to be a' seeing miss, if I do say so."

She had grimaced at the idea of thousands of dead and wounded men, but she couldn't let that bother her. "Well, I'm sure I will make it just fine," she said, holding her head up. "Thank you very kindly for your help, Cal. I hope you have a safe trip back home."

"Yeah, miss, you have a safe trip, too. And I would be careful if I were you. There are lots of Confederate skirmishers around the closer you get to Springfield. I don't think they'd harm you on purpose, but make sure they know what it is you're a'doin'."

Cordia drove on. Part of her was very glad that she had run into Cal Markson. Now they had a better idea of exactly where they needed to go. But, then, the only news he had given her was bad news. So, on she drove, knowing the quicker she got there, the quicker the agony of the unknown would be over.

By nine o'clock, it was pitch black. The horses were exhausted, and Frieda was insisting that they stop for the evening. The house Cordia's father had recommended was left behind in the miles they had crossed that day. They had stopped to rest the horses only twice, and Cordia had spent the whole time pacing, urging Frieda to let them continue. Now, she, too, was feeling weary from their long journey. And she did not like the idea of driving into war-torn country in the darkness. She finally consented to pulling over into a hollow in the trees for the night and trying to get some sleep in the wagon. They decided it would be safer if they slept in shifts, and since this was the first time in days that Cordia actually wanted to rest, Frieda was fine with taking the first watch.

Normally, Cordia had trouble falling asleep in strange places. But this night, she was so fatigued; it only took her a few minutes to drift off. However, it was not a peaceful sleep. Not long after her eyes shut did she begin to dream.

Once again, she was on the battlefield. This time, she was in the thick of battle. She looked around her and could see men in gray uniforms charging ahead at an unsuspecting crowd of blue. She was wearing the same green dress she had been wearing that day, but now it was covered in dirt and ash. Yet, she seemed caught up in that wave of gray, and she, too, was charging at those unsuspecting Union soldiers, who just stood there, nonchalantly, some of them even chit-chatting idly. Then, she realized that she was carrying a rifle. And as she drew close enough to those boys in blue, she aimed her weapon along with the rest of the charging Rebels. She felt the rifle kick, throwing her backward as she fired. She watched the path of the bullet, moving in slow motion. Then, her eyes widened in horror as she realized where it was headed.

Will was standing right in the bullet's path. He was laughing, talking to Frank Glen, not even noticing the bullet coming right at him. She began to scream, "Will! No, get out of the way!" But he could not hear her. And then, right before the bullet struck him, he turned and saw it coming. His face deformed in an expression of horror. As it impacted him in the chest, he was flung to the ground. She ran to him. His uniform was covered in blood. The other Confederates were sweeping over them, pushing the Union soldiers before them. As they flew by on either side, she dropped to her knees, lifting his head carefully in her arms. "Will, Will, I'm so sorry! I didn't mean to hurt you!" she cried. She had never imagined a person could bleed so much.

There was blood all over him. Blood all over the ground. Blood all over her. "Oh, Will! Please don't die," she whispered. "I love you!"

He was looking at her then, his brown eyes seeming to fade as the life drained out of him. She noticed, then, that he had a strange look on his face. And to her astonishment he opened his dying blue lips and asked, "Who are you?"

Cordia shook awake, violently. Her eyes flew open, and again, she had to place herself outside of the dream. Where was she? And then she remembered. She was in the back of the wagon. They were on their way to Springfield. She looked around. The night was pitch black, no moon in the sky. She couldn't really see anything. Feeling around in the darkness, she finally found her bag. She found one of the candles she'd brought and lit it. Strange that Frieda had not said anything when she started making such noise. She crawled up to the front of the wagon and could see why. Frieda had fallen asleep at her post.

Fairly annoyed at this (after all, Confederate pickets could have shot them) she shook the older woman, who was also snoring. "Frieda!" she said in a furious whisper. The caregiver only gurgled a little so she shook her harder. "Frieda!!" Finally, she sat up straight, looking surprised. One of the horses whinnied, and she seemed to suddenly remember where she was.

"What's the matter?" she asked, yawning.

"What's the matter?" Cordia repeated, climbing over the seat back to sit beside the other woman. "You fell asleep! That's what's the matter!"

Frieda stretched, "Oh, I was only dozing. I would have heard if anyone would have approached us."

"Really?" Cordia asked. "Then why did I have to shake you twice to get you to wake up?"

"Well, I'm sorry," Frieda began, "But I am too old to be sitting up half the night in the middle of nowhere, waiting to see if we are going to get shot at!" Then, she began to start up again about what a foolish idea this was in the first place.

But Cordia cut her off. "All right—enough! I am awake now. Go back in the wagon and go to sleep. I will wake you at first light, and we're driving out of here."

She did not have to tell Frieda twice. She hopped down, went around, and climbed into the wagon, shaking the whole vehicle as she proceeded to make herself comfortable. Cordia decided to leave the candle lit. She was carrying a watch with her, and she dug around in the dim light to see what time it was. Only 2:30. She would have to sit there for four hours and be haunted by the memories of her vivid dreams. These last few days had by far been the longest of her whole life. But, in just a few hours, all of her worrying and waiting would be over—for better or worse.

Again, the minutes ticked by so slowly. Finally, a glimmer began to lighten the sky at the edge of the horizon. That was good enough for Cordia. She stretched her aching back and shoulders. "FRIEDA!! Wake up. We're moving out!!"

Chapter Eight

No amount of preparation could possibly have equipped Cordia Pike for what she saw as she neared the hospital outside of Wilson's Creek. Though she had been warned by telegraph, and by Cal Markson, that this was not a pleasant place, until her eyes actually took in the sights, until her nose actually whiffed the stench, she could not have comprehended the horrors that were war and the catastrophic wake it left behind.

She had been surprised at the few number of Confederate troops there were patrolling the area. She assumed that was because most of them had fallen back to Springfield, which was still about ten miles ahead of them. One of the young men had come close enough to the wagon that she had asked him for directions to the hospital. He had simply pointed in a general direction. She thought it was possible that some of the wounded had been moved to other locations on the battlefield, so as she pulled up to an area lined with a few tents and a few scattered buildings, she wasn't certain that she would find the answers to her questions somewhere amongst this rabble. Cordia was compelled to try, however, and she would keep searching until she found the information she was so desperately looking for.

It wasn't as if there was truly a hitching post or a good place to stop the wagon. Frieda finally just pulled it over off of the road. They both hopped down, and Frieda tied the horses to a tree as Cordia's eyes took in the scene. Men were lying around on the ground, those in the open tents on tables or cots. Some of them had white bandages stained red with blood on their heads, arms, or legs. Others were on makeshift crutches, trying to hobble around. In one of the larger tents, there was a man, whom she assumed must have been a doctor, giving directions to a few other men and even a couple of women. They each nodded and went on their way. The man leaned against the tent pole, wiping his head with the back of his hand wearily. The ground here was fairly torn up. She could see puddles of red water around the tents, which she knew must be blood. The stench was overpowering. Flies buzzed by in swarms. Frieda joined her and they walked slowly across the road. She could hear someone screaming now. She couldn't quite make out what he was saying, but it sounded much like, "Please don't take my leg!" She was horrified at the thought of someone losing a limb, but then she realized, many of the men who were sitting around underneath the trees were missing arms or legs, one of them an eye. Then she saw one of the most dreadful things she could possibly ever imagine. Over beside one of the tents, there was a large pile of body parts stacked up on the ground. Arms, legs; the sight was revolting. Her stomach turned over, and for a second, she thought she was going to be sick.

Frieda must have felt the same way. "This is just dreadful," she said. "I never imagined...." Her voice trailed off. She didn't need to say anything else; Cordia knew exactly what she meant.

Cordia looked around for someone to ask for help, but she didn't feel right asking any of the wounded. A few orderlies walked by, but they were carrying a litter, and it looked like there must be a corpse on it as there was a human form beneath the bloodied sheet. She wondered why they would bother with the sheet when other corpses littered the ground all around them, but this one they carried off out of sight, behind a building.

Finally, she saw a young man who looked like he was not too busy to help them. "Excuse me," she said. He looked confused at first, as if he didn't know why she would be speaking to him. "I'm sorry," she said walking closer to him. "I was wondering if you could help us."

He was chewing on a piece of straw, and while he had on a Confederate uniform, he also had a white apron tied around him, spattered with blood, which marked him as some sort of doctor or nurse, she assumed. When they were right up on him, he seemed to realize she was, in fact, talking to him. "Miss, nurses and volunteers are to report to Dr. Mitchell, in that tent over there. He'll get y'all straightened out."

The two women exchanged glances. "No, I'm sorry, let me explain," Cordia said as politely as possible. "We're not here to help...." How rude that must have sounded. She started over. "I mean, we've come a long way, trying to find out what has happened to some of the boys from our town...." She could tell by the look on his face he didn't quite understand.

Luckily, Frieda was more direct. "Listen," she started, "Do you know where we can find Lt. Jaris Adams, Confederate Army?" Cordia nudged her then, and she added, "Or Pvt. Will Tucker, Union Army? They're supposed to be here, at the hospital."

"Oh, I see," the young man said, though neither woman was very sure that he did. Perhaps the long hours of attempting, and often failing, to save lives had left him a bit daft. "No, I don't know those names. Let me see," then he turned and yelled at another orderly who was happening by. "Roberts, hey Roberts, these women are looking for a Lt. Adams and a Pvt. Tucker. Do you know them?

"Yes," this man, Roberts, answered, much to Cordia's relief. "I know where one of them is. Back in the outbuilding, behind the main house." He was gesturing as if he expected the other man to lead them there. But Roberts seemed to know this other man a little too well. "Never mind," he relented, walking over to them. "I'll walk them down."

He motioned for the two women to follow, which they did, after a brief thank you to the first useless orderly. Roberts didn't say anything as they walked along. He looked exhausted, and Cordia wondered how long he had been here, with no rest, taking care of the wounded. She was not brave enough to ask. He seemed to be leading them in the same direction that the two orderlies carrying the litter had been going. They passed a farmhouse, which Cordia took to be the "main house" Roberts had spoken of, and then a couple of small buildings. They walked through uncountable soldiers spread out all over the ground, propped against trees, talking in little groups of four or five. All of them seemed to grow quiet as the ladies passed by, their eyes following them in wonderment. Finally, they reached a smaller building, and Roberts swung open the door. Though nothing about this hospital smelled particularly appealing, the air coming out of the tiny space was overwhelming.

"I apologize for the smell," Roberts said upon seeing the looks on their faces. "I'm kind of used to it, I'm afraid. Your friend is in here."

He motioned for the ladies to go in, but Cordia hesitated. She had never smelled a dead person before, but she was quite certain that the odor she was encountering could not possibly be coming from living souls. At least one of the men that she loved was in that building—dead—but she didn't even know which one. She hesitated there, at the threshold. She thought of the life she had known until this time, now separated from the life she would lead from this next moment to come. Though she knew her anguish would now at least partially be over, she could not seem to get her feet to move forward. Finally, it was Frieda, rough and tumble Frieda, who took her gently by the arm and led her inside.

There before her, she saw the bodies of about eight men, spread out on tables of various shapes and sizes. This building seemed to have been a shed of sorts, in its life before it was a morgue. If Frieda had not been gently pulling her forward, there would have been simply no way that her feet were going to move.

Roberts had followed them in. It was difficult to see in the dim light provided by one dirt-caked window, but they saw him gesture farther into the room. They continued their slow trod forward, until finally, there, near the end of the somber row, Cordia saw his face.

It seemed Frieda was having a harder time of it at first. She slumped back against the wall. Cordia put her hand to her forehead, closed her eyes for a second, not sure what to do. Her lips began to tremble. And then she could feel tears spilling slowly down her cheeks.

After a few seconds, she found the strength to step forward. She needed to touch him, needed to see that it really was him—that this wasn't a dream. She took his hand gently in hers, pressed it to her heart. It was ice cold. And yet, his sweet face looked so peaceful. His eyes were closed, as if he were only sleeping. He even looked like he might have a smile on his face. She ran her hands through his hair. It was so hard to believe, even standing here, that she was never going to speak to him again. Then, she glanced down at his uniform and could plainly see where he had been shot. She stood there for a moment, just staring at him. Eventually, Frieda gathered her wits about her enough to come and stand behind her, which Cordia was thankful for because she wasn't exactly sure how her knees had kept from buckling.

After a few moments, she turned back to Roberts, who had been standing there watching, quietly, she thought in case one of them fainted and needed some assistance. "Do you think he suffered?" she asked.

He seemed a little puzzled at first, not sure how to respond. "Well," he said, thinking, "I wasn't there when he was wounded, but I would say probably not for long. Generally, gunshots like that don't take too long to put a man to rest."

She nodded. That comforted her, in some small way. "He wasn't alive when they brought him to the hospital then?"

"No, no, he died on the battlefield." Roberts replied. "Died leading his men in a charge, I hear. Friend of mine helped carry him in. Said we lost a fine man that day. Yes, he died on the battlefield, just as they were loading him on the litter. But, I recall, my friend said something odd."

Cordia had been staring down at his face, but now looked back at Roberts as he paused in thought. "What's that?" she asked.

"Well, my friend told me he had said some strange word, just before he passed. Wanted to know if I knew what it meant. Now, let's see," he scratched his head, straining to think. "Caridy, or Coridy, or something...."

She looked at this man she had just met with a stunned look on her face as he tried to come up with the word. "Cordia," she said quietly.

"That's it! Cordia," he acknowledged. "What's that mean? Cordia?"

Now she couldn't hold back the tears. Bloodstain or no, she threw herself on top of his body, shaking and sobbing. But as she lay there lamenting, Frieda made a realization. "No, darling, no," she began, squeezing Cordia's shoulder. "You don't have to cry. Don't you see? Don't you see why he is smiling? Cordia, when he was dying out there, he wasn't hurtin'. He was happy. He was happy because he was thinkin' of you."

Cordia rose, wiping the tears out of her eyes so she could see his handsome face. "You're right, he is smiling," she said to Frieda. Then, she leaned over, kissing him gently on the forehead. She rested her head there, next to his for a moment, and then, whispered softly into his ear, "See, I told you I would come to get you, Jaris. I told you I would."

After another moment, Frieda had her arms around her, pulling her away. "Come on, darling, let's not stay here anymore."

Roberts stepped forward. "I reckon you'll be wanting to take him back home then?" he asked.

"Yes," Frieda nodded. "We brought a wagon. Is there someone that can help?"

Cordia glanced down at the body of her fiancé one more time, and then they proceeded out the door. As she heard Frieda and Roberts talking about the wagon, it suddenly dawned on her that she was not finished. "Will!" she exclaimed. "Frieda, I need to find Will."

"Darling, after what you've been through, you go back to the wagon and rest. We'll get Lt. Adams loaded up, and then I'll go see about Julia's brother."

"No," Cordia insisted. "I have to find him myself. I have to talk to him. He's not just Julia's brother, he's . . . my friend. Roberts, are you sure you don't know where I could find a private in the Union Army?"

The orderly contemplated the question for a moment. "Union Army?" he repeated. "You might find him in the church, over across that field."

Cordia could see the building behind a line of trees. Without another thought, she took off running. "Cordia!" Frieda yelled. "You can't mean to run all the way over there, the condition you are in!"

Actually, she had meant to. She needed to see him as soon as possible. What better place than a church to give her hope that he was alive? "I'll be back!" she yelled over her shoulder.

It really wasn't that far, but she was running as fast as she could, tears still streaming down her face, pulling the bottom of her gown up she wouldn't trip. By the time she reached the little white building, she was gasping for air. Under normal conditions it would have been diffi- cult, but it was even more challenging for her to regain her breath when all that she sucked in stunk of death. Her side was throbbing, she now realized. She bent over, trying to get enough air so that she could ask someone for help. Finally, she caught her breath enough to get some words out.

A young woman was approaching the church from the general direction that Cordia had come from, though at a much more practical pace. "Excuse me," Cordia said, still panting. "I'm looking for someone."

The young girl's eyes widened. She looked at Cordia as if she thought she were mad. "Yes?" she asked, bewildered.

"I'm sorry," Cordia said, finally breathing fairly normally again. "I'm looking for William Tucker. Do you know him?"

The girl seemed to think for a second. "Oh, Will," she acknowl- edged, shaking her head. "Yes, he's in the church." She started to walk away, but Cordia grabbed her arm.

"I'm sorry," she said again. She had waited long enough. "Is he alive?" She was not about to walk into a church of deceased men and try to pick him out. If she never had to choose from a lineup of dead men's faces again, it would be far too soon.

The girl's expression became increasingly strange. "Of course, he is. Why else would he be in a hospital?" she asked. Then, shaking her arm free, she strolled into the church and began to tend some of the men.

Cordia looked up at the sky, a sigh of relief washed over her, and she could feel a mound of weight lifted from her still broken heart. "Thank you, sweet Jesus," she said. Then, she turned and entered the church. It looked like they had turned the pews into beds, roughly sawing off the backs of some of them. There must have been thirty on each side, and some men lying up toward the pulpit. They were moaning and groaning, coughing, some of them mumbling. How was she going to find Will in this mess?

Perhaps it was the look of anguish on her face, or perhaps it was to avoid any further conversation, but just then, the girl from outside walked over, tapped her arm and pointed.

Cordia's eyes followed in the direction of her finger. The first true smile she had felt in days spread over her face. There he was. "Thank you," she said over her shoulder as she walked quickly over to where he was lying on one of those makeshift beds toward the back of the church.

His eyes were closed. But he was breathing. She could tell that by the way his chest was rising and falling. She stood there for a moment, gazing down at him. It had been so long since her eyes had fallen upon his face. Though an overwhelming sadness for dear Jaris was still eating away at her insides, she could not stifle the happiness that she was finally feeling in this moment of knowing that Will was alive.

As if he could feel her looking at him, he began to stir. Then, his eyelashes started to flutter. She moved from where she had been standing at the foot of the bed, and knelt down beside him, hovering just above his head.

Will had an overpowering feeling that someone was looking at him. It was so prodigious that it woke him from one of the soundest sleeps he could recall enjoying in months. He opened his eyes slightly and then closed them again. There appeared to be a woman crouched beside him. At first glance, he thought it was Cordia. But that was not possible. She was all the way up in Lamar. He started to fall back to sleep, but then he decided he had better check again. He lifted his heavy eyelids one more time and then closed them. It was Cordia.

"Hello," she said quietly.

After a few seconds, he mumbled, "You're a dream." He scratched his face but did not open his eyes.

"What?" she asked, cocking her head to the side.

"I said, 'You're a dream,' a fabrication. You can't be real."

She laughed then. How long had it been since she had done that, laughed? "I am real," she reassured him. "Open your eyes, and you'll see."

"Nope," he said stubbornly. "No use in torturing myself."

Cordia laughed again, "Come on," she said. "I have driven all this way to see those deep brown eyes of yours, and now you won't open them. Now who is being tortured?" She glanced down just long enough to find his hand, clasping it gently, and when she looked back up, his eyes were open and fixed on her. "Hello," she said again.

He was smiling back at her now. "Hi. Miss Cordia Pike. Didn't know if I would ever see you again."

She nodded, understanding what he was hinting at. "How are you?" she asked, still studying his face.

"Well," he began, "can't complain too much. Been better. Could be much worse." He was still holding her hand, but now he reached over with his other and gently began to play with her hair. "Don't your ma throw fits when you don't put this up?" he asked teasingly.

She shook her head at him. "Well, you can't be too bad. Feeling good enough to be ornery."

Now he began to laugh, at least as much as he could in his condition. "I'm sorry," he said. "I'm sure you didn't come all this way so that I could give you trouble."

"No, no I didn't." Then, she changed the subject back to his injuries. "Where are you shot?" she asked.

"Uhm, one here, in the shoulder," he said pulling the top of his shirt open so that she could see, "and one here near my collarbone."

She grimaced at both wounds, though they were bandaged. Still, the idea of getting shot was not a pleasant one. "Did it hurt really badly?" she asked quietly.

"Actually," he said, "I don't recall. I passed out from losing too much blood pretty quick. Hurt something awful later on when the doctor dug the bullets out." She covered her face when he said that, which for some reason, almost made him laugh again. "Don't feel so good right now, either. But I reckon I'll be all right."

"I can't imagine what it must be like to be shot and then have someone digging around inside you with a knife and no anesthesia trying to find the bullets," she mutters, shaking her head. "No chance you're going to get an infection or pneumonia or anything is there?"

He shook his head. "Nope, I'll be just fine. Y'all can't get rid of me that quickly. Take a few weeks or so to heal up, that's all. Doctor did say I was lucky that the bullet that hit me in the collarbone had already went through something else though, otherwise it probably would have killed me."

Cordia's eyes were wide with amazement. "Really?"

"Yep, but I'm okay." He paused for a second, studying her face. "How are you?"

He could tell by the look she was giving him that she must know what happened to Jaris then. He hadn't known if he should tell her or not. "You hear? About Jaris?" He nodded. "Glad I don't have to tell you," she said, dropping her voice. "After all, it probably isn't the best idea to tell a wounded man that his cousin.... But, I'm glad you know because it don't seem right keeping it from you either." Will nodded, and Cordia took a deep breath. "I don't know how I feel." She sat back on her heels. "I guess it ain't sunk in yet. I feel. . . very strange."

He nodded his head in agreement. "Yeah, I guess a day or so is not quite long enough for something like that to settle on ya."

"A day or so?" she repeated. "Will, battle news around here spreads slower than watching paint dry. When I left home yesterday morning, all I knew was that you and Jaris were both casualties. I bet news of who's living and who ain't probably still hasn't made it back to Lamar."

He was shocked. "Then, you mean to tell me you just found out that Jaris was dead when you got here?" She nodded. "My God, Cordia," he exclaimed, looking up at the ceiling. "How is it that you aren't crying your eyes out right now?"

She seemed to question herself for a moment. "Perhaps I should be. Somehow, though, I don't even think that's what Jaris would want me to do." She let out a sigh and readjusted as if she wasn't sure what to say. "When I first saw him, I cried my heart out," she explained. "I did mourn him. I will mourn him." After a moment of thought, she admitted, "I was just so happy to hear that you were alive that I couldn't really think of anything else, presently."

Then he realized just how much anguish she must have been in the past few days, not knowing if either of them was alive. "Oh, Cordia, I'm so sorry," he said. "All that you've been through." She shook her head, as if he needn't be thinking of her now. She realized he had been through much more himself. After a moment, he added, with conviction, "He was a good man."

She nodded her head and repeated him. "Yes, he was a good man." The tears were threatening to empty over again, now. "I will have plenty of time to think on Jaris on my way home. I do not have too much longer, however, that I can spend with you. Tell me, what do you mean to do when you are all healed up?"

He was holding her hand in both of his now, and it was all he could do to keep from reaching up and touching her face. "Well, I am a Confederate prisoner right now. However, word has come through the line that we have all been exchanged, and as soon as we are healed, we will be released. My enlistment was for ninety days, which I have served. So, that leaves me with a few choices. I could go back and join my unit in Rolla, or I could go east where the 'real fighting', as we're told, is happening. I don't rightly know just yet what I plan to do."

"This seems real enough to me," she declared. He nodded, and he assumed she recognized he had been being sarcastic. She reached up and smoothed his hair as she talked, a gentle touch that calmed him like nothing else had for days, years maybe. "I don't reckon there's any chance you would consider coming home, then?"

The question just seemed to hang there between them for a moment. "Cordia," he began, and he could see in her eyes that she knew the answer was no. She pulled her hand down now, rested it on his, which was still clinging to her other hand. "My duty isn't over yet. Just 'cause I got shot, don't mean I get to go home and sit out the rest of the war."

She was exasperated. "Twice, Will. You got shot twice."

He looked away from her again. "I know, Cordia. I know I got shot twice."

"Then come home. Please, please come home," she was beginning to cry now. "I didn't know if I can bear going through this again."

The look of anguish on her face made him want to hold her. He tried to sit up, but could not do it, no matter how hard he tried. Frustrated, he reminded her, "Cordia, the thing is, I don't really have a home."

Cordia looked at him and in her eyes, he saw the clear message, "I'll be your home." She was quiet for a moment before she asked, "What about your sister?"

"What about my sister?"

"Well, you should have seen her the other day, not knowing if you were alive. Crying her eyes out."

He nodded his head slowly, "I am very sorry for that. I am very sorry to both of you for that. But Julia's strong. Not as strong as you, but strong enough."

"I find it almost comical to hear you say that I am strong when I am pleading for you to come home so that I won't have to 'be strong' anymore. But I know a thing or two about bull-headedness, and the look on your face tells me I am not going to change your mind."

No longer able to meet her gaze, Will looked away for a long moment.

"All right," she finally acquiesced. "But, maybe you will consider coming home for a few days before you head off again? I know Julia would like to see you. I wanted to bring her with me, but I didn't know how she would handle . . . the smoke." He was sure she was going to say "handle the trip," but she likely didn't want to let him know she thought his sister might have actually made herself sick over him.

Turning back to face her, he nodded, letting her know that he would consider what she had to say.

"Well," she said, standing, "I hate to go, but, there's a lot of people back in town waiting to hear what I have to say. And I am sure my mother's probably worried to death by now." She caught herself on those last words. Funny how something you might say a hundred times during normal circumstances sounded so wrong when it slipped out in a situation like this.

"Wait," he said, grabbing her hand. "I have something for you."

"You do?" she asked, her expression showing she had no idea what in the world it could be.

"Yes," he strained to reach down inside his pocket. He had placed his letters to her in there just before the battle. Reaching them with his fingertips, he pulled them out and handed them to her. "Here you go."

She looked at them as if she had never seen paper before. "What's this?" she asked.

"One of them, I have to apologize, I should have mailed a long time ago. The other one, I wrote just the night before the battle."

"Oh." Cordia turned the papers over again and again in her hands. Though he had held her hand and played with her hair, she had questioned whether or not he was doing these things out of kindness, and familiarity of seeing a face he recognized. She had been sure that, if he truly reciprocated the emotions she had articulated in her letters, not only would he have written her back—and sent the letters—but upon seeing her, he would have expressed his undying love for her, or something of that nature. His refusal to return to Lamar only served to further convince her that he did not feel the same way about her as she did about him and she was just beginning to wonder how she was possibly going to go on with Jaris gone and Will rejecting her. Now, she didn't know what to think. Though these letters could certainly be only friendly in nature, she dared to hope that maybe he cared for her a little after all. "Thank you."

"Sorry I didn't write more."

She nodded again, not sure what else to say. "Well, I had better go find Frieda," she said, starting to turn to the door, the letters still hanging from her hand; she had no idea what to do with them.

As she turned to go, he said her name. She paused at the foot of the makeshift bed. Now, somehow, he found the strength to prop himself up on his elbows. "Cordia, please forgive me for saying this right now. After all, you just found out your fiancé has passed on, my own cousin, and you're standing there with his ring on your finger. But I did want you to know...." Will paused, an expression of torment on his face, as if he wasn't sure whether or not to continue.

"Yes?" Cord asked, hope bubbling up insider her that perhaps she would hear the words she'd been longing to hear for months. He was staring at her, as if he was trying to memorize her face.

"I'm sorry to look so hard at you, Cordia, but it had done me well to do so on the last occasion I was able to gaze upon your face."

Cord felt the heat rising in her cheeks.

"I apologize for my forwardness," he said, looking away from her for a second. "I've never said this to anyone before."

"That's all right," she said, her eyes wide with wonderment, holding her breath as she waited for him to find the words.

"Cordia Pike, I do love you."

At first, she thought her ears were deceiving her, but by the look on his face, she knew she had heard correctly. And just as she was about to run back to his side, throw her arms around his neck, kiss him a thousand times—proper or not—she felt Frieda's hand on her arm.

"Here you are!" she was saying, as if she had searched the world twice over. "Running off like that, couldn't believe my eyes. You shock me every day, Cordia Pike."

Cordia turned to look at her, as if she had never laid eyes on the woman before. "Please don't think me improper for being concerned about a friend," she said smartly.

"Oh, Cordia, you deal with this however you need to, child. Now, come on, we've got the lieutenant loaded up. We need to go home." Then, as if she hadn't even noticed him until now, she turned to Will and said, "Oh, good. You're alive."

Cordia sighed. "I'll be out in a minute."

"But, Cordia..."

"I said I will be out in a minute!" That was enough to shut even Frieda up. She threw her hands up in the air, turned on her heels, and stormed out of the church.

"You'll be hearing about that all the way home," Will said.

She was walking back over to him now, nodding her head. "Yes, but I don't care. I will think of you every day, every minute, every second," she said taking his hand in hers.

He nodded, "Just try to pay attention to others while you're doing so," he smiled.

"How do you know me so well already?" she asked.

"I don't know, but I do. Send Jules my love?"

"Of course. Get plenty of rest, and don't get out of that bed—pew —whatever it is—until the doctors say you can."

"Anything you say."

"All right, I really have to go now." She leaned over and kissed him quickly on the forehead, but that wasn't enough for him, and as she started to stand back up, he gently nudged her head back down, finding her lips with his. Relief washed over her as she breathed him in, thinking of all the days she'd longed to feel him again, just to know he was alive.

As much as Cordia wanted to stay there with him, to never let him out of her sight, she feared Frieda may come looking for her again. Reluctantly, she pulled away. "Goodbye, Will Tucker," she said squeezing his hand.

"See you by and by, Cordia Pike," he replied, still looking longingly into her hazel eyes.

As she made her way out of the church, she tucked Will's letters into her waistband. It was not going to be easy to keep from reading them on the way back, but she couldn't let Frieda see them. She glanced back at him one last time, and he lifted his hand slowly. Cordia took a deep breath and turned away.

When she stepped outside, she was relieved to see that Frieda had pulled the wagon over in front of the church so she didn't have to cross back through that field. Despite missing Will already, Cordia was as ready to get out of that horrible place as she could possibly be. As she climbed into the wagon seat, she couldn't help herself but to look into the back. Frieda had wrapped the body in one of the sheets she had brought with them. It was still very hard to believe that her dear friend was gone. "Let's go home," she said, taking the reins.

IN A VERY REAL WAY, the journey home was, for Cordia, almost as difficult as the initial trip had been. Though she no longer felt the heavy burden on her heart of waiting, she was now fully aware that it would be her duty to inform the Adams family that their proud soldier son was, in spirit, no longer with them. Though she had somehow obtained this reputation of being strong enough to handle most everything, she didn't know how in the world she was going to find the words to look Margaret Adams in the face and say those few words, "Jaris is dead."

An idea crossed her mind, and that afternoon, as they neared a small town in Green County, she asked Frieda if they could stop by the post office and see if they had a telegraph machine. At first, Frieda had argued with her, saying how important she thought it was to reach Jasper County, and the safety of some family friends, before the sun went down. However, after a small amount of pressing from a desperate girl who could not fathom looking that mother in the eye and saying those words, Frieda gave in, warning that they probably wouldn't have a telegraph there anyway.

Luckily, she was wrong. The old man behind the counter was very obliging. Cordia filled out the message, addressed to her father, and watched as he sent it through.

August 13, 1861

Father, I wanted to let you know that we have reached the hospital in Springfield and are returning. Awful. Please tell Julia that Will is wounded but all right. Please inform the Adams family that we are bringing back Jaris's body. Love, Cordia

"Did it go through all right?" she asked as the man seemed to be finishing up.

He was about as old as anyone Cordia had ever laid eyes on. He was squinting at the paper, but he seemed well skilled on the telegraph machine. "Yes, miss. Been doing this a while, e'en in New York City. Your pa will get the message." He spit some tobacco juice into a can nearby.

That was by far enough for Frieda. "Miss Cordia, we've got a lot of miles to cover and not much time to do it in."

Cordia nodded, grabbing the copy of what she had sent. "Thank you," she said before turning and following Frieda back to the wagon.

They made their way back across the same ground they had covered the day before. Cordia could feel those letters burning a hole through her waistband. When Frieda wasn't paying attention, she plucked them out and stashed them in her bag. But, there was no helping the fact that she would not be able to read them with Frieda next to her. She tried to think of something else, but she couldn't think about Will without wondering what it was he had to say.

Occasionally, her mind wandered back to Jaris. Thinking of him only left her with an overwhelming sadness. She tried to keep him out of her thoughts, too, but it was very difficult, as she had an overpowering awareness of his lifeless body in the cart behind her. There would be no question they would have to find a place to stop that night. She couldn't possibly drive the entire distance, having not left Springfield until around noon, and there was no way they could sleep in the wagon under the present circumstances.

Her mind kept going over the events of the day. She didn't think she would ever be able to lose the memory of walking into that shed, that tomb, seeing those bodies lying there. She had realized as soon as she entered that horrific space that each of those men was wearing the uniform of a Confederate officer. An overwhelming amount of anguish still lingered in her heart for Jaris, and she also felt compassion for the families of those officers and all of the other dead men she had seen that day. It seemed there were just too many people to cry for and not enough tears for each.

Feelings of guilt also pervaded her mind. She had never felt quite right not being honest with dear Jaris, especially not after she realized she had feelings for Will. And now, here she was, playing the part of the grieving fiancée, when she knew she really should only be playing the role of a grieving friend. She felt dishonest. She wasn't being sincere to their families, to herself, to Jaris. These thoughts tugged at her conscious. And now, she would never get the chance to come clean with him. She was beginning to wonder if she was ever going to feel right again.

Frieda had taken the reins some time ago, and now Cordia could see they were approaching a farmhouse. It was a large, two-story wooden structure, and Cordia could see some little girls playing in the yard. At the approach of the wagon, their mother flew out the door, and the girls ran to her side. "Where are we?" Cordia asked her companion.

"Well," Frieda said, "This should be the Shaw place, according to your daddy's directions. It's getting to be about six o'clock, and I don't want to drive the rest of the way in the dark."

Cordia agreed. She could see that the look of alarm on the woman's face turned to inquiry as the wagon with the women approached. "Hello," Cordia yelled waving. "Are you Mrs. Shaw?"

The other woman nodded, and as the wagon slowed, she came over cautiously. "Can I help you?" she asked.

Cordia smiled, trying to put her at ease. "My name is Cordia Pike. This is Frieda, my caretaker. My daddy is Isaac Pike, the president of the bank in Lamar," she waited to see if the woman showed any sort of recognition. She was delighted to see the woman's face change. Mrs. Shaw did know who they were, and she nodded her head. "We were wondering if you might have some room for us to spend the night. We've come from Springfield, retrieving the body of my fiancé."

"My goodness," the woman exclaimed, her eyes peering into the back of the wagon. Then, she remembered herself. "Of course we have room. Jessie!" she yelled. The older of the girls came running over. "Go out into the field and find your pa. Tell him we have company."

The Shaws had taken care of them as if they were family. They had handled the wagon and horses, even the precious cargo, provided them with a meal, and finally, a place to sleep. Cordia was exhausted. Luckily, they had given her a separate room from Frieda, and she was alone at last. Though she could hardly keep her eyes open, she knew she could not rest until she read Will's letters.

She brought the lantern over to the little bed in the corner of the room and climbed underneath the covers, letters in hand. Setting the lantern down on the nightstand beside her, she pulled the first paper out of its envelope. They were both dirty and wrinkled, some of the ink running a little bit, even a little blood on them, it seemed. But, she knew she would be able to decipher them.

July 6, 1861,

Dearest Cordia,

Please forgive me for not writing to you sooner. I am not so good with words, and your skill has intimidated me some, I am afraid. I have taken much solace in your letters. Your words have captured the feelings within my heart, and it brings me peace, even now as I have just come from an awful battle, to know that you are out there waiting for me. I was at first concerned about your relationship with Jaris. I wish that I could advise you on what you should do so as not to hurt him, but I do not rightly know the best thing to do either. I do know that war seems to change people. Perhaps, when all this fighting is over, you will find your answer. In the meantime, I must tell you it is only the thought of building my life with you that carries me through the hardships we must each endure. How many times in these past weeks must I have thought back to that kiss? I dream of the day I shall return to you as your one true love.

Forever yours,

Will

She read over each word several times. Finally, she pressed the precious paper to her heart one last time and unfolded the other letter. This one, it seemed, was a little worse for the wear, as he had not had time to put it in the envelope. Still, she was able to struggle through the words enough to make them out.

August 9, 1861

My Dearest Cordia,

Again, I must apologize that you have not received word from me. Several times I have intended to mail a letter to you and have not done it. Yet, I have received several encouraging compositions from you. Each time I hear the words "mail call" I run over in the hopes of receiving even the shortest of messages from you. You are the angel that lifts my spirits. You are the keeper of my heart. How much more cruel would this war be without the memory of your face?

I think there must be a battle a brewing for tomorrow. No one has said, but there is something hanging in the air over our camp tonight. I could not rest until I let you know how, even in this darkest of times, you shine a light for me. I know that, no matter what obstacles stand before me when the morning comes, I will get through them because of you. I can still smell the lilac perfume you were wearing the last time my eyes fell upon your perfect face. You are a beacon to me, guiding me home, even in these dark, uncertain places. Please know that, no matter what is to come, I will always return to you.

All my eternal love,

Will

Again, she read his words several times before placing his letters safely away. She put out the light and tried to make herself comfortable enough to fall asleep. So many thoughts, however, saturated her mind, and it was very difficult to find peace. She continued to mill over the conversation she had, had with him, these letters, even the few times they had spoken before he was off to war. "When was it," she asked herself, "that I fell in love with Will Tucker, exactly?" She could not think of the time, and her thoughts began to jumble as sleep finally overtook her. One word finally came to her mind as an answer. "Always."

The cornfield needed harvesting. It was plain to see by the height that it was time for it to come in. She looked around at the tall stalks, stretching to the sky, and wondered why Mr. Adams had not come to gather it up. She was not standing in the cornfield itself, but in a little lane between two sections of field. Off in the distance, up the path, she could plainly see the farmhouse. Behind her, there were some trees, and in those woods, there was a little creek, which had often been the spot where she would be trapped and could no longer run.

Just now, however, she was not running. She was standing there, peering into that cornfield, wondering how so much work was going to get done. Just then, she heard a wrestling within the stalks. They started to bend and twist, and she became aware that someone or something was climbing out of them. At first, she was startled, wondering if now was the time to run. But she didn't move, and then she could see that it was Jaris.

He was standing in front of her now, wearing his Confederate uniform. But, there was no blood on it. He was alive. He was still smiling.

"What were you doing in there?" she asked, hearing her own voice as if it was floating by on the wind.

"Waiting for you," he said, with a matter-of-fact tone.

Suddenly, she could see that he had something in his hands, but she couldn't tell what it was. "Why?" she asked.

He chuckled then, and Cordia found some comfort in the sound of that familiar laugh. "I have something for you."

"What is it?" she asked stepping toward him. She could hear something now, coming from the space between his hands. They seemed to be throbbing, a consistent rhythm pouring forth. She stared at them intently, wondering what he could possibly have.

"I have something that belongs to you," he continued. "It isn't mine. I tried to take it from you, but it wasn't mine to have."

Her eyes lifted then, from his hands to his face. She looked into his eyes, and in that familiar shade of blue, she saw something amazing. There, behind his eyes, she saw clouds floating by, saw a shiny golden gate. Behind his eyes, she could see the way to heaven. How had she never noticed this before?

"Jaris," she started, wanting to ask him about this new revelation.

"Never mind that now, Cordia," he said. "This is more important." He raised his hands in gesture, and her eyes returned to what he was holding. "This is why I have come."

There seemed to be something alive in there. As she watched, he began to separate his hands. There, wiggling around, pulsating wildly, was a human heart. Though it was fully functioning, it was not bloody or gross, and she suddenly felt a longing for it. She started to reach out her hand, but hesitated, looking into his face again. "Yes, take it," he reassured her. "Take it. It's yours. It belongs to you. I shouldn't have it."

Now she understood why he had come. He was releasing her from her contract. He wanted her to go, give her heart to someone else. To be happy. To be free.

"Are you sure?" she asked.

He was still smiling. "Yes, of course. I should have never tried to steal it from you in the first place."

She reached out her hands and took it from him. "You know I do love you though, don't you?" she asked, beginning to feel the vibrations in her own hands now.

"Yes. Yes, I do," he leaned over then and kissed her gently on the head, as if he was her older brother, her caretaker, her guardian angel. "You're free now—free to give your heart away to whomever you choose."

He smiled at her again, tipped his hat, and then turned to walk back into the cornfield. She stood and watched him disappear, and then the pounding of her heart overtook her. She felt her whole body pulsating along with its beat as it became louder and louder.

Once again, she was thrown violently out of the world of sleep. This time, however, she was not sweating; she was not frightened. She even remembered where she was. She looked out the window next to the borrowed bed she was sleeping on. For the first time since she could remember, Cordia rolled over and went back to sleep.

Chapter Nine

TRAVELING along the crudely cut wagon rut of a road the next morning, Cordia felt an overwhelming amount of solace. They had been
riding along for an hour or so, just entering into Barton County, when
Frieda remarked on how peaceful she seemed.

"I am at peace," she agreed. "And I am happy to be nearly home."

Frieda seemed putout that Cordia was willing to admit she was no
longer beside herself with grief. She "humphed" about it and gave the
reins a violent shake.

Cordia's forehead furrowed in surprise. "What, would you have me
bawling all the way home?" she asked.

"No," Frieda relinquished. "But, still, don't you think you should be
feeling a little distraught, considering what it is we are a'haulin' here?"

There really was no way that Cordia could explain to Frieda why it
was that she now felt such contentment. Ever since she had dreamt of
Jaris, she had felt as if her burden of guilt and even, in many ways, her
feelings of grief, had alleviated. She wasn't quite sure what it was about
this particular dream that had made it seem so real. She was quite sure
that the other visions that had come to her the nights prior were only
fabrications of her imagination, but she had an overwhelming feeling
that Jaris had actually come to her the night before and released her

from her weight of sorrow. It wasn't totally unheard of, people saying they had been visited by spirits in their dreams. Still, Frieda was not the kind of person who would understand something like that. Perhaps the only one who would believe Cordia was her overly superstitious friend, Susannah. "I'm sorry," she finally said. "I am distraught over the fate of our dear Jaris. I am, however, looking forward to the comfort of my family and friends"

Though this answer didn't exactly seem to satisfy Frieda, she didn't say anything else. Eventually, they reached the outlying areas of town, and they rode by many familiar homesteads. They agreed that their first stop should be the Adams Farm. Cordia was counting on the fact that her daddy had already informed the family of their loss, and she was eager to get Jaris home. Though she hated putting her father in that position, he was very good at such things, always knowing exactly how to comfort people in their time of need. Still, if he had not gotten the telegraph, she would be the one who had to speak those words. It didn't even cross her mind to be fearful of her parents' wrath for sneaking out, considering the conditions in which she was returning. She knew she was likely to receive a lecture about providing for her own safety, but she did not anticipate any sort of a punishment.

In a short amount of time, they approached the lane that led to the farm. Cordia felt sadness welling up in her throat. No amount of relinquishment, real or dreamt, could keep her from feeling the pain of this family who had lost their pride and joy. But, as they approached the hitching post near the road, they were surprised to see a number of wagons and horses already tied up. The gate to the lane that led to the house was open, and Frieda decided to go ahead and drive up toward the house. Then, Cordia saw a great crowd of people gathered in the yard. "They must have come to comfort the family," she thought. But, as she got closer, she thought it looked more like a celebration than a group of mourners. What could it possibly be? She looked at Frieda, who stared back at her, just as confused.

The crowd seemed to realize it was them approaching now, and they began to run over, Jaris's younger brothers practically skipping over in delight. Cordia's eyes fixed on one face though, the face of Margaret Adams. She had been dreading facing that woman since she left Springfield. Now, here she was before her, a wide smile brightening, beaming a path before her.

Cordia could not for the life of her figure out what was happening. Then, Zachariah called from beside the wagon, "Where's Jaris? Where's my brother?" The boy also looked confused. He climbed up the side of the wagon and peered in. As if he hadn't realized what he was looking at, he climbed back down, and looked into Cordia's face.

Frieda had pulled the horses to a stop. Cordia got a sickening feeling in her stomach. Surely, this could not be what it appeared to be.

Margaret called, "Where is he? Don't tell me he's fallen asleep in the back?"

But Cordia couldn't answer. She now realized her father was standing nearby. He, too, was smiling. She began to shake her head. Finally, her voice made it past the lump in her throat. "You received my telegraph?" she asked.

"Yes," Arthur said, smiling from where he stood next to his wife. "You said Jaris was coming back with you. Well, is he here?"

"My God!" Frieda gasped beside her.

Cordia's knees buckled. For a second, she thought she might fall clean out of the wagon. She heard the youngest boy, John, clambering up the back of the wagon now. "What's this?" he asked his hand reaching for the sheet.

"No!" Cordia yelled, but it was too late. She watched, as if in slow motion, as the little one's hand pulled the sheet off. His eyes widened in the horror that Cordia was feeling to the core of her soul. He fell backward then, off of the wagon. Luckily, Zachariah caught him. Cordia grabbed the sheet, throwing it back over the remains of the child's dear brother. Tears flooded her face now, and she asked herself, "What have I done?"

Like a rippling wind, the realization of the misunderstanding seemed to pervade the crowd, until each one stood there, still and silent, keenly aware of the truth. And then, Cordia heard one voice of disbelief. "Where's my boy?" she heard Margaret say, in the tiniest voice imaginable. Arthur moved to wrap his arms around his wife, but she pushed him away. "No," she said, walking toward the wagon. "I want to see my boy."

In her mind, Cordia was moving to stop Margaret from lifting that sheet. But, physically, she could only stand and watch as the woman hoisted herself up the side of the wagon. And as Margaret began to scream, members of her family rushed to comfort her, to keep her from falling. Cordia could not even bear to look. She turned and climbed down off the wagon. Her father's arms were the only solace she could find, and she buried her head in his chest, sobbing again.

Later, in her own home, she stared at the plate of food her mother had set before her, blankly. How could she eat after what she had done? If only she would have had the courage to tell the family herself, they never would have received the wrong message. Imagine, all of them standing there, waiting for the triumphant return of their soldier boy, off at war. Instead, they were faced with the shocking reality that they would never speak to him again.

Finally, as if reading her mind, her father said, probably for the hundredth time that afternoon, "Cordia, darling, it was not your fault."

She knew that what he said was technically true. Still, she felt that she should have handled things differently. He had shown her what it was that the old man had sent to Mr. Ward.

August 13, 1860

Father, I wanted to let you know that we have reached the hospital in Springfield and are returning. Awful. Please tell Julia that Will is wounded but all right. Please inform the Adams family that we are bringing back Jaris. Love, Cordia

If it had been any other word that would have gotten left out, it would not have been half as awful. But her father, assuming she would have said so if Jaris was dead, went and told his parents exactly what Cordia had sent. How happy they had all been! Margaret had spent the entire evening before and much of that morning planning a celebration and letting the folks in town know. And they were all so happy to hear that one of their proud boys was returning. Many of them still didn't know the condition their own sons and sweethearts were in. They were hoping that Jaris would bring word. Likewise, they were anxious to hear exactly how the battle had unfolded. In Cordia's mind, her act of cowardliness had taken an entire town from the epitome of glee to the very depths of despair.

CORDIA HAD NEVER BEEN to a funeral before. Most of her grandparents had died before she was born. Her Nana Pike passed away when she was about three or four, but she had stayed home from the funeral with Frieda. She had read about such things in many books, so it was a little surprising to her when she awoke that Saturday morning to see the sun shining in the sky. After all, in every story she had ever read, the sky was always dark and gloomy, wind blowing a driving rain, as all the mourners, dressed in black huddled around the coffin.

As her family followed the procession of other carriages and wagons out to the cemetery on the edge of the Adams Farm, she thought it fitting that the sun was shining. Though it was still August, and therefore, still hot, there was a nice, gentle breeze blowing. Jaris's parents had asked Cordia and her family to sit with them directly in front of the coffin. She took her place there, beside what would have been her mother-in-law. Margaret smiled through her tears and took her hand. Of course, she was not angry with Cordia over what had happened with the telegraph. Arthur sat on her other side, along with the three boys. Cordia's heart went out to them. Zachariah, trying to be a man, still wanting to cry like a little boy. Peter, sobbing his eyes out. And John, not quite able to comprehend what was going on around him.

Rev. Jacobson took his place beside the closed casket. A Confederate flag was draped over it along with some fresh flowers. He waited a few moments for others to make their way down the little walking path. Finally, he began, over sobs and wails of those come to give their last goodbyes.

"Dear friends and family, we are gathered here this August day to say goodbye to a brave and courageous young man." People did not hesitate to verbalize their agreement, throughout the reverend's speech, saying such things as "Yes, yes" and "Amen." The reverend continued. "In a time like this, it is so easy to ask the Lord, 'Why, why this young man? Why now, struck down so young, so much in the prime of his life, so useful to so many.' And, yet, we cannot ask God why. No, that is not our place. We must trust in the Lord's judgment

...." The sermon continued for about fifteen minutes. The reverend quoted scripture, read from the Bible, and blessed the family in prayer, including Cordia, who he described as, "Not yet a wife, but the love of Jaris's life, and the truest of friends."

Then, to Cordia's surprise, Rev. Jacobson asked her father to say a few words. Apparently, he had planned to do this, as he pulled a small piece of paper out of his jacket pocket. He nodded his thanks to the reverend, and then addressed the crowd. "As you all know, I was given the honor of spending an enormous amount of time in this fine young man's presence. We have been blessed in these trying times with many strong, courageous young men. But, I don't think there are any who could champion Jaris Adams in his convictions, nor in the ability to stand up for what was right. I was looking forward to walking my daughter down the aisle to take his hand and join these two families into one. I would have been so proud to call my daughter Cordia Pike Adams. To me, we will always be bound to the Adams family in this special way, but I thought it was fitting, at this time, to share with all of you some of the words that Jaris spoke to me on the night he asked me for my daughter's hand. He said, 'Mr. Pike, I know there is a war a'brewin.' I know that I may be called upon to do my duty. And if that time comes, and I have to leave my family and your dear daughter to answer that call, I will do so with knowledge that I am fulfilling my destiny. But please know, I will love your daughter with all my heart, always, no matter what may come to pass.'" Cordia couldn't help but to begin to weep, listening to her father's words. He closed with a few more remarks about Jaris's strength of character and then returned to his seat, squeezing his daughter's hand.

After another prayer, the reverend closed the ceremony. The flag was folded and handed to Mrs. Adams, and then Jaris's coffin was slowly lowered into the grave. Cordia, along with the rest of his family, said there last goodbyes, tossing flowers onto the lid. Then, Cordia numbly made her way back to the carriage and to her life, without Jaris.

A FEW WEEKS INTO OCTOBER, the sky finally began to change, the wind seemed to shift, and the sun seemed to lessen in intensity. To the citizens of Barton County, it seemed that this cruelly hot summer might finally be over. They were all looking forward to a crisp, cool fall. And, hopefully, the cessation of fighting.

That didn't seem too likely, however. Everyday seemed to bring more news of battles and skirmishes within the state. Lexington, Butler, Warrensburg, all of these towns were scenes of heavy fighting. And then, there were more stories of raiders, working their way along the Missouri-Kansas border. Word had it homes were being burned with little warning, families attacked. There was even news that bands of guerrilla warriors were milling about, looting and robbing, taking whatever it was they wanted.

So far, the closest the fighting had gotten to Lamar since the Battle of Carthage was Butler in Vernon County. Still, folks were becoming very cautious, especially those who lived farthest away from town. The militia was still drilling on the square every day. Some folks said it was just a matter of time before war reached right into their own backyards.

But for now, Cordia was looking forward to spending a nice fall day with Julia at the Adams Farm. It had been a rough September for her dear friend. Julia had not quite recovered from the effects of not knowing Will's fate. She had spent a great deal of time in bed lately, coughing, choking, too weak to get up. Cordia had been extremely concerned for her. She had been to see her every day. Sometimes she just sat by and watched Julia in a restless sleep. Other times, she would read to her, or they would share stories about their childhoods. At one point, Julia's fever was so high, Dr. Walters wouldn't let Cordia, or anyone else besides Mrs. Adams, even go into her room. Finally, it had broken, after about three days.

Since that time, about a week prior, she had seemed to be doing much better. Since it had cooled off a little, she was even spending some time outdoors in the fresh air. Cordia had sent word to Will about his sister's condition, but she had not heard from him since she left the hospital that day, over two months ago. He had sent a letter to Julia, however, in early September, letting her know that he was recovering. He did not speak of any plans at that point, so Cordia wasn't even sure if he was still in Springfield, or if he had gone back to his unit. For all she knew, he could have died of pneumonia, or got back to fighting and gotten shot again. Once more, she was in a state of not knowing, which was almost intolerable.

As she made her way up the path to the Adams's house, she was delighted to see Julia sitting on a swing underneath an oak tree reading a book. She looked up and saw her friend coming and waved. Cordia smiled and waved back. "Nice to see you outside already," she said as she sat down beside her. "How are you feeling today?"

"Good," Julia said, and Cordia could tell by her smile that she was telling the truth. She seemed to have a glow back to her cheeks today, something she had been missing for a long time. It was nice to see.

"What are you reading?" she asked.

Julia filled her in on the newest novel she had found stashed away in an old cabinet in the back of the house. It was an extremely exciting romance story that Julia said she could hardly put down. Once Cordia was up to speed on what had happened so far, Julia began to read the rest of the story to her.

After an hour or so of reading about pirates, treasures, and how Sir Camion would love Miss Sicilia to the end of time, Julia paused. "My throat is dry," she said. She coughed a little, which alarmed Cordia.

She started to get up. "I'll go in and get you some water," she said.

Julia's hand pressed her down. "It's okay, Cordia. I can get it. Thank you." Cordia took the book and let her go, but she was still concerned. It was going to be tough for her to let Julia start doing things on her own again. She knew that Julia had worked on a farm her whole life, knew she was a very strong young lady at times. But to Cordia, she was so fragile, she needed to be protected.

She stared down at the cover of the book. It was tattered and worn, either from use or from being cast aside. She glanced up momentarily, back at the book, and then paused. She raised her eyes again. Off in the distance, she thought she could see someone traveling up the lane by foot. She squinted her eyes and shielded them, as if the sun was tricking her. At first, she thought it looked like Will. But she knew that couldn't be possible. Unless. . . what was it that Susannah had told her?

Dropping the book on the ground, she flew to the house, pulling open the door frantically. "Julia!" she screamed.

Julia, who was standing right in front of her, looked at her curiously. "I'm right here, Cordia. What is it? You look like you've seen a ghost."

Cordia was so panicked, she didn't know what to think. Had she seen a ghost? "Julia—I thought I saw... but that's not possible.... Susannah said that when someone dies sometimes you think you see them... but how could I...."

Julia grabbed her by the shoulders. "Cordia—you're not making much sense. Did you see Jaris?"

Cordia shook her head. How could she tell her dear, fragile friend that she thought she just saw the ghost of her brother? "No," she finally stammered. "I thought I saw Will."

But, to Cordia's disbelief, Julia did not get upset. "Will?" she repeated. "You saw Will?" She started out the door.

"But Julia, that's not possible," Cordia was saying.

Julia wasn't listening. She ran through the yard, her eyes peering out past the hitching post. Then, she started to scream.

"Julia?" Cordia said following slowly behind her.

Cordia didn't think she had ever seen anyone run so fast in her life —sick and all--there she flew across the yard, out the gate, until she finally reached her destination, her brother's arms.

Cordia, on the other hand, was still not quite sure what to think. How could he possibly be here? She continued in their direction, but much more slowly, much more cautiously. Not that she thought he was a ghost anymore; she just wasn't sure why he had come.

When she finally reached them, she could plainly see that Julia had done herself no good running out across the field like that. She was still breathing heavily, coughing occasionally, yet trying to talk. Cordia didn't catch all that she said, but she heard enough to know what she was saying. "I think she thought you were a ghost!"

There he was, standing in front of her, desperately needing a shave, a change of clothes, a bath. She just stared at him for a moment, not sure what to say. Finally, he spoke first. "Cordia Pike. Nice to see you."

"Nice to see you, too, Will Tucker. Got to say, we weren't expecting you."

He nodded his head. "I know. I'm awful about writing."

"It's just fine," Julia said, arm in arm with her brother as she led him back to the house. "We're just so happy to have you home."

"Home. There was that word again," she thought. She was behind them now, walking more slowly. How difficult it would be to have him here and to pretend to everyone that they were just acquaintances, just friends. Yet, as she noticed Mrs. Adams coming out the front door to greet him, she knew she had no other choice. They all went inside, and she lingered in the yard a moment, trying to get herself together. It wouldn't be the first time she denied the way she really felt. She guessed she could do it again.

Margaret was smiling and laughing, but it wasn't the same as it had been before Jaris was killed. Now, her face seemed to have a gray tone to it. Even when she was truly amused, it never quite left her. She had gotten Will something to drink, and was trying to force food upon him, though he insisted he had eaten while he was making the trip from the train depot to the farm. He had walked the two miles, which seemed like nothing to him now, he was saying, having marched all over Southwest Missouri.

Julia was hanging on his every word. Now, she was asking questions about army life. He was explaining as best he could without getting into the more horrid details. Cordia stood over by the fireplace, just listening. Finally, Margaret said, "Cordia, don't you want to sit down and join us?"

How long had she been standing there, she wondered. It hadn't seemed that long, but they had been talking for a while. She had been studying Will's face the whole time and not once did he even look in her direction. Now, he had stopped his story and was looking at her, too, waiting to see if she was going to oblige them.

Though part of her knew it would be easier to go home and not have to pretend, she could not bring herself to leave his presence just then. She went over and sat down in a chair beside Mrs. Adams, about as far away from him as she could possibly be. He continued his story without looking at her, which made her believe either he had lost feelings for her, or he was just incredibly good at acting like she was practically a stranger.

And then he was saying her name. She looked at him, questioningly. Apparently, she had not been listening. "What?" she asked. All three of them were looking at her.

"I said there were lots of men wounded much worse than me, ain't that right, Cordia?"

"Oh," she said, nodding. "Yes, that hospital was a horrible sight."

He finished telling them about how he had been in the hospital until the end of September when they finally said he was well enough to go. Then, he told them how he had decided to come back to Lamar for a few days before going off to join the Union Army in Tennessee.

Cordia thought maybe Julia would protest, but she didn't. She seemed to understand that it was his duty to go off and fight again. His aunt simply said, "Well, you be mighty careful." Then, she excused herself back to the kitchen and some pies she had been starting to bake earlier.

Of course, Cordia wanted to protest—wanted to tell him she was never going to let him leave again. But she couldn't exactly say that just now. Maybe she would get a chance to talk to him about it later. At that moment, she tried to concentrate on being happy he was there.

And then, a sort of a miracle happened, or at least it seemed like one to Cordia. "Julia," Margaret was calling from the kitchen. "Could you come here for just a moment, please?"

Julia hopped up to go help her aunt. "I'm so glad you're home, Will!" she said kissing his cheek as she bounded out of the room.

As she was leaving, Cordia was trying to think of exactly what she was going to say to Will in the few seconds she had. But before she could even open her mouth he said, "I wanna kiss you so bad, Cordia Pike."

Her eyebrows went up with surprise. "What did you say?" she asked.

"Nothing," he said, smiling but looking away from her. "How are you?"

"I'm fine. Thought you might a lost a hand, though, having not heard from you."

He looked a little ashamed. "I did write," he finally said. "Just didn't mail it."

"Doesn't do me much good then, does it?"

"Nope. But I'm here. For a while anyway."

She nodded, not knowing what to say. Then, she heard Julia coming back into the room. Just before she came in, he slipped a folded piece of paper across to her. She grabbed it, wide-eyed—and shoved it into the only place she could think of in such a short amount of time—down her bodice.

At first, Will looked a little shocked. But then he began to chuckle. Cordia tried to look angry that he would laugh at such a thing. After all, what was she supposed to do with it? But, she ended up laughing, too. Of course, Julia wanted to know what was so funny, and neither one of them had an explanation. Eventually, she let it go and sat back down to hear more about Will's experiences in the army.

"Well, I think I should probably be heading home," Cordia said after a few more minutes. "I'm sure you want to spend some more time with your brother, and you don't need me hanging around for that."

"You don't have to go," Julia protested.

But Cordia couldn't sit there across from him any longer and control herself. How she wanted to reach out and touch him, something she simply couldn't do with Julia there. Then she had an idea. "You know, Will, my daddy has been itching to hear as much as he can about what it's like being in the army. He would have enlisted himself if he wasn't too old and too important to this town. Maybe you and Julia could come over after dinner and fill him in on your experiences?"

"That would be a lot of fun!" Julia exclaimed. "I haven't left the house for so long."

"All right," Will agreed. "Sounds like a good idea to me."

"Good," Cordia said, smiling. "Then I will see you both around 7:00?" They both nodded. "All right, then." She peered into the kitchen. "Goodbye, Mrs. Adams!"

The other woman shouted her goodbyes, and then Cordia turned and walked out the door, smiling. "I can't believe Will Tucker is back in Lamar," she said to herself as she climbed up into the carriage. "Now if I can only get him to stay."

CORDIA SAT through dinner doing everything in her power to act nonchalant about Julia and Will coming over later that evening. Her father had been so excited himself, he was bubbling with glee all through their meal. "It will be so nice to hear from someone who has actually been in battle," he was saying.

Cordia wasn't really eating. It was more like she was conducting some troop movements of her own, maneuvering the various items of food around her plate so that it looked like she was consuming it. Her mother had noticed though. Finally, she said, "Cordia, dear, you don't have to eat it if you aren't hungry. I know it must be very sad for you to see Will. Probably just a reminder of your dear Jaris."

If that's what it took to get out of pretending to eat, then she was willing to accept it. "Yes, mother," she said. "May I be excused?" Her mother consented and she went upstairs to re-read Will's letter. It wasn't quite 6:30, so she still had over a half an hour of time to kill before he arrived. *They* arrived. Julia was coming, too; she mustn't forget.

September 21, 1861

Dearest Cordia,

I have tried to write to you several times these past weeks but I have not been strong enough in my shoulder to sit up and still write. Now, I am finally able to do so. Please forgive me for not sending word some other way, but I didn't think you would want me to dictate a letter to you the way that I have dictated a letter for my sister. I have had plenty of time to think about you while I have been lying here in this makeshift hospital bed. It has seemed like an eternity since the day I saw your face. I hope to look on you again soon. I do plan to take your advice and come home for a few days when I am well. But, I hope that, when I do, you will not try to talk me into staying. Please know that I would give anything to be able to settle down with you now and start a life. But it wouldn't be right, and I would spend my time loathing myself, rather than enjoying being in your company. So, I will come for a few days and hopefully find some way to spend a few moments alone with you. It will be unbearably hard to see your lips and not kiss them, but it will be better than not seeing your face at all.

All my love,

Will

She must have read his words over ten or fifteen times before she finally heard noise downstairs. They were here. She tucked the letter away for safekeeping along with his other letters and then ran to the landing. She could see her father leading them into the parlor. She smoothed her hair and then ran down the stairs to join them.

At first, her father said he thought the ladies might be more comfortable off by themselves, after all, talk of war and fighting was not exactly proper discussion in front of ladies. But Cordia insisted that it wouldn't be fair to Julia to take away any of the time that she had to spend with her brother, so he finally relented, and they all sat down in the parlor together. Will and Mr. Pike were sitting in chairs, while the ladies were situated on a small sofa across from them, although Cordia's mother spent a great deal of the evening bustling around, refilling tea, taking care of other minor household duties. Frieda was not there that evening. She spent a few evenings a week over at a friend's house at a quilting bee.

After a little while, Cordia began to feel sorry for Will. Her father was asking a barrage of questions—complex ones, too, for that matter. He wanted to know what Will thought of Lyon's decision to attack, how he had felt standing there with the rest of Sigel's men, watching those gray uniforms get closer, what he thought of this U. S. Grant and this campaign into Tennessee. But Will was able to handle every single question tossed his way, and with surprising skill, Cordia thought. For someone who claimed he never knew what to say, he sure was holding his own with her father—a man known for being quite the debater.

As the evening wore on, it became fairly apparent that Will's shoulder was bothering him. Ever since Cordia had visited that hospital, she had been compelled to learn about nursing so that, if there should be a battle nearby, she would be equipped to help. Dr. Walters had been training her a couple of hours each week. She could plainly see, though Will was trying his best to hide it, that it was really starting to hurt him. Finally, she had to say something. Her father had just asked another difficult question, but before he could answer, she said, "Will, when was the last time that bandage was changed?"

All evening long, Will had been trying his hardest to pretend he was not aware that Cordia was in the room. He had looked in her direction a few times, but he had to be careful because, after all, this was her doting father he was speaking to. So, he was a little surprised when he heard her talking to him. "What's that?" he asked.

"I'm sorry to interrupt, Daddy," she said to her father. "But, Will, it looks to me like your shoulder is bothering you. I have some ointment."

"Did you know Cordia's been studying to be a nurse?" Julia asked her brother, happy to finally have a chance to speak. She had been listening for ages, it seemed.

"No, I did not know that," Will said. "Isn't that interesting?"

"I could change the bandage if you want," Cordia said, hoping that no one would volunteer to help her.

"All right," he said standing. Then he turned to her father. "I'm sorry—I can answer that when I return."

Her father nodded obligingly, and Will moved to follow Cordia out of the room. "So, Julia, you must be excited to have your brother home for a little while," she heard her mother saying as they entered the hall-way. She was relieved then; neither her mother nor Julia were going to follow them.

She was storing up a supply of bandages, as well as other medical supplies, in a little cupboard in the corner of a room off behind the staircase. Even though she didn't feel it would be proper to shut the door, she didn't think anyone would be coming back that way, and they would have a little privacy. She took one of the lanterns out of the foyer as she passed so that she could see to light the lamps in the room. For some reason, she felt a little nervous as she entered. She went about the business of lighting the place up and getting out her supplies.

"Where do you want me?" Will asked.

"Well," she said looking around the room, "why don't you have a seat on the table there so that I can see it a little better."

He did as he was told, and she slowly walked over, setting her supplies and the original lamp down beside him.

"I was wondering how I was ever going to get you alone," he said quietly.

"Probably only have a few minutes before someone comes looking for us," she said, giving him a bashful smile. She was standing so close to him now, she could smell that familiar scent of his cologne. She had spent so much time remembering that smell. And she could see that he had shaved and cleaned himself up since his long journey. "You're probably going to have to take off your shirt," she said, shyly.

Lost in her eyes, he had temporarily forgotten the purpose of their rendezvous. Nodding obligingly, he began to unbutton.

Cordia didn't know if she should help him or just wait. She looked up at him and saw how intently he was staring at her. He unbuttoned the last button and took his arms out of the sleeves.

His chest was just as she had imagined it would be. Strong and muscular. Even with his bandaged shoulder and the scar on his collarbone, she could not have imagined a more perfectly formed man. "Oh, my," she said under her breath. She could tell by the expression on his face that he had heard her. Crimson spread up her neck, warming her cheeks. Timidly, she smiled and tried to clear her mind so that she could perform the task at hand. "All right," she said. "I'm going to have to remove this old bandage. It might hurt a little."

"I know, Cordia. It has been changed a few times before," he said quietly, grinning at her.

She nodded, knowing he was just giving her trouble. As she slowly removed the old bandage, trying her best not to hurt him by pulling off the scab, she became extremely aware of his breath on her neck. She had to stop for a second. "You're making this a little difficult," she said quietly.

"You're making this intolerably difficult," he replied.

She attempted to continue removing the old bandage, but just as she almost had it off, he began to kiss her lightly on her neck, then beneath her ear. She leaned into him, their arms around each other. She ran her fingers across his chest and down his stomach as his lips finally found hers. She kissed him back, passionately, completely forgetting what it was she had come there to do—until, her hand caught the old bandage and ripped it right off, along with part of the scab that had been covering the wound.

Will sat up sharply, obviously in pain. He didn't say anything, but then he didn't have to. She knew what she had done. He looked at her face then and could see that she was about to cry. Her hands covered her mouth, her eyes wide with alarm. "I'm all right," he said, and then he had to smile because she was looking at him as if she had nearly killed him.

"I am so sorry," Cordia said. She was also embarrassed. She had never kissed a man like that before, certainly never had her hands on a man's bare chest—and she had been anything but graceful doing it.

"I'm not harmed," he assured her. "Are you all right?"

She nodded then. "Yes. Here, let me finish this before I accidentally poke your eye out or worse."

That he couldn't help but laugh at. "I'm sorry, Cordia. It was my own fault for kissing you when you weren't expecting it."

"I should have been more careful," she muttered as she gently rubbed the ointment on his now slightly bleeding wound. "Can you imagine me doing something like that to a freshly injured soldier?" she thought aloud.

"Well, I should hope you won't be doing *that* with any other soldiers," he replied, being careful to give her more room to finish her job so that he didn't reach over and kiss her again.

She rolled her eyes at him. "That's not exactly what I meant," she said—knowing full well he knew what she was trying to say. She neatly finished replacing the bandage. "There,' she said. "That should hold for a while, but I will probably need to change it again tomorrow. I don't think it did much good to rip it open like that."

"I guess if I have to let you change it again tomorrow, then I'll just have to find a way to bear it," he said smiling. He started to put his shirt back on.

"Do you think having the wound reopened was worth it?" she asked slyly, turning around to put her supplies back in the cupboard.

He finished buttoning his shirt and crossed over to where she was standing. "Cordia Pike, I'd be willing to get shot every time you kissed me if that was the price I had to pay."

She turned to face him, his hands on her waist, and she was looking deeply into his eyes. "Well, Mr. Tucker," she said softly, "I will remember you said that. I'm a pretty good shot."

"I bet you are," he said kissing her one more time.

Hearing footsteps in the hall, she pulled away, just in time.

"Cordia? Will?" It was her mother. "There you are. I was wondering if you needed some help, it was taking so long."

"Hi, Mama," she said, hoping her hair was all in place and that her mother could not tell what it was that had made them tarry. "I had some trouble getting the old bandage off. But I got it. We're done."

"Good. I know your father would like to talk for another hour or so, but don't you think Julia probably ought to be heading home? She's starting to look a little tired, and I know you wouldn't want her to get worn out," she said as they walked back toward the parlor.

"I'm sure you're probably right, Mama," she said. Sure enough, Julia looked like she was about to fall asleep.

They all said their goodbyes, and Mr. Pike said he would like to do this again before Will went back to join the Union forces. He had found Will's insight fascinating and had enjoyed talking with the young man. Cordia suggested that they all have dinner together the next evening and invite the Adams family, which they all agreed to. Then, Cordia stood outside and watched them as they rode into the distance. She knew she would sleep well that night, dreaming of Will Tucker.

Chapter Ten

IT WAS ALMOST unbearable for Cordia to know that Will was in town but that she could not see him. She realized she could have found an excuse to go over to the Adams Farm. But she also thought that she should give Julia some time to spend alone with her brother. Likewise, she had found out the day before how extremely difficult it was to be in the same room with Will and just pretend he was a simple acquaintance, the brother of a friend, the cousin of her lost love.

Instead, she spent the day with Susannah. Her friend had not been the same since her husband went off to war. Susannah had always been one to worry about every little thing, but now, she was sure that her husband had been killed or was going to be killed soon. Every day that went by without a letter from James brought more horrifying images to his wife. And it didn't seem to matter how many times Cordia explained to her friend that the post moved very slowly these days, especially out of moving army camps, she still insisted that he was dead or dying. Needless to say, spending her time with Susannah was not something that Cordia enjoyed anymore, but it did give her something else to think about. And seeing the two boys run around and play in the yard, so carefree, gave her hope for the future. Still, she spent the whole day sulking, thinking about how unfair it was that Will was so close, and yet, she still could not even see him until dinner that evening.

Mrs. Adams had stopped by on her way to the market that morning to tell Jane that they were all happy to be invited to dinner and that they would be bringing one of her famous apple pies for dessert. They would be stopping by around 6:00. To Cordia, that seemed like a lifetime from now. Standing in Susannah's kitchen, helping her fold linens and clean up after her two sons, she began to dream of what life would be like for her and Will someday, after this cruel war was over.

"So, was it hard for you, seeing his cousin and all?" Susannah was asking.

Cordia had, once again, not been listening. "Excuse me?" she asked.

Susannah was used to her friend's ways. "Always lost in your thoughts, Cordy. Have you heard a word I have been saying?"

Now, Cordia really had not been listening for at least a half an hour, but she took a stab in the dark. "Of course. I know how much you are missing James," she said.

Susannah nodded, and Cordia felt relieved that her guess was accurate. "But what about Will? I asked if it was difficult for you to see Jaris's cousin and not miss him something awful."

"Oh," Cordia sighed. Pausing from the stack of tea towels she was folding, she looked down at them, studying the embroidery. It was so difficult for her not to be completely honest with Susannah. Since they were about five years old, they had shared every secret. Even when Susannah got married, she told Cordia exactly what to expect on her wedding night—something no one had ever even mentioned to her before, not even her own mother. Keeping a secret of this magnitude from Susannah was one of the hardest things Cordia ever had to do. But she also knew she couldn't bear to tell Susannah the truth either. So, she thought about Jaris for a few minutes, trying to remember how sad she had been when she first heard that he had been wounded. "Yes," she finally said, a few tears streaming out of her eyes. "It is difficult for me to see Will, but I am happy that he is home."

"When is he going back?" she asked, wiping the dinner table off with a damp cloth.

Cordia thought for a moment. He hadn't really said. If she had her way, he wasn't going. But she could hardly say that. "He didn't say," she answered.

"Well, maybe while he's in town, we can introduce him to Sally Canes. You know how awful it was for her not having a beau leaving when all the rest of us did. Too bad her mama's such a good cook. She has such a lovely face."

"I don't think he will be in town long enough for anything like that," Cordia replied. She glanced into the small living area of the house at the clock. Only two o'clock. How could she possibly last another four hours? And then, to make matters worse, Susannah started talking about how difficult it was going to be for her to find another husband after poor James died in battle.

Finally, at half past four, Cordia could take it no longer, and she went home to help her mother and Frieda prepare dinner for ten. As she walked the half mile to her house, she was thinking about various ways to get Will all to herself. She was hoping that no one would volunteer to help her change his bandage again; that was one way. Surely there must be something else that she could do.

She had to cross over a bridge that spanned a large fork of Muddy Creek and through a wooded area behind her house. Though Lamar was being settled fairly rapidly, the area right behind the Pike house had yet to be occupied, mostly because of the creek and the fear of flooding. Still, it was easier for Cordia to make her way from Susannah's house through this little scenic area than to stick to the city streets. The little narrow footbridge that crossed the creek here was one of only four bridges that spanned this waterway that encircled the town from the northwest. There was one more just as narrow a few miles down the stream and then two that carriages could cross, one just west of town, one just to the north. Though Cordia didn't think any raiders would try to invade Lamar soon, she often wondered, if they came from the direction of Kansas, which of these bridges they would choose. As she made her way gingerly across the creaking wood, she hoped it would not be this one. The raiders would end up directly in her own backyard.

As the two-story brick structure came into view atop a gently rolling hill, Cordia's mind left the idea of war and marauders and again her mind returned to Will and the idea that perhaps, someday, they would have their own home and family, once this war was over.

DINNER WAS JUST AS AWKWARD as Cordia had imagined it would be. She spent what seemed like an eternity trying not to look at Will and could tell by his avoidance of making eye contact with her, he was trying just as hard. Finally, as the meal was ending, she suggested that she have a look at that bandage. Alas, Margaret chimed in that she had already changed it just a few hours ago. Cordia felt her heart sink, having no earthly idea how she was going to get to see Will alone now. She could see by the disappointed look on his face that he had not been a willing patient for his aunt either.

"Well," Isaac proclaimed, standing up, "That was a fine meal. Now, let us gentlemen retire to the study to finish our discussion of politics and warfare—ideas the woman can surely do without."

The men, including Zachariah who was nearly 15, all stood up to follow Mr. Pike into the study. It had occurred to Cordia that Margaret would not want to join them and be reminded of the horrors of war. Yet, Cordia was hoping to somehow be included. Her father, however, did not ask her to join them. Soon, her mother was leading Margaret, the two younger boys, and Julia into the ladies' parlor, and she was expected to follow. Reluctantly, she went along, as her mother's singsong voice described to Mrs. Adams how beautifully Cordia was able to play the new sheet music her father had finally gotten in from New York.

Just as Cordia was about to shut the parlor doors, she saw Will walking through the hallway. Hoping her mother would somehow fail to notice she was absent, she darted out and closed the doors behind her.

"Hello," he whispered, stopping halfway through the room, seemingly surprised to have run into her.

"Where are you going?" she asked, tiptoeing across the wooden floor.

"Your father is out of brandy, and he is sending me down to the cellar to get some more."

Just as Cordia was about to ask if he needed any help, her mother flung open the doors to the parlor. "Cordia? What are you doing, dear? Mrs. Adams would like to hear your new song."

Cordia sighed. "Be careful on the stairs. They can get slippery when it's humid out."

Will smiled at her and continued on his way as she went back into the parlor and shut the glass-paneled French doors. She tried to smile as she crossed to the piano and sat down, but she couldn't help but slam the lid into place as she lifted it up to reveal the well-worn keys. She had played this song so many times; she didn't really need to look at the music. Instead, she looked past it, out into the hallway, watching to see when Will would go back to join her father. But she never saw him. Could she have missed him? She didn't think so. What could he possibly be doing?

Cordia concluded the song. The ladies and the two young boys clapped. "Thank you," she said, standing up.

"Oh, play something else," Julia implored. "You know how I love to hear you play."

"I will in a moment," Cordia assured her, "But first, I think we are almost out of wine. Mother, I am going to go down and get us a fresh bottle."

Her mother looked disagreeable. "Cordia, it gets slick down there. Let's send one of the men, dear. I would hate to see you slip on those stairs."

"Don't be silly, mother. I can manage." She picked up one of the lanterns off of a little table by the door and quietly made her way through the hallway. There was a small storage room off the dining room where a little door concealed the stairs to the cellar. She could tell that Will had not come back up because the cellar doors were still open. She thought it strange that he could be gone so long without her father sending someone after him.

The stairs were slick, and the musty smell of darkness and rotting wood hit Cordia as she began to carefully pick her way down the steps.

The light was only so much help. It bounced off the cobwebs hanging overhead and illuminated the dust she was stirring up around her. She wasn't exactly sure what she would find when she reached the bottom. Maybe he had fallen and broken his neck. Maybe a marauder had crossed the bridge behind their house, snuck inside, and hidden in the basement. Perhaps a wild animal had burrowed its way in. As she reached the last few steps, she whispered "Will, are you down here?" No answer.

Carefully, she made her way across the uneven dirt floor, trying to shine the light into the shadows. There was no sign of him anywhere. She peered over into the far corner, thinking maybe she saw something there, or perhaps it was her own shadow. An eerie feeling came over her. Suddenly, she felt someone grab her from behind. A hand over her mouth kept her from shrieking, and she nearly dropped the lantern.

"Shhh!" a whispery voice said in her ear. "Ghosts don't eat apple pie, and they don't drink brandy."

Cordia spun around, and he let her go. She had been planning on hitting her "attacker" when she wasn't sure who it was, and now that she knew it was Will, she was just about mad enough to strike him anyway. "Do you think that is funny?" she exclaimed, raising the lantern so he could see the terror in her eyes. "You're lucky I didn't...."

"Didn't what?" he asked, unable to keep from laughing at her. "I'm sorry—I didn't think I would scare you. Who else did you think it would be? Didn't Jules explain to you that I am not a ghost?"

"Yes!" she huffed. "But usually people announce themselves. They don't just sneak over and grab you."

"I apologize," he said, and seeing that she was calming down, he took her free hand. "Will you forgive me?"

She nodded her head. It would be impossible for her to stay mad at him, that she knew. "Why are you still down here?" she asked.

"I was waiting for you, of course. But, it took you so long to come down; I didn't think you would ever make it. I'm sure your pa must think I have just decided to leave town."

"Well," she started, "Everyone wanted me to play for them. I couldn't get out of it."

"You play divinely," he said. "I could hear you through the floorboards. Best piano playing I ever heard."

"Thank you," she said. He leaned over and kissed her softly on the lips then. She couldn't help but kiss him back. In just a few seconds, however, they heard footsteps at the top of the stairs. It was Zachariah, calling Will's name. Cordia sighed.

"I'll be right up. I couldn't find the right bottle, but Cordia happened by, and she helped me."

They heard the young man walking away then. Will leaned over and kissed her one last time before bounding up the stairs, bottle in hand.

"Wait!" Cordia called. She didn't want him to go, not yet. But she knew she couldn't keep him down there with her either. It was too suspicious. He was looking at her, a questioning expression on his handsome face. "Will, when are you leaving? You haven't said."

He sighed. He had been trying to keep it from her so that she wouldn't be dreading it all along and would try to enjoy the few moments they had together. "Tomorrow. Train leaves at ten o'clock in the morning."

Cordia had suspected as much. Her shoulders slumped. "Fiddle," she whispered, looking at the ground. Once again, he turned to go, his head hanging, knowing she was disappointed.

"Wait!" she cried again. He turned and walked back a few steps so that he could see her face. "There's an old bridge in those woods behind my house. Will you meet me there tonight? At two o'clock?"

Cordia wasn't sure who was more surprised at her words—him or her. She hadn't planned on making this proposition, but at the same time, she couldn't bear the thought of letting him go without spending any more time with him. He nodded at her again and turned to walk up the stairs. He took a few steps and then turned back to see if she was going to call him again. She was still watching him, but she didn't make a sound, and he finished his ascent. She made her way over to the wine racks and found a bottle she knew her mother would appreciate and made her way up the stairs.

As she reached the top, she was a little surprised to see Julia standing there. "Cordia," she said, a peculiar expression on her face. "There you are. We were beginning to wonder if you had fallen down the steps and hurt yourself, dear."

Cordia pulled the cellar doors into place. "No, I'm fine. It's just difficult to see down there, that's all."

Julia nodded, and the girls crossed back into the parlor. But there was something about the look on Julia's face that made Cordia think that maybe something wasn't quite right. Surely, Julia hadn't heard what Cordia had said to her brother? If she did, wouldn't she say something? Cordia didn't know, but one thing was for sure—Julia was acting a little strange.

❀

CORDIA PIKE HAD NEVER EVEN IMAGINED DOING anything like this before in her whole life. Except for her rash trip to Springfield, she had always been extremely honest with her parents—almost to a fault. Now, here she was, lacing up her boots at 1:45 in the morning to sneak out.

She had wondered, at first, about the possibility of going out her bedroom window. There was a tree branch that overhung the roof, and she had thought it might be possible to swing onto the top of a little shed from there and then jump down. Though Cordia usually found it hard to admit, she really was scared to commit such daring feats. So, she decided she would do the most obvious thing and take her chances sneaking out the back door. She was too frightened to bring a lantern with her. Instead, she used what little moonlight fell across the stairs to navigate her way down them and into the hallway. Her parents' bedroom was upstairs, as was Frieda's, and none of them seemed to be following her as she made her way out the back door. One slight creak of the screen door, and she was free. She took off running across the backyard, the sweet smell of freedom before her.

She ran all the way to the little bridge, dodging tree branches, tree roots, and mud holes as she went. When she finally reached the modest structure, she paused to catch her breath and waited for Will —half afraid that he was going to sneak up on her again.

He didn't though. In a few minutes, she saw him appear out of the shadows of the trees. He was walking very slowly, cautiously, as if he was unsure that it was really Cordia waiting for him.

He stopped at the far end of the bridge. Though the moon was not full, they were certainly illuminated standing out in the open. Cordia decided maybe they would be better off beneath one of the stately pine trees, and she walked briskly over, grabbed his hand and led him away from the rickety old bridge.

"Hello," she said when she could finally pause to look directly at him.

His deep brown eyes seemed to peer right through her, as if he was studying her very soul. He was holding both of her hands in his and the look of serenity on his face calmed her nerves and assured her that what she had done, even if there were consequences, was right.

She leaned back against the trunk of the tree. The lowest branches were still several feet above their heads, and for a moment, they could pretend that they were safe from the rest of the angry world. Finally, he spoke. "I wasn't sure you would come," he said, still studying her face. "Your parents... if they found out...."

Cordia shook her head. "I don't care," she explained. "I couldn't let you go without...." She paused, trying to collect her thoughts, yet distracted by the closeness of his perfect lips. "Without seeing you in private."

He nodded, his hands moving up her arms and then encircling her. Instinctively, her hands went to his chest, and for a moment they just stood there, looking longingly at each other. "Cordia, I am so sorry that it has to be this way. I'd give anything to stay."

"I know," she interrupted. "I know. You don't have to explain. It's just that, I will miss you so much. Every day that passes without being with you, my heart feels heavier and heavier, until it's like a rock beating in my chest. And I don't know when I will see you again. It might be...." She paused again, not wanting to say the word. She realized that tears were sliding down her cheeks. "It might be years."

He pulled her to him now, holding her in his strong arms, one hand tangled in her hair. "I know." He couldn't help but agree with her, having no idea when he would be back. Not only was he leaving the state, but he had enlisted for two more years. "But Cordia," he said, pushing her back enough to look into her face again, "I will return to you. You must know that. I will always return to you."

Somehow, she believed him. She nodded. And then he began to kiss her. Each time his lips fell on hers, she locked that moment away in her mind, trying to remember each detail of how he felt, how he smelled, how he tasted. She knew she would need these memories to get her through the long journey ahead.

He kissed her ear and then her neck. They slid down the tree to the ground, still locked in an embrace, barely able to breathe as their love became a passion. Cordia had lost herself in this man that she loved. In this moment, she was ready to become his wife, preacher or no, regardless of what others might think. And just as she began to grow certain of Will's intentions, he pulled away, as if suddenly waking from a dream.

"Will?" she asked, looking at the almost stunned expression on his face. "What's wrong?"

He sat back on his heels, leaving a few feet between them. "I'm sorry Cordia. I almost got carried away," he said. Though he wanted more than anything in the world to be with the woman that he loved before he left for battle, he knew he couldn't do it. Not like this. She was the most angelic person he had ever met, and he could not disrespect her in such fashion. He smiled at her, "Well, now I will certainly have something to return for."

She smiled at him, the distance clearing her own head. She knew that, if he had not stopped, she would not have either. Part of her was relieved, the other part knew that she would not have been as remorseful as one would have expected. She was beginning to see that, in times of war, even those virtues that people know to be their very core believes are sometimes questionable.

"Cordia," he said, after what seemed like a very long period of silence. "I do have something for you." He reached into his pocket and pulled out a narrow gold band. "It's nothing fancy. Doesn't even have a diamond on it. But it was my ma's, and I would like for you to have it." He held it up for her to see, the moonlight glinting off of its shiny surface.

She gasped in surprise and held out her hand. "It's beautiful, Will!" she exclaimed. Somehow, it didn't matter what it looked like. It was from him. It was perfect.

"I know that you won't be able to wear it publicly right away," he said, as he slid it on her finger. "But, I thought, maybe, someday, when I come back, you would consent to wearing it—and being my wife?"

Cordia's eyes darted from her hand to his face. She felt the tears streaming over once again. This time, she also knew she was beaming. "Yes," she said, leaning over and hugging him. "Of course, I will be your wife."

"I know it might be difficult to hide our relationship from everyone, but I think we should do so, until the war is over, and I am home for good. Otherwise, people might not understand."

Cordia nodded her understanding. "I will wait for you," she promised.

They held each other for several minutes then, melting into each other. Finally, Will began to stand up, pulling Cordia with him. "We should get back to where we are supposed to be before anyone notices we are gone."

Cordia nodded, not wanting to let him go but also not wanting to prolong the inevitable. "I love you, Will," she said, wrapping her arms around his neck again.

"I love you, too," he said. He kissed her lips one last time, and then pulled away, reluctant to release her hand until her outstretched arm could no longer reach. "I'll see you at the train station in the morning."

Cordia watched as he disappeared into the shadows. She heard a faint whinny and then hoof beats leading away. She stood for a moment beneath the branches of the pine tree to gather her thoughts and try to remember exactly what it had felt like to be kissing Will. Finally, she straightened her hair and began to pick her way back toward her house.

It was a little slower going this time. Not only was she walking up hill, but no longer was her heart light with the idea of meeting Will. Now, the trip back to the house seemed endless. She thought she had only been gone for about an hour or so, and she was hoping that everyone was still sound asleep. As she reached the back door, she pulled it open as quietly as possible. She peered inside and was relieved that no one was standing there waiting for her. She carefully made her way across the dining room and to the stairwell. She paused for a moment, listening. Not a sound. Cautiously, she began to climb the steps. With each new height, and no bedroom doors being flung open, she felt she could claim a small victory. Finally, she reached her bedroom door. She slowly drew it open, stepped inside, and closed it gingerly behind her. She released a deep sigh of relief and turned on her heels to make her way back to bed.

"Where have we been Miss Cordia?"

Cordia jumped. Someone was sitting in the shadows on her bed!

Will had seen the militia out making patrol rounds as he made his way toward the Adams Farm. They had not seen him or else he would have probably been interrogated and would have had to lie so as not to tell them where he had been. He finally made it back to the barn to tie up the horse, relieved to see that there were no lamps lit in the house. He snuck in the back door and made his way to the makeshift bedroom he had been sleeping in. However, as he crossed the kitchen, he saw Julia sitting up in her bed in the room beyond. He sighed, and she stood up to follow him into his room.

"Well?" she asked, closing the door behind her.

"Well, what?" he asked, taking off his hat and coat and throwing them over the back of a chair.

"Aren't you going to tell me where you've been?" she asked a bit too noisily.

"Not so loud!" he said, sitting down on the cot and taking off his boots. "Why do you care where I've been?" he asked, as any older brother would. "Shouldn't you be asleep?"

She crossed over to stand in front of him. "Will, how do I know you didn't just ride off to set the courthouse on fire?"

He couldn't help but chuckle at that. "Why would I do that?" He looked at her and could see by her expression that she was seriously concerned. "I was just out for a ride," he finally said.

She did not accept his explanation. "Why would anyone get out of a warm bed and go for a ride at 1:30 in the morning when they are supposed to be on a train in a few hours?" she asked.

"Julia," he said, plopping himself back to lie on the bed. "I wasn't tired. I went for a ride. Now I am tired. Please stop asking me questions, and let's get some sleep." He closed his eyes, hoping that she would acquiesce and leave the room, but she didn't budge.

Instead, she pulled a chair closer to the bed and sat down. He opened his eyes and could tell by the solemn expression on her face that something was truly bothering her. Finally, she spoke, "Will, I was standing behind the door when you and Cordia were in the cellar. I heard what Cordia said to you. I know where you went. I just don't know why."

He sat up then, shocked to know she had been eavesdropping without him realizing it. "You heard that?" he asked.

She nodded her head. "How could you do something like that to Jaris?" she inquired. "How could Cordia? I just can't believe you would betray your own cousin by sneaking off with the woman he loved."

Will shook his head. He had been doing everything he could to avoid this conversation, but now here it was. How was he going to make Julia understand that he wasn't just fooling around with Cordia? "Jules, it's not what you think," he began.

But she wasn't finished. "Can you imagine if it would have been Aunt Margaret who overheard that, or Uncle Arthur? Even Jane or Isaac? They would have likely shot the both of you! How could this have happened in such a short amount of time? You've only been back a couple days, and you didn't even see Cordia that much." She was shaking her head slowly back and forth, bewildered.

"It didn't," he began again. "It didn't happen in a couple days. I mean, not that it took long to happen when it did," he said, thinking back to how quickly it seemed he had given his heart to Cordia. "Julia, you don't understand. And I'm not sure if this will make it better for you or worse, but I fell in love with Cordia before I even left. And she was in love with me then, too."

"What?" Julia gasped. "She was in love with you before you left for the war? But what about Jaris? She was engaged to be married!"

"I know, I know," he tried to explain. "But Julia, she didn't love Jaris. I mean, she loved him—they were the best of friends—but she wasn't in love with him."

"Why didn't she just say 'no' when he asked her to marry him?" Julia said, folding her arms across her chest.

"It's complicated. Their families expected it. She felt trapped." Will wasn't sure that Julia was mature enough to understand the situation, but he was hopeful she had read enough romance books to comprehend.

"Well," Julia began, "I can't believe I am about to ask this about someone I thought of as my very best friend, but was she hoping he would die?"

Will gasped. "Of course not!" he proclaimed. "No, not at all. She was planning on telling him after the war, before the wedding, but she didn't want to send him off to fight all demoralized. She didn't want to marry him even before she met me. But then, when we met, well, we kind of just fell in love." He stared intently at his sister's face. She seemed to be a little bit more accepting of what he was saying than she had been before. "We were writing each other—well, she was writing me, and I was writing back but not sending the letters for one reason or another—but Jaris didn't know. He had no idea. Of course, I felt bad about it, but I also understood her reasoning. I can't imagine what it would be like out there fighting and finding out that your girl doesn't really love you after all. But Julia, you've got to believe me. I love Cordia, and she loves me. We got engaged tonight. I'd like to shout it from the mountaintops, but we've got to consider everyone else's feelings. And we are. No one else knows. Please, just try to understand."

Julia listened without saying a word. When he was finished, she still sat and looked at him for a few minutes before she finally spoke. "It's just..." she began, "it's just a little hard to grasp." He studied her face for a few moments, seeing her work over everything he had disclosed. Finally, giving a small smile, she reached over and hugged him. "I guess, the most important thing to realize is that my big brother is engaged to be married. Congratulations!"

CORDIA GASPED. Barely any light was coming in through her bedroom windows, but she thought the form and the voice were familiar. Finally, she said in a very meek voice, "Frieda, is that you?"

The shadow shifted a little bit, and the voice boomed, "Yes, it's me. Where have you been child?" She stood up now and reached over and lit the lamp next to Cordia's bed.

Though Cordia was about as frightened as she had ever been, she suddenly became very aware that she was still wearing Will's ring. She slid it off before Frieda turned back around and shoved it down the top of her dress. She decided to play nonchalant. "Oh, Frieda," she said smiling, "don't you know I sometimes like to go for walks? I was just out for a little stroll."

Frieda didn't seem to be buying the story. "At two o'clock in the morning? You were out for a little stroll? Miss Cordia, I saw you coming out of those woods, and I am pretty sure I heard a horse. Now, are you going to tell me what you were doing, or am I just gonna have to assume you've been giving information to a spy?"

Cordia's eyebrows furrowed. "Spy?" she repeated. "Why in the world would I be talking to a spy?"

By now, her parents had, apparently, been awakened, and Cordia could hear them scurrying around next door. Frieda continued. "You been out giving information to raiders and marauders, haven't you?" The door came open just in time for Cordia's parents to hear the last words.

"What?" Cordia asked, amazed. "Frieda, you have known me my whole life. Do you honestly think I would be out giving information to spies? That's ridiculous!"

Now her parents were demanding to know what was going on. Frieda began her accusation again, but Isaac and Jane were looking at Cordia, so she began to tell them the story she had fabricated earlier, just in case she got caught. "I woke up around one o'clock from a terrible nightmare about Jaris. It was awful. So much blood." She could tell her parents were sympathetic. Her mother was making a *tsk tsk* sound with her tongue. "Well, I couldn't go back to sleep, so I decided to get dressed and go for a walk around the yard. But, when I got outside, I thought, it was such a pretty night, I would just walk down and look at the creek. That's all. I didn't see anyone else, and I certainly didn't hear any horses."

Frieda began to protest again, but Mr. and Mrs. Pike were tired and obviously unwilling to take the more complicated side of the story. "Come on Frieda," Mr. Pike said, ushering the servant woman out the door. "What an imagination you have."

"Get some sleep, dear," Mrs. Pike, said hugging her daughter. "If you have any more bad dreams, you know your father and I are right next door. Wake us any time, darling. But please don't go outside in this dew. I don't want you getting sick."

Cordia nodded and kissed her mother's cheek. Finally, everyone cleared the room and Cordia was able to get back to bed. She did feel bad using Jaris as an excuse, but she also knew that her parents thought she could do no wrong the moment his name was mentioned. And besides, it's not as if he had never gotten her into trouble to save himself when they were children. She changed into her nightdress and slipped the ring back onto her finger, tucking her hand under her pillow where no one coming into her room might see.

NORMALLY, Cordia loved to hear the sound of the train whistle. Today, as she stood outside in the rain watching black smoke billow from its iron lungs, she thought it must be the most lamentable sound in the world. She had wanted to wear black to match her melancholy mood, but she knew that would be questionable. So instead, she put on one of her best gowns and tried to make herself as beautiful as possible so that Will could remember her as such. She was quite sure, however, that he would look into her eyes and see that her true feelings were anything but the light, airy mood she was trying to suggest.

She had not had a chance to hug him at the train depot. His aunt, uncle, cousins, sister, even her own mother, had been able to. She waited in the back, trying to make herself unnoticeable, trying to make herself seem only as dismayed as one should be who was saying goodbye to their good friend's brother. He had said all of his goodbyes, looked at her momentarily, and waved, before jumping lightly aboard the train. She stood there, umbrella in hand, watching him go, wanting to hold on to him for even one more second, if that was possible. She held Julia's hand in the guise of comforting her friend as the train became smaller and smaller, and finally disappeared. Julia had tears streaming down her face, and Cordia was hoping that Julia would think the solitary drop that ran down from one eye was purely sympathetic. She quickly wiped it away, looking to see if Julia had noticed. She didn't seem as if she did, and slowly, the two girls turned and followed the rest of their families back to the waiting carriages. Finally, Cordia turned to Julia and said sympathetically, "You are going to miss your brother a lot."

"Yes," Julia agreed. "And you are going to miss your new fiancé."

Chapter Eleven

"LET the blessings of spring be bountiful, and let our hearts be open in this time of new life and new promise. In Jesus blessed name we ask these things, Amen."

Cordia had been trying to listen to Rev. Jacobson's sermon, but her mind was full of turbulence these days, and she was having trouble concentrating on the outside world. Thankfully, she had been hearing from Will on a regular basis. Throughout the winter, there had been little need to worry, as his unit had not been very active, only a small skirmish from time to time. Yet, as the days started to grow long again, and all things dead seemed to reawaken, she grew more worried that the spring would change its role from bringer of life to the season of mourning. With warmer weather, more battles were apt to happen, more lives likely to be lost. And though Will had promised he would return, part of her still agonized over the idea that he might not be able to keep that promise.

Cordia followed her mother out of the narrow pew, her father behind. Her mind was still lost in thought, and it wasn't until she was outside of the double doors that she realized someone behind her had been calling her name. She turned around and glanced behind, her but whoever it was must have still been inside. Continuing on her way, she was suddenly caught by the arm from behind. She whirled around to see familiar, icy eyes staring into hers. "Why, Carey Adams, you frightened me."

He smiled at her now, which Cordia thought quite strange. Carey had never seemed to have anything but torture in mind when it came to her. "Cordia Pike, you are still the picture of beauty," he said. He was wearing his military uniform, a cape draped around his shoulders.

"I am quite surprised to see you. I thought you would be gone for the duration, as much as you like to hurt things." She couldn't help but be a little sharp-tongued. She was not exactly fond of this man.

But Carey was not offended. He threw back his head and laughed. "I would still be a'fightin' with the rest of them, miss, but they sent me home."

It was then that Cordia got a glimpse of what was underneath that cape. She could not help but gasp in horror at the sight of Carey's pinned-up, empty sleeve. For a moment, she almost thought this was another one of his mean tricks, just to make her feel sick. But she could tell by his expression that he had truly suffered this calamity and now would have to go through life with only one arm. "I am truly sorry for your loss," she finally managed to say.

He nodded his head in agreement. "Many have given much more," he said as solemnly as Cordia had ever heard him speak. Then he added, "I am surprised to see you wearing such a bright colored dress. Shouldn't you still be wearing black?"

Cordia was momentarily confused. Then, she realized what he was implying. "Oh," she began, looking down at her bright blue dress. "I was never required to wear black. Jaris...." She was slowed by the look of amazement on his face. She continued, "Jaris wasn't my husband."

Carey's face seemed to grow sterner, a look Cordia was more familiar with. "Yes, I know," he stated. "But, as much as the two of you loved each other, well, I expected you would be in mourning, regardless of the fact that you never actually stood before the preacher."

Cordia could feel the heat rising in her cheeks. Why was it any of

Carey's concerns whether or not she was wearing black? "I am in mourning, Lt. Adams," she said sharply. "I will be in mourning for years to come. That does not mean that I am required to wear black. Believe me, the loss of such a fine man has marred the hearts of many in this town, my own included. Now, if you will excuse me, I think my parents are waiting for me." Fortunately, they were, and she was able to climb aboard the waiting wagon and leave without him following her. At least not on foot. She could feel his cold blue stare trailing her until they rounded the corner onto Broadway Street. She shuddered.

Her mother must have thought the March wind was getting to her because she wrapped her own shawl around Cordia's shoulders. "Here, dear. Don't want you to catch cold."

"I'm fine, Mama," she said, but her mother didn't seem to agree as the shawl stayed in place.

"Saw Carey Adams talking to you," her father began. "Fine soldier. Too bad about his arm. Hear he is going to be placed in charge of the city militia, though. That'll be good for us." Despite the fact that her father was a Union man, he had the utmost respect for the entire Adams family, Carey included.

Cordia didn't comment. She didn't want to think about having to see Carey Adams every day for the rest of her life. She began to consider how completely unfair it was that someone like Carey got to come home while Will was still out there fighting. But then, she remembered the awful sight of that pinned-up sleeve and was hopeful that, when Will did come home, he would come home all in one piece.

The next day, Cordia was elated to receive a letter from Will. She immediately took it over to Julia to share its contents with her friend. Though Julia had not been able to completely understand the rapidity of Cordia and Will's relationship, she had, in the months following Will's departure, accepted the fact that her brother and her dear friend were in love. And even though Cordia still made the same efforts toward Julia as she always had, she could tell that Julia did not see her in the same light as she had before. Nevertheless, she still spent many days at the Adams Farm, passing time with her would-be sister-in-law. Through the winter, Julia had been battling her tuberculosis off and on. Now that spring was arriving, she seemed to be feeling better. Still, she had not been able to make it to church the day before. Cordia would also need to relay her conversation with Carey Adams. She knew that, when it came to Carey, she and Julia shared a common sentiment of loathing.

When Cordia arrived, Julia was sitting on the swing under the oak tree, a light blanket wrapped around her to help combat the cool March breeze. She looked pale; her eyes had dark circles under them. Cordia wasn't sure she should even be out of bed, but she knew it was no use trying to tell Julia that. "Mornin'," she said as she approached. She sat down next to her friend who acknowledged her arrival with a smile. "How are you feeling today?"

Julia peered off beyond the horizon for a few moments. Finally, she said, "I feel all right. I didn't want to stay in that stuffy bedroom anymore. Aunt Margaret finally said I could come outside for a spell, but only if I stayed wrapped up."

Cordia could plainly see the agitation on the young woman's face. She knew that Julia was a very capable person, and as hard as it was for Cordia to see her a prisoner of her own body, it must have been exponentially harder for Julia to accept her own limitations. "Well, I have something that might cheer you up," she said, the smile on her face giving the news away.

"A letter from Will!" Julia exclaimed. Her excitement, however, caused a fit of coughing that Cordia had to help her control before she could continue with the letter. After a few moments, she was able to calm down, and Cordia opened up the letter.

February 19, 1862

Dearest Cordia,

I received your last two letters, dated January 3 and January 5, just a few days ago. I am sorry I have not been able to answer them until now, but my unit has been particularly busy. I don't know if word has reached you yet of the battles we have been engaged in, but rest assured I am uninjured. We were able to take both of the Confederate forts near where we are stationed with little trouble at all. Fort Henry and Fort Donelson by name. This U.S. Grant is something else. All the men are cheering him, saying, if we put him over in Washington City, this war would be over by now.

I cannot tell you where we are now marching to, but we hope to have some rest. Both forts fell within ten days of each other, and we are intolerably tired for it. But we will press on and drive these Rebels out of Tennessee sure enough.

I have told you previously of the antics of my friend Gene. Well, he has gone off to see the doctor, not as a result of battle, but as a result of his own clumsiness. During the mild fighting we have encountered lately, he managed somehow to put his bayonet into his foot, rather than into his rifle. They expect him to be released soon, however. I am sure he will do something to get himself right back in there if he ain't careful.

Tennessee is very beautiful. I should like to take you and Julia here someday, after the war is over, assuming we don't destroy it. The trees are just beginning to get their leaves back. We can finally hear the birds singing again, which is a nicer thing to awaken to than the sounds of gunfire or other men snoring.

Every night I fall asleep dreaming of your face. I don't know when I will see you again, but I take comfort in the memories that I have of you. I will not say more, as I am sure you are sharing this correspondence with my sister, and I do not wish to embarrass either of you. Still, know how I long to be with you again.

Please give my love to Jules and let her know I miss her.

All my love,

Will

JULIA BEAMED, so delighted to have heard from her brother at last. She asked Cordia to read the letter again, which she did. "I do hope that this war is quickly over," Julia declared. "I long to see Will once again."

Cordia agreed. "Me, too," she said softly, her arm around the young girl's shoulders. "Me, too."

Then, remembering her conversation of the day before, Cordia added, "Guess who I saw at church yesterday."

Julia seemed to think for a moment but then said, "Carey Adams?"

Cordia was surprised. "However did you know?"

"Aunt Margaret told me," she admitted. "She's been so excited that he's come back in town, although she is very regretful about his arm."

Cordia considered this information. It would make sense that Margaret would know her nephew had arrived in Lamar.

Julia continued, "Heard he spent some time conversatin' with you, too," she added.

Cordia looked down at the younger girl, her eyes widening, attempting to understand precisely what Julia was implying. "He spoke to me briefly after service," she admitted. "Believe me, it was nothing to take note of."

"If you insist," Julia muttered under her breath.

"Now, just what does that mean?" Cordia demanded, turning to face Julia a bit more.

"Nothin'" Julia said, sitting up a bit straighter. "It's just, my understanding that Carey has taken an interest in you, since Jaris is no longer with us, and of course, no one else knows about you and Will."

Cordia felt as if she might be sick. It took her a moment to regain her composure before she could speak. "Whomever did you hear that from?" she asked.

"Aunt Margaret," Julia replied. "She mentioned it at the supper table last night. Don't know what's been said by whom, but she seemed to think it was something Jaris might appreciate, you still bein' an Adams and still marrying in to the family."

Cordia considered this piece of information. It could be valuable in the future, once Will had returned and they were able to profess their love publicly. After all, he was every bit as much a relation to Jaris as Carey. But as for now, if this meant that Carey Adams was going to be attempting to court her, well, he had another thing coming.

"Let's just hope Cousin Carey knows what he is getting himself into," she said slyly.

He had heard that some were calling this place Shiloh after a church nearby. However, from his vantage point, Will could see nothing peaceful about it. The day before, he and the rest of Grant's men had been bivouacked near the river, waiting for reinforcements from Ohio. They knew that P.G.T. Beauregard and his troops were in the area; however, they had no idea that they were so incredibly close.

The Rebs had been successful that first day, pushing them back toward Owl Creek. The ground had been terrible, like fighting in a pile of fresh horse manure, the mud clinging to their shoes and their pants, weighing them down and making any sort of a hasty retreat impossible. Luckily, the enemy had seemed confused, and Will and the men he was fighting with were able to drop back to a better position. It seemed like the Sunken Road they chose for cover was good ground, and it proved to be so when the Confederate Army could not make its way through what they were now calling the "Hornet's Nest."

Despite being caught off-guard, the Union Army was able to hold the field that first day, and with the arrival of reinforcements the next morning, General Don Carlos Buell of Ohio and his additional men, Grant's forces were victorious. Though Will's unit had seen some tremendous action the first day, they were able to fall back the next day into reserve and let the new arrivals feel the brunt of the burden of war.

The following morning, when the fighting was over and Beauregard had taken his Confederate forces and disappeared, Will heard the sound of bugles, letting them know it was time to move out. The carnage left in the wake of the battle was like nothing he had ever seen before. There was nary a sound from those troops considering themselves lucky to still be marching, despite the number of their comrades who littered the ground around them.

One sight in particular was especially disheartening to Will. As they continued along their way, they eventually came to a small pond. The bodies of the dead and wounded lay so thick around this shallow vessel of water that the blood had tinged the surface a sickening red color. For these poor souls, the pond had been their one hope for relief from their agonizing wounds. Most of them would find solace here eventually, as they faded out of this world and into the next.

As they passed through this dismal place, Will overheard one of his companions say, "War is hell."

"Yes, it is," he thought to himself. *"Yes, it is indeed."*

THE REMAINDER of 1862 included several more major engagements for the Union Army of the Tennessee. Gen. U. S. Grant realized that, if he was going to be successful in securing the Mississippi River for the

Union, therefore cutting off a major artery to the Confederates, he would have to capture the fort city of Vicksburg. Will saw action at several battles and skirmishes along the river, some successful, though many only resulting in high casualties, particularly for the North. It wasn't until the spring of 1863 that Grant began to make significant progress toward his goal. By then, Will had become quite the veteran soldier, though he still refused any offer of promotion. He had earned a reputation as one of the most reliable gunmen in his regiment and was occasionally called upon as a makeshift sharpshooter when needed. He wrote to Julia and Cordia as often as possible and relied on letters from home to soften the hardships of war. The horrendous sights of the battlefield cast images his mind would not soon forget, memories he knew he would carry with him long after the cruel war was over, should he be so fortunate as to find his way back home.

The summer and fall were particularly difficult for Julia who spent much of her time in bed, tuberculosis consuming her lungs. Cordia visited as often as possible, but many times Margaret advised against a lengthy stay since Julia needed to rest, and Cordia was helpless to ease the debilitating cough. Dr. Walters frequented her bedside and prescribed laudanum to help Julia sleep. As far as curing the illness, there was little he could do. She fared better in the winter when the cool air helped to open her lungs, but even then, she was not herself, and Cordia began to fear the worse. She wrote to Will to let him know that his sister was doing her best to contend with the sickness but that she was legitimately concerned for Julia. When he acknowledged her apprehensions, he did so as positively as possible, though the health of his sister was consistently on his mind.

Over the course of the year, Carey Adams made both his presence and his intentions well known. He had started off slowly, catching Cordia after church or at social events, speaking to her briefly, flashing her his charming Southern-gentleman smile. Cordia was neither impressed nor amused. She wasn't sure what made him think that a few kind words now could make up for years of verbal abuse and ill-well. He may have fooled the rest of the citizenry into thinking he was an upstanding young man, but Cordia had seen him do the unthinkable —cruelly kill small animals, leave insects in precarious positions to die, not to mention all of the horrific ways he had tormented her over the years. She knew that, deep down inside, he would always be the same degenerate, self-centered boy who loved to torture her as a child.

Yet, the more visible he became in the community, the more pleasantries he spoke to her parents, the more he began to wind his way into her everyday life. In fact, her mother began to grow quite fond of him. She would even go out of her way to speak to him whenever she had the opportunity to do so. It wasn't long before Cordia found herself sitting across from Carey at her very own dinner table, an occurrence that simply made her lose her appetite.

"Tell us, how are the city militia boys keepin' up?" her father asked, a large piece of pot roast poised on his fork.

Carey chewed a bit before answering. "Very well, sir," he replied. "We are in fine shape to hold off even the most deliberate of guerrilla raiders. Why, I assure you, even Quantrill himself would not be able to step foot within our city limits without our forces crushing him and his men. Not even the army of Gen. Grant would stand a chance against our fine Lamar fighting troops," he continued, his chest puffing with pride.

Cordia couldn't help but snicker. "Do you mean the same Gen. Grant who has Braxton Bragg and his forces high-tailing it to Chattanooga? That must be quite some force of farmers and merchants you've put together there." She had begun an intricate process of moving small portions of her food from one part of the plate to another, which only allowed her to glance briefly in his direction.

"Cordia!" her mother exclaimed, her face turning a slight shade of red. "Don't be rude to our guest!"

"Now, now, that's quite all right," Carey assured her. "I understand Miss Cordia is skeptical. She is certainly entitled to her opinion. One of the traits that I have always admired about you, Cordia, is your inquisitive mind, even when it is tinged with cynicism. We would do well to have more like-minded women. Perhaps us gentlemen would be less impulsive and more compassionate."

"Here, here!" her father said, raising his glass and gesturing for Carey to toast, which he did. Even though Isaac had always been pro-Union, he still admired Carey's service for the cause he believed in.

And, now that Carey was in charge of the city guard, he would be defending the citizens of Lamar against anyone who may attempt to harm them, regardless of Union or Southern sentiment. Carey came from an upstanding family. He was well spoken and polite. For Isaac, accepting Carey back as a member of their community was just the first step in moving past the divisions the war had created. As more and more young men returned from battle, it did not matter which side they had fought for. They were still members of their social circle, and the town could not survive if people continued to take sides. That was Isaac Pike's view, at any rate, and he was doing all he could to spread that idea throughout the town he was so influential over.

Cordia looked away in disbelief. Did her own father actually believe that Carey Adams felt that women should have any influence over politics or any other social issues? Though she was compelled to voice her opinion regarding his true sentiments, she bit her tongue. She could see no reason to begin a debate about women's rights at this point in the evening at her parents' dinner table. Hopefully, this meal would be over very soon, and it would never be repeated. She had not been able to stomach one bite of her food, and the longer this event dragged out, the less likely she was to be able to convince her mother that she was actually eating.

"Speaking of Gen. Grant," her father said, between bites, "Do you think that he is on his way to Vicksburg? Do you think he'll be able to take it?"

Carey seemed to consider the question for a moment. Having fought for the Confederate Army for over a year, it would be difficult for him to say that he thought Grant would be able to take the southern Mississippi town. "Well, Mr. Pike, sir," he began, wiping his mouth with his napkin. "I would say that will be quite a feat for Grant, considering that Pemberton is most likely to receive support from Gen. Johnston. Though Pemberton is greatly outnumbered without current support from other Confederate forces, it is highly unlikely that the Southern Army would abandon Vicksburg. It is one of the most important defensive strongholds on the Mississippi, and if it should fall into Union hands, well, then, control of the Mississippi River would also be sacrificed."

Clearing her throat, Cordia asked, "Don't you think that the victories at Port Gibson and Raymond might just give U.S. Grant the momentum he needs to swing right on down and march Pemberton and his men out of Vicksburg and directly out of Mississippi? I hear those victories were pretty sizable."

"I guess I didn't realize you were following the war effort so closely, Miss Cordia," Carey replied, finishing up what was left of his dinner. "Tell me, what do you think about Gen. Grant's chances of taking the capital at Jackson then?"

"I am following very closely, Lt. Adams. You know, some of our Lamar boys are fighting for Grant, and I, like many of their wives and families, have a sincere interest in hearing of their victories." She couldn't help but be a bit sharp with her answer. She had taken his comment to imply that he felt she was uneducated, something she did not take to lightly. Continuing, she added, "I feel that Gen. Sherman and Gen. McPherson should have the upper-hand, particularly if the same number of troops are still protecting the capital in a few days when they arrive as are guarding it now. The Southern soldiers will be outnumbered and facing better-armed men. I think they will crumble and fall apart, retreating to the higher ground of Vicksburg. 'Course, it will only be a matter of time before Grant marches in there, too."

"Cordia, darling," her father said, looking at her as if he were seeing her with new eyes, "Wherever are you getting all of this insightful information?"

"Well, Daddy, the men send letters. I read the newspapers. Telegraphs come in from friends and family in Mississippi. It isn't difficult to stay well informed when one has a mind to." Looking down at her nearly full plate, she realized she could no longer stand to sit and stare at the food anymore without the possibility of becoming sick. "May I be excused?" she asked, praying her father would consent.

But it wasn't her father who replied. "Actually, Cordia, I was hoping you would join me on a stroll in this nice May weather we are having," Carey said, an actual smile, grazing his handsome face. For once, he looked almost kind, something Cordia had never noticed before. Still, the queasiness in her stomach became even worse with the thought of joining him for anything, and she began to formulate a declination.

However, she wasn't given the opportunity to do so. "Oh, how lovely!" her mother gushed. "I'll go grab your shawl!" She stood up from the table more quickly than Cordia had ever remembered seeing her move, meeting Frieda on the way out, and gently squeezing her arm as if they shared some secret that Cordia was not privy to."

Cordia closed her eyes in concentration, trying to come up with any polite excuse she could think of. As her mother wrapped her shawl around her shoulders, nothing came to mind. She heard Carey push his chair back from the table, and she realized she was trapped. Her eyelids fluttered open to see him offering her his hand, and she reluctantly pushed her chair back and stood. Her mother grabbed her shoulders and squeezed.

Refusing to take his hand, Cordia turned and made her way to the door. Carey followed, smiling at her parents and giving her mother a cordial nod. He made it to the door before Cordia, and politely opened it for her, allowing her to pass through first. The air was still a bit chilly for an early May evening. The sun had set, but a full moon and several stars were enough to light the path in front of the Pike house. It had been a very long time since Cordia had been invited on a stroll with a gentleman suitor, and the thought of walking down the lane with Carey, the same way that she had done so with Jaris, brought back melancholy memories, so she remained in a somber silence for a few moments before he finally spoke.

"Lovely evening, isn't it Miss Cordia?" he asked. He was walking on her left side so that his right arm, his only arm, was near her, and she anticipated that, eventually, he would offer it to her. Despite his disability, Carey seemed to do everything any other man could do, and it was quite easy for her and others to forget that he had returned from war less than whole.

She peered up at the stars for a moment, considering the question. If he were speaking of the works of God that surrounded them, then, yes, it was a lovely evening. If he were referring to the company, her answer would be far different. Finally, she replied simply, "The sky is gorgeous."

"So it is," he agreed without so much as glancing up. "As are you, Miss Cordia," he added, trying a bit of charm.

Ignoring his comment and hoping to remind him a bit of the sorrow that hung over her now as she made a familiar journey with a less familiar individual, she responded by saying, "Sometimes, when I look up at the stars, I pretend that one of them is Jaris, lookin' down at me from heaven. It's my way of keepin' him right here with us." She was staring intently into the heavens, one eye slightly closed as if squinting would somehow help her to focus more on whichever star she believed to be Jaris.

Carey did not feign sympathy. By nature, he was uninterested in pretending to be empathetic when he was not. Coldly, he stated, "It's been over a year-and-a-half now, hasn't it? I'm sure that Jaris has found happiness that you are moving on with your life, and despite missing him, as I do, he knows that you cannot possibly spend the rest of your life dwelling on losing him."

"Ah, and there it is," she gasped, slowing her stride for a moment and staring at him as intently as she dared. "I knew the true Carey Adams was still in there and had not been replaced by the chivalrous leader you are pretendin' to be. Oh, you may think you can fool everybody—my mother, my father, the rest of the town. But don't you forget, I know you."

"I haven't the slightest idea what you're implying, Miss Cordia," he replied, placing his hand on her arm rather forcefully. "I'm not living any charade. I am who I have always been. Perhaps you have never noticed the good in me because, for so long, you've been hung up on who I was as a boy. Well, that, my dear, was longer ago than I can even fathom, and if you insist on thinkin' of me as a youngster picking legs off of crawdads and shootin' at birds with my sling-shot, then, yes, I am always goin' to seem like a cruel and devious individual to you. But that is not who I am today, my dear. I wish you could see that."

It was all she could do to keep from laughing in his face. "Carey, I can remember you torturing animals as a teenager, which wasn't all that long ago. You trapped me down by the river when I was eight and you were fourteen, and you wouldn't let me go back to the house unless I showed you my knickers! If Jaris hadn't come along, I don't know what you would've done. Oh, I know who you really are; I know plenty." The feeling of his hand on her arm was almost too much for her, and it was all she could do to keep from knocking it away.

"I wasn't going to harm you, Cordia," he said as calmly as he could muster. "I only did that because I liked you, not because I was trying to scare you or injure you. I was jealous, jealous of how much you seemed to like Jaris and of all the time he spent with you. That's all. It was completely innocent."

Cordia's memory served her well, and she could distinctly remember fearing that he was going to hurt her in some way that she could not, at the time, even understand. She refused to believe his story now; yet, she also knew it made no difference. Whatever his intentions were, and she shuddered to think of what they might be, he was not going to be able to persuade her in his favor regardless of what sort of sweet talking he might resort to.

"Listen, Cordia," he began, slipping his arm through hers. She fought the urge to keep from jerking her arm away. "I have had my eye on you for years. When Jaris was here, of course, I said nothing. I would never consider trying to come between my own cousin and the woman he loved. Now that he is gone, however, well, I think you should know, I am interested in pursuing you as my wife. And I intend to ask your father for his permission to formally court you."

With that, Cordia halted, and spinning to face him, responded, "You're going to need more than just my father's permission for that, Carey Adams. You're gonna need mine, too, and I can tell you right now, the answer is no. There's no way in this world that I would ever consider courtin' you, certainly never marry you. I am not at all interested. Now, if you'll excuse me, I am not feeling well, and I will be headed back to my home and to my bed."

As she turned to go, he abruptly caught her arm and slowly but firmly pulled her back to face him. "Cordia, why do you have to make everything so difficult? Don't you know how much your parents admire me? The idea of having you still marry within the Adams family is all they want for you. Of course, your father will give his permission. And, of course, you will consent, because you're a respectful daughter who loves her parents. And let's not forget, you're getting of an age now where your options are beginning to dwindle. Do you think that anyone else in this town is going to dare pursue the fiancée of the beloved Jaris Adams? Now, let's not be hasty, darlin'. I can provide a nice life for you. In return, you will be my beautiful little wife. Perfectly dressed, perfectly spoken, the hostess of all major events in this town, and a loving mother to our numerous children. It may not be what you think you want for yourself right now, but you have my assurance, there's no one out there lingering who is going to make a more suitable husband for you."

The words she longed to spit into his face were choked in the back of her throat. How she yearned to let him know how incredibly wrong he truly was. And yet, she could not. She had promised Will she would say nothing, to any one, until he returned. As difficult as it may be to keep that promise, she intended to do so. Biting her tongue, she pulled her arm away from him, and hurried back toward her house. He followed a few steps behind her, saying no more, a knowing smirk on his handsome face. For Carey, it was just a matter of time before Cordia would be his at last.

THE BATTLES LEADING up to the siege of Vicksburg were bloody and had put a strain on Will's division. He had recently been promoted to captain and was leading a company. Though the position had been offered to him several times before, he had not accepted because he did not want the responsibility of having the lives of other men in his hands. However, after the Battle of Raymond when they had lost their captain, he had been all but ordered to assume the responsibility, so he had reluctantly accepted this time. Now, perched on a hill outside of Vicksburg, congregating with other leaders, he wasn't sure exactly what he had gotten himself into.

It was May 21, 1863, and the plan they were devising was to be carried out the next day. From the beginning, all involved had known that it would not be an easy assignment. Yet, they recognized that, if they could find a way to force Pemberton and his troops out of Vicksburg, they would have the port city at last, and with it, control of the Mississippi River. Controlling the river meant monitoring supplies, and without being able to use the waterway to transport materials, weapons, and troops, the Confederate Army would be all but defeated in the Western Theater.

The plan was to begin a cannon bombardment at approximately six o'clock the next morning. After that, part of Sherman's division would advance down a narrow road, known locally as Graveyard Road, and attempt to use ladders and makeshift planks to infiltrate the fortress around Vicksburg. By concentrating all of their attacking forces in a small area, they hoped to overpower the lesser Confederate forces. However, though the Rebels were outnumbered, they held the high ground and were entrenched behind substantial fortifications.

Will was grateful that he had not been included amongst the 150 men chosen to make the primary attack. Instead, his company, under the command of Colonel T. Kilby Smith, awaited orders to attack for quite some time. Once they began to move forward, Brig. Gen. James M. Tuttle's men were only able to come within about 100 yards of their objective. Smith's were placed near Green's Redan, which was near the southern flank of Stockade Redan. From their location, Will ordered his men to pour heavy fire into the Confederate line. Though they were successful in covering the Confederates with plenty of rounds of ammunition, it made no difference for the assault as a whole. A series of miscommunicated information between Gen. Grant and his field commanders led to an unsuccessful attempt from the Union Army in moving the Confederates from their highly fortified position. By the evening of May 22, it was quite clear that Grant and his men needed to prepare for a siege.

May 30th, 1863

Dearest Cordia,

I hope this letter finds you well. We are held fast against the fortifications of Vicksburg, Mississippi, unable to go forward through the Confederate battlements and not inclined to fall back until this city is ours. Gen. Grant seems quite determined to take Vicksburg back into Union hands and regain control of the mighty Mississippi River.

So we are digging in. Our orders are simple—dig. I believe our generals are under the impression that we can find a way to burrow under Vicksburg and poke our heads up near the center of town, sneaking up on the enemy thusly. I don't suppose this will work, but I do think we are well enough supplied that we can wait the Rebs out. We still have reinforcements cutting off the exits to the south of the city. This will leave Pemberton and his men little choice but to surrender or start an unhealthy diet of stray dogs and shoe leather. While I have little sympathy for the fighting men of the Confederate cause, I do feel very sorry for the citizens of Vicksburg who find themselves trapped between two warring armies. I do hope that none of the innocents are hurt or killed by the bullets and cannon fire we continue to rain down on our enemies.

So, my love, it appears I will be spending the next several weeks, if not months, digging and shooting and praying that the enemy surrenders. Should you have some free time on your hands, please consider visiting Vicksburg. It is a lovely town, if you like the stench of rotting horses. I jest of course. I hope this letter finds you safe at home with your friends and family.

I cannot tell you how badly I long to see your beautiful face, to smell your sweet perfume, to hold your soft hand in mine. If only Lincoln would take our Gen. Grant and let him take his turn against Gen. Robert E. Lee in the east. Then, perhaps, our competent commander could finally successfully end the victories for the Army of Northern Virginia once and for all, and this war would finally be over. As you know, my enlistment is up in a few short months. At this time, I do not know if I will be compelled to stay or if I shall return to Missouri for a spell. I will look to hear from you how my dear sister's health is treating her before making that decision. As much as I would like to cast this cruel war aside and be done with it, it is very difficult to leave these men who have fought alongside me so bravely.

I have received several letters from you of late, all of which are greatly appreciated. Thank you for sending word of Julia and the rest of my family. I hope to see all of you very soon.

All my love,
Will

Chapter Twelve

AUGUST 1863

JULIA SOUNDED AWFUL. Even though Cordia had brought letters from Will to read to her, the poor girl had coughed and gasped most of the way through them. Eventually, Margaret had sent Cordia home, telling her it wasn't safe for her to be in Julia's presence while she was having one of her spells. Now, with the scorching August sun blazing overhead, she made her way back home, hopeful that Julia would soon recover and considering whether or not she should send word to Will, though she did not want to worry him if she didn't have to. She knew there was very little he could do for her from Mississippi, and she was hopeful that Julia could hold on until he returned. She believed wholeheartedly that Julia would make a full recovery if only she had the opportunity to see her loving brother again.

As Cordia pulled into the drive that led to the barn, she noticed a familiar horse tied outside of the stables. She found it rather odd that Carey Adams would be at their house this early on a Wednesday afternoon. It wasn't quite super time yet, and though he had been a frequent guest of late, he usually didn't arrive until much later in the day. She also noticed that her father's cart was in the barn, which meant that he was also home. At first, her heart caught in her throat, afraid they had some terrible news to tell her. But then she realized that no one had any idea that she was in love with Will. If something happened to him, she would have to find out from Julia or his aunt. Her parents would never think to break such news on her lightly.

Neither would Carey Adams. He would probably be sufficiently delighted to find out that something awful had happened to Will, simply because Carey seemed to be pleased anytime another human being suffered. The thought of entering her own home and being faced with him was enough to make her sick to her stomach.

He had been courting her for months now. She knew her father had approved, and while she had protested several times, her mother always ended up in tears, and Cordia reluctantly gave in. After all, he was always polite, never tried to kiss her or acted inappropriately; he only tried to hold her hand and told her stories about how perfect their life would be someday when they were married. He had visions of a legion of children she would have to birth and care for, and since she was fully aware of how those children would have to come into existence, she quickly changed the subject each time he broached it so as to keep any mental images at bay. Now, as she climbed down from her seat and began to put the horses and wagon away, she saw Frieda coming out of the side door to the house either to help her or move her along. Either way, she knew Frieda's assistance would allow her to join Mr. Adams inside more readily, so she did her best to dilly-dally.

"Miss Cordia," Frieda said, marching over as quickly as her short, stocky legs could carry her, "Your father requests your presence inside directly." She took the reins from Cordia's hands and proceeded to take over.

"That's quite all right," Cordia replied, attempting to usurp her way back into the process. "I don't need any help."

Frieda knew exactly what was happening. "Now, Cordia," she insisted, stopping in her tracks and turning to face her young mistress, "You best just go ahead and make your way in there now. Ain't no use in prolonging the situation."

"What does he want this time?" Cordia asked, almost afraid to hear the answer.

Frieda shook her head. Though she didn't always agree with Cordia's headstrong ways, she did want the girl to be happy, and she was very much assured that Carey Adams was not the one who could make her so. Nevertheless, she was under strict orders to get Miss Cordia inside as quickly as possible. "Well, darlin', why don't you go ahead and make your way into the house and find out already?"

Cordia sighed. She knew that stalling would do her no good in the end. Hanging her head, she slowly turned and made her way inside. She used the same side door that Frieda had exited through and was hoping to have the opportunity to at least freshen her dress and make herself a bit more presentable before announcing her presence. As much as she didn't care what Carey thought of her appearance, it would give her the opportunity to take a little more time before having to face him. However, her mother heard the door closing and yelled for her to join them in the parlor.

Making her way into the room, Cordia could see that her mother was serving both her father and Carey tea from their best service. "There you are, darling," she said sitting down the teapot and making her way over to Cordia. She took her gently by the arm and led her over to the duvet where Carey was sitting. "Lt. Adams is here to see us. Isn't that nice, Cordia?"

Carey nodded politely in her direction, holding a teacup in his hand. Her mother poured a cup for her as well and handed it to her before sitting down in a chair next to her father. He was smoking a cigar, a grin plastered across his face, and Cordia couldn't help but look from one to the next, wondering what was going on.

"Cordia," her father began, setting his teacup down on the small table next to his chair. "Carey stopped by to see me this afternoon at work. We had thought about waiting until after church Sunday to share the good news with you, but the more we discussed it, the more I realized, life is short. Why put off until tomorrow what can give us joy today?"

Cordia was confused. She shook her head slowly, indicating to her father that she didn't understand what he was saying. Carey spoke then, also setting his teacup down. "Cordia, I was sharing with your father how wonderful it has been for me to get to know you again these past several months. You and I have spent quite a bit of time together recently, and you should know how fond I've become of you." He reached for her hand and, though she was bewildered, she offered it to him, unsure as to precisely what he intended to do. "Cordia, you are a remarkable young lady. Beautiful, intelligent, and an important member of the community. Your father and I have spoken, and he agrees that you and I make a fine match."

A shriek of delight from her mother caught Cordia's attention for a brief moment, and she turned her head to see her mother was crying. Feeling as if she were in a dream, Cordia glanced at her father, who was also beaming, and then back to Carey. He had a gleam in his eye, as if to say, "I always win." He let go of her hand for just a moment and began reaching around in the inside pocket of his uniform. "Cordia, darling, will you make me a very happy man by consenting to be my wife?"

Even as he was slipping the ring on her finger, Cordia's mother was up out of her chair, flying across the room and embracing her. "Oh, Cordia, I'm so thrilled!" she gushed. Her father was standing now, patting Carey on the back and shaking his hand.

Cordia sat on the sofa, frozen, glancing at Carey over her mother's shoulder. Suddenly, there was a noise at the door, and neighbors began to pour into the living room. Cordia stood, shocked to see so many of her friends and acquaintances. Each of them stopped to hug her and tell them how very happy they were for her. Even Margaret Adams was there, and though it was evident she had been crying, she congratulated Cordia and told her she was so glad she would be a part of their family at last.

The next few hours were a whirlwind of gifts and baked goods, congratulator hugs, followed by a meal, piano playing, and dancing. Cordia was obligated to dance with her new fiancé though it was awkward to say the least, not just because of his missing arm but more so because she could not stand to be held so closely to him. Everyone clapped and cheered, some insisting that the new couple kiss, to which Cordia was able to draw the line, based on her own modesty.

At the end of the evening, the visitors slowly started to file out. Cordia had found her way out to the porch swing, where she was sitting with Susannah, who was going on and on about how unfair it was that Cordia's husband would never have to go off to fight again. Cordia was lost in her own thoughts and barely noticed exactly who was stopping by to tell her they were leaving until Susannah finally stood and hugged her goodbye, her little ones pulling on her skirts as they made their way down the porch steps.

Carey slowly sauntered over and took a seat next to her on the swing. He said nothing at first, giving her a moment to gather her thoughts. When she did not acknowledge him, he finally said, "Well, I hope you understand that this is for the best."

She could not help but chuckle. "Whatever do you mean? I didn't even say yes."

"Well, of course you did," he replied smartly. "All of those people think you did anyway. Now, what are you going to do? Call off the wedding and break your poor mother's heart? Don't be ridiculous."

Cordia said nothing. All she could think about all evening was how she was going to find a way to get out of this sham. She also knew it was imperative that she write to Will immediately, in case word got to him that she was engaged to Carey. She needed to make sure he understood precisely what had happened so that he was not at all confused or concerned. "I've got to hand it to you, Lt. Adams," she said indignantly. "You sure did find a way to manipulate this situation into your favor."

Carey smiled and nodded. "I always win, Cordia," he replied smartly.

Her immediate response was, "Tell that to the Union soldier who took your arm," but she did not say it aloud. There was no point. Instead she said quietly, "I'm going off to bed. If I don't see you again for quite some time, that will be all right with me."

He chuckled softly, knowing she would be seeing a lot of him for the rest of her life. "Have a lovely evening, darling," he replied. Then, standing quickly and grabbing her arm, he pulled her in closely and said, "I look forward to the day when we shall retire to the bedroom together."

Cordia yanked her arm away in disgust. Again, holding her tongue, she turned sharply and made her way inside. Her mother was standing nearby, arms open wide, ready to congratulate her again. Cordia only glanced in her direction before climbing up the stairs and slamming her bedroom door.

"Must have had a lover's quarrel," her father supposed, patting his wife on the shoulder. "I'm sure she'll get over it. You know our Cordy."

Though she was disappointed and a bit concerned, Jane nodded and went about helping Frieda clean up, completely oblivious to the tears her daughter was shedding upstairs.

Cordia did everything she could to keep from completely saturating the paper with the teardrops that were streaming from her face as she began to write to Will. She knew his enlistment was almost up, and she had been praying desperately for months, for years even, that he would return home once he was free to do so. She knew that it would be difficult for him to walk away from the men he had been fighting alongside for years, but she could see no other way to escape Carey's clutches without breaking her poor mother's heart and disappointing so many people.

Dearest Will,

I hope this letter finds you safe and well. While I am generally inclined to keep my correspondence light and positive, there is a situation I must relay to you, and I hope that it neither finds you offended or dismayed. It is difficult to explain precisely the events that have led to the current situation, but I will do my best to elucidate the occurrences as they have transpired. Some months ago, Carey Adams asked my father for permission to court me. He has fooled many a soul by portraying himself as an outstanding member of the community, and my parents were thrilled at the opportunity he provided me to finally find a replacement for dear Jaris. Reluctantly, I gave my consent, not because I find him any less repulsive now than I ever have, but because I knew that, should I decline, my poor mother's heart would break. So, I have been doing my due diligence, allowing him to accompany me on strolls and carriage rides, that sort of thing, for several months. I assure you that there has been no romantic sentiment exchanged whatsoever. I have had (and still do have) every intention of confessing our relationship to my parents upon your return. However, I have said nothing to them or to anyone else, as we have discussed. Your dear sister and I have hardly spoken since this charade has begun, and I am not sure if she is even aware that Carey believes that I am his betrothed. Nevertheless, this evening, Mr. Adams found a way to ask me for my hand and persuade the entire town that I had said yes, when in fact, I never answered at all. There was a party with singing and dancing and all sort of celebration. And there I sat, with this hideous ring upon my finger knowing full well I had never consented—nor shall I ever consent—to be his wife. I shall put off coming clean until you return unless you decide to re-enlist, at which time, I will be forced to speak the truth so as to avoid becoming the wife of Lt. Carey Adams. I hope that you will forgive me for not carrying our secret, though I'm certain you can understand why. Please, my love, write back soon so that I know my actions have not upset you and that you understand why I have done the things that I have done. I look forward to hearing from you soon, and I pray that your heart will lead you home directly so that we may begin our life together.

All my love,

Cordia

The next morning at breakfast, Cordia's mother wanted to know if everything was okay between herself and Carey. Though it seemed like a prime opportunity to completely enlighten her mother, Cordia did not do so. She simply replied that nothing had changed between herself and Lt. Adams; their relationship was just as it had always been. Jane took this as good news and finished the meal with a smile on her face.

As soon as the post office had opened that morning, Cordia had been there, letter in hand, ready to inform Will of everything that had transpired. "Good morning, Mr. Wheeler. How are you this morning?"

The older man smiled at her, his spectacles sliding down his nose. "Just fine now, my dear. Long as this sun don't burn me alive!"

It was intolerably hot outside again already, and Cordia completely understood the sentiment. "Yes, I am certainly looking forward to some nice fall weather! Mr. Wheeler, I need to get this letter out right away, if you don't mind, sir," she said handing over the letter she had penned to Will just the night before.

"Yes, Miss," he replied, taking it from her and checking the postage. "It'll go out this afternoon. It was lots easier to get mail to Grant's folks when they weren't movin' around so much. Now that Vicksburg has fallen, well, might be a little tougher," he added, glancing down at the recipient.

"Yes, sir. Thank you, kindly," she said, nodding and smiling at the sweet older gentleman. She briskly made her way out the door and back toward home. Though she had considered going to call on Susannah, she decided not to. The last thing she felt like doing was discussing her wedding plans.

Just as Cordia turned the corner, the door to the post office flew open again. Mr. Wheeler looked up, and realizing who it was said, "Oh, you just missed your fiancée!"

Carey nodded, surveying the room to see who else might be present. One customer was turning to exit, and he knew he would have the opportunity to rather candidly discuss with Mr. Wheeler why he had come. "Yes, I know," he replied. "May I ask what my love was doing here so early on a Thursday morning?"

Mr. Wheeler chuckled. "Same thing most people do here, mailing a letter."

Carey wasn't amused. "Yes, I sort of inferred that. Can you please tell me who the recipient is?"

Mr. Wheeler looked a bit confused but saw no reason to withhold the information. "She writes to her friend Julia's brother quite often, Will Tucker. You know 'm, Jaris's other cousin."

Of course, Carey knew precisely whom he was speaking of. He had watched Cordia go in and out of the post office dozens of times while he was drilling on the adjoining square. Being a suspicious man by nature, and an incredibly jealous one, he realized he needed to get his hands on that letter. "Mr. Wheeler," he said, leaning in and lowering his voice to just above a whisper. "I am going to need to confiscate that letter and any other letters that Ms. Pike may attempt to send to Mr. Tucker. I have reason to believe that the safety of the town may be at stake."

Mr. Wheeler's eyes widened. "Due to Miss Cordia Pike? Your fiancée? You don't say?"

Carey's patience was waning. "Dammit, Wheeler," he spat, banging his hand against the counter. "Do not ask me to disclose confidential military information. It is vital that you follow my directives. Otherwise, I don't want to think about the possibilities. Please, do not jeopardize the safety of our citizenry!"

Stunned, Wheeler handed the letter over to Carey, his eyes frozen open in astonishment. Carey took the letter and slipped it into his shirt breast pocket. "Thank you," he said gruffly. "I will be back weekly to check for more correspondence. Be sure to collect all of them; do you understand?" The old man nodded obediently. "Very good."

Carey turned to leave, the letter burning a hole in his pocket. Just as he reached the door, he turned back to face the postmaster who still had not moved. "And, Wheeler," he added, "this information is highly confidential. Do not disclose the matters of this conversation to anyone. Understand?"

Mr. Wheeler nodded his head again as Carey flew out the door, practically running into his Aunt Margaret in the process. "Oh, Carey!" she said smiling. "How are you?"

Carey was extremely disgruntled at finding out that Cordia had been corresponding with Will and in a hurry to read the letter. The last thing he wanted to do was exchange pleasantries with his aunt. Nevertheless, he had a reputation to uphold, so he took a deep breath, plastered a winning smile on his face and declared, "Aunt Margaret! How lovely to see you!"

"Yes, you as well. I was just about to drop a letter to Will. I mentioned you in it!" she teased.

This had Carey's attention. "Oh? How's that?" he asked.

"Yes, I let him know all about how you and Cordia are engaged. He'll be so happy for you both, I'm sure. Cordia's become such a good friend to Julia these past years. It's a shame she can't come and visit, what with Julia's illness flaring up. Hopefully the cooler weather this fall will improve her disposition."

Carey had stopped listening after the first sentence, a broad smile brightening his face. "Oh, yes, lovely," he exclaimed, hoping that his response fit his aunt's entire comment and not just the first portion. "Well, if you'll excuse me, I have to get back to the troops."

Margaret was a bit puzzled, not exactly sure what Carey thought was "lovely," but she nodded. "Have a pleasant day!" she called after him as he made his way back toward the men he commanded.

Carey chuckled quietly to himself. Not only was he holding the only potential cry for help his betrothed could possibly hope to muster, his aunt had taken care of sending word to his possible rival that Miss Pike was no longer on the market. Though he was still curious to read Cordia's letter and see precisely what was going on between the two of them, he was assured that, once Will received his aunt's letter, it would no longer matter.

He had a feeling that Cordia's letter would leave him a bit nauseated, however, and after reading through it quickly and finding his suspicions were true, he crumpled it in his fist. He had not quite reached the soldiers he had left drilling on the square, and as much as he wanted to rip the paper into tiny pieces, he had no way of disposing of them just now. He shoved the document back into his pocket, planning to watch it burn in his wood stove later that evening.

AFTER VICKSBURG HAD FALLEN in early July, Will's company was back to its usual routine: travel around a bit, encamp, engage the enemy, repeat. Though there were no major battles, there were plenty of skirmishes and plenty of opportunity to get shot. His enlistment would be up on September 1, and should he choose to do so, he could go home. Back to Missouri—back to his sister and to Cordia. Though he longed for the familiarity of home and the peace it would bring, he could not help but feel that he had not yet found atonement for his brother's death. As long as even one Rebel stood against the Union, he found it hard to leave the war effort.

And, yet, he knew Julia was not doing well. His sister did not write as much as she used to, and when she did, the correspondence was not as long. Clearly, she was struggling. Cordia did not mention her as often, which led him to believe she was not able to visit as frequently, probably due to Julia's illness. His Aunt Margaret also avoided the subject of Julia, which led Will to the conclusion that she must be fairly ill.

It had been a few weeks since he had received a letter from Cordia, so when the mail carrier stopped him on his way back to his tent, the late August sun beating down upon him, he was certain this letter must be from her. But it was not. Since it was from his Aunt Margaret, he was not as hurried to read it and placed it in his pocket to look at later.

It wasn't until much later that evening that he pulled the letter out to read it by the light of a kerosene lantern. As he read the later portion of the letter, the devastating news almost overwhelmed him, and it became extremely difficult to control himself and not to have an emotional outburst in front of his entire company.

August 8, 1863

Dear Will,

I hope you are doing well. I know it is intolerable hot out there, and I can't imagine what it must be like, walking around in those wool uniforms, carrying everything you own, with the threat of engaging the enemy around every corner. I pray that you are doing well and that the Lord walks beside you wherever you journey.

Your Uncle has finished planting the west fields, and they will be ready for harvest before too long. It took all three boys a'helping him this time around. They are getting so big and strong. It's hard to believe that Zachariah is now old enough to enlist. Of course, I will not allow him to do so. Still, he has become a strong young man, much like his older brother, and I am very proud of him in so many ways. The younger two boys look up to him and try to be like their older brothers, and I find it amusing to see them strut around as if they were grown men. They miss you very much and send their love.

Julia longs to see you. She is doing her best to hang in there and stay strong, but she is having a difficult time of it these past few months. I know that seeing your face would do her well. If there is a way that you could come, even just for a bit, before you re-enlist, if that is your plan, I hope that you will consider it. I know how important this war is to you, but I hope you will remember your poor baby sister at home who is alone and ill. She would find great strength in seeing you again.

On a lighter note, Jaris's other cousin, Carey, has become engaged to be married recently. I find it a bit trying that he will be marrying Miss Cordia Pike, Jaris's previous flame, though I am very happy to have Cordia in our family at last. Still, I can't help but think of what might have been. But I guess that's what any mother would be thinking. Cordia is a fine young woman, and Carey is lucky to have her. He is also doing extremely well as commander of the city guard, despite losing his arm in battle. I hope that, should you choose to return here, you may have the opportunity to get to know him better as I am sure the two of you could be very good friends.

WELL, I suppose this letter is long enough for now. I hope that you are well and that we will see you soon. You know you are always welcome in our home for as long as you may need to stay.
All of my love,
Aunt Margaret

WILL TOOK a deep breath and lay back on the one tattered blanket he owned. He read and re-read that paragraph so many times, not believing he could possibly be seeing it correctly. He felt as if he had been punched in the stomach, and it took him several hours before he could even respond to his bunkmates, who could plainly see something was wrong. He was finally able to assure them that everything was fine, and he just wasn't feeling well. He certainly could not tell them that his fiancée had moved on since no one had any idea he even had a sweetheart waiting for him at home.

The next day, Will woke up early with a new resolve. Despite feeling as if his entire world had crumbled around him, Will had to find a way to go on. He knew he must simply put Cordia out of his mind. He had no earthly idea how she could possibly do such a thing to him. He was under the impression that she loathed Carey Adams, and now she was engaged to marry him without so much as a letter to let him know she was no longer interested in being his wife. And yet, a small part of him felt that, perhaps, he should have seen this coming. After all, wouldn't Jaris have found himself in a similar position should he still be alive?

Even though he never wanted to see Cordia Pike again, he knew what he needed to do. If Julia was so sick that his aunt was asking him to come home, he had to make arrangements to do so. As much as he wanted to stay and see this bloody war to the end, now may be his only opportunity for years to take advantage of his freedom. His colonel had been asking him for weeks what he intended to do, and now he knew for sure. He needed to return to Julia as quickly as possible. As soon as the other men were stirring about, he made his way over to his colonel's tent to inform him of the decision he had made.

Chapter Thirteen

THE FIREPLACE BLAZED AWAY as Cordia sat in the straight-backed chair in her bedroom, her mother brushing out her long plaits of hair, just as she had done when she was a small child. The dressing mannequin across the room was an ominous presence, dressed as it was in the now nearly finished wedding dress. It had been almost two months since she had sent word to Will asking him for his consent to let her disclose their relationship so that she could terminate her engagement to Carey, and yet had heard nothing. Every day, she stopped by the post office, hopeful that Mr. Wheeler would have some news for her, but each time, he shrugged, reluctantly. Cordia was curious to know whether or not Julia had heard from her brother, but she had been so ill recently, Cordia had scarcely been allowed to visit. The one time she had stopped by a few weeks ago, she hesitated to mention him because Julia was already struggling to breathe, and she didn't want to upset her.

As Jane ran the brush through her hair, Cordia contemplated bringing up the subject of Carey. Perhaps she could find a way to break off the engagement without mentioning Will at all. Yet, knowing how much her mother wanted this marriage to take place made it extremely difficult for Cordia. She didn't want to disappoint her mother. Though she wasn't sure how she would react to knowing Cordia was in love with Will, at least, she thought her mother would have some satisfaction in knowing Cordia wouldn't die an old maid.

Jane began to braid Cordia's hair, a sign that she was almost finished, so Cordia decided to broach the subject and feel her mother out. "Mama," she asked quietly, "Were you in love with Daddy when the two of you got married?"

The brush paused for a moment. "Oh, Cordia, what a strange question," Jane replied. "Now, don't you worry about your daddy and me. We may have our differences, but we get along just fine."

Cordia sighed. "No, Mama, that's not what I meant at all. I was just curious how you knew he was the one for you."

"Well," Jane pondered, "Your daddy was a fairly persistent suitor. He used to come a'callin' at least once or twice a week. Course, we didn't court that long before we got married. None of this goin' on for almost a year like you and Lt. Adams. I believe I loved your father when we first got married. But love is a peculiar thing, Cordia. Sometimes you don't know exactly what it is at first, and then it begins to grow on you."

Cordia gave that a bit of thought and realized, if that were truly the case, her mother had no idea what true love really was at all. There had never been a question in Cordia's mind that she was in love with Will Tucker. She knew that from the very beginning. In a way, she felt a little sorry for her mother. Perhaps, she had married her Jaris. "Mama, I'm just not sure . . ." she began.

But Jane was finished with her hair and had changed the subject. "There you go, darling. You look so beautiful," she said studying her daughter's face in the mirror in front of them. "I can't wait to see you walk down the aisle. You're going to make the loveliest bride the folks of Barton County ever did see!" Her mother bustled about the room, putting the hairbrush away and tending to the fire. "Now, you get on to bed so you can get some rest. We've got a lot of work to do tomorrow for the wedding. It's less than three weeks away!"

Sighing, Cordia climbed into bed. She could hear the howling wind out her window, and she couldn't help but feel it was crying out a warning to her. She had less than three weeks to call off a sham engagement to a man she couldn't tolerate and to find some reason as to why her true fiancé was not responding to her letters. As she lay in her warm bed, she began to think about how much better off she was than the poor troops in their encampments and hoped that Will was sleeping safe and sound, wherever he might be. She was resolved that, in the morning, she would pay a visit to the Adams Farm and inquire as to whether anyone in his family had heard from him. At least, she may be able to answer one of her questions.

The next morning, Cordia was up with the sun, baking a loaf of pumpkin bread to take with her to the Adams Farm. She wished that she could ask Margaret the same question she had asked her mother the night before, as she thought she might receive a more suitable answer; however, considering Cordia had almost married Margaret's own son, she didn't feel as though it was a suitable topic for discussion. She was certainly going to find out if Margaret or Julia had heard anything from Will, no matter what suspicions her questions might gather.

The ride out to the farm was a bit chilly. Cordia had her coat wrapped tightly around her. Despite the fact that it was only late October, the weather seemed particularly ferocious already, perhaps a sign of a hard winter to come. She pulled the wagon in and tied the horses up to the hitching post. Though it was still rather early in the morning, the Adams family was certainly awake. She could hear the sounds of family chores being performed both inside and outside of the homestead. She climbed the porch and knocked on the door, hoping she was not intruding, though she had always felt welcome here.

A few moments later, Margaret opened the door, a broad smile on her face. "Cordia!" she exclaimed. "It's so nice to see you!" She embraced Cordia warmly, gesturing for her to come. "How are you, dear? I bet you've been so busy planning the wedding. It seems like it's been ages since we've had a visit from you.

Cordia stepped in, offering the bread to Margaret before taking off her coat and hanging it near the door. "I know, I have been busy. I've also been hoping to give Julia some time to recuperate. How is she doing?"

Margaret took the pumpkin bread. "Oh, thank you! You didn't have to do that. You're so thoughtful." She paused for a moment, considering Cordia's question. "She has her good days and her bad days. She has not fully recovered from her last spell, but the doctor does say he thinks she is on the mend. He says any alleviation of stress and strain is a positive for her, so we are hopeful that things will continue to improve."

Cordia was glad to hear that Julia was making progress, though she wasn't quite clear she fully understood what Margaret was referring to. "Would it be possible for me to see her?" she asked, hopefully.

Margaret sighed, walking in to the kitchen to put the pumpkin bread on the counter. "I think a short visit would be just fine. I do worry that she is contagious, however, so that's something we'll have to be careful of. I'm not sure if you might be able to catch that cough from her or not."

Julia's room was in the back of the house, and the women had to cross the kitchen to get there. Margaret tapped lightly on the door before opening it just a hair and peeking her head in. Julia stirred a bit, and Margaret opened the door more widely, allowing Cordia to step in.

Seeing who it was, Julia attempted to sit up a bit, still groggy with sleep and clearly not feeling well, as Cordia could see from the color of her pale skin. Still, she smiled with excitement. "Cordia!" she said as she entered. "It's been so long since I've seen you! How are you?"

Margaret came in as well and stood near the door. Cordia crossed over and sat down on the edge of Julia's bed, keeping her distance but reaching the vicinity of her friend. "I'm well, darling! How are you?"

Julia nodded, "I'm doing much better now. It's so nice to see you! What have you been doing?" She coughed a little then, holding a hand-kerchief over her mouth. Cordia was happy to see that there were no droplets of blood on it when she pulled it away. Still, any coughing spell at all was a strain on Julia, and she looked more tired just from those few moments of exertion.

Cordia wasn't sure if Julia knew about her engagement or not. She was wearing Carey's ring on her finger, but she had her hands folded, as she usually did, so that no one could see the ring. She glanced up at Margaret, who shook her head, as if to indicate that she had not told Julia about the upcoming wedding. Cordia wasn't sure why that might be, but she saw no reason to mention it now, not until she had the opportunity to talk to Margaret in private. "I've been busy, that's certain. I've been working with Dr. Walters, honing my nursing skills. I've been knitting blankets and socks for the troops, spending time with Susannah, gathering information about the soldiers, that sort of thing. Thinkin' on you, for certain, prayin' you'd be feelin' better soon."

Julia smiled. "I've missed you, but I know they didn't want you to come while I was so sick. I understand that."

Margaret chimed in. "And she can't stay too long this time either, Julia. You need your rest."

Julia shook her head and then began another coughing spell. This one was worse than the last, and Margaret rushed over to steady her frail body as she gyrated with the intents spasms. When the coughing finally came to an end, Margaret said, "I'll go get your medicine," and stepped out into the kitchen to retrieve it.

Not knowing what to say, Cordia just smiled at Julia with concern. Julia was attempting to slow her breathing and did not speak either.

"Here you go," Margaret said, crossing the room and pouring a spoonful of liquid for Julia to swallow. Even from a distance, Cordia could smell the pungent medication, and the odor was revolting. She was glad she was not the one being called upon to force it down. Julia swallowed it quickly and then took a drink from the glass of water next to her on the nightstand.

"This medicine makes her very tired," Margaret remarked to Cordia.

Julia already looked as if she was about to fall asleep, and she had just swallowed the dose. "And it tastes like shoe polish," she added.

Clearly, Cordia would not be able to stay and visit with Julia any longer, as she was starting to doze off. Margaret seemed to indicate that Cordia should exit with her as she went back into the kitchen to put away the medicine. Cordia was reluctant to go. Not only did she miss her friend, she had been hopeful that she would have the opportunity to ask Julia if she had heard from her brother. As she stood to go, she reached over and lightly touched Julia's hand. "Get some rest, sweetheart," she said. "I will come back and visit you soon."

Julia's eyes had glazed over a bit. She was no longer sitting up but had begun to roll back onto her side, away from Cordia. However, as Cordia withdrew her hand, she murmured softly, "Oh, your ring. You're finally wearing it. Will must be so happy." Then, her breathing stilled, and she was out.

Cordia turned quickly to see if Margaret had heard Julia's remark. She was standing in the doorway, one hand on the doorknob, the other pressed against the doorjamb. She had a curious expression on her face, but she did not say anything. Cordia thought, perhaps, she had not caught the last part.

As Cordia entered the kitchen on Margaret's heels, she peered around anxiously, hoping to find a way to engage Margaret in a conversation so that he could ask the question she'd been longing to have answered. As if reading her mind, Margaret began to slice the pumpkin bread and poured two cups of coffee. "Have a seat, darling. I don't get too many opportunities these days to visit with you. I'd love to hear how the wedding planning is a'comin' along."

Cordia went around the side of the table and sat down in the chair she had always sat in when she was visiting. It seemed like so long ago, in those carefree days when she would come in from running around in the backyard, hair a mess, covered with dirt, and sit down for a glass of milk. Those days were long gone now, as was the friend she had played with so hard.

Margaret set coffee and a slice of bread in front of Cordia and sat down across from her. As Cordia studied her face, she realized she appeared to have aged rather quickly these last two years. The weight of the war, the loss of Jaris, the burden of raising a sick niece, had all worn her down. Cordia longed to ask what the true prognosis might be for Julia, but in a way, she feared hearing the answer. If Dr. Walters thought Julia was not going to make it, she didn't really want to know.

Sighing, Margaret spun her coffee cup around on the table, not drinking it. "It gets better, then it gets worse. Some days she's practically normal; other days she can't even sit up. It's . . . hard. It's just very hard to see her struggling."

Cordia nodded, taking a sip of her coffee. Though she had made the pumpkin bread herself and thought it sounded good at the time, she had no appetite. Margaret took a bite, attempting to be polite, but Cordia could tell that she really did not feel like eating either. "We will continue to pray for a quick recovery," she said solemnly.

Again, Margaret nodded. "I had thought that havin' Will come back would fix her, but, I guess I was hoping for a miracle. She's a little better. She really is. But she's got a tough road ahead of her."

Cordia was puzzled. Margaret's words were a bit cryptic, and she wasn't quite sure what she could infer from that statement. "I'm sorry," she said, "Did you say that you thought Will coming back would make her feel better or that you *had thought?*" The tense in such a sentence was critical, and Cordia's confusion was mounting by the moment.

Margaret opened her mouth to explain, an equally confused look on her face, but she did not have to. As she began to speak, the back door opened behind Cordia, and she turned in shock to see Will standing there before her.

Cordia pushed her chair back slightly, her astonishment keeping any words from coming out of her mouth. He glanced in her direction, a look of apprehension on his handsome face, but not of surprise. It seemed he had been working outside the entire time Cordia had been there and had not come in to greet her. He crossed the kitchen, disappeared briefly into an adjoining room, and then walked back outside without so much as speaking to her. Cordia's eyes followed him, but she said nothing, confusion and disbelief crowded her mind, and she was not sure at all what to make of the situation.

As he closed the door behind him, she turned back to Margaret, who also looked similarly confused. Finally, Margaret said, "He's been back for a little over a week. Is there something I should know?"

Cordia felt her heart racing. How was it possible that Will had been back for more than a week, and he had not come to see her? For two years, she had envisioned a tearful reunion, professing their love for each other to the world, and starting their lives together. He hadn't so much as written her to let her know he was coming home. For months, she had worried that something awful had happened, and he had been out of harm's way since at least the beginning of September when his enlistment was up. She could not fathom what could have possibly transpired to make him act this way. Without answering Margaret's question, she flew up from the table, nearly knocking her chair over in the process, and flung open the back door, oblivious to the sharp October wind.

He was chopping wood just a little way from the house, his hat pulled down over his eyes so that she could not even see them. She paused by the lilac bushes a few yards away, not exactly sure what to say and having difficulty holding back her emotions. He seemed to notice that she was there, but he did not stop swinging the ax to acknowledge her, nor did he speak.

Cordia could feel the tears in her eyes. "Will!" she yelled between swings of the ax. He didn't pause to look in her direction, and she began to feel even more frustrated and angry. "Will! Please, come and talk to me! I had no idea you were even home!"

He stopped then, resting the head of the ax on his boot, choosing his words as carefully as he could. "I guess I didn't realize you'd want to know," he replied, two months' worth of exasperation evident in his voice.

Before he could resume the task at hand, she rushed over, completely perplexed as to what he was insinuating. She left a few feet of distance between them, aware that he clearly wanted to keep his space. "Will, what are you talking about?" she asked in dismay. "I've been waiting for you for two years!"

"Really?" he asked, pausing for a moment, one hand resting on the ax, the other on his hip. "Your finger says otherwise, Cordia."

Cordia's eyes widened as she glanced down at the ring on her finger. "What?" she asked, realizing at last what the misconception must be. "You know I don't have feelings for Carey. I wrote you. I told you, I never even said yes."

Will had spent ample time imagining how this conversation might go on his long and arduous trip home. His emotions had gotten the best of him several times, and he had run the gamut from extreme anger at her deception to despair. Now, face to face with the woman he had spent so much time thinking of and longing for throughout the course of his service, he couldn't help but think of what might have been, if only she had been honest with him. There was one thought that kept returning to him time and again, and now, faced with the opportunity to voice it to her, he hesitated. Yet, he couldn't help but say, "I guess I should have known better than to ever get involved with someone as fickle as you Cordia Pike. I realize now, however, that I deserve this. If this is what we were about to put Jaris through, well, then in some ways I envy him that he escaped this torment."

Cordia looked at him in astonishment, her mouth open. "How can you say that?" she asked after a moment. He had turned away from her and was concentrating now on the wood he still needed to chop. It was as if he had not heard a word she had said. "I told you, Will. I don't love Carey. I never have. I hate him! Why won't you listen to me?"

Though Will wanted to believe her, he couldn't, not while she was standing there wearing Carey Adams's ring. After months of lamenting losing her, it wasn't so simple to come home and accept that it was all a misunderstanding. If she truly loved him, how could she ever consent to be someone else's wife? He turned and glanced in her general direction before walking toward the barn, saying only, "Goodbye Cordia. Good luck with the life that you've chosen."

Exasperated, Cordia started to follow him. However, he was walking much faster than she could, her heavy gown weighing her down, and he had made it quite clear that he did not want to speak to her anymore. She could feel the hot tears splashing down her face as she watched him go. Still in a state of disbelief that he was actually home but that she still could not be with him, she realized that, regardless of whether or not Will ever forgave her poor judgment, there was one situation she needed to take care of immediately.

As she turned to walk back to where she had parked the wagon, she realized that Margaret was standing in the yard, near the back door. The expression on her face let Cordia know she had heard everything. For a moment, Cordia considered walking past her without saying a word, but she couldn't do that. The least she could do was apologize, though she knew it would carry little weight. Without meeting her eyes, she whispered, "I am so sorry," before making her way to her wagon and leaving the Adams Farm, possibly forever.

As she rode back to town, she knew she truly was sorry. Not for what had happened between Will and herself; she could never be sorry for that, not even now that it was apparently over. But she was truly sorry for the grief she would have caused to Jaris if he had lived. And, now, she was sorry for the pain she must have caused Margaret and the rest of his family, to learn the truth in such a star-tling and unexpected way must have made the realization that she had never intended to marry Jaris far worse than if Cordia and Will had sat the family down and explained everything to them, the way that Cordia had been intending to do these past two years. None of the conversations she was having this day were anything like she had pictured they would be. The next one probably would not be either, though the rage she felt brewing inside was a consolation for that. She brought the horses to a gallop as she turned them down the road that led to the home Carey shared with his father. Will was certainly correct about one thing, she never should have allowed herself to be placed in such a compromising position, and she had been far too polite for much longer than she should have been. Her parents would just have to accept the fact that she was not marrying Carey Adams. Whether or not this would be enough to bring Will back around, she could not say, but it was a step in the right direction.

The wind was picking up, and Cordia realized she had forgotten her coat. The anger building up inside of her was enough to keep her from becoming too cold, however, and she pressed on, eager to finally have the opportunity to say the words she had been thinking for so very long.

She continued to go over the brief words she had exchanged with Will and was still in disbelief that he had thought for these past two months that she was truly engaged to Carey, that she had picked that scoundrel over her one true love. She still could not fathom how her letters suddenly stopped being delivered to him while, clearly, he was receiving word from someone in town, most likely his Aunt Margaret. Just as she pulled the horses to a halt in front of Carey's house, she realized there was only one person who would be devious enough to confiscate her mail.

She jumped down from the carriage and stormed her way up the short walkway to the front door, giving it a good pounding. She was not sure if he would be home for the noontime meal yet or if he would still be at the square. Either way, she would track him down and set things straight, regardless of who may be present.

Fortunately, she did not have to search further. "Cordia!" Carey exclaimed smiling that wicked smile of his as he pulled open the door. "Whatever brings you here this time of day?"

She didn't bother to come inside. Even as he spoke, she was pulling the ring off of her finger. "How dare you?" she exclaimed, throwing the small circle of gold at him and hitting him squarely in the chest. "You are the most despicable person I have ever met, and please listen carefully when I tell you I never want to lay eyes on you again. Ever!"

He looked puzzled, watching the ring bounce off and roll across the porch. "Now, Cordia, whatever has gotten into your little mind now?" he asked, belittling her.

Cordia could not keep the tears from trailing down her cheeks. The anger and devastation were welling up in her now, and she didn't know if she could even find the words to tell him off. "You know full well what has gotten into my 'little' mind." She shook her head in anger and turned to go.

Carey caught her arm and pulled her back around, forcefully, but Cordia shook her arm loose. Though he was still smirking, his eyes showed that he was beginning to grow angry, and for the first time in several months, he thought there was a possibility she may be serious this time. "Cordia, whatever it is you think I've done, I assure you, you're mistaken. Is this about Will Tucker?"

"You knew he was in town, didn't you? You confiscated my mail. You meddled in my affairs. You had no right to...."

"No right to what? Prevent my fiancée from philandering with another man?" he said, the anger apparent in his voice. He reached out and grabbed her upper arm again, this time with even more intensity, and Cordia winced in pain. "I have every right to do whatever it takes to control you, Cordia Pike. You see, you're mine now."

Cordia attempted to shake her arm free again but could not do so. "I've never been yours!" she said, shoving him away with her free hand. He took a step backward but did not let go. "I have been engaged to Will for two years! I never even agreed to marry you!"

"Yes, yes you did," Carey replied. "When you consented to wear that ring, you became my fiancée, my wife for all intense and purposes, my property. Some poor dirt farmer returning does not change that, Cordia, and I'll see you both in hell before I see you married to anyone but me."

Cordia slapped him across the face, the rage she felt inside finally surfacing in one crescendo. She hoped that he would finally release her, physically and emotionally, that the blow would be enough to let him realize she was serious in her assertion that she was leaving him.

Carey didn't let go, however. Instead, he laughed, a menacing sound echoing through the air, and Cordia could see that evil presence she had noted as a child peeking out at her from behind his eyes. Though she was still outraged, she also began to grow fearful of what he might do, and she felt the urge to get away from him as quickly as possible. "You've ruined everything, Carey," she said, staring into those malevolent eyes. "Will doesn't want to have anything to do with me now."

He smiled back at her in triumph, releasing his grip just a bit. She took advantage and shook her arm free. "That had to be difficult for you," he snickered. "See, it's fate telling you that you're destined to be with me."

Cordia did not reply. Now that she had her physical freedom, she wanted to flee as fast as she possibly could. She began to back toward the steps, hoping he would not follow.

"You just need some time," Carey said, sure that he would be able to find a way to re-entrap her, particularly if Will Tucker had washed his hands of her. He stooped down to pick up her ring off of the porch and held it up so that she could see it. "You'll be getting this back soon, Miss Cordia," he added, placing it securely in his shirt pocket.

Cordia continued to back away, not feeling at ease enough to turn her back on him. Once she made it to her waiting wagon, she climbed aboard, taking her eyes off of him only briefly enough to climb into the seat without tripping. As she picked up the reins with one hand, she dug into her own pocket with the other. "If I can't wear this engagement ring, I won't wear any at all," she assured him, holding the ring that Will had given her up for him to see.

Even from that distance, she could see the anger growing in his face as he began to turn a bright crimson color, and his eyes darkened. She did not wait around to see if he would come after her again. Slipping the ring onto her finger where she realized it had always belonged, she flicked her wrists, and the horses were off. She prayed that this would be the last time she ever saw Carey Adams, though she was quite certain that it would not be.

When Cordia arrived home, she went straight upstairs. She ignored her mother's call to join her in the parlor. Though she knew she would have to explain everything to her parents eventually, she couldn't bear to do it just then. Tears were already threatening to pour as she hastily made her way into her bedroom, and she knew she would be spending the next several hours rereading every single letter Will had ever sent to her and crying in anguish.

As she drew the hatbox out of her closet, the one where she had hidden his correspondence, she let the tears flow freely. All of this time, all of those days of missing him and praying that he was safe, every night dreaming of the day when he would return and they could start their lives together. Now, all of those hopes were dashed to pieces. She knew it was all her fault. If only she had been courageous enough to do what she felt was right instead of attempting to protect the feelings of others, perhaps she would not be in this situation now. Her entire life, she had been told how strong-willed and opinionated she was. Now, when it had counted the most, she had bent to the will of others, and this is where it had gotten her.

She re-read every word he had ever sent to her, her heartbreaking as he confessed his undying love for her again and again. When she had finished, she carefully placed the lid back on the box and slid it to the foot of the bed, sobbing uncontrollably. Surely, if the words he had written were true, even a mistake as enormous as the one she had made could not completely change his feelings for her so drastically. She began to doze off, praying that she would find a way to show him she had never meant to betray him and that she wanted to be with him more than anything in the world.

❀

IT WAS clear to Will as soon as he entered the house that his Aunt Margaret had at least some inclination that he and Cordia had been involved romantically. He was not sure precisely what she knew or how she had come to gain this information, but he could tell by her expression and her shortness that she had come to realize that she had been deceived and that she was pondering both the nature and the duration of their relationship.

At dinner, a heavy silence hung over the entire table. The boys could plainly see that their mother was upset about something and almost thirty years of marriage had allowed Arthur the ability to read his wife very well. In this situation, he found, it was better not to speak than to risk becoming the object of her frustration.

Will joined in the silence, knowing eventually he would have to talk to Margaret about Cordia but thinking now was not the best time. He had been contemplating his conversation with Cordia the majority of the day, and he was beginning to realize that there was a distinct possibility that the emotional hell he had been going through these past two months was greatly due to a lack of communication. Nevertheless, he was still extremely upset that Cordia would be willing to wear another man's ring while he was off fighting. He had been completely unaware that she was spending time with someone else.

About halfway through dinner, Margaret's disturbance got the best of her, and she decided to alleviate her curiosity. Considering her sons were present, she attempted to be cryptic, knowing she may have to send them out of the room if she failed to keep her composure. She decided to begin the conversation with some general questions and then work her way into what she really wanted to know. "Will, did you get much work done on the house today?" she asked.

Will had been working to restore his family home in Vernon County when he wasn't helping out at his uncle's farm. He was hopeful that he would eventually be able to move Julia there and lessen the burden on his extended family. When he had first returned from the war, he went to see his parents' and Nolan's graves, thinking surely the house would have been burned to the ground by marauders some time ago. But it was still standing, and he began to focus his attention on repairing it. If nothing else, it took his mind off of Cordia, or at least it was an attempt to do so. Today, he had found little relief from her memory and had gotten next to nothing accomplished. "Not much," he replied, still leery of joining into a conversation with his aunt at this point.

She nodded. "That's too bad. I know how much it means to you. Though I still don't think it is a good idea to be moving Julia out there until she is fully recovered. I guess you had an eventful day, one way or another," she added.

Hoping to avoid any further questions, Will simply nodded and chose not to respond. He refused to even look in her general direction and tried to concentrate on finishing with dinner so he could excuse himself before Margaret began to ask the more difficult questions.

His silence was even more aggravating to Margaret, so she continued. "You can imagine my surprise when she flew out of here so quickly to chase after you."

Now, Will realized that there was nothing he could do to escape this conversation and that his aunt had chosen this moment to have it, despite the confused looks on the faces of the others present. "Yes, I can imagine that was surprising," he admitted.

"How long?" she asked bluntly. No one was eating now, and the younger boys looked especially bewildered, as if they wished they could melt into the floorboards and disappear.

Will considered the question. How long? Not long enough? Too long for Margaret's liking? He finally said, "It's over, Aunt Margaret. It doesn't matter now."

She cleared her throat and placed her napkin in her lap firmly. "I want to know how long," she repeated, trying to keep her calm.

Will just shook his head, "You won't understand," he replied quietly.

Margaret banged her fist on the table. "How long?" she demanded.

"Two years." He watched her eyes widen before adding, "Yes, the answer to your question is yes," he replied as calmly as he could.

She buried her face in her hands, and her family became genuinely concerned. Arthur looked at Will as if he was just realizing this information would affect him as well. He glanced back at his wife who was beginning to recover from the shock of the information. "How could you?" she asked quietly, without looking up. Then she added, "How could she?"

Will looked around the table, not sure exactly what he should or should not say in front of his younger cousins. "It wasn't intentional. We were waiting until I came back to let you know.... to let everyone know. But, clearly, I got what I deserve because I'm exactly where. . . he would have been," he said, continuing to choose his words carefully.

Arthur realized exactly what the conversation had been about now, and he gasped in shock. "What?" he asked quietly, looking at his wife whose eyes confirmed his suspicions. "Boys, why don't y'all run upstairs, and let us have the rest of this discussion in private."

As if they had been released from prison, all three boys took off up the stairs as quickly as they could. Arthur waited until they were out of earshot before he asked, "Do you mean to tell me you were having an affair with Cordia while Jaris was still alive?" He was doing his best to control his tone, but he was aware that the anger was building as he completed the sentence, and he was doing all he could not to come undone.

"It wasn't an affair," Will said defensively. The way his uncle put it made it sound like they had been involved in some seedy carnal relationship. "It wasn't like that. Nothing physical happened, not really. We just. . . fell in love." He looked from one face to the other, the looks of anger morphing into perplexed stares. "She told me that she never really loved him," he explained as gently as he could. "She said she didn't want to send him off to war that way, knowing that she never intended to be his wife. We were going to wait until the war was over and then...."

"And then what?" Margaret asked in an angry whisper. "Shatter his heart into a million pieces? After years of deception and lies?" She leaned back in her chair, folding her arms. "I never, ever thought I'd find a reason to say this, but I am almost glad he isn't here to hear this. I just can't imagine how he would have ever overcome such devastation."

"I know," Will said quietly. "I know exactly what you are saying, Aunt Margaret, believe me."

The expression on his face made her realize his words were true. Even though Margaret was outraged at her nephew's behavior, she couldn't help but feel compassion for him, considering all that he had been through and how much she loved him. She realized just how much he was hurting. The same amount of anguish she had just envisioned for her son was now clearly staring back at her through the eyes of his cousin. She could tell by her husband's expression that he was not feeling as forgiving as she was, however, and she realized, if this riff was to be repaired, she would have to be the one to mend it. After a few minutes of silence, she finally said, "It sounded to me like she was telling you that she doesn't want to marry Carey, that she really wants to be with you."

Will snickered, his head in his hands. "I don't know what to think," he replied. "I don't know what to believe."

Margaret nodded, understanding. If she would lie to Jaris, perhaps she would lie to Will as well. However, reflecting on Cordia's disposition these past few months, and the history she had with Carey, she began to think that perhaps Cordia was telling Will the truth. "Well, there's really only one way to find out," she replied.

"How's that?" Will asked, wondering if the change in conversation meant that his aunt wasn't about to throw him out of her house and tell him never to come back.

"Go talk to her. If she intends to marry Carey, I'm sure she will let you know. If she doesn't, well, then I think you have your answer," she explained.

Will shook his head. "I just don't understand why she would consent to marry him if she truly loved me," he replied, a look of anguish on his face.

It was Arthur who responded this time, "Why do women do anything that they do?" he asked, ignoring the gasp from his own wife.

"Honestly, Will, if you can figure that out, please, enlighten the rest of us."

Margaret glared at her husband before chiming in. "Her mother has been so overjoyed about the wedding. It's been all Jane can talk about. Maybe she felt as though she would be disappointing a lot of people if she didn't say yes."

Will just stared at her for a moment, wondering if she would realize the gravity of her words. He saw her expression shift a bit and recognized that she knew those words would apply to both Cordia's situation with Carey and her relationship with Jaris.

Clearing her throat, Margaret said quietly, "Perhaps Cordia is more vulnerable than any of us have ever realized."

After a moment, Will stated, "I don't know what to do. I guess, I'll give her a few days and then try to talk to her."

"I wouldn't wait too long," Arthur replied. "If she really does love you, she's probably over there crying her eyes out."

Will considered that for a moment. Of course, he would hate to think of Cordia that upset, but at the same time, he couldn't help but think perhaps she deserved it after putting him through such emotional turmoil these past several weeks. Still, if it had not been intentional, he wouldn't want to see her suffer if he could prevent it. "I'm not sure she'd want to see me right now. I wasn't exactly kind to her earlier today."

"It's never a bad time to apologize," Margaret advised. "Besides, she left her coat here earlier, so you have a legitimate reason to stop by."

Will considered her words, suddenly feeling the urge to run out the door. However, he also did not want to be too impulsive. "How do you think her parents will react to me showing up at this time of evening?"

"They aren't home," Arthur replied. "They're having dinner with the Peltzers. Isaac mentioned it when I saw him at the bank this afternoon. I guess Cordia might have gone with them but probably not if she's upset."

Nodding his head, Will stood and began to clear the dinner table, still pondering whether or not he should pay Cordia a visit. As he continued to help his aunt and uncle remove the dirty dishes, something his aunt had said earlier came back to him. "I do want to say that

I am very sorry for causing both of you any sorrow through my actions. I hope you know that it was never my intention, and I greatly apologize."

Margaret sat the plate she was carrying in the sink and stretched open her arms to hug him. "Will, I love you like a son. I know that, I truly do. Though I can't say I'm not thoroughly surprised, I do know that love causes us to do strange and sometimes terrible things. We forgive you."

CORDIA'S MOTHER had awoken her around seven o'clock, just before she and her father left to visit some friends of theirs for dinner. She had invited Cordia to come along, but she explained that she wasn't feeling well, and Jane could see that certainly did not look up to coming. She had volunteered to stay home with her, considering that Frieda was out with her friends at the quilting bee, but Cordia insisted that she would be all right, so her parents had left her alone for the evening.

An hour or so after they left, Cordia descended the stairs in search of something to eat, realizing she had not eaten anything all day. She lit a lantern, but the house was mostly dark except for the fire in the hearth in the parlor. The kitchen was toward the back of the house, and as she made her way into the room, she began to hear the floorboards creaking behind her. At first, she thought she was imagining things, but the further she walked, the mores she realized someone was in the house. She felt panic beginning to well up inside as she hurried to where they kept the knives. Grabbing the largest one she could find, she turned to face her assailant.

The grin on his face was enough to let her know his intentions. Clearly, he had been drinking, and his only purpose for breaking into her home, knowing full-well she was there alone, was malicious. Holding the knife between them and attempting to keep her voice as calm and steady as possible, she asked firmly, "What are you doing here, Carey Adams?"

He was wearing his full uniform, including his dress sword which hung on his right side, and he drummed the hilt with his fingers as he measured her up with his narrowed eyes. "Cordia, my love," he replied, his speech slightly slurred by the alcohol she could smell on his breath, "I came to see you. I thought it was time we made this marriage official."

Cordia gasped. Though she still held the knife firmly in her hand, she realized that he also had his pistol, and she knew she would not be able to protect herself easily against an armed soldier. "Carey, you've been drinking. I think you should go home before you wake my parents."

Chuckling, he took another step in her direction. "Cordia, I know your parents aren't home. You're here all by yourself, darlin'."

She was pinned against the counter, but she thought, if she could get to the back door, or perhaps passed him and into the dark hallway that led to the front door, possibly she could get away. Still, there was only a foot or two of space between them, and it would be difficult to get by. She contemplated attempting to stab him right now, before he expected it, but the thought of doing so made her queasy, and she didn't know if she would be able to actually plunge a knife into someone else's flesh.

As if reading her mind, he said, "Cordia, put that knife down before you hurt yourself. We both know you're not going to stab me."

She glanced at the knife and then back at him. He was probably right. And yet, she certainly wasn't going to just stand by and let him take her either. Distracting him by pulling the knife over to the side near the counter, she raised her knee rapidly and connected right between his legs, leaving him bent over in pain. However, it wasn't enough to put him out of commission, and before she could get around him, he pressed her back against the counter, grabbing her wrist and pounding it on the edge, knocking the blade free. It clattered loudly to the floor out of her reach.

"Now, why in the world did you go and do something like that?" he asked, still grimacing in pain.

"Leave me alone," she replied between gritted teeth. He still had her wrist and it was beginning to throb. His body was pressed against hers, and she began to realize she was running out of both time and options.

"I told you, Miss Cordia, I'm here to take you as my wife. Now, we can do this the easy way or the hard way."

Just then, Cordia heard the cock of a pistol, and realized they were not alone. "I prefer the hard way," Will interjected, stepping out of the shadows, his gun drawn and pointed directly at Carey's temple. He closed the short space between them before Carey even had time to react, and Will's revolver was pressed firmly against Carey's head preventing him from drawing his own weapon from its holster.

Cordia held her breath, relieved that Will had come to her rescue but uncertain about what might still transpire. She stood perfectly still, waiting for Carey to back away from her so that she could put some distance between herself and her assailant.

Will could see that Carey's hand was resting on the butt of his gun. "I wouldn't do that if I were you," he said, the control in his voice a clear result of years spent in similar situations. Carey moved his hand back, and Will reached around with his free hand and took his pistol, handing it to Cordia, who accepted it without hesitation and slid away from Carey, keeping his own weapon trained on him as she did so.

"I think this has been some sort of misunderstanding," Carey said, raising his hand in the air.

"You think so?" Will asked sarcastically. "I think I know exactly what you were up to, Lt. Adams, and I think you better head right on out of here while you're still capable of walking."

Carey glanced nervously at the gun out the corner of his eye. "Listen, you just happened to walk in on a spat between me and my fiancée. That's all. You're overreacting, Mr. Tucker."

"Your fiancée?" Will repeated, glancing at Cordia who still had the gun trained on Carey. "I don't believe that's your ring she's wearing," he replied, realizing that she was wearing the ring he had given her.

Carey had not noticed the ring before, but he saw it now. Despite the realization that a trained killer had a gun pointed to his head, he could not help but moan in disgust. Feeling the cold steel pressed against his temple, he snapped back to attention. He began to recognize that his best option at this point was to escape and find a way to gain his vengeance later. "All right," he said, reluctantly, "I see. Just give me my pistol, and I'll get out of here."

Cordia cocked the gun, an indicator that she had no intention of returning the firearm to its previous owner. Though she had mostly fired rifles, she knew exactly how to use the handgun, and even with the trepidations she had about the possibility of actually using a weapon to assault anyone, she was not afraid to use it to intimidate him.

Will pulled the gun back away from him slightly, giving him enough room to start his retreat. He was aware of the sword and kept his eye on Carey as he began to back out of the room, toward the back door.

Carey kept his hand in the air until he reached the doorknob. As he pulled the door open, he said, "This isn't over. You'll both regret this." Before either of them could respond, he bolted through the door toward his waiting horse, which was tied to a tree nearby.

Will went to the door, making sure he had no other weapons and that he actually left the premises. Despite the darkness, they both saw him ride by the kitchen window and down the street, pressing his horse to go as fast as it could run.

Cordia could still feel her heart racing, but as Will approached her, she realized the pounding was not just due to the situation with Carey. She opened her mouth to speak, but before she could say anything, his mouth was on hers, his arms around her, pulling her close. She had waited so long to feel his lips against hers, to feel his strong embrace. As she returned his kiss, she concentrated on every sensation; the feel of his breath against her skin, the scent of his cologne, the taste of his mouth, the way his hands caressed her. His lips began to trail down her neck, his hand cupping her face. "Will," she said quietly as his mouth settled between her shoulder and her throat, "I'm so glad you came back to me. Thank you."

He looked up at her, as if he was going to say something, but instead he pressed his lips against hers again, more hungrily this time, and Cordia leaned in to him, longingly. After a moment, he released her, suddenly realizing there was a possibility that Carey could return, potentially with reinforcements. "Cordia," he began but her lips were on his again and he paused to kiss her, pulling back after a moment and trying to speak once more. "Cordia, this might not be over," he said, as she kissed him again.

Cordia was contemplating what he said as her lips explored his. Finally, she let him go, resolving to restrain herself. "What do you mean?" she asked, staring into those eyes she had missed for so long.

He rubbed her cheek softly with his thumb as he studied her face. "He's the head of the militia, isn't he? I'm wondering if he would dare to call them in to action," he explained.

Cordia contemplated the possibility. "Why would he do that?"

"I don't know," Will replied. "But if he wanted to throw me in jail for a while, it wouldn't be too difficult. It would be our word against his. I wouldn't put it past him."

She nodded in agreement. "We should go," she replied. "Get away from here for a little while until he simmers down and sobers up."

Will nodded in agreement. "We would probably be safe at my house. It's not in Lamar, not even in Barton County, so technically, he wouldn't have any authority there, not that that would necessarily stop him, but he probably wouldn't know where to find us."

"It's worth a try," Cordia agreed. "Do you think I have time to pack a bag?"

"I believe so," Will replied thoughtfully. "I'll go get your horse saddled up. Western style though, none of that sidesaddle business. We're riding out of here like men."

She giggled, the thought of an adventure with Will sounding extremely appealing to her. "I'll be right down," she said, kissing him quickly before she bounded toward the staircase, gathering up her skirts so she could climb them even faster.

Throwing a few dresses and some essentials into a bag that would fit easily on the saddle horn, she noticed the wedding dress, still standing guard across the room. Her first impulse was to take the pair of scissors on her dresser and slash it to shreds, but she knew her mother had worked hard on that dress. The more she considered the garment, standing there staring at her, the more she began to realize there was truly only one way to ensure that Carey Adams gave her peace at last. She gave the gown one last glance as she headed back toward the stairs, wondering how she could possibly tactfully broach the topic with Will.

He was back inside when she reached the bottom step, waiting for her near the door, keeping an eye on the street, though he certainly noticed her as she approached him. She realized he was holding the coat she had left at Margaret's. He had come over to return it and ended up saving her from Carey in the process. He smiled at her, and it was all she could do to keep from throwing herself back into his arms. Knowing that would certainly occupy their valuable time for a while, she held back, surveying the house quickly, wondering whether or not she should leave the fire and the lantern lit.

"Are you ready?" he asked, still looking out the door.

"Yes," Cordia replied. "Just about. Do you think the fire will be all right?"

Will glanced at it and saw that it was fully contained by the fireplace. "Yes," he responded. "Let's put out the lantern."

"I'll get it," Cordia said, dropping her bag and moving toward the kitchen. She spotted an inkwell and pen on the counter, the one her mother used for quick correspondences and lists, and realized she needed to find a way to let her parents know where she had gone. After she had taken off to Springfield with Frieda, they had reprimanded her fairly sharply, and she had promised never to leave again without letting them know where she was going. She paused for a moment and wrote a short explanation. Then, she realized, if Carey was able to find a way to gain entry into her home once, he could do it again. She placed the note in the one location she didn't think he would ever look, and she knew her father most certainly would find it.

She put the lantern out and returned to the foyer where Will was still waiting, though a bit less patiently. "All right," she said. He held her coat open for her to slide into.

"Let's go," he said, kissing her quickly before picking up her bag, taking her hand, and leading her out the door.

Chapter Fourteen

CAREY ADAMS WAS NOT a man to be trifled with. Even before he had left the Pikes' yard, he was already formulating a plan to seek his vengeance. He galloped off in the direction of the county jail, seeking Sheriff Don Dickerson, intending to let him know that he had walked in on Will Tucker accosting his fiancée. He knew Cordia would deny it, of course, but if he could find a way to have Will arrested for even a few days, perhaps he would find the opportunity to make Cordia pay for rejecting him. Otherwise, he would have to take his vengeance a step further. Will needed to be eliminated, one way or another, and if he needed to call out the militia to do it, so be it.

By the time Cordia and Will left her house, Sheriff Dickerson and his men were already on the way, riding at full speed toward the Pike house, intending to rescue Cordia from her attacker. Upon their arrival, Sheriff Dickerson charged into the home, his gun drawn. After a quick survey of the house, he realized it was empty. "No sign of them," he explained to Carey who was standing near the doorway.

Carey sighed, a look of despair on his face. "Perhaps, he has carried her off?" he asked, the words catching in his throat as he was overcome with emotion.

Sheriff Dickerson nodded, believing that was the only logical explanation. "We'll gather up a posse and ride out looking for her. Don't you worry, now, Lt. Adams. We'll find her."

The sheriff and his men did a search of the home, looking for any clues that may let them know what had happened. They saw the knife on the ground and believed that Cordia must have attempted to use it to protect herself. They found no other evidence and were just about to wrap up their investigation when Mr. and Mrs. Pike returned.

From the moment the house was in view, Jane had been extremely agitated, pressing Isaac to drive the horses faster. She was certain something terrible had happened to Cordia. As soon as the horses came to a halt, she clambered down and rushed inside, Isaac right behind her. "What's going on?" she asked, stepping inside and seeing the look of anguish on Carey's face.

"Mr. and Mrs. Pike," Sheriff Dickerson said, approaching them. "I'm afraid we have some difficult news. It seems that your daughter, Cordia, has been abducted."

"What?" Isaac exclaimed, his wife gasping beside him. "By whom?"

Carey embraced Jane as she began to cry. He had tears in his eyes as well. "It was. . . Will Tucker," he stammered, pulling Jane in closer.

"Will Tucker?" Isaac repeated. "But, why would he do such a thing? How do you know?"

Sheriff Dickerson relayed the story. Carey had come over to check on Cordia because he understood she was not feeling well. When he arrived, Will was inside the house, a gun pointing at Cordia. Carey had come unarmed so he had no way to defend himself or his fiancée. Will had threatened to shoot him if he didn't leave immediately. Carey had raced straight to the jail to retrieve the sheriff, but by the time they had arrived, it was too late. He explained that his men were out rounding up anyone who would be willing to ride out and begin searching for Cordia, adding that he had every confidence that they would find their daughter safe and sound.

Isaac shook his head in disbelief. "We have been friends with his aunt and uncle for more years than I can possibly count. How is this possible?"

"I don't know," Sheriff Dickerson replied. "But we are wasting valuable time. Now, you all wait here, and we will be back just as soon as we have news. We will head straight for the Adams Farm and see if they have any information. Perhaps we will find Cordia there."

As the sheriff and his men left the premises, Carey led Jane into the parlor. She was still crying inconsolably, and Carey was doing his best to comfort her. Isaac couldn't help but search the house himself, though he knew there was no way his daughter was there somewhere and the investigators had missed her. Once he had satisfied himself that she had not been overlooked, he returned to the parlor and joined the vigil. Frieda also arrived home shortly, hearing the devastating news at the quilting bee and rushing to the house to be with Mr. and Mrs. Pike.

It was almost ten o'clock when Arthur Adams heard horses in his front yard and peeked out the window to see several riders approaching. He had heard there were some marauders in the area and he ordered his sons to grab their weapons and brace themselves for a fight.

When Sheriff Dickerson knocked on the door, Arthur had his gun at the ready. "Who's there?" he yelled before throwing the locks.

"Sheriff Dickerson," the older man replied.

Stunned, but recognizing the voice, Arthur motioned for his sons to stand down, and he unlocked the door. Margaret was also in the room, and she took a few steps toward them, the worst possible scenario entering her head as she imagined they were there to tell her something awful had happened to Will.

Sheriff Dickerson nodded a greeting as Arthur opened the door. Five armed men stood behind him, their guns at rest but an imposing sight nonetheless. "Sorry to disturb you at this time of evening, Arthur," he began, "but we have it on good authority that your nephew, Will Tucker, has been involved in the kidnapping of Cordia Pike, and we were wondering if you might have any information as to his whereabouts."

Margaret gasped. "What?" she said, stepping forward. "No, that's not possible. Will would never do anything like that. If Cordia has disappeared with Will, then she did so by her own choosing."

Sheriff Dickerson could sympathize with the woman, but he did not believe her story. "Your other nephew, Carey Adams, witnessed Mr.

Tucker holding Cordia at gunpoint in her home. Now, they are both gone. We have every reason to believe Lt. Adams. Do you have any idea where Tucker might have taken her?"

Arthur looked at Margaret who was shaking her head in disbelief. She was well aware that Carey was fully capable of treacherous activity. She had not been completely ignorant of his forte for torturing animals as a child, nor had she missed the way he had spoken to Cordia since they were small children. She had been surprised that Cordia had ever consented to marry Carey for just that reason, and now she had much more evidence to support the idea that Carey had fabricated a story than to believe that Will had actually kidnapped Cordia. She shook her head no and said, "I can't think of any place. You're welcome to check our home if you think it would relieve your suspicions, but I guarantee you won't find a trace of either of them. Check our barns, our sheds, whatever you like."

"What about his parents' home?" Sheriff Dickerson asked. "Didn't they have a place in Vernon County?"

"They did," Arthur replied. "But it was burned to the ground by guerrillas years ago. There's nothing left." He told the lie with such conviction, Margaret almost believed him herself.

The sheriff shook his head. "There's no reason to check your home; we believe you," he said. "However, if you truly don't mind, I would like to look in your outbuildings, just in case he's hiding her in one of them, and you are unaware."

"Certainly," Arthur replied, nodding in agreement.

"Thank you, kindly," Sheriff Dickerson replied. "And if you hear anything from Will, you let me know right away," he ordered.

"We will," Margaret promised as Arthur closed and relocked the door.

"What in the world?" Arthur asked, crossing over to his wife and taking her in his arms.

"I'm not sure," Margaret replied, "But I know that Carey is at the center of this, and I pray he comes clean before someone gets hurt."

THE SKY WAS FAIRLY CLEAR, and the stars were shining brightly as Cordia and Will made their way around the outskirts of town, away from major roads and populated areas, before turning north and heading for Will's home, near Nevada in Vernon County. The wind had died down, but it was still rather chilly, and Cordia was thankful to have her coat. Will was used to being outside in all kinds of weather and was just grateful that he had a horse to ride on this journey, rather than walking the twenty-five miles or so they would cover that night.

They didn't speak too much at first, afraid that doing so might lead to their discovery. However, as they wound their way out of town, they became more confident in the success of their escape, and Cordia couldn't help but engage him in conversation. She had so many topics she had wished to discuss with him for so long, and having him here at last was almost too hard for her to believe. "If Carey went to the sheriff or called out the militia, do you think they will visit your aunt and uncle's place?" she asked riding along beside him.

"Most likely," he replied, pulling his hat back on his head so that he could see her better. They were not pushing their horses, wanting to ensure they made the whole distance with no difficulties. Should they believe they were being followed, they would need to press them, so for now they traveled at a slow gallop.

She considered his answer a moment before continuing. "What do you think they'll say?"

"I'm not sure," he admitted. "We had a bit of a falling out this evening. Aunt Margaret said that she forgave me, but she may be inclined to tell the truth. I'm sure that, if she tells the authorities my house is still standing, it won't be too long before we have company."

"About what?" Cordia asked, although she had a suspicion she already knew the answer. She pulled her coat closer against the cold.

Will sighed, not really wanting to relive the conversation but realizing she needed to know. He also understood that he had a lot of explaining to do to Cordia as well, though she didn't seem to think he owed her an apology. He believed he did, however, and he hoped to get to that before they reached their destination. "She overheard our conversation today, at least part of it. She wanted to know how long you and I had been involved together."

Even in the dim light, Cordia could see his eyes. She swallowed hard; this lump in her throat had been growing for years. "I see," she said quietly. "What did you tell her?"

He contemplated the question for a moment before responding, "I told her the truth. I thought they deserved to know."

She nodded, not sure if he could see well enough to know she was doing so. "How did she respond?"

"Better than I thought she would," he admitted. "Uncle Arthur knows, too. I was a little afraid they would throw me out, but they said they forgave me, forgave us I suppose."

"God," Cordia whispered. "I've feared that conversation for so long, and you had to have it all by yourself. I'm so sorry you had to do that alone," she said, reaching for his hand.

He gave her hand a quick squeeze before letting her go. "Thank you," he replied, shaking his head, "but it was my fault I was alone. If I had believed you, we would have been able to talk to them together as we had planned. Cordia, I am so sorry that I didn't trust you."

"You're sorry?" Cordia repeated, her eyebrows raised in disbelief. "Will, if anyone should be sorry, it's me. If I had been courageous enough to stand up for myself in the first place, this would have never happened."

"No, Cordia," he insisted, "I told you I didn't want anyone to know about our engagement until I returned. I understand now why you did what you did. I just wish I would have known these past two months that you weren't actually planning on marrying Carey."

"Carey was absconding with my mail," she explained. She saw his eyes widen even in the near darkness. "He must have threatened Mr. Wheeler or something, but he was stopping my mail to you from leaving the post office."

"Unbelievable!" Will exclaimed. "How can someone be so malicious?"

"I have been asking myself that question for years," Cordia admitted. "I don't know, and why he would want to marry someone who hates him as much as I do...."

"Well, that's an easy one," Will interrupted. "He thinks he deserves the best, and you are certainly the most beautiful woman in Lamar, or anywhere for that matter."

She was glad he couldn't see that she was blushing. "Oh, please," she said modestly.

"Seriously, Cordia. Who wouldn't want to marry you?" he asked, staring at her a bit longer than he intended to. "I know I want to," he added quietly.

"Thank goodness this is your ring on my finger then," she replied, a teasing lilt to her voice.

He chuckled softly. "When did you put that on?" he asked, watching it glint in the moonlight.

"As soon as I took his off and threw it at him earlier this afternoon," she replied.

"Oh, I see. So, you paid Lt. Adams a visit today as well?" he asked, previously unaware of what had set Carey off.

"Yes, I did," she explained. "As soon as I left the farm, I drove straight to his house and told him off, once and for all. I've got a nice bruise on my arm to prove it, too, if you'd like to see," she added, still feeling the sting off his fingers on her arm.

"That bastard," Will mumbled. "He's lucky I didn't shoot him when I had the chance."

"Me, too," Cordia agreed. "Or I could have stabbed him right in the face, right in the smirking, smarmy face."

Will raised an eyebrow and looked at her intently. "Thought about that before have you?" he asked a bit amused, despite the seriousness of her remarks.

"Thousands of times," she admitted. "But I guess I'm just not a violent person."

"Thank God for that," he replied, "or else I might be a bit worried riding around out here in the dark with you, not a soul nearby to hear my screams."

She laughed but his statement did raise a question for her. "What are the chances we're going to run into marauders?" she asked.

"Tonight?" he clarified. "Not very likely. We should be able to hear them coming, same as anyone following us from town. I will admit I worry about them coming back, though, when I'm at the house, probably because the memories I have of the morning Nolan was killed are so vivid. But you don't need to worry, Cordia. I will protect you."

"I know you will," she said, believing it wholeheartedly. Off in the distance, she could see a cluster of lights from what appeared to be a small town. "Is that Nevada?" she asked.

"Yes," he replied. "There's a road up here that turns left and it goes back toward the house. If we go the other direction, we will arrive in Nevada in about a half-hour or so."

Cordia was a bit confused. "Why would we go to Nevada instead of your house?" she asked, wondering if, perhaps, he was concerned that they were being followed.

Will pulled his horse to a stop and turned to look directly at her. She also stopped and turned to face him, a puzzled expression still on her face. "Cordia," he began, reaching for her hand, which she gave to him. "It's been two years. After spending the last few months thinking I would never have the opportunity to be with you again, I'm done waiting. I'm done taking chances. I want to marry you. I want to take you to my house, to our home, as my wife."

She had not expected this at all, and her expression changed from confusion, to shock, to overwhelming happiness. "You want to marry me?" she asked, watching him nod his head. "Right now?"

"Yes," he confirmed. "I want to ride with you into Nevada, find the pastor who used to stop by once in a while and check on us after our folks died, and marry you tonight. Right now. What do you say, Cordia Pike? Will you agree to be my wife? Again?"

Cordia couldn't contain the smile that broke across her face as she nodded her head. "Yes, of course, I will!" She leaned over and kissed him quickly before giving her reins a snap. "Let's go!"

They galloped in near silence until they were at the outskirts of town. By the time they began to reach the houses on the perimeter, their horses were beginning to grow tired, and they decided to slow them. Will was hopeful that the pastor still lived with his family in the small house behind the rectory. Even though it was nearly one o'clock in the morning, and there was the possibility that they could awaken the whole town, he was hopeful that the pastor would consent to conducting the marriage immediately.

As they approached the pastor's home, they noticed a light burning in the front window. Finding that a bit odd, Will cautioned Cordia to stay back a ways and let him check it out. He dismounted and quietly walked over to the house, knocking softly on the door. After just a few moments, the door opened and a middle-aged man peered back at him, a Bible in one hand, the other on his holster. "Can I help you?" he asked cautiously.

"I'm so sorry to disturb you, Pastor Bryant," Will said recognizing the man from his last visit just a few years ago, though it seemed like an eternity now. "I'm not sure if you remember me but. . . "

"Will Tucker!" the man exclaimed. "Of course I recognize you! How are you, son?" he asked, removing his hand from the pistol and offering it to Will.

Will shook his hand, relieved that the reverend remembered him. "I can't complain," he replied. "How are you doing, Pastor?" he asked politely.

"Strangest thing," the pastor responded, a bit lost in his own thoughts. "I could not sleep tonight. I went to bed with my wife a few hours ago, but I just couldn't fall asleep. Finally, I got up and began to read the Good Book. I felt my heart leading me to a certain book, chapter, and verse, one I had not paid too much attention to these days, with all the trouble going on around us. But I knew the Lord wanted me to study on His word and on these very verses. Perhaps, He will unveil His plan to me soon so that I may know His purpose."

Will had never been too religious, but he listened respectfully to the pastor's story. "I see," he replied, nodding his head. "Well, I'm glad we found you already awake so that we didn't rouse you from sleep, but I was hoping you wouldn't mind doing me a quick favor."

By that time, Cordia had realized the pastor was not going to harm them and had dismounted and tied both horses to a hitching post. She was on her way over toward the house as Will was speaking, and Pastor Bryant was aware of her presence.

"This is my fiancée, Cordia, and we would like for you to marry us, tonight, right now, if you would be so kind as to do so. I'm happy to compensate you for your services," Will explained as Cordia slipped her arm through his.

The pastor began to giggle with glee. "The Lord always provides!" he exclaimed. Cordia and Will looked at each other, smiling but confused. "You see, children," he began, "The verses I was called upon to study tonight are from Proverbs 31:10-12. This is where the Lord speaks of the value in marrying a good wife. And now, here you are, showing up on my doorstep in the middle of the night, a good wife on your arm. Isn't the Lord amazing? Does He not lead us with His own divine presence?"

Cordia had goose bumps on her arms. She had always been strong in her Christian faith, and she took this as a clear sign that she and Will were doing the right thing. "Amen," she agreed.

"Come in, come in," Pastor Bryant said, stepping back out of the doorway. They were aware that the pastor's family was sleeping nearby so they attempted to be as quiet as possible. The ceremony was simple and short. Pastor Bryant even had a marriage certificate, which he filled out and signed for them. Though there were no other witnesses, with his signature the document was binding by law and would be recognized by the church. Cordia was disappointed that she did not have a ring for Will, but he assured her that his father's ring was buried safely at home and that he could wear that one, once he could retrieve it. Pastor Bryant insisted that he would not charge to marry two people so obviously joined by the Lord but he did allow Will to make a donation to his church.

As the pastor closed the door to his little home, Cordia and Will approached the horses, hand in hand. A wave of relief washed over them both as they knew now, no matter what Carey may try to argue, they were married, and no one could change that. Cordia was so over-joyed, she couldn't help but giggle like a schoolgirl. Will spun her around in a circle, dancing with no music, the light of the moon gleaming off of Cordia's perfect smile. He pulled her in closely and kissed her, almost unable to believe that this day was here at last.

Will helped Cordia mount her horse and untied both of them from the post. She could not take her eyes off of him, and once he was atop his own steed, she leaned over and kissed him again. "I can't believe you are finally my husband," she whispered, still smiling.

"I can't believe you're finally my wife," he agreed, kissing her once more before they rode off to the home they would share together, married at last.

❦

SHERIFF DICKERSON and his men searched the Adams Farm thoroughly. They found no trace of Will or Cordia. They began to ride out into the outlying areas, stopping at houses, and asking if anyone had heard anything suspicious. No one had noticed anything out of the ordinary. Around two o'clock in the morning, Sheriff Dickerson ordered his men to go home, planning to reconvene at first light. He returned to the Pike home to let Cordia's parents and Carey know they had come up empty handed.

Carey's performance had been extremely convincing. As Sheriff Dickerson explained that the search had not been successful, the brokenhearted fiancé began to weep. Jane also broke into tears, and Isaac did his best to comfort his wife. Frieda asked to be excused to her room so that she could mourn in private, unwilling to speak her theory that, perhaps, Cordia had ridden off with a band of marauders. She had held her suspicions since the last time Will was in town, and it was difficult to convince her otherwise.

After the sheriff and his men had gone out, promising they would reconvene at first light, Isaac proposed that the rest of them get some rest as well. Tomorrow promised to be a difficult day for all. Though Jane offered to let Carey stay in a guest room, he decided he needed to go home and check on his father who was probably very worried about him.

As Carey exited, his tears dried up immediately, and the malevolent grin reappeared on his face. A thorough search of the house had produced nothing, which meant that Cordia had not been wise enough to let anyone know what he had done. Now, as soon as Will thought it was safe to come home, he would be arrested. Even if Cordia attempted to convince the sheriff that she had gone of her free will, the Pikes would be so angry they would insist on pressing charges anyway, he was sure of it.

"Did you check her room well?" Jane asked, hoping there was a possibility a clue had been left behind and the men had just overlooked it.

"I believe so," Isaac said, thoughtfully. "But, darling, if you'd like to go up and check it again, perhaps you should do so."

As Jane stood and approached the stairs, she asked, "Did he even let her take a dress or her essentials?"

"I hadn't noticed," Isaac admitted. "I was looking for additional items, not any that had been removed."

Jane nodded, not too surprised. "I will see if any of her dresses are missing. I hope he was at least kind enough to let her take some things with her. I just cannot imagine Will acting this way. He has always been so pleasant."

"I know," Isaac agreed. "Perhaps the war has changed him." He was leaning against the banister, watching his wife ascend the stairs and thinking how very little of this situation made any sense. A rumbling in his stomach reminded him of how late it was and how food always had a way of making him feel better. He went off to the kitchen to see what he could find.

Jane opened Cordia's bedroom door cautiously, hopefully. Maybe, if she concentrated, Cordia would be there, somehow. Of course, when the door opened, her daughter had not manifested. Jane went to her daughter's closet and moved her dresses around on the clothes rack. She noticed immediately that Cordia's light green dress, one of her favorites, was not there. She looked around on the floor and did not see it there either. Turning back to the closet, she double-checked, realizing there was another dress missing, the pink one, and Jane's suspicions began to grow. She looked up at the shelf on the top of the closet. Though she was short, she could see that Cordia's overnight bag, the smallest of her luggage items, was gone. There was a gaping spot open in the top of the closet, and it looked like, perhaps, more than one article had been removed. Quickly, she went to her dresser drawers and realized Cordia had packed some other items as well. She surveyed the room, noticing other articles that were out of place. Cordia's hairbrush, her favorite hair comb, both gone. Seeing none of these items on the floor or on the bed, she became certain that Cordia must have taken them with her. Now, why would a kidnapper allow his prisoner to pack a bag?

Then she noticed something else. A hatbox on the bed. Though it was possible Cordia had just removed it when she was taking items out of the closet, she decided to investigate. Pulling the top of slowly, she saw that it was full of letters. She had no idea that Cordia had received so much mail. She picked up the one on top and saw immediately that it was from Will. Before she even opened it, she glanced through the rest of them. There must have been at least two or three dozen of them, all from Will. Pulling the top letter out of the envelope, she read over it quickly. At once, she could see that it was a love letter. Cordia and Will had been corresponding this entire time! They were courting, even while he was off at war? Jane looked quickly through the dates on the letters, trying to determine if there was any evidence of what might have gone wrong. The last letter she could find was dated in August. Was it possible that Cordia had written to Will, informing him that she was breaking off their engagement to marry Carey? In a rage, he had returned and absconded with her, planning to force her to become his bride? As fast as her stout legs could carry her, she grabbed the hatbox and hurried down the stairs to find Isaac.

He was standing in the kitchen, crunching on an apple, peering out the window. At least the last time Cordia had disappeared, he knew that Frieda was with her, and he knew where she had gone. He had been concerned about her for certain, but at least she had not been accompanied by a trained soldier who had possibly taken her in a jealous rage.

"Isaac!" Jane exclaimed, carrying the hatbox into the kitchen and sitting it on the counter. "Look at what I found in Cordia's room!"

Puzzled, Isaac peered over his wife's shoulder as she took the lid off, revealing what looked like letters. "What is it?" he asked confused.

"Love letters from Will Tucker!" she exclaimed. "He must have found out that Cordia was planning to marry Carey and returned to seek his vengeance!"

Isaac did not feel any less confused. "Now, why would he do that? And even if that is why he returned from the war, Arthur mentioned he'd come back over a week ago. Why wait until now? Hasn't Cordia been over to the Adams Farm recently? Certainly she has. That makes little sense to me, Jane."

Jane was upset that Isaac had blown so many holes in her theory. "Well, what do you think happened then?" she asked smartly.

Pondering the question, Isaac picked up one of the letters. It was the most recent one, dated in August of this year. "I'm not sure," he admitted. "Did you read any of them?"

"Just that one," Jane conceded. "It just talked about how the war was going, how he wasn't sure if he was going to come home at the end of his enlistment, and how much he loved her and missed her. Nothing unusual."

Isaac knew he did not want to read any of the letters. What a young man wrote to his daughter regarding his love for her was none of his business. "What's the date of the first letter?" he inquired.

Jane sighed. "That's the thing, Isaac. It's August, 1861." Jane watched as her husband did the math. "That's right, before Jaris died. Can you believe that? Can you imagine what Margaret is going to think when she finds out?"

"Did you read it? Maybe they didn't start this courting business until later," Isaac said, wanting to give his daughter the benefit of the doubt.

"Not yet," Jane replied, "But I intend to. I intend to read all of them. There may be some clues in here!"

"Now hold on there," Isaac said, picking the box up and pulling it away from her reach. "These are our daughter's private correspondences. There's nothing in here that's going to let us know anything more than this last letter. And if you've read that one, then we don't need to read the rest."

"Are you serious, Isaac?" Jane implored. "We need to turn these over to Sheriff Dickerson. There may be some valuable information in there!"

"Oh, horsefeathers," Isaac replied, putting the lid on the box. "How would you like it if I handed over our love letters to Sheriff Dickerson? No good can come of it, Jane."

She considered his statement and agreed that she certainly wouldn't want anyone else reading the letters Isaac and she had sent to each other before they were married. "Well, what if there's some important information right under our noses, and we miss it?" she asked in anguish.

"If there is, it's not in here," Isaac replied, matter-of-factly. He took the hatbox and put it high up in one of the cabinets where no one else could reach it. "Now, come on, let's get some rest," he advised, nudging her in the back and steering her out of the room. As he passed by the counter with the cookie jar, he began to consider how much better a gingersnap always made him feel. He pulled the lid off of the container, a waft of sweetness filling the air.

"Now Isaac," Jane began, "You don't need a cookie this time of night."

Considering her remark and thinking about the extra weight he had been putting on as he aged, he realized she was right and put the lid back on the jar. "Tomorrow," he whispered. "I shall see you tomorrow, dear Ginger Snap."

EACH TIME WILL STOPPED to consider the spot in the yard near the door to the diminutive log cabin, the place where Nolan had fallen and lost his life, he was taken aback. It was never easy to cross by there, and even tonight, with his new bride, he was consciously aware, as he led Cordia to the door, of what had transpired here such a short time, an eternity ago.

Cordia was also aware that this may be difficult for him, and she said nothing as they approached the house. He was carrying her bag and held her hand. As he drew near the door, he opened it, setting her bag inside, and turning back to face her. She looked into his eyes, confused as to why he had not entered.

"Cordia," Will said quietly. "This house isn't much, not yet, but I intend to make it a nice home for you and for Julia."

Cordia smiled. "Will, it doesn't matter to me where we live, as long as we are together."

He leaned in and kissed her softly before sweeping her into his arms and carrying her through the doorway. Setting her down gently, he lit a lantern that sat on a small table by the door. In the dim light, it was difficult to see, but Cordia could make out a couple of beds, a dining room table, and a fireplace. After the long ride in the cool night air, she was happy to see the fireplace, and Will set about getting a blaze going.

Cordia took off her coat and hung it on a hook by the door. She turned back around to see Will had the fire started and was removing his own coat. She was suddenly very aware of the larger bed in the corner of the room. Though she had certainly spent quite some time thinking about her wedding night, now that it was upon her, she could feel the butterflies fluttering around in her stomach.

He was standing next to her now, a shy smile on his face. "Cordia," he said quietly, "I know it's late. We do have two beds."

Cordia glanced away from him but only briefly. As she spoke, she looked directly into his eyes. "Will, I've been waiting two years to be your wife. I will admit I'm nervous, havin' never done anything like this before, but I'm ready."

He could tell by the sincerity in her voice that she meant what she said. "Well, all right then," he replied, his smile broadening. He took her hand and led her over to the larger of the two beds. Kissing her gently, he began to undress his new bride. Once she was down to her undergarments, he guided her onto the bed, pulling the blankets down for her to slide beneath. In the light of the flickering fire, he undressed himself and climbed in beside her. "I love you, Cordia," he said looking into her eyes.

Leaning over and kissing him passionately, Cordia conveyed how deeply she returned that love. Will responded to her kiss with conviction, and with the light of the moon shining through the windows of the small cabin, he proceeded to make Cordia his wife at last.

ISAAC PIKE WAS UP EARLY the next morning, despite having gotten little rest. He had been aware that Jane had dozed off just a few hours ago, her light snoring an indicator that her sobs had finally trailed off enough for her to rest. He knew she would be angry later that he did not wake her, but he also realized she needed her rest, and there was little she could do to locate Cordia, so she may as well sleep.

He made himself a quick breakfast, a bit surprised that Frieda was also still sleeping. The house seemed intolerably quiet, and he was thankful when a knock on the door ended the eerie silence. He rose to see whom it was, fairly certain he would find Sheriff Dickerson there.

Surprisingly, it was Carey. He looked a bit haggard himself, as if he had gotten little sleep. "Good morning, Mr. Pike," he said, stepping in the door. "Any word?"

Isaac shook his head no, gesturing with his hand toward the parlor, inviting Carey inside.

"No, thank you, I can't stay," he replied. He looked a bit nervous, and Isaac couldn't tell if it was because he was anxious to find Cordia or something else. "I've just received word that a company of Union soldiers has set up an outpost at the courthouse over night. Most of my men have elected to join them, but being a former Confederate officer, I'm reluctant to do so. It seems I've lost my command, and my fiancée in the same day."

Isaac had been hearing rumors for several weeks that the 8th Missouri Cavalry was in the area and that they had been charged with guarding the county courthouse against raiders, which were also known to be nearby. Though plenty of able-bodied men had been protecting the town for years as part of the city guard that Carey had headed up, these troops were regulars, and since Missouri was still part of the Union, their authority would usurp Carey's for certain. "I'm sorry to hear that," Isaac responded, though he was actually glad to hear that cavalry would be keeping them safe now. His understanding was that cavalry could be much more effective against the likes of the guerrilla raiders that had hit towns in nearby counties. Ever since the raid in Lawrence, Kansas, just a few months ago, the entire area had been on alert. Any extra soldiers would be welcomed by Isaac and his fellow citizens, though he could also understand why Carey would not be the first to applaud their presence.

"Any word from Sheriff Dickerson?" Carey asked, still standing near the door.

"No, I haven't seen him yet this morning," Isaac replied. He was wondering if it were possible that the good sheriff was meeting with the commanders of the 8th now, possibly seeing what information they might have regarding the possibility of a local raid. If that were the case, Cordia's whereabouts may no longer be a priority.

Carey ran his hand through his shaggy blond hair. "I'm planning to ride out this morning, survey some of the surrounding areas, see if I can find any trace of her. Some of my men, former Confederate soldiers, will be riding with me. We may be gone for a few days. I'll check back in once I return to town. Hopefully, I will find Cordia and bring her back safely to you very soon."

Isaac nodded. He could understand why Carey would want to go out and conduct his own search, particularly since it seemed that the sheriff was preoccupied. "Be careful," Isaac warned. "Rumor has it that devil Quantrill is out and about."

Carey was fully aware that Quantrill was nearby. In fact, he was a bit suspicious that Isaac had so quickly named his true objective. "I will be careful," he promised, reaching for the doorknob. He nodded a quick goodbye and made his way back to his steed, which was tied to a tree close to the front porch. He would meet the four men he had recruited early that morning at a prearranged location east of town and then ride out to see if they could find Quantrill and his men. If the devil truly was considering a raid on Lamar, as rumor had it, perhaps the notorious guerrilla could use some information. Carey had grown weary of the likes of Isaac Pike and his spoiled daughter. It had been two years since he had been engaged in warfare, and he longed for the smell of battle. If the 8th Cavalry wanted a fight, he would bring them one.

Isaac watched as Carey rode off, peering down the street to see if there was any sign of Sheriff Dickerson. He saw none and was resolved to go find the peace officer himself if he did not show his face soon. Though he was getting up there in years, he wasn't too old to ride out and begin searching for his little girl.

Walking back past the stairs, he paused for a second to see if he could hear either Jane or Frieda stirring. He heard nothing, so he sauntered off toward the kitchen, fully aware that the night before he had made a date with a sweet little morsel named Ginger Snap.

IT WAS late in the morning when Cordia awoke. Will was no longer next to her, but she could hear him outside. The fire was blazing, and she knew he must have gotten up to tend it and possibly find something to eat. She was suddenly aware that she was famished. She was also aware that she was still undressed, which brought back memories of the night before, bringing a smile to her face. She hurried to pull on her clothes before rushing outdoors to find her husband, and hopefully, an outhouse.

She didn't see Will until after she had finished using the only facility they had available. He was on the other side of the house, chopping wood, and for a moment, she paused to consider how different her life had become since she had watched him perform the same task just the day before. As she approached, he put the ax down and walked toward her, smiling broadly.

"Good morning, Cordia," he said embracing her and kissing her on the forehead.

She had not put her coat on before she had come out, and she felt much warmer now, wrapped in his arms. "Good morning. You're up bright and early, aren't you?"

Will glanced up at the sun. "It's almost noon, love," he replied. "You slept in. But, we went to bed pretty late last night and," he added with a sly smile, "I think I may have worn you out."

She hit him gently on the arm, laughing. "I think you just might have," she agreed. He leaned down to kiss her, and she brought her mouth up to meet his. After a few moments he finally released her, and she could not help but smile at him. Despite the events of the day before, she could not believe she was standing there next to him, at last. As her stomach began to rumble, she remembered just how hungry she was. "Do we have anything to eat?" she asked.

"Yes, got a rabbit this morning. Brought a few other things from the farm. Let me finish up this last cord of wood, and we'll get it on the fire."

Cordia was relieved that he was willing to help her as she had never cooked over an open fire before. "All right," she agreed. "Is there something I can do to help you?" she asked.

"No," he replied, "just go inside where it's warm."

She kissed him again before she turned and walked back to the cabin. She glanced around the small space, trying to determine if there was anything she could do to put herself to good use. It seemed that Will had recently repaired much of the chinking in the log timbers that made up the exterior of the house. The fireplace also showed signs of recent repair. Despite the fact that the house had not been lived in for years, it was very clean, and Cordia could see just how much Will loved this place.

The bed needed straightening, but Cordia realized the sheets would have to be washed. If there had been any question in Will's mind as to whether or not he was her first, there could be none now. She was pondering just how one did the laundry out here when she heard him at the door behind her. "That was fast," she said turning to smile at him.

He was carrying the rabbit, which was skinned, and set it down next to the fireplace. "I was almost finished when you came out," he replied. He could see that she was puzzling over the sheets so he crossed over to where she stood. "What's the matter?" he asked.

Cordia could feel her face flushing. "How do you wash the clothes?" she asked.

He saw the problem and couldn't help but laugh just a bit. "Well, Ma and Jules used to get water from the well and use the wash basin, which is hangin' on the wall over there. You think you're up for that?" he asked, realizing Cordia had probably never had to do the laundry ever before in her life.

"Do you think that I am not capable of fulfilling my wifely duties?" she asked, turning to look at him, a sly smile on her face.

"Oh, I have no doubt that you are fully capable of that, my dear. Or else, we wouldn't have this problem now, would we?" he asked, leaning over to kiss her.

Once he released her, she walked over to the wall and pulled the basin down. It was heavier than she had expected, and she almost dropped it. He moved as if he was going to help her but could see by her expression that she wanted to do this herself. Despite its weight, she managed to get it outside. She knew that the well in the front of the yard was dry, so she glanced around and saw a second one in the back of the house. She was confused, however, with how to get the water from the well to the basin. Will opened the door, handing her another bucket, a bar of lye soap, and the sheets.

"I was just coming to get that," she said, matter-of-factly.

"I'm sure you were," he replied, smirking.

"Hmm," she said, placing the sheet in the washbasin, tossing in the soap and taking the bucket over to the well. Being a frontier wife was harder than she had expected.

IT WAS all Isaac could do to keep from yelling to wake Jane up. He had flown up the stairs, faster than he had moved in years. She was still asleep, and he didn't want to startle her, but she needed to know what he had found immediately. "Jane," he said, sitting down on the edge of the bed and shaking her gently.

Jane began to stir, her snoring growing louder before finally ceasing. Her eyes fluttered, and when they finally opened, she realized that she had slept too long and that she needed to get up. Cordia was still missing.

Isaac placed his hand gently on his wife's shoulder. "It's all right, Jane," he said in as calm a voice as possible. "I found a note from Cordia. She's fine."

Jane couldn't believe her ears. "A note?" she repeated. "Let me see!" She took the paper from his hands and read it over, her face turning from shock, to surprise, to rage.

Dear Daddy,

I am so sorry for worrying you, but I could not risk putting this note anywhere that Carey Adams may look to find it. I have left town tonight with Will Tucker. I love him. I have never loved Carey Adams. I broke off my engagement to Carey earlier today, and he came here tonight to attack me. Will saved me, but we fear that Carey will do his best to seek vengeance. I'm not sure

*where we are going, but you will hear from me soon, I promise. Do not worry
about me. I am safe and sound with Will.*

All my love,

Cordia

"That scoundrel!" Jane shouted. "We need to find him immediately
so that Sheriff Dickerson can put him behind bars."

Isaac nodded, "I know, darling, but he's gone. He stopped by the
house earlier to say he was riding out of town. Said he was going to
look for Cordia. But I'm wondering now if that's true. Union cavalry is
in town, and I'm wondering if he didn't just disappear, afraid he'd get
himself into trouble with the Northern soldiers. Or maybe he thought
he'd be found out."

"But what if he does go look for Cordia? What then?" Jane
implored, still afraid that her daughter might be in danger.

"I'll ride over to the Adams Farm in a bit and see if they have any
idea where Will might've gone. I also need to go alert the sheriff that
we were lookin' for the wrong fellow."

"All right," Jane agreed, leaning back against the headboard, only
slightly more relieved than she had been the night before. "Where did
you find that letter, anyway?" she asked.

A guilty look flashed across Isaac's face. "Well, you weren't awake to
get me breakfast, so I may have had a cookie, or two."

"Isaac Pike," Jane declared. "Thank goodness your daughter knows
about your sweet tooth or else we may have never figured out what
happened to her."

"Did you have to do a lot of cooking for yourself when you were
encamped?" Cordia asked, finishing up the rabbit stew Will had
prepared for her while she was out scrubbing the bedding. The sheets
were hanging on a makeshift laundry line now, her efforts successful.

"Sometimes, if we could find something to cook," he replied.
"Spent most of the time eating hardtack though." The memory made
him grimace, and he was thankful, once again, that the army life was
behind him.

"Well, this was very tasty," Cordia said, finishing up and wondering what she was supposed to do with her dishes. At home, they had a sink with a water pump. Clearly, she would be doing more washing in the basin outside.

"Thank you," he said smiling. "You like to cook though, don't you?"

"I do," she said, nodding. "But we're gonna have to figure out how to get a stove in here if you want me to cook. I've never cooked on an open fire before."

"We can get a stove," Will assured her. "I'm planning on building on. We'll need a private space for Julia. I saved up most of the money I earned over the last few years, so we should be able to make some improvements around here."

Cordia tried not to look too relieved. "That's good," she said. "I was wondering if Nevada was close enough for me to get a nursing job there."

"Possibly, if you want to," Will said, not realizing she had considered working outside of the home. "It's certainly something we can look into if you want. But I don't want you to feel like you have to work. I'm more than prepared to provide a good life for you, Cordia. We'll just have to get some things worked out."

She nodded, hoping she hadn't offended him. She was sure he could take care of her just fine. Working with Dr. Walters had given her the opportunity to help others, and she found that she really enjoyed nursing. Of course, once they brought Julia to live with them, she would have the opportunity to take care of her, at least until she was strong enough to take care of herself.

"Speaking of Nevada, what do you think about riding over and sending a telegraph to your parents and one to my aunt and uncle?" he asked, stacking their dishes together.

"Do you think that will alert the authorities as to our whereabouts?" she asked.

"They'll know we are near Nevada but not exactly where. Besides, if we let them know you're safe and sound, hopefully, it will dissuade them from sending out any further search parties."

"All right," Cordia agreed. She had been extremely worried about her parents. Though she had written the note, there was a possibility that her father had lost his appetite if he had been considerably worried about her. It was also possible that Carey had found the note.

"We'll have to make sure we're back before dark, though. It's Halloween and that might lead to some rambunctious behavior for some folks," Will explained, taking the dishes outside to wear Cordia had left the wash basin to dry.

She grabbed the bucket and followed. "Do you think that the devil's holiday will stir up any devilish behavior?" she asked.

"Hope not," Will replied, taking the bucket and going to retrieve enough water from the well to wash the dirty dishes.

Cordia stayed behind, wondering exactly what the devil was planning to do.

CAREY ADAMS WAS STARING the devil in the face. William C. Quantrill himself, the ex-school teacher who had abandoned Gen. Sterling Price's division and rode out to form his own band of guerrillas. He had become famous for many of his raids in the area but none so much as the one on Lawrence, Kansas, in August. Now, he was on his way back from northern Missouri, headed to Texas for the winter and pondering whether or not to stop by the county seat of Barton on his way, just to cause a little mischief.

Carey had also served with Price, but he had never met Quantrill. Some of the men he was riding with had, however, and the assured the commander that, despite his disability, Carey was one he would want to have on his side. "Name sounds familiar," Quantrill mentioned, looking Carey over.

"I believe you knew my cousin, Lt. Jaris Adams," Carey explained. "Died at Wilson's Creek."

Quantrill nodded. "Hell of a fighter, that one. You're his cousin? You're all right by me then. Tell me what you know about the defenses set up at Lamar."

Carey smiled. He knew plenty, and he wasn't afraid to sell his soul to the devil in the name of revenge.

MARGARET WASN'T SURPRISED to see Isaac standing at her door. She let him in and invited him to the kitchen for some coffee. He accepted and waited until she joined him at the kitchen table before starting the conversation. "Do you know where they are?" he asked simply, taking a sip of the warm beverage.

"I reckon I do," Margaret admitted, stirring a small amount of milk into the steaming cup. "You know he didn't take her against her will, don't you?"

Isaac nodded. "She left a note. Looks like Carey was up to no good, and Will defended her."

"Sheriff still looking for him?" she asked, finally taking a drink.

"No, straightened that out this morning before I headed over here. They're keeping an eye out for Carey, but he done disappeared," Isaac explained.

"We should have known Cordia never intended to marry Carey," Margaret sighed. "Why ever did she agree to do so?"

"I've been thinking about that a lot," Isaac admitted. "You know, looking back on it, Cordia never did say 'yes.' He put that ring on her finger, and we threw a party. I guess she felt obligated. Sure wish I'd known about Will, though. This whole time, she kept that a secret. Feel like I missed out on two years of her life, having no idea what she was going through, worrying about him, missing him. I just wish she would have trusted me enough to let me know," he took his hat off and brushed his thinning hair back before replacing it.

Margaret felt herself beginning to get emotional and did what she could to prevent it. "It wasn't you she was afraid of hurting, I don't reckon," she explained. "I think she was afraid of offending me and Arthur. And rightly so. It wasn't the easiest thing I ever heard, you know, to find out she never loved Jaris, that she was corresponding with Will before he was even gone."

"I know, I know," Isaac assured her, nodding his head. "And I am truly sorry for that. She loves you and this family dearly. And I know she loved him, too, she truly did. Just not in the way she was supposed to, I guess. If she'd'a never met Will, maybe she would have gone through and married Jaris and learned to be happy, the way so many do. But Cordia's never been one to acquiesce. That's why I find this situation with Carey so confusing."

"Maybe she was scared," Margaret reasoned. "Scared that he would try to hurt her or another member of your family if she didn't consent. Maybe she was just waiting for Will to get back."

Isaac nodded his head. "Maybe so. And I guess she had reason after what transpired last night." He took another sip of his coffee, considering the statement. "Now, where do you think they might be?"

"I suppose they're at Will's folks' house, up by Nevada. But I don't think you should ride out there, not just yet. I figure they'll let us know where they are when they're good and ready."

"But her mother. . ." Isaac began.

"Tell her mother that we heard from her, and she's fine. She'll believe you. Otherwise, you're walking into a situation where you're not welcome, and you'll just end up stirring up trouble. She's twenty-one years old, Isaac. She's a grown woman. Give her some space. She ain't seen him in two years. Let 'em be." Margaret seemed fairly certain in her convictions, so Isaac nodded. Just then, there was a loud fit of coughing from the adjoining bedroom, and Margaret jumped up to go tend to Julia.

"I'll let myself out," Isaac said, walking back toward the front door. "Thank you, kindly, Margaret." He thought he heard her acknowledge him as she attempted to help Julia bring her coughing back under control.

THE TRIP into Nevada took about thirty minutes each way. Besides sending the telegraphs, they had also gotten some much-needed supplies. Will was anxious to hear how Julia was doing, and he didn't want to stay cut-off from his family for too long, but he also wanted to make sure that Cordia's father had the opportunity to receive the telegraph and calm down the authorities some before they headed back to Lamar. That was assuming that anyone was even looking for them. They weren't even sure that Carey had reported anything to the sheriff at all. They decided to wait about a week before venturing back to the Adams Farm to ascertain the situation.

They had done their best to avoid as many people as possible, particularly other riders. The fewer people who knew the old Tucker homestead was occupied again, the better, especially since the town was alive with whispers and rumors of guerrillas and marauders. Despite the fact that the house she was staying in had been marked by vigilantes only a few years ago, as she returned home, Cordia felt safe. She felt that Will could protect her against anyone. And she knew how to use a gun, too, if necessity called upon her to do so.

Returning home before dark, they went about the evening chores, such as taking care of the horses. One of the first things Will had done was repair the old barn, and they were able to keep their horses in there until he had the chance to finish up repairs to the fence around the pasture. The soil had come back some these past two years, though it had been fairly unproductive the last several years his father farmed it. It was too late in the season now to plant much, but he had every intention of turning these 150 acres back into a working farm come spring. He explained his vision to Cordia over dinner, and she agreed to help him however she could, excited at the idea of having something that belonged to them.

They retired as soon as the sun went down, despite sleeping in so late that afternoon. Cordia was not so nervous now, and she was just as eager as he was to climb into bed. Even though she no longer lived in an enormous house, no longer had her parents and Frieda to take care of her, and she had left most of her worldly possessions behind, she was as happy as she could ever remember. She had found her home in Will's arms, and that was all that mattered to her now

ISAAC HAD RETURNED from the Adams Farm, stopping by his house just long enough to assure Jane and Frieda that Margaret had heard from Will and Cordia and that they were safe. Both women were relieved. They had several questions, none of which did Isaac feel like answering, so he had made his way to the bank. It was afternoon by the time he had arrived at his office, but he would much rather sit at his desk and do some work than be bombarded with questions he would have to invent answers to.

He hadn't been there long when a light knock on his door drew his attention. "Come in," he yelled, looking to see whom it might be. He expected one of his colleagues to come through the door, but to his surprise, it was Mr. Ward from the courthouse.

"Afternoon, Isaac," he said, holding a paper in his outstretched hand. "Wanted to get this to you right away. I know you been lookin' for your girl."

Isaac quickly grabbed the paper, reading it before Mr. Ward even let it go.

Daddy wanted to make sure you know I'm safe. Carey is the assailant. We will be back as soon. My love to you and Mama. Cordia.

Isaac nodded, rereading the short message. "Where did she send it from?" he asked.

"Vernon County's all I know," Mr. Ward replied. "You think that's true, what she says there about Carey?" he asked. Of course, he had to read the telegraph as he was taking it down, but Isaac was a bit annoyed that he was prying into his personal business.

After a moment, Isaac replied, "I believe my daughter, if that's what you're asking."

"Oh, no, of course. You don't think Will Tucker forced her to send that message, do you?" Mr. Ward said a bit defensively.

"Of course not," Isaac responded. "We had already figured out this morning that Carey was the perpetrator here. If he hadn't disappeared out of town, I'd be sending the sheriff after him now."

"Unbelievable," Mr. Ward muttered, shaking his head. "Leader of the militia. And now he's taken off to join Quantrill."

"What's that?" Isaac asked, his eyes snapping up from the telegraph and back into Mr. Ward's face.

"Yep. Brandy Nance stopped by a bit ago, checking to see if she'd gotten any telegraphs from her husband, Bill. Said he rode off this morning with a band of fellers who was upset about the cavalry arriving in town. Said that Carey was leading them out to meet up with Quantrill," Mr. Ward explained.

Isaac absently rubbed his head. "I'll be," he finally whispered in disbelief. "Well, I guess that answers any questions we may have still had about Lt. Adams's character, doesn't it?"

"Yes, indeed it does," Mr. Ward agreed. "I just hope he isn't planning on leading them in here," he added. "Carey knows this town pretty well. Surely, he won't allow them to raid Lamar."

Isaac considered the possibility for a moment. Shaking his head, he said, "No, not even Carey is that malicious. If nothing else, it may be a reason Quantrill decides to bypass Lamar on his way down south and leave us alone. Maybe Carey will be good for something after all."

"Hope so," Mr. Ward said, turning to go. "By the way, Will sent word to his aunt and uncle, too. Says they're planning on coming back in a week or so, unless Julia gets worse, and then to let him know. So, I figure that means somebody out there knows how to find your daughter, if you're wantin' to hunt her down."

"Thank you," Isaac said, already having that piece of information. At least with the telegraph, he would have something to refer to when Jane started asking questions. He wouldn't have to lie anymore. If it wasn't on the paper, then her guess was as good as his.

CAREY WAS ENCAMPED with Quantrill and his band of raiders, which numbered nearly two hundred, in a wooded area north of Lamar, for several days before they finally rode out to meet up with a few stragglers who had been out visiting family. Quantrill had been corresponding with Col. Warren Lewis of the Missouri State Guard, and they both had their eye on the outpost located in Lamar at the courthouse. On November 4, Quantrill gathered up his forces and began the ride north. Carey and the few men who had come along with him were instrumental in giving information about roads and the location of troops, etc. Carey also suggested that they try to take out the prominent businessmen in town and their families. Quantrill agreed. Any permanent scars they could leave on the face of the town would be well worth it. Carey sketched a rough map of the town, placing an "X" on the homes of the town leaders, and Quantrill made sure his marauders knew precisely where to strike.

After one last night of planning, Quantrill began to get his men into position. It was agreed that he would bring his troops in from north of town. Lewis's men would come in from the south. They would convene on the town square around ten o'clock that night. The plan was to raid the outpost, set fire to the courthouse, and burn as many other houses to the ground as possible on their way out of town. Quantrill would take his men south, as they would be on their way to Texas for the winter.

Knowing they would have to cross Muddy Creek, Carey attempted to convince Quantrill to use the smaller of the available bridges, explaining that it was located in a portion of town where there were fewer houses and that there would be less possibility of detection. Quantrill considered the possibility, but in the end, he thought the bridge was too narrow. He would use another avenue of crossing Muddy Creek, though he wasn't opposed to his men using that secondary bridge as an escape route. They had specific orders of where to meet up once the raid was over.

Bill Nance was frightened for the safety of his wife and children. Carey had assured him that their own homes wouldn't be harmed, but he did not know how it was possible to be so sure. No one seemed to notice when Bill snuck off later that afternoon, compelled to warn the 8th Cavalry and get his family to safety before the Devil rode into town.

Chapter Fifteen

CORDIA WAS STARTING to feel comfortable with her role as the frontier housewife. She was beginning to do some of the cooking, could handle the cleaning, and even helped with some of the repairs on the outside of the house. Despite missing her family and friends, she was perfectly content to live out here alone, with only Will to keep her company, for the rest of her days. Even after spending almost an entire week seeing and speaking to only each other, they were every bit as much in love as they had been over the course of the two years when they had not seen each other at all. She had never doubted her love for him, and now she was assured that they made the perfect couple.

Thursday, November 5 was a chilly day. In fact, it seemed to be growing colder as the day grew long. They had attempted to work on gathering firewood and mending another section of the fence, but they had not made much progress before noon when they returned to the warmth of the little cabin and a stew that Cordia had put on that morning.

"My fingers are frozen," Cordia complained, bending her fingers over and over again as she stood by the fire.

"You were wearing gloves," Will replied, questioningly.

"I know," Cordia admitted. "Maybe I need some new ones."

"Maybe you should knit some mittens," Will said, teasingly, making a gesture as if his fingers were all stuck together except for his thumbs.

She couldn't help but laugh at him as the blood began to course back through her hands enough for her to ladle out the stew. "I'd be a lot of help to you out there with no fingers," she declared. "Not that I'm that much help to you now," she remarked setting the bowls and spoons down and pulling out her chair.

Before she could sit down, he wrapped his arms around her from behind. "You are an amazing help," he said quietly, kissing her softly on the cheek.

She wrapped her arms around his and smiled. "Oh, yeah?" she asked, enjoying the feel of his lips as he continued to kiss her.

"Most definitely," he confirmed, his teeth tugging gently on her ear.

Just as she began to think perhaps the stew could wait, they heard an approaching rider outside. Will grabbed his rifle from where he kept it mounted on the wall and gently pushed Cordia behind the door. He opened it cautiously and peered outside. Realizing it was his Uncle Arthur, he set the gun down and motioned for Cordia. He felt a lump growing in his throat as he stepped outside. There was only one reason why his uncle would be there.

"Better come quick," he said without dismounting.

Will nodded and looked back at Cordia, who already had tears in her eyes. Without saying anything, he went back inside to put the fire out and grab his revolver, just in case they ran into any guerrillas on the way to Lamar.

THE RIDE from the Tucker house to the Adams Farm was nearly silent and forced. The horses were spurred on in a full gallop for as long as they could bear it. Arthur did not have to say anything more for Will to know that, if Arthur was riding out to retrieve him, Julia must have grown much worse.

When they arrived, Zachariah came out and took their horses. Arthur helped Cordia dismount but by the time she was off of her horse, Will was already inside the farmhouse, flying toward the back room. Cordia caught up with him at the door of Julia's room, where he paused to compose himself before entering. She put her hand gently on his back, giving him the assurance he needed to enter the room and survey his sister's waning condition.

As they entered the room, they could see Dr. Walters sitting on a chair next to her bed, Margaret at the foot of the bed but within reach of her niece. Julia's breathing was labored, but she was breathing. Her cheeks were flushed and her forehead looked clammy. Both the doctor and Margaret rose when they realized Will and Cordia had arrived, and they moved to the back of the room so that Will could speak to his sister. Cordia wanted to give him some time, so she stayed by the foot of the bed as Will sat next to Julia.

"Jules?" Will said quietly, taking her frail hand in his. "How are you feeling?"

Her eyes were just slits, but she recognized his voice at once and smiled. "Oh, Will. You're home at last! Is the war over?"

Will considered the question, and since the war had ended for him, he replied, "Yes, dear sister, it's over."

"Did we win?" she asked, her raspy voice just a whisper.

"We did," he replied, brushing strands of hair away from her moist forehead.

Julia sighed. "I'm so glad. I knew we would win." She was clearly heavily medicated and was having trouble staying awake. "Did you see Cordia?"

Will glanced back at his wife, who had tears gently streaming down her face. "I'm here, Julia," Cordia replied, a slight catch in her voice. "I'm right here."

Julia smiled again. Her eyes didn't quite focus on Cordia, but it was enough to know she was in the room. "Oh, good. I can't wait for the wedding. You're going to be such a beautiful bride."

Will glanced down at their father's ring, which he had been wearing for the past few days, hoping she wouldn't notice. "It will be a beautiful ceremony," he assured her. "And you'll have a spot right next to Cordia, to stand with her in a position of honor."

"Oh, yes, it will be lovely. And I will wear a pink dress with lace," Julia muttered. Her breath was very labored now. Will could feel tears in his eyes, realizing that she did not have much longer, and he was not sure exactly what to say to her. Guilty thoughts began to flood his mind. He had not been there for her these past two years; he had not been there for her even this week. Now, she would soon be gone, and there was nothing he could do to make it up to her.

As if she was reading his mind, she turned to him, opening her eyes as wide as she could, and looking directly into his. "Will," she began, "I want you to know how proud of you I am. You went off and fought for the cause, defending the name of our Nolan. You are the best brother a girl could ever hope for, and I am honored to call you my own." The statement had seemed to take all of her energy, and she began to cough a bit.

Wiping the tiny splatters of blood from her mouth, Will could no longer hold back the tears. "Thank you, Julia," he said, his hand smoothing her cheek. "It is I who should be grateful to have the opportunity to be your brother. You are such an amazing girl. I can't tell you just how very much I love you."

"I love you, too, Will," she mumbled, her eyes completely closed now. "I'm so tired. . . could we talk some more tomorrow?"

"Yes, yes of course," he replied, adjusting the blankets around her. "You rest now, Julia, and we will talk again by and by."

He waited a few moments until she was asleep before standing and walking to the back of the room to consult with the doctor. Cordia wrapped her arm through his, both of them doing all they could to hold back their tears.

Dr. Walters spoke in a hushed voice, so as not to disturb her. "She doesn't have much time, maybe a couple of hours," he began. "She was suffering something awful, so I gave her a considerable dose of laudanum, which has relieved her coughing and her pain. Of course, with that comes the extreme fatigue. But, you understand, it is for the best."

Will nodded, not able to speak at first. "No, I don't want her to be in any pain," he finally managed to get out. He had watched his parents suffer from consumption, his father coughing up blood and pieces of lung for days before he finally succumbed. His mother had attempted to take care of her children up until the very last, and she collapsed outside one day, her dress covered in blood. She never awoke. No, he did not want to see Julia suffer, not if it could be helped.

"I believe she will pass in her sleep," Dr. Walters continued. "If she does wake up, I recommend we give her some more medication. Eventually, her lungs will simply quit functioning, and her breathing will stop."

Will brought his free hand to his eyes and squeezed the bridge of his nose, not quite able to grasp what the doctor was saying. "And you think this will be in a few hours?" he clarified.

Nodding, Dr. Walters said, "It might be as long as ten or so, but it could be as few as two. It's hard to say. She's been fighting it for so long. She's tired. I believe she's ready to go, son," he added, patting Will on the upper arm.

After a moment of consideration, Will responded. "All right. Do you mind if I speak to my wife outside for a moment?" he asked, taking Cordia's hand. He didn't seem to noticed the slightly surprised looks on the doctor's face and his aunt's as he led Cordia out of the bedroom, through the kitchen, and out the back door.

Before he could say anything, Cordia wrapped her arms around him and buried her head in his shoulder. She was sobbing, and it was all he could do to keep from letting his emotions overcome him as well. He stroked her hair and rubbed her back, doing his best to comfort her. Eventually, her sobs lessened and he began to speak. "I think you should go to your parents' house for the evening," he said quietly.

Cordia looked up at him in surprise. "What? Why?" she asked, a few tears still streaming down her face.

Will wasn't exactly sure he had the words to explain his thinking, but he was content to try. "Cordia, I know how much you love her, I do. And she loves you, too. I just feel like this is something I need to do on my own."

"But, Will, we're married now. You don't ever have to do anything on your own," Cordia replied.

He sighed, brushing a tear from her cheek. "I know that, darlin'. But I'm not sure how well I'm gonna handle this, and I would rather just get through this night on my own and work through the rest of it with you. I can't begin to explain how extremely guilty I feel for leaving her these past few years."

"Will," Cordia said gently, "You heard what she said. She's proud of you. She knows why you were gone."

"I know, I know," he replied. "But that doesn't change how I'm feeling, not right now. Please, Cordia, just do this for me. Your family wants to see you, and I need to do this my way."

Reluctantly, Cordia nodded. She wanted to do whatever she could to make this as easy on him as possible, and as much as she loved Julia, she couldn't bear to think of watching her die. Spending some time with her parents would do her good, and she missed them terribly. "All right," she said. "I'll go."

"Thank you," he said, leaning down and kissing her. "I'll ask Zachariah to ride over with you." It was starting to get dark outside, and he didn't feel that it was a good idea to let her go alone, particularly since there had been rumors of so many marauders in the area recently.

Zachariah was obliged to ride Cordia over to her parents' house in town, and Will watched her go until he could see her no more before turning and walking back inside. When he got back to the kitchen, he found his aunt sitting at the table, staring at a cup of coffee, the doctor in with Julia, listening to her hearts and lungs.

"Your wife?" she asked as he entered the room, not looking up from the black liquid steaming from the cup in front of her.

He paused behind her chair, just a few steps from his sister's doorway. "Yes," he replied quietly. "We got married that first night," he explained. "Rode straight to a pastor's house in Nevada, and he performed the ceremony." He walked around behind her, stopping at the doorway to Julia's room.

She turned to look at him over her shoulder now. "Congratulations," she said, managing a smile. "Seems you two really are meant to be together."

Taking a few steps back, he placed his hand on her shoulder, and she reached up and gave his hand a tight squeeze.

"Thank you," he replied quietly, watching as the doctor stood and crossed over to the door.

Dr. Walters was shaking his head. "I don't think it will be too much longer," he said sadly. "Her lungs sound so weak, and her heartbeat has slowed considerably."

Sighing, Will said, "Thank you for all you've done, Doctor." He offered his hand, and the doctor shook it. Will left him to his aunt's care and went in to sit with Julia. He sat in the chair next to her bed so as not to disturb her and began to do something he rarely did anymore; he began to pray. He was not imploring the Lord to let her stay, rather to give her a comfortable passage, to gather their family to greet her, and to keep His arms wrapped around her so she would feel no more pain. He was not sure if his prayers were of any use to Julia, but he found strength and comfort in repeating his request, so he continued to do so as he watched Julia's angelic face.

CORDIA'S PARENTS were elated to see her, though hearing of the circumstances that brought her diminished their joy significantly. They invited Zachariah in, but he declined, thinking his mother may need him back at the house. He knew that, once Julia had passed, his mother would be extremely emotional, and he wanted to be there to comfort her.

Once Frieda had greeted her, she disappeared into the kitchen, pouring drinks and preparing something for Cordia to eat. Though she protested that she was not hungry, Frieda insisted that she would need her strength. Cordia joined her parents in the parlor, feeling awkwardly like a guest in what was, until very recently, her own home for so long. She sat on the duvet across from her parents, who sat in their usual chairs. The fire was blazing in the fireplace, and Cordia suddenly became very aware of how cold she had been, despite her heavy winter coat.

"Well, Cordia, dear," her mother began. "How have you been? What have you been doing this past week?"

Cordia had lost track of time and did not realize it had been almost a week until her mother said so. "Well, we've had plenty to keep ourselves busy out on the farm. Will did a lot to fix up the house and the barn before I got there, but we've been working on the fence, getting firewood ready for the winter, that sort of thing." Though she did not mind relaying her experiences to her parents, she could not keep her mind completely focused on the discussion. Her thoughts kept wondering back to Julia and to Will. She would have no way of knowing if and when her friend passed, but the doctor had seemed fairly certain it would be soon, and Cordia had lost any hope that she may actually improve.

"That sounds like a lot of hard work," Isaac admitted. He had never known his daughter to thrive on physical labor, but he was proud of her for her willingness to pitch in.

"What is the house like?" her mother asked. "Is it a farmhouse?"

"No," Cordia explained. "It's just a little log cabin for now, but we intended to build on. Will wants to build a few more rooms in the back and add a second story. Course, one of those rooms was going to be for Julia...." she said, her voice trailing off.

"How many rooms does it have now?" Jane asked. Isaac reached over and gave her arm a squeeze, an indication to Cordia that her mother was getting at something, though in her distracted state, Cordia wasn't sure exactly what.

"Just one," she replied, an eyebrow arched. Suddenly, she realized why her mother was making such odd inquiries. She had not given them the most important news of all. "Oh, Mama," she said her hand flying to her forehead. "Forgive me, I've been worried for a week about how to tell you this, but now, considering the circumstances, it doesn't seem like such a trial after all. Will and I are married." She paused for a moment when her mother gasped, covering her mouth with both hands. "The night we left here, we went straight to a pastor in Nevada, one Will knew from before the war. He married us that night. So, you don't have to worry about your little girl living in sin."

The sound of her father's chuckle was not lost on Cordia. She couldn't tell if he was laughing at her last remark or at the situation in general. She had not been as worried about her father accepting the fact that she had eloped; she was much more concerned about her mother's feelings.

Jane took a few moments to recover from the news. "Well," she began, "I am certainly relieved to hear that you were proactive in your decision making," she replied. "But I must say I am thoroughly disappointed that we did not get to see you married. You know how much your wedding has meant to me."

Thinking on her feet, Cordia replied, "Will and I have talked about having a local ceremony or a reception of some sort. I could wear a weddin' dress to that, and you can certainly help plan it. How does that sound?" There had been no such discussion, but she was sure that Will would do whatever she asked him to do if it would make her mother happy.

Sighing with relief, Jane nodded. "Yes, that sounds wonderful," she said. "I think that would be lovely." She smiled at her husband who returned the gesture. He had been listening to his wife complain about his daughter committing a deadly sin for days now, and he was relieved that Cordia was wiser than his wife had given her credit for and thankful that Jane would now have something else to throw her energy into.

"What became of Carey?" Cordia asked after a few moments, praying they would tell her he was rotting in jail.

Isaac glanced at Jane before answering. "He rode off the next morning. Stopped by here to tell me he was going out to look for you, but rumor has it he actually rode out to join Quantrill."

Cordia was shocked. "Quantrill?" she repeated. "Why on earth would he do that?"

"Don't rightly know," her father admitted. "But Bill Nance's wife said that's where they were a'goin' that morning when he left."

"So, Quantrill really is in the area?" Cordia asked. She had heard the rumors in Nevada, but she was hopeful that they weren't true.

"I suppose so," Isaac replied. "Not quite sure where he might be, but we keep hearing reports that he's out there somewhere. Some folks say he's interested in the outpost here in town, thinks he can get some provisions there or somethin', but I can't imagine he would spend too much time on our little old town."

Cordia nodded. Surely Quantrill had his eyes on a bigger prize than the little sleepy town of Lamar, Missouri.

❀

A FEW HOURS into Will's vigil, he realized that Julia's breathing had changed. The door to her bedroom was ajar, and he could hear his aunt bustling around, keeping herself busy. "Aunt Margaret," he said as loudly as he could muster. "I think you should probably come in here."

Margaret had been present at quite a few deaths over the years. Thankfully, most of them had been the passing of elderly members of her family, such as her grandparents, though she had watched her mother breath her last at the age of fifty-two. She had always regretted not being there for her brother and his wife, Will's parents, but they had lived such reclusive lives. She didn't even know they were sick until after they had passed. Entering the room, she could tell immediately that Julia's time had come. Her breathing was very shallow and uneven. Several seconds passed between breaths. Catching Will's eye, Margaret nodded solemnly.

He moved from the chair to the bed then, taking her hand in his. Already, her diminutive hand was icy, her fingertips a light shade of blue. He leaned forward and kissed her softly on the forehead. "Good-bye, sweet sister. May the angels guide you as you take flight. You will be at peace at last," he whispered softly into her ear.

Julia took one last breath and then she was gone. Will kissed her one more time before folding her hands across her chest and framing her hair around her face. He couldn't help but think how angelic she truly did look, her sweet face resting peacefully at last. Despite having witnessed the horrors of war, seeing his friends blown to bits on the battlefield before his very eyes, the realization that the last of his family had left him brought him to tears, and he began to sob uncontrollably. His aunt was there then, wrapping her arms around him and allowing him to be vulnerable, allowing him to grieve. She said nothing, just held him, wiping her own tears away. Julia had come to be the daughter she had always longed for, and it would not be easy going on without her. They would have to pull together as a family to make it through yet another loss of one so young.

It was quite some time before Will was able to regain his composure. This was precisely why he had asked Cordia to go to her parents' house. Though he knew she would not judge him for being human, he did not want his new wife to see him so full of despair. He was thankful, however, that his aunt was there to comfort him. When he was finally able to speak, he wiped away his tears and looked up at her, saying, "Thank you, Aunt Margaret. I don't know what we would have done without you these past two years."

"There, there," she replied, still rubbing his back. "Y'all are my family. We love you dearly. We were so lucky to have been able to spend the time with sweet Julia. She really was a gift from God."

Will nodded, unable to speak again. He glanced back at his sister and realized, the longer he stayed in this room, the more tears he would shed. "I think I need to get some air," he said, standing.

Margaret let him go. "Take your time. We'll wait until morning to let Dr. Walters and the proper parties know. Ain't no use in bringing anyone out this time of night."

Will nodded his understanding, but he did not turn around. He walked through the kitchen and the side room that used to hold his cot, onto the small porch on the side of the house. Upon opening the door, the smell of pipe smoke hit him in the face, and he realized his uncle was sitting there in his old wooden rocking chair, staring up at the stars.

Will said nothing but sat down in another chair, wishing he had taken up smoking or that he had a stiff drink. Since he had neither, he settled for gazing up at the sky, letting the cool November wind blow away his tears.

Arthur wasn't precisely sure how to ask the question that was hanging on his tongue. Finally, he said simply, "All over then?"

Will nodded, knowing that words were dangerous just now.

Pondering his answer for a few moments, Arthur eventually said, "I'm so sorry to hear that. We'll miss her somethin' awful."

Again, Will mustered a nod. Over the past two years he had grown accustomed to missing Julia. Now, he knew that, from time to time, he might forget that she was gone, might catch himself thinking he would see her again someday, when he came to visit his aunt and uncle. Those were the types of thoughts that often ended up being the most painful, and he was not looking forward to such situations at all.

They sat in silence for quite some time and, in the darkness, Will began to realize just how much he missed Cordia. He was certainly thankful she had not been present for his emotional breakdown, but he had become acclimated to having her nearby. He knew this night would be endless and restless either way, but at least, if Cordia were there, he would have someone to comfort and distract him. He began to ponder the possibility of showing up at her parents' house but assumed that they were probably all in bed as late as it was. How he was ever going to make it through this night alone, he was not sure.

Just then, he caught a whiff of smoke on the air. Not pipe smoke, but something else. He looked at his uncle who sat up straight in his chair, obviously smelling it, too. "What's that?" Will asked, standing.

"Not sure," Arthur replied also jumping out of his chair. They both walked down off of the porch, out into the yard. It didn't take them long to see where the smell was coming from or what had started the fire. A band of horsemen rode off into the night, leaving their mark on the Adams Farm.

CAREY WAS FURIOUS. "This is my aunt and uncle's farm!" he was yelling, bringing his horse between the torch men and the shed they had just lit on fire. "You have direct orders from Quantrill not to touch any of our property or our relations'!"

"Sorry! We didn't know!" an older crosseyed soldier spat back before riding off. Though it was too late for this particular shed, Carey was hopeful that he could save the rest of the farm from a similar fate. He was leading a small band of marauders into town. Quantrill had split his men into smaller groups so that they could enter the city limits a bit more stealthily. They would meet back up at the court-house directly. Carey had given very specific directions to everyone as to which houses were to be spared, this being one of them, but apparently these outlaws had not listened as closely as he would have liked, and he began to fear for the safety of his father who was likely sleeping in the home they had shared. He contemplated whether or not he should break away and warn his father or continue to ride with this pack. As much as he hoped his father and their home would make it through the fray, the idea of gaining vengeance won out, and he led the men through his uncle's property, riding directly between their home and the large barn that housed all of their horses, out to the road that led into town.

WILL and Arthur stayed in the shadows but ran around to the other side of the house to watch the horsemen ride past, ensuring none of them stayed behind to wreak further havoc. "We need to get that fire out before it spreads!" Arthur cried, running back to the house to retrieve his sons.

There was only one thought on Will's mind, however. "I've got to get to Cordia!" he yelled, running for the barn to get his horse. He didn't wait to hear if his uncle had any words of wisdom. As he saddled up his horse, he realized he had neither of his weapons, having taken them both inside with him upon arrival. Climbing upon his stead, he hastened back toward the house. Though Arthur and his older two sons were running toward the blazing outbuilding, buckets in hand, John was coming toward Will, carrying his pistol and his rifle. Will slowed the horse only long enough to snatch the weapons out of his cousin's hands, nodding his thanks, and he took off, headed straight for Cordia's house, praying he could find a way to avoid the marauders as he went.

CORDIA WAS LOOKING FORWARD to sleeping in her bed, even though she was missing her husband. Still, her mattress was so much more comfortable than the one at the cabin, and she was wondering if it might be possible to move her entire bed out there, though it would take up most of the room. Perhaps, once they built on they would have enough space for it.

She was just about to wish her parents goodnight when they heard a loud commotion outside. Isaac ran to the parlor window to see what was going on. Suddenly, a rock came flying through the dining room window, directly across the foyer from where they stood, followed by a burning torch. Cordia heard her mother screaming behind her, but she wasted no time in tearing down the curtains from the window and smothering the torch before it could ignite anything else.

Despite Cordia's success in putting out the flames, the noise outside was an indication that they were not out of danger yet. Gunshots rang out in the air around their house, the cool night air bringing the sound in through the broken window. Jane was still screaming, and Isaac contemplated giving her a good, hard slap across the face to make her shut up as he crossed in front of her, hurrying to the gun cabinet. He didn't have time, however, so she continued to fill the room with terrified yelps.

Frieda was up now, rushing down the stairs in her nightclothes, demanding to know what was happening.

"We're under attack," Isaac said as calmly as he could. "Jane," he continued, crossing the room to hand Cordia a loaded rifle. "Go with Frieda into the crawlspace under the stairs. Lock the door, and don't come out until Cordia or I tell you to—unless you smell smoke."

Jane's feet weren't moving until Frieda grabbed her by the arm and began to pull her in the direction Isaac had indicated. The screaming stopped after a few moments, or at least they were far enough away that Isaac and Cordia could no longer hear her.

Cordia cocked the rifle. The thought of using the gun on a human being was revolting to her, but when it came to protecting her family, she would not hesitate to do so. The cacophony outside was growing louder, and the smell of smoke was wafting in on the breeze blowing in through the broken window. Isaac positioned himself next to the window in the parlor, and Cordia ducked down next to the broken window, pushing the shattered glass out of her way with the butt of the gun. Their house sat back away from the road a bit, so anyone who wanted to assault them again would have to cross through the yard. If there were not too many of them, Cordia and her father should be able to get a few rounds off before they got close enough to throw another flame. However, if there were enough of them, or if they snuck around the back of the house, there was no guarantee that they couldn't reduce the house to ashes.

WHEN WILL TOOK off from his aunt and uncle's farm, he avoided the main road out front, choosing instead to pass through the yards and farms that would take him directly to Cordia's house. This was risky, however, because, if a neighbor mistook him for a marauder, it was possible he could find a bullet in his back before he had the opportunity to explain. He made his way to the outskirts of town without incident. However, as he began to near the center of town, he realized the situation was far worse than he had even suspected. The sound of gunfire was all around him, and he could smell the smoke pouring off of houses north of town. He knew he would need to avoid the town square since it sounded as if most of the gunfire was coming from that direction.

He rode up on Tenth Street, one of the roads that led to the square, and couldn't believe his eyes. Almost every house was on fire. Citizens were fleeing their homes, most of them in their nightclothes. There was no sign of the guerrillas, as they had apparently ridden on toward the square and the outpost stationed there. He was only about four blocks from the square, and the commotion coming from that direction was steadily growing. As much as he wanted to help these destitute people, he could think only of his wife and her family. He turned his horse south, concluding that, if he could ride a few more blocks in this direction, he could turn back west and cut over toward Cordia's house. The further south he went, the fewer houses, and the less likely he was to draw the attention of the raiders, though it was more likely that these citizens would be ready to shoot anyone on a horse.

Riding south but glancing down the streets he passed, he saw several other structures on fire. Passing Twelfth Street, one of his most grave concerns came to pass as one of the civilians in his yard took aim at the only figure on a horse he could see. Will did not waste time trying to explain that he was one of the good guys, nor did he need to coax his horse to run faster as it took off with the sound of the bullet whizzing by so closely.

Hunkered down over the neck of his horse, he spurred him on, rounding the corner near Fourteenth Street, headed west toward his wife's family home. A new sound spooked his horse now, a sound that Will had hoped he never heard again, the sound of cannon fire.

THE GROUP of men Carey was leading were pyromaniacs, apparently. His understanding was that Quantrill wanted them to converge on the square, take the outpost, and then light the town on fire as they made their escape. These men spent a great deal of time throwing torches through broken windows, and it seemed that they would never make it to the heart of the battle unfolding on the square a few blocks away.

At last, Carey gave the order to ride on, and then did so, not caring who followed. He could see that a large contingency of the men had accompanied him, while only a few stayed behind to torch the houses along Tenth Street. He covered the few blocks to the square quickly, hoping to get in on the fight. It had been almost two years since he had tasted battle, and he was eager to feel the rush of assault again. However, once he got to the square, he realized Quantrill and Lewis had not organized their attack as well as he had hoped. The 8th Cavalry appeared to be ready for them, cannon drawn and ready to fire. Anytime Quantrill's raiders attempted a charge at the Union soldiers, there was heavy return fire, and the marauders had to back off. Granted, the aim of the cannons was such that they frequently missed the mark, but the threat of grape pouring into them was enough to make Quantrill's men rethink their strategy.

Carey saw Quantrill in the distance and hurried his horse off in the direction of the famed leader. He saw a weakness that he hoped the raiders could use to their advantage. "Quantrill, sir," he said as he drew close enough to speak. "Most of the munitions are stored on that side of the courthouse over there, near the gazebo. If we can set that on fire, we might have an opportunity to bring down the courthouse."

Quantrill simply nodded, leaving Carey to move forward with the plan. He rode off to find one or more of the prolific torchers who had accompanied him to this point.

CORDIA AND ISAAC saw several riders pass by in a hurry down Broadway. Some were headed toward the foray on the square, but most were fleeing. There was even a carriage or two that went shooting by, likely families hoping to escape the raiders. They watched carefully for riders approaching their home but saw none for quite some time until Cordia realized a single horseman had crossed out of the shadows on the other side of Broadway and was heading through their yard.

Peering closely, Cordia was quite certain the rider posed no threat. It wasn't until she heard her father cock his gun that she realized that, despite his weakening eyesight, her father also had the rider in his crosshairs. "Stop!" she yelled as Isaac trained his gun.

Isaac had a nervous trigger finger. He had shot plenty of game in his younger years but never a person. Yet, faced with protecting his family, he was prepared to fire on anyone or anything that moved. "What?" he asked. "Why?"

Cordia wasn't certain she was looking at her husband making his way cautiously across her yard, but she was nearly so. Still, she was guarded as she went to the door opening it just wide enough to peer out.

Will was well aware that he had at least two rifles trained on him as he neared the front of the house. He raised both of hands in the air to show that he meant no harm. He saw Isaac withdraw his rifle, and Cordia peek out the door. "It's me, Will," he said as loudly as he dared, not sure who else may be hiding in the darkness around the house.

Isaac breathed a sigh of relief, not willing to think about what he might have done if Cordia hadn't spoken up when she did. Cordia motioned for him to hurry inside and though Will was reluctant to leave his horse tied up in the yard so close to the street, he had little choice. He grabbed his weapons and hurried inside, overjoyed to see that his wife was safe.

Throwing her arms around him, Cordia planted a kiss on Will's lips, not carrying that her father was present. "Thank God you're here," she said releasing him and rushing over to the window.

Will could smell the scorched wood immediately as he knelt down next to her. "What happened?" he asked, surveying the broken glass and the burn mark on the wooden floor.

"They broke the window and threw in a torch," Cordia explained, her eyes still trained on the street.

Will could see the charred curtain tossed in the corner as well. "Who put it out?" he asked, also peering intently out the window.

"I did," Cordia replied, nonchalantly.

Will snickered. "Of course you did," he replied, truly not surprised. He knew his wife was capable of just about anything.

"Is it Quantrill?" Cordia asked only glancing at him as she spoke.

"Believe so," he replied. A rider went flying by just then, but he did not slow and posed no threat. "Good part of the town seems to be on fire," he added.

Cordia gasped. It was difficult to judge exactly what was going on based on the scent pouring in the window. "What about the Adams Farm?"

"When I left it was just a shed, but if they go back that way, who can tell?" Will remarked, praying they exited south of town and didn't ride back through the way they had come.

Cordia wanted to ask about Julia but didn't think this was the right time to do so. The noise from the square was growing. The Rebel yell echoed through the air, a chilling sound that left Cordia shuttering and Will bracing himself against the memories of hearing that cry in battle. Cordia stretched over and put her hand on his knee. He squeezed her hand to let her know he was okay. Just then, an explosion rocked the entire house. The china in the cabinet behind them shook, some of the pieces breaking, and the remaining glass in the window shattered. Will instinctively threw himself on top of Cordia, both of them covering their heads with their arms.

The shaking was over in just a few seconds, and when they believed it was safe to do so, they both looked up, checking to see if everyone was all right. Though Isaac was shaken, he appeared to be fine. "What was that?" Cordia asked, her ears ringing.

"I believe that was the munitions arsenal," Will replied solemnly.

CAREY'S PLAN WAS WORKING. The cavalry was not prepared for an assault on the munitions, and when they blew, it shook the entire square. Glass shards flew through the air, people went flying, horses darted off, some with riders still holding on. The explosion had caught the wooden steeple and roof of the courthouse on fire, and the structure was going up in flames. Within a few moments, the entire top of the building was burning.

The Union troops realized that their focal point was rapidly disappearing. While this was certainly devastating to their purpose, it did suddenly create a sense of mobility to the commanders. No longer tied to a structure to protect, they began to pour out in formation, engaging the enemy where they were, rather than waiting for Quantrill and his men to come to them.

Quantrill recognized this problem almost instantly. He had hoped to acquire some of the weapons and munitions that had been stored there, but at least they would no longer be in Union hands. Seeing his objective melting away before him, he gave the order to begin retreating. His men knew, however, this meant to pillage and burn as they went, not to simply hightail it out of town.

Carey took this as his opportunity to carry out his own devilish plan. Spurring his horse, he called to some nearby men to follow him and took off down Broadway.

His ride would not be an easy one, however. Broadway was one of the major thoroughfares headed south, and a great deal of Quantrill's men were now using it to make their escape. Most of them were aware of the bridge behind the Pike house, which they could use to cross Muddy Creek. While the presence of his fellow raiders was not an issue, the attention they garnered from the Union Cavalry was problematic, and the next thing he knew, Carey was dodging cannon fire as he neared his objective.

It was never the intention of the Cavalry to rain cannon fire down on the citizens. However, in the smoky conditions mistakes were made. Grapeshot or canister would be the most effective against men on horseback, but most of those munitions had gone up in flames with the grand explosion. Thus, they had resorted to cannonballs. It was one such cannonball that went through the roof of the Pike home, shaking the structure once again, firmly implanting itself into one of the thick wooden beams in the attic.

The timing couldn't have been better for Carey. The cannonball hit just as he and his handful of men reached the yard. The jolt was enough to bring the occupants to the floor again, and by the time Will, Cordia, and Isaac recovered, Carey and his men had found shelter in the trees directly in front of the porch. The first victim of their assault was Will's horse, which served only to provoke him.

Carey was not a stupid man, and seeing a horse tied up outside of the Pike house made him realize that his betrothed and her new romantic interest must be inside. "Cordia!" he cried. "Come on out, or else I set your folks' house on fire."

Cordia gasped at the sound of his voice. She knew there were marauders in her yard, of course, but she was not expecting Carey to be one of them. She looked at Will, her eyes imploring him to tell her what to do.

He was not looking at her, however. His eyes were trained on the trees outside. She could not see what he was looking at, but just a few seconds after Carey spoke, the quick pop of Will's rifle left her guessing no more. The only sound they heard from outside was a sharp thump as one of the raiders dropped to the ground.

Carey glanced over at where the man had been standing just a second ago. "Nice shot, Will," he admitted, realizing the victim had been one of the less intelligent of his men, thinking perhaps he had made a stupid move, and that's the reason he now found himself face down on the ground. Nevertheless, Carey was sure to stay well hidden behind the tree. He had four men left, and all of them seemed both impressed and terrified by Will's marksmanship, and he was hopeful that none of them would panic and run.

Cordia was also impressed. No longer wondering if she should step out of the house, she began to realize that her husband truly was going to take care of her. If any of those men dare move out of the shadows,

Will would shoot them down immediately. He had one bullet left in the rifle, but she was able to hand her gun off to him if need be, and he still had a loaded pistol. If no more raiders showed up at her doorstep, they should be just fine.

Carey also realized that Will could pick any of them off at this angle. If any of his men stepped forward to throw a torch at the house, that man would be a sitting duck. However, Carey wasn't above trying out this theory. He signaled for one of the other men to light a torch and toss it at the window where Will's rifle shot had generated.

The man hesitated. He was one of Quantrill's men, as were all of these fellows, not one of the men that had served with Carey in the city militia. As much as the raider feared Will's aim, he also wanted to see the large brick home gutted. In the end, the thrill of the flame won out, and he lit the torch. Essentially, he provided Will with an illumi- nated target, and before he could even raise his hand to toss the torch, he fell to the ground, as did the unlucky bastard who had been standing next to him.

Aware that there were only two other men left, Carey began to rethink his strategy. He could hear a commotion on the road behind him, realizing that not only were the rest of Quantrill's men fleeing the city, but that the cavalry was now beginning to make their way up Broadway behind him, he knew he was running out of time. Glancing over his shoulder, he saw blue uniforms steadily coming up the street. Gaining his men's attention, he gave a quick hand signal, and almost instantaneously, the remaining guns were emptied on the windows of the house.

Cordia and Will ducked down in time. However, Isaac had been under the impression that the marauders did not see him as a threat, so he was surprised when the fire rained down on him as well. He fell backward as a bullet entered his shoulder, broken glass falling down on him as he tumbled.

Seeing that her father was hit, Cordia began to panic. Stifling a scream, she crawled over toward him, no longer concerned about the three trained killers in her yard, leaving her husband to cover her back.

Will reacted swiftly and violently. Unsure whether or not the raiders had other weapons, he gambled that they would have to reload.

While Cordia had her back turned and could not see what he was doing, he sprang to his feet and flew out the door. Betting that it would take Carey slightly longer to reload because he only had one arm, he fired at the other two men first. They both looked shocked that he had dared come out to face them and neither of them was prepared for the assault, even though one of them did, in fact, have a loaded pistol in his holster. He fell to the ground just as easily as his unarmed colleague.

Will had his revolver trained on Carey now, who quickly raised his hand in surrender. He hesitated to shoot him, thinking of his Aunt Margaret and the rest of the family that they shared. This man had been Jaris's best friend. Despite the awful things that he had done, shooting him just didn't seem right.

Carey could see the hesitation in his face and took advantage of it. "Will," he said, "I'm unarmed, and I am surrendering. You don't want to shoot me."

"If I let you leave," Will began, "Where will you go? What will you do?"

"I promise," Carey assured him, "You'll never see nor hear from me again. You have my word."

Will didn't think Carey's word was worth much, considering how he had just betrayed his entire town. As he was contemplating what action to take, a volley of gunfire rained down in their direction, coming from the Union soldiers on the street, who were firing at some of Quantrill's men who were disappearing around the side of the house, near the barn, attempting to cut through to make it to the bridge.

Carey took this opportunity to duck into the shadows. The gunfire was aimed more in Will's direction, and Carey managed to get around the side of the house before Will was able to come out from behind the tree he had used as shelter. Even as he took off on foot, Carey whistled for his horse. He had a second pistol as well, this one strapped inside his boot, and though it was just a derringer, anything might help at this point. He pulled it out as he ran, hearing his horse closing the gap behind him, the bridge in view in front of him.

It was completely unexpected when Cordia stepped out from

behind the back of the house, rifle in hand, pointed straight at his head. "Where you goin' Carey Adams?" she asked. "Drop the pistol. Now!"

The horse ran straight by, seeing the other riders off in the distance, and Carey knew he was trapped. Will was certainly behind him now. He dropped the derringer to the ground, hoping compliance would be beneficial. His only option was to find a way to get close enough to Cordia to take that gun away and use her body as a shield. "Cordia," he said as sweetly as he could muster, "you're not going to shoot me," he smiled at her, nonchalantly. "Go ahead and step out of the way, darlin' so I can join my men."

"You and your men shot my daddy," she replied, her voice filled with hate.

Carey swallowed hard. It had never been his intention to physically harm her father. "I'm sorry to hear that," he said quietly. "Your father and I have always been such good friends. I'm sure he would understand why you would let me go."

It was a stretch, and they both knew it. Yet, as he spoke, he stepped forward and Cordia could see that he was closing the gap between them now. He was only a foot or two away. Her finger was on the trigger, all she had to do was pull it, and Carey Adams would no longer be her concern. She had hated him her entire life, for as long as she could remember. Even as a small child, she had somehow known the evil he would someday bring down on her. Now, faced with the opportunity to take him down once and for all, she could not bring herself to do it. She was not a trained killer. She was just a young woman caught up in a war that no one seemed to understand.

"Cordia," he said in that singsong voice, the one he used to charm her mother and the other ladies. "Beautiful Cordia. Step aside now, darlin'." As he spoke, he began to reach for the rifle. She realized what his intentions were just a split second too late. Before she could pull the trigger, he grabbed ahold of the barrel and turned it away from himself, pulling her toward him. In that split second before her body completely covered his, there was a flash. Cordia was so close she could feel the heat of the bullet as it flew by, the spray of blood as the metal hit its mark. She jumped back, her heart racing as she watched

Carey tumble to the ground, a look of shock and dismay frozen on his face. His head collided with the brick wall behind him, jarring his eyes closed as he landed against the hard ground.

Cordia's hands immediately covered her mouth. Before she fully realized exactly what had happened, Will stepped out of the shadows and wrapped his arms around her, whispering, "It's all right. It's all over. He can't hurt you anymore."

She hadn't even known he was there. Somehow, he had managed to put himself in a position to take Carey out from the trees to her left, and she had never even seen him come around the side of the house. "How did you do that?" she asked, once she had regained her ability to speak.

He shook his head. "It's just. . . what I do," he replied.

The noise from the street reminded them that they were not necessarily safe just yet, and they hurried back inside. "How's your father?" Will asked once they were standing in the kitchen and the door was locked. He could see a few more horsemen flying across the bridge behind the house.

"I think he's going to be okay," she replied, hurrying back into the living room to check. He was lying on the duvet, Jane at his side. Cordia had had enough time to check the wound and see that the bullet had passed cleanly through his upper shoulder before she realized that Will had gone outside to face the marauders. She had applied pressure to her father's injury while watching from the window until she saw Carey disappear around the side of the house. She had been tempted to let him go but could not do so. On her way to the back door, she yelled for her mother and Frieda to go help her father, which they had done as quickly as possible.

Isaac was awake, and Frieda offered him a shot of whiskey, which he downed. Cordia went into the other room to get her nursing supplies, aware that, if Dr. Walters was safe, there was no way he was coming out to help tonight. Both of them would be very busy the next day taking care of the wounded. So many people would be left homeless. It would take a lot of time and cooperation to rebuild their little town of Lamar, but Cordia had no doubt in her mind that it would happen.

Once her father's wounds were dressed and the bleeding had all but stopped, Will helped her assist him up the stairs and to his room. There was just an occasional gunshot outside now, no more cannon fire, no more pounding of horses' hooves. While she was working on her father, Will had gone outside and dragged the bodies of the dead away from the house and over toward the barn. Jane had gone in to take care of her husband and Frieda went down to make sure the house was locked up and find a way to cover the broken glass in the windows. She said she couldn't rest with the whole house exposed.

Cordia took Will by the hand and led him into the bedroom she had called her own her entire life. Well aware that her parents were right next door, her intentions were only to find solace in his arms, and hopefully, eventually fall asleep. She sat on the edge of the bed and began to pull off her boots. He stopped her, however, taking them off for her. "Thank you," she said quietly as he slipped off the first and moved on to the other. "I don't know what I would have done tonight if you hadn't shown up."

"I told you, I will always protect you," he replied smiling at her gently.

She nodded her head, wrapping her arms around him. She sat quietly for a few moments, content to relish in the long-awaited solace, before she finally asked, "Is Julia gone?"

Throughout the events of the night, the thought of his sister had been at the forefront of his mind, despite the chaos unfolding around him. "Yes," he said quietly, nodding his head.

Cordia sighed. "I'm so sorry to hear that," she said. She knew the next days, weeks, and months would be full of tears for her dear, sweet friend whom they had lost far too young, but for now, she was too exhausted to cry.

"Me, too," he replied, looking up into her eyes. Smoothing back a lock of her long brown hair, which had come loose he added, "You're the only family I've got now, Cordia. But you're all I need."

"For now," she said smiling. "But someday, hopefully, we'll have lots of little Wills running around causin' all sorts of mischief."

"And lots of little Cordias?" he asked. "I'd love to have a little girl who looks just like you."

"What if she acts just like me?" Cordia laughed.

"Ah, well, then, I guess you'll get what you deserve then," he teased. "Strong willed little girl, just like her mama."

"You're the only Will I need now," she said raising her eyebrows.

He couldn't help but chuckle as he pulled her in and found her lips with his. "I love you, Cordia Tucker," he quietly proclaimed.

That was the first time anyone had ever called her by her married name. Cordia liked the sound of it. "I love you, too, Will Tucker," she replied, kissing him once more before collapsing on the bed in his arms. Outside, the war may have raged, creating a dangerous and uncertain world. But at last, Cordia had found her peace and solitude. Cordia had her Will at last, and he was all she would ever need.

THE END

Keep reading about the Tuckers in the new sequel, *Cordia's Hope: A Story of Love on the Frontier*

A Note from the Author

Thank you so much for reading *Cordia's Will: A Civil War Story of Love and Loss*. If you enjoyed it, please consider leaving a review. People decide whether or not to give a book a chance based on reviews, so your words are very powerful. Leave your review on Amazon here.

If you loved Cordia and Will's story, you will also enjoy *Cordia's Hope: A Story of Love on the Frontier*.

Hope Tucker is a school teacher looking for adventure. When she moves to Texas to tame the frontier, she finds a fairly settled town. Until she meets Judah Lawless. Everyone warns her to stay away, but that just makes Hope want to get to know him even more. Are the rumors about Judah true? Could Hope's life be in danger?

Get *Cordia's Hope: A Story of Love on the Frontier* here.

Please consider signing up for my newsletter! You can download several of my books for free when you sign up. Find the link and discover your next favorite book here:

https://books.bookfunnel.com/idjohnsonnewslettersignup

Thanks again for your support!

Also by ID Johnson:

Stand Alone Titles

Christmas Memory

(sweet contemporary romance)

The Doll Maker's Daughter at Christmas

(clean romance/historical)

Pretty Little Monster

(young adult/suspense)

The Journey to Normal: Our Family's Life with Autism *(nonfiction)*

Duology

(psychological thriller/literary fiction/women's fiction)

Beneath the Inconstant Moon

The First Mrs. Edwards

Forever Love series

(clean romance/historical)

Cordia's Will: A Civil War Story of Love and Loss

Cordia's Hope: A Story of Love on the Frontier

The Clandestine Saga series

(paranormal romance)

Transformation

Resurrection

Repercussion

Absolution

Illumination

Destruction

Annihilation

Obliteration

Termination

A Vampire Hunter's Tale (based on The Clandestine Saga)

(paranormal/alternate history)

Aaron

Jamie

Elliott

The Chronicles of Cassidy (based on The Clandestine Saga)

(young adult paranormal)

So You Think Your Sister's a Vampire Hunter?

Who Wants to Be a Vampire Hunter?

How Not to Be a Vampire Hunter

My Life As a Teenage Vampire Hunter

Vampire Hunting Isn't for Morons

Vampires Bite and Other Life Lessons

Gone Guardian

Death Doesn't Become Her

Ghosts of Southampton series

(historical romance)

Prelude

Titanic

Residuum

Heartwarming Holidays Sweet Romance series

(Christian/clean romance)

Melody's Christmas

Christmas Cocoa

Winter Woods

Waiting On Love

Shamrock Hearts

A Blossoming Spring Romance

Firecracker!

Falling in Love

Thankful for You

Melody's Christmas Wedding

The New Year's Date

Reaper's Hollow

(paranormal/urban fantasy)

Ruin's Lot

Ruin's Promise

Ruin's Legacy

When Kings Collide

Princess of Silence

Collections

Ghosts of Southampton Books 0-2

Reaper's Hollow Books 1-3

The Clandestine Saga Books 1-3

The Chronicles of Cassidy Books 1-4

Celestial Springs Collection

Heartwarming Holidays Sweet Romance Books 1-3

Heartwarming Holidays Sweet Romance Books 4-7

Websites: https://books2read.com/ap/xX7ZD8/ID-Johnson

and

nextbookboyfriend.com

For updates, visit www.authoridjohnson.blogspot.com

Follow on Twitter @authoridjohnson

Find me on Facebook at www.facebook.com/IDJohnsonAuthor

Instagram: @authoridjohnson

Amazon: ID Johnson

Follow me on Bookbub: https://www.bookbub.com/authors/id-johnson

Made in the USA
San Bernardino, CA
12 August 2020